ALWAYS DANGEROUS

Dee J. Adams

Copyright © 2015 by Dee J. Adams

All rights reserved. No portion of this book may be used or reproduced in any manner without the written consent of the author.

This book is a work of fiction. The names, characters, places, and incidents are products of the writer's imagination or have been used fictitiously and are not to be construed as real. Any resemblance to actual events or locales or persons, living or dead, is entirely coincidental.

Published by Totally Irish Productions
First print edition October 2015
ISBN-13: 978-0-9892452-7-2

Edited by Melissa Johnson
Cover Art by Croco Designs
Interior Formatting by Author E.M.S.

Published in the United States of America.

Books by Dee J. Adams

THE ADRENALINE HIGHS SERIES

Dangerous Race
Danger Zone
Dangerously Close
Living Dangerously
Imminent Danger
A Little Danger
Always Dangerous

HIGH STAKES SERIES

Against the Wall
Over the Top

Dear Reader,

It's been fun bringing you the Adrenaline Highs, and I hope you enjoy this last book in the series. I wanted to come full circle with Kim and Leo, who were in books one and two, respectively. I loved giving questionable characters their happily ever after. Kim and Leo have been through a ton and I think they deserved each other. (I mean that in the best way possible!) They've seen the rougher sides of life in their different ways and they're possibly—and probably—a little jaded.

Love may not be easy, but these two show that it's worth fighting for! You'll see one or two references to *Dangerous Race* since that's where it all began. And there might be one or two other characters you recognize along the way.

More than anything, I want to thank you for taking the time to read any of the books in this series or my High Stakes series. There are a lot of books out there today and I'm thrilled you chose one of mine.

I love to hear from readers, so feel free to email me at deej.adams1@gmail.com.

I hope you enjoy Kim and Leo and their adventure in *Always Dangerous*!

Best,

Dee J. Adams

Acknowledgments

I have to thank recently retired Detective Joel Price of the Los Angeles Police Department for his help with procedure, and for his patience with my questions, not only on this book, but on *Imminent Danger* as well. Thank you, sir, I appreciate all your time!

A big thank-you to stuntman Casey O'Neill for all his help with the horse stunt. You were very generous to talk to me during your vacation, so I thank you for that as well!

Thank you to stuntman Rex Reddick for allowing me to use his name and likeness in the book. You guys have seen Rex in dozens of movies, you just don't realize it's him. Among his many talents, his motorcycle and driving skills are the absolute best in the business.

Thank you, Debra Neil-Fisher for all your expertise in editing and the film world in general. I didn't mean to ruin your vacation with all my questions! You are a true gem!

I'm especially happy to have contest winner and friend, Dan Lora, in this book. The man patched me up on set on several occasions and it was fun when he won my contest to be a character in *Always Dangerous*. He's been waiting very patiently for this book to come out. Hope you enjoy seeing your name and likeness in this book, Dan!

My thanks to Jerome Butler, because he's an awesome man and he has offered invaluable help during my audiobook narrations. He may not have a hand in writing the books, but he definitely has a voice—no pun intended—when it comes to the narrations.

An additional thank-you goes to Helen Hong for her help in voicing a character in my recent narration. If you get a chance to catch Helen's stand-up routine, you should see it. The lady is crazy funny!

As always, this book wouldn't be here without the amazing eye of my editor, Melissa Johnson. Thank you, Melissa, for being the consummate professional. I'm so glad you're so much smarter than me! (And I mean that from the bottom of my heart!)

Thanks to Sean and Katelyn, because they are always my biggest support. I couldn't—and wouldn't—be doing this writing thing without you. I love you both immeasurably.

Any mistakes are my own.

Dedication

This one is for my daughter, Katelyn, and sister Eileen,
two ladies who mean the world to me.

Eileen, you taught me to be strong. Thanks, Sis. Love you.

Katelyn, you continue to teach me about compassion and
selflessness every day. I couldn't be any prouder of you.
I love you with all my heart.

Chapter One

The high-pitched shriek woke Leo Frost with the finesse of a jackhammer and his pulse skyrocketed until he defined the source. Cats. Exhaling a slow breath, Leo blinked at the moonlight filtering through the curtains and the strange room came into focus. Right. His new bedroom. Would it ever be home? A few small pieces of his espresso colored furniture filled the room, but his custom headboard hadn't fit against any of the walls so he'd had to settle for the queen size bed that had been in his guest room.

Outside, the felines battled for the King of the Wall separating his property from the next and he winced at the high pierced *reooows* that cut through the night like warped buzz saws. Not only had he barely slept in days, but despite his exhaustion, he'd had a hard time *getting* to sleep when he had the opportunity. He'd finally drifted off—he glanced at the clock—twenty minutes ago and now *this?*

A fresh battle of meows screeched loud enough to wake the dead. "Shut up!" he yelled before slamming the pillow over his head.

As if life wasn't bad enough. He'd lost his beautiful house, his gorgeous sleek Porsche, most of the movie memorabilia that meant anything to him and now he'd even lost a peaceful night's sleep.

The cats screamed again because apparently he wasn't miserable enough.

Frustration and rage snapped the last threadbare string of his patience. "Dammit! That's it!" Leo tossed the covers off, dug his feet into his mammoth cross-trainers and stalked out of the room wearing only his nylon basketball shorts. Who had cats in the hills anyway? Weren't they hawk or eagle bait? At this moment, he wouldn't mind a couple of winged animals hauling away the culprits.

Leo turned the doorknob when all hell broke loose outside. *What the hell?* Table legs scraped against the patio cement, the cats screeched bloody murder. He fumbled for the outside light and ran to break up the ruckus. Cool October air hit his bare chest and legs. Seemed like an awful lot of noise for...

"Holy shit!" he muttered, his tired brain now fully awake and taking in the picture. More than just fucking cats. A coyote had one cat in his mouth and another one cornered. A fucking coyote! Leo's heart pounded harder and sweat prickled his skin. "Hey!" he shouted, picking up a nearby broom leaning against the wall. "Get out!"

The coyote turned on him, a low growl rumbling in his throat. Jesus, coyotes weren't supposed to be aggressive unless they were in a pack. Unless this guy was sick. Or just damn hungry.

Fresh sweat dotted Leo's spine, but he wasn't going to give the animal a chance to pounce. He lifted the broom. "Out!" He rushed the coyote as the cornered cat swiped with vicious claws and scary white teeth. The cat in his mouth wasn't going without a fight either and it did a good job of marking up the coyote's face before the animal decided to cut his losses. Yelping in pain and dropping the cat, the coyote hightailed it back up the terraced yard and into the hills above.

Leo chased the coyote to make sure it disappeared. Breathing hard, he squinted into the dark hills. By the time he got back to his side yard, only one cat remained. The one the coyote had nearly had for its midnight snack.

The cat's matted black fur was slick, a mixture of blood and saliva. Hell, his whole patio was full of blood and fur. What a mess. Both cats must have given the coyote a good chase. A couple potted plants were turned over and dirt was spread across the pavers. God, he didn't want to deal with this now. Or ever for that matter. He had enough on his plate without this mess.

The feline gazed at him with helpless eyes as it panted. Probably waiting to see if Leo was another monster out to hurt him. Poor little guy was in bad shape.

"Shit," Leo muttered. "I don't do cats."

He'd just moved in so he didn't know his neighbors. Not that he could ring anyone's doorbell in the middle of the night. He also couldn't just leave it here. Who knew if the coyote would come back?

Leo had never owned a pet. He'd begged his mom for a dog for years, but she'd categorically refused. Once he'd started working, he'd been traveling too much to keep a dog. Leo crouched next to the cat. "Okay. How about I call animal control? They'll fix you up."

Meow. The softest little sound he'd ever heard. *Meow.*

His heart took an uncharacteristic thump. "Gonna play dirty, huh?" He touched his thumb behind its ear and the cat closed its eyes and pressed subtly into the rub. He reconsidered the cat's sex. "You must be a girl. I know your type," he murmured. He sighed. *Damn.* Cat needed help and sitting here wasn't going to accomplish anything. "Give me two minutes to call animal control. Be right back." He stood up and stopped. "Nope. Can't leave you out here alone, can I? Cujo is probably waiting for a chance to finish the job."

Leo grabbed the towel sitting on the stationary bike under the awning and gently eased it under the cat, before scooping it all up in his arms and walking inside. "Okay, let's see what the Internet will tell us."

After setting the kitty in an empty moving box stacked in the corner of the laundry room, Leo opened his laptop on the kitchen counter and found the number for animal control. A phone call later, he discovered their only unit was out dealing with an emergency, so he couldn't even get a time frame for arrival. The officer on the phone gave him the address of the nearest emergency vet clinic and Leo hung up the phone.

"The emergency room?" he asked the cat, glancing around the small, dim galley kitchen. "I'm really taking you to the emergency room?" Of all the stupid, aggravating... Leo fought the urge to throw an adolescent fit. He just wanted to sleep. Was that asking too much? "I don't take anyone to the E.R., cat. Do you know who I am?"

The cat blinked slowly with heavy eyes and Leo's heart melted a little more. "I'm Leo. Leo Frost. I was in *Dangerous Race*. I won an Oscar and Emmy during the same season." But even as he spoke, he realized what he had to do. "I've got two

People's Choice awards too." He walked as he spoke, grabbing keys and throwing on a clean, but wrinkled as hell T-shirt from the pile on top of the dryer.

"Let's go, cat," Leo said, picking up the box and heading out. "You owe me. Big time."

The cat mewled a response and Leo's heart took another hit. "Oh no you don't," he said, balancing the box and closing the door to the garage behind him. "I'm not falling for that shit." Then he glanced at the pitiful ball of fur with the heavy eyes and bloody coat. "Hold tight, cat. I may not be a hero in real life, but I play one in the movies. Let's see if I can't get you to the doctor in time."

It didn't even take Leo twelve minutes to get to the vet. It would've been even faster if he'd been driving Stella. But now he was stuck in a previously owned—oh how far he'd fallen—old-model Mercedes. At least it was black. About the only thing it had going for it. Between the middle of the night hours and no traffic—and maybe the fact that he went about seventy on Ventura Boulevard—he made it in "American Racing Organization" time. He knew learning to drive an open-wheel Arrow car during the filming of *Dangerous Race* would come in handy.

After squealing into a parking spot, he scooped up the box and rang the bell to be admitted inside. Luckily the place wasn't packed. Just one guy sitting on a long bench with a very dejected look on his face. He barely glanced up and the stuffy smell of dirty fur assaulted Leo's senses.

"Hi," Leo said, setting the box down on the counter at the reception desk.

The young brunette behind the desk stood up and looked inside the box. Her green hospital scrubs hid any hint of a figure, not that he cared. There was only one figure burned into his brain and it currently belonged to a woman eighteen hundred miles away. "Aw. Who's this? What happened?" she asked.

"Don't know who it is. It managed to get attacked on my patio. Coyote."

She rubbed the cat's head. "Poor baby." She looked up. The tiny stud in her nose caught the light and her brown eyes widened as she recognized him. "Oh. Um. Hi." Her cheeks burned bright red. "Leo Frost, right?"

"Yeah. Hi. And you are...?" All he wanted to do was drop off the fur ball, but he never dissed a fan. If being nice to this girl got the cat faster care then he was fine with that.

"Rebecca. Rebecca Marx. Hi." She looked around and seemed to realize there was a bleeding cat between them. "Oh, I should...here." She handed him a clipboard from her desk with papers and a pen. "You need to fill out some paperwork."

Leo put his hands up. "Oh, no. Not me. I'm not filling anything out. Not my cat." His mistake was looking at the animal in question when he said it. The fur ball tried to move and let out a very pitiful whine. "What?" Leo said to the cat. "I'm not responsible for you. Hell, I can barely take care of myself."

The cat blinked another slow, deliberate time.

"No," Leo told it.

Meow. Meow. Meooowwww.

Dammit, he wasn't made of stone. "You don't play fair, cat. I'll remember that." Leo snatched the clipboard. "This is stupid. I don't know anything about the cat. If he had a collar the coyote got it off him."

"Maybe she has a chip," the receptionist or technician—or whatever she was—said.

"It's a she?" Leo looked up from the papers. He hated leaving a damsel in distress. Force of job habit.

"From what I can see, yes." She took the box. "Go ahead and fill out what you can and I'll take her back to the doctor. He's almost done with his current patient. Shouldn't take long."

Leo might've growled as he took a seat and looked over the questions. Aside from the contact information, he couldn't check any boxes or fill in any blanks when it came to the feline's prior health. Half these diseases he'd never even heard of. "Pointless," he muttered.

"You can't leave her here," the guy on the opposite bench said.

Leo looked up. The twenty-something guy sitting across from him had out of control brown curls wigged out in every direction. Wearing sweats and a stained AC/DC T-shirt, he seemed as if he'd also been pulled from his bed. "You talking to me?"

"Yeah. You can't leave the cat or they'll just send her to the pound where she'll be put down. You can't leave her."

Leo didn't especially appreciate being told what he could and couldn't do. It wasn't like he didn't have a heart. "It's not my cat. Look... I don't do cats." That definitely sounded a little cold, but he had valid reasons. "Sometimes I'm not home for months at a time. I can't have pets."

"Don't you have an assistant? I thought all big time actors had assistants."

He used to, but times had changed. Not that he planned to tell this guy anything...and wasn't it *nice* of him to bring it up. "That's not the point. An animal needs love and companionship. I'm hardly home. I don't do pets. I never have."

"That doesn't mean you shouldn't start." Persistent dude.

"Look..." Leo leaned forward, hoping to get it in this guy's skull that he wasn't in a position to own a pet, but the door opened and a different technician—male, bald and with a colorful tattoo sleeve on his right arm—wearing the same green-colored scrubs appeared.

"Mr. Seaton, you can come back now," he said. "Chocolate is bandaged up and ready to go home."

Chocolate? A dog? A cat? Leo really didn't care. But as the door closed behind the guy, Leo felt the hard stab of guilt slam into his chest. *She'll be put down.* The words kept bouncing around in his head and the longer he sat there, the more they made him sick.

He'd worked with a golden retriever once years ago and ran into the trainer a few months back who told him that Sam had been euthanized because of kidney failure. Leo had been sad, but figured at least the dog wasn't suffering anymore. But this: an animal that could be nursed back to good health, but might die because he walked out the door...that made him feel like a flat out dick.

It was another forty minutes of arguing with himself about the cat's well-being before the same technician opened the door and called him back. She showed him into a small sterile room where the feline was laid out on her side, bandaged and breathing hard.

A bald technician moved out of the room as Leo came in. "The doctor will be right with you," he said and closed the door behind him.

Leo would've protested, but he couldn't take his gaze off the injured animal. Her yellow eyes looked up at him, soulful and sad. Leo stroked the same spot behind her ear and she purred. She fucking purred.

"Yeah, you and every other chick that comes my way, huh, babe."

The door opened and the doctor came in, his blue scrubs differentiating him from his staff. Buzz cut gray hair, chubby cheeks and round glasses over brown eyes. "Hey, there. I'm Dr. Soledad. Nice to meet you. I took special care of your girl. I'm a big fan." He smiled and winked.

"Great. But she's not really my cat. She just managed to get attacked on my patio."

He nodded and smiled as if he understood completely. "But you're taking her home right? She can go home. Nothing's broken. I stitched her up. She'll be moving slow for a while, but she's a tough cookie. Living one of her many lives, I guess. Judging from her teeth, she's about two. If she spreads out the drama, she should be around a long time." He made notes in a chart.

Sighing, Leo tried again. "I don't really have room in my life for a cat. I can't take care of her right now..."

"Ah. Shooting a new film?" the doctor asked, glancing up.

Didn't he wish? He'd been up for two big budget films and both had gone to other actors. He'd been banking on at least one of them to come through because he needed the money. "Uh. Well. No. Not at the moment."

"Going out of town?" the man asked.

Leo hadn't felt this cornered since standing in the high school principal's office after he'd been caught feeling up Mary Kate McGee behind the bleachers. "Uh...no." Shit. Why didn't he lie?

"Oh, well good. It shouldn't be a big problem." The vet kept talking then. Explaining the injuries and the treatment and the stitches, and Leo couldn't get a word in edgewise. To compound the problem, the cat kept looking at him like he was a god. And the damn thing purred every time he set a finger on her. She looked pretty pitiful with a big white bandage wrapped around her torso. With all that black fur sticking out on either end, she reminded him of an Oreo.

"You can bring her back here or take her to a vet in a week or so to have the stitches removed."

"A week or so?" Leo's eyes bugged out wide. "You don't understand. I don't want the cat. I'm not taking care of the cat."

Meow.

Dammit. Leo addressed the cat. "Look. I don't have any cat things, okay? No food, no milk. No cat things."

"Cats really shouldn't drink milk," the vet said, narrowing his brows. "I'm happy to send you home with a sample bag of food. Should last you a few days. It'll give you time to get to the store."

Clenching his jaw, Leo held back his frustration. He couldn't blurt out that he didn't have the money to feed an extra mouth. That realization pissed him off. Plenty of people had less than he did and they not only fed pets, but kids too. So what if he'd never had any animals before. So what if he never saw himself in this position. So what if he was a dog person and not a cat person. Ugh. "Fine. I'll take the cat."

Minutes later, he got a crash course in kitty care and the doctor even gave him a small gray mesh carrier and a blue plastic litter box along with the food. *Great.*

Leo got back in the car after setting the cat paraphernalia in the trunk and looked down at the cat. "Well...you need a name," he told her. "No. Scratch that. You won't be staying long enough to need one. "This is a temporary situation, cat. Maybe Vivienne will take you home." He still kept in touch with his former assistant. "She's nice. Most of the time," he amended. He started the car and headed home.

Chapter Two

"Hi. Kim Jacobs. Nice to meet you." Kim took in the deep maroon and gold accents in the posh office as she shook the lawyer's hand. A large mahogany desk sat on one side with a sofa and two large leather seats placed adjacent. It was a power office and nothing like what she expected for Tucson, Arizona. She caught her reflection in the mirror on the sidewall and looked away from the faint darkness beneath her eyes. What a month.

Hell, she never expected to be in a lawyer's office at all this trip, but once again, life had laughed at her plans and dictated a whole new path.

"Nice to meet you. Your aunt spoke very highly of you." Gary Cohen, her aunt's lawyer, gestured to the empty chair next to her cousin, Wilson. "Have a seat," he said, opening the last button of his dark suit coat and taking the chair across from both of them at his desk.

Wilson gave her a quick hug before they faced Mr. Cohen. He pushed up his John Lennon glasses in a nervous tell that Kim had come to recognize, and her own stomach took a recently familiar spin. His sandy blond hair still made him look like a surfer dude despite never spending a day at the beach. The circles under his eyes had become more prominent in the last few weeks and showed the strain on his handsome face. His tan sport jacket and pressed jeans marked a change from the usual worn T-shirts she'd seen him wearing lately. But they'd both been working hard in recent weeks.

Kim had no idea her aunt had been so sick. They'd talked often over the years, but Carolyn had been closed mouth about her cancer diagnoses until it was too late. It still came as a shock.

Kim and Wilson were the last two of their immediate family.

"Can I get anything for either of you before we get started? Water or coffee?" Mr. Cohen asked. They both declined and Kim noticed the lawyer openly staring at her. When she lifted her eyebrows in question, he stammered. "I'm sorry. You just look so much like your aunt. The resemblance is uncanny."

This wasn't news to Kim. Their whole lives the family joked how Kim should've been Carolyn's daughter instead of Susan's. Though they were thirty years apart, pictures of them growing up showed them nearly identical at every age. The lawyer flushed and lifted the manila folder. "I'll just…" He opened the top. "All right then. Let's get started."

Feeling even greener around the edges, Kim crossed her legs and took a deep breath. Her aunt didn't have much so this shouldn't take long. Now with the funeral over, she could get back to Indiana and back to her business partner and her end of much neglected business.

Mr. Cohen pulled out the pages inside the folder as he spoke to them. "Your aunt had a trust, so you won't have to worry about a probate. She was a smart woman. I respected her greatly." The papers crackled as he flipped through them. "Miss Jacobs, I'm not sure if you're aware that your aunt made you the trustee of her trust."

A trust? Kim's stomach took a full on header as she glanced at Wilson. He looked just as surprised. "No. I didn't know. I didn't realize she had a trust." Most people didn't think ahead to protect their property from taxes.

He gave her a reassuring smile. "She did. She hoped to make it easier for her family when she passed and she entrusted you to make sure her wishes were carried out." He adjusted his glasses and looked down. "Let's see. Here it is." He began reading.

"Well, no one lives forever, so if you're reading this, then my time here is over. Don't mourn my life, kids. Celebrate it. And celebrate your own lives. I want you to know that I loved you both as if you were my own. You may be my sisters' kids, but we all have the same blood. That includes you, Wilson. I never let your adoption keep me from thinking of you as family. I've thought long and hard about what I've done, so I don't want you to think that the decision I made came easily or without a certain amount of heartache. But I did what I thought was right. It's the way I lived my life and the way I'm doing it in death."

Next to her, Wilson fidgeted in his chair and pushed up his glasses again.

"What I'm about to say may sound harsh, but I think it's important so you know where I'm coming from."

Kim couldn't begin to guess why all the build-up. Her aunt owned a modest—albeit beautiful—house in an upper middle class neighborhood in Arizona. Nothing too fancy. She'd always been a frugal woman and Kim had learned to live similarly after losing a fortune a handful of years ago.
Mr. Cohen continued reading.

"Kim, for many years I worried about you. If a party existed, you went to it. If a man offered you something, you took it. I always wanted the best for you, but you never gave yourself any credit and it hurt me to watch. I was proud when you got your own business off the ground and I thought you'd come into your own and gain confidence. But it took the worst to bring out the best in you. You lost everything, but I think you found your self-respect. You've come a long way in a few short years and I'm so proud of you."

Mr. Cohen flicked his gaze up and smiled before looking back at the pages in his hand.
Heat flushed Kim's cheeks and her stomach rolled at the mini recap of her life until now.
The lawyer went on,

"Wilson, This is going to come as a shock to you. But I know you know my secret."

Kim glanced at Wilson whose tired brown eyes had gone round. Aunt Carolyn had a secret? Was she talking about the trust or something besides that?

"But, Wilson. I know *your* secret."

Kim stared at her older cousin, the only son of the oldest sister. Seemed everybody had a secret, but her. Apparently her quick rise and quicker fall had been family headline news and thanks to Carolyn's letter, her cousin and this lawyer knew about her party ways so many years ago too. Nope, no secrets here.

The lawyer read on.

"I know why your wife and daughter left you. I know why you lost your house. I know why you began calling and coming over so often the last few years, offering to go to the market or run errands for me."

Mr. Cohen paused.

"I know you have a gambling addiction just as you know that I have money."

Now it was Kim's eyes that went wide as she looked at her cousin. Wilson had a gambling problem? Aunt Carolyn had money? How much money? Living in Indiana sure kept her out of the loop.

"Wilson...I know you hoped to profit from my death. Don't worry, I know you didn't kill me. The cancer did that well enough. But the more I thought about it, the more I couldn't enable your addiction with money. I can't do that to you. What I will do is give you a roof over your head. Free and clear. Wilson, you get my house and all of its contents. Maybe all the heirlooms will help you realize the importance of family. The house is worth about three hundred and fifty thousand dollars since I remodeled. It's not huge, but it's a good place and you don't have a mortgage. Whether you take out a mortgage or sell it to fund your addiction is up to you and your decision to make. I loved that house and hope you have many happy years there if you choose to keep it."

The lawyer cleared his throat as Wilson's mouth dropped open wide.

"But, Wilson, I know that's why you started sucking up to me. You didn't think I'd find out that you answered my phone and talked to my accountant, but I did. He told me you asked questions, pretending that you were relaying them from me. But that was never the case, was it? You just wanted to know in case I could loan you money. I was disappointed in you. I wanted to see you quit gambling while I was alive, but I only watched you lose everyone around you and nearly everything you owned. I'm sorry, honey, but I won't enable more of that behavior."

Kim's heart pounded as if she'd run five miles and sweat prickled under her arms.

The lawyer continued.

"I've set up a trust fund for Amanda and she'll receive five hundred thousand dollars upon her twenty-fifth birthday."

Kim's eyes nearly bugged out. *Five hundred thousand dollars?* God, if Wilson's daughter invested that right, she could be set for life. Where did all that money come from?

Mr. Cohen glanced up before going back to the will.

"I've missed seeing her since Chloe moved out of town, but I believe she's in a better environment than she was here. She still has a lot of growing up to do and I hope you become a man she can look up to."

Wilson looked as pale as a cotton ball.

"To my niece, Kim…"

Another flush chased up her cheeks and she focused on the lawyer. Her turn.

"As I said, I watched you grow and I couldn't be more

13

proud of you. You decided to live your life and be an independent woman instead of thinking you needed a man to give you what you wanted. I leave the rest of my estate to you, which includes stocks, bonds and liquid assets equaling about ten million dollars."

Ten what?

The lawyer went on, but Kim didn't hear a single word. She felt Wilson's penetrating stare and couldn't look at him. It was too much to take in, too hard to believe.

The lawyer must have finished because he set the papers on his desk and stood up. "I'll get you both some water and give you a few minutes to talk. I'll be right back."

Talk? Talk? Like she could come up with words? Was he kidding?

The door closed behind him and Kim finally chanced a look to Wilson.

"What just happened here?" he questioned with such emphasis that Kim felt she had to answer.

"I have no idea." A few weeks ago, not long after she got home from her trip to Los Angeles, her aunt had mentioned not feeling well. Kim had flown to Arizona, surprised to find her robust aunt flat on her back and frail. She'd lost a ton of weight and her skin had been pasty and white. Her aunt had died a few weeks later. That made all three sisters gone, and she and Wilson were the only ones left. Kim had been under the impression that they'd all lived middle class lives—but maybe the one sister with no kids could've lived life large, but just chose not to. Kim had a few questions of her own. "How long has she had money? When did you find out she had money? She rarely spent a dime. I don't get it."

"How do you think I feel? I've been living in the same city, helping her for years and she does this?" Wilson shot to his feet and started pacing. "Unbelievable. She may as well have sliced off my balls one at a time."

Kim cringed at the picture. "It's not that bad, Wilson. You have the house. It's beautiful."

His brown-eyed gaze slid to hers slowly. "You're kidding me, right? She just unloaded ten million dollars on you. *Ten million!*"

"She also gave a huge chunk to Amanda." Her young cousin

was only eight, so by the time she came into her inheritance it would be worth a lot more if invested correctly. Kim might be able to help with that.

Wilson lifted his arms in a WTF gesture. "Great. Five hundred grand that we can't use for college, which means a bunch more debt. Can't wait." His sarcasm wasn't lost on her. "It's all a little unbalanced, don't you think?"

"She outlined why she did it," Kim said quietly. God, what if she hadn't straightened herself out four years ago? Would her aunt have left all her money to Amanda, to a charity or one of the other distant cousins they'd lost touch with?

"I don't believe this," Wilson said, clenching his fists and pacing some more. "Chloe left me, then I lost the house a few years ago, and Carolyn could've fixed it with a little loan." He shook his head, stuck his hands through his thick hair and took a deep breath.

Mr. Cohen returned with glasses filled with ice water. "Here you go," he said, handing them over.

Kim nearly guzzled hers in one swallow. This was too surreal. The rest of the meeting went by in a blur as the lawyer talked about the trust and the details involved. A half hour later, Wilson and she stood at their cars parked in front of the building.

"I'm sorry, Wilson. But you know I didn't expect this."

He snorted. "Huh. That makes two of us."

"I didn't know about…" She couldn't even say it.

"My gambling problem," he mumbled. He looked totally defeated and Kim felt terrible. A rumble sounded from his chest as he stared at the sky and yelled, "I stopped! I told you I stopped!" He slammed his palm on the roof of the car. "I ran my ass off for her for the last three years. I dropped everything at a moment's notice for her and all she did was leave me her house?" He finally stopped and dropped his head. Then he started laughing. He laughed so hard, his eyes filled with tears. "Her house? She left me her house? And she left you ten million dollars." He pulled himself together and finally studied her with an eerie calmness. "How's it feel to be a millionaire, Kimbo?"

A millionaire. It didn't seem possible. "Honestly, I don't really think this is for real. I think it's a dream and I'm about to wake up any minute and discover—"

"It's not!" he shouted and Kim almost flinched at his

outburst. Then he wiped the spit off his chin. "It's not a dream," he said more calmly. "This is as real as it gets." He opened his car door and slid behind the wheel. "I'll give you a call later. Sorry. I just need to process. I need some space, okay." He cranked the engine and backed out before she got a word in.

"Yeah," she said to his departing car. She'd rather have her aunt back than have her money and deal with a side of her cousin she'd never seen. "I wish she wasn't dead either."

Wilson slammed on the gas and zoomed down the street, weaving around slow cars and doing his best to get his cousin and that damn lawyer as far behind him as possible. Heat had made the car an instant sauna and sweat prickled from every pore. "A house," he seethed softly in his old-model Ford. "No, Wilson," he said, mocking his aunt's voice. "'A house worth a whole three hundred and fifty thousand dollars. I remodeled, you know. That tacked on a good hundred thousand dollars to the place.'

"But you had to give Kim everything else, didn't you, you old bag. You couldn't even give Amanda her money for college. You fucking…" He swallowed back bile. "I know your secret," he mocked. "You don't know shit, Carolyn. You have no clue what you just did.

"Ten million dollars? Are you kidding me?" he seethed. All her accountant had said was that her investments were doing very well and she'd be set for a long time. But ten million dollars was over and above his wildest expectations. And she hadn't given him a cent of it.

After a fifteen-minute drive, Wilson found himself at his aunt's house. His house. She'd given him a key when she'd gotten sick, so he let himself inside and looked around the place. Boring white walls and stupid knick-knacks on every surface. It smelled like her…a combination of flowers and must. She still had ancient furniture on her shiny hardwood floors.

"What's the point of having money if you never spend any of it?"

Anger filled him fast and hard. "You will not get away with this, auntie. I guarantee you will not." He paced the living room. There had to be something in this house worth a few bucks.

Jewelry!

Wilson strode to Carolyn's bedroom and went straight to the jewelry box on her bureau, a smile creeping on his lips. Her late husband must have had money. He'd gifted her with some amazing rings and necklaces. He'd seen her wear them on special occasions. Taking a deep breath, Wilson opened the top. His grin faded at the empty box. He quickly opened the small drawers, pulling the thing apart as each space came up just as empty as the one before. Carolyn had cleaned the thing out. He'd lay odds it all sat in the damn safe deposit box she'd left to Kim.

Fucking bitch.

A burst of anger erupted in his chest and Wilson threw the empty box across the room. It shattered the free-standing mirror in the corner and glass splintered everywhere. He started pulling open drawers and tossing them, looking for any hidden stashes Carolyn might have forgotten about.

Nothing.

Didn't old people hide their cash under mattresses or in their underwear drawer?

Fucking bitch. He couldn't even rely on her to be a regular old bat.

Breathing hard, Wilson collapsed on the floor, his heart hammering. Now what?

He needed to find a way to get his hands on that money, that's what. Not only did he have child support payments, but he owed a bunch of people a hell of a lot of money.

Cousin Kim used to be his best pal. They'd practically grown up together. Seemed like it was time to renew that relationship. And maybe take it a step farther. There was a time in high school when he thought their relationship might shift, a time when they shared their secrets. They weren't blood relatives after all. Then one of the football players had asked her out and she'd drifted away from him. Those days were long gone, but he was pretty sure his cousin wasn't dating anyone now. If he played his cards right, he might get his hands on that money yet.

Chapter Three

Kim walked through her office doors a few days later. A new small desk had been added near the entrance. There had to be a reason for that... They rented the building and made the most of the space. By sharing a large office, they could use the other room as a conference area.

Baby paraphernalia dotted the cream Berber carpet and espresso wood of the office furniture. All that was per usual. Still, she felt an elemental shift in the air. With this inheritance, her life was her own. She didn't have to do anything she didn't want to do anymore. Like work for people she didn't want to work for or spend long hours calculating how to make the most of their finances. But the last thing she wanted to do was ditch Chelsea. They'd been in business together from the very beginning. They'd been best friends since college.

Chelsea looked up from settling a blanket over the baby sleeping in a portable bassinet in the corner of their shared office and smiled. Sophie's dark hair peeked out from a knit pink cap and her full bowed lips and puffy cheeks were Gerber-baby cute.

"Hey, stranger!" Dressed in a floral skirt, a solid matching green top and flats, Chelsea greeted her with a hug. Kim had thought about telling her the news over the phone, but she wanted to see Chelsea's face, so she'd kept her mouth shut about the inheritance.

"Shh," Kim hushed. "You'll wake the baby."

"No way. I'm teaching her to sleep through the sounds of life. I refuse to tiptoe and get her used to waking at the drop of hat." Concern filled her eyes. "How are you? I'm so sorry about your aunt. I thought you were going to take some time off. Life's been crazy lately. You should take a break."

"I thought L.A. was my break."

"Hardly," Chelsea scoffed. "Losing all your belongings in a house fire is not a break. Besides, L.A. seems like a lifetime ago." She stood back and studied Kim carefully. "You feeling okay? I hate to say it, but I think the last few weeks in Arizona took a toll."

"It did." Kim set her bag in the big drawer of her desk, avoiding Chelsea's eagle-eyed stare. The bags under her eyes hadn't disappeared beneath makeup because that would've been too easy. "I've been fighting something for weeks too. A cold or flu. I'm getting ready for it to hit full force any day now."

"Really." She said it as a statement, not a question and her brows scrunched together. "Hmm."

"Hmm?" Kim repeated. Her phone rang and she pulled it from her bag, glanced to see Wilson's name pop up on the screen and set it on her desk. "What's hmm?"

"Don't you want to get that?" Chelsea asked, tipping her chin toward the sound.

"Not really. It's my cousin again. He's been calling nonstop since I left Arizona. Now tell me what that hmm meant."

"I just wondered how long you've been feeling this way?" Chelsea asked, resting her ass against her desk and crossing her arms.

Kim thought back. "I don't know... I was home for a few weeks before Aunt Carolyn called me. Then I was in Arizona for a few weeks. I guess the middle part of my trip I started feeling weird. I chalked it up to being around Carolyn and knowing she was dying. That's not going to make anyone feel good. Seeing her so queasy and sick kind of rubbed off on me."

Chelsea nodded then lifted a dark eyebrow. "You're probably right. I mean, you're not...um...late, are you?"

"Late?" Kim checked her watch. "I always get here this time in the morn—" She jerked her gaze to Chelsea as her friend's tone registered in her brain. She couldn't be thinking... "You're not talking about what time I arrived this morning?"

Chelsea shook her head no.

A full body flush crept up from Kim's center all the way to her forehead. Did Chelsea mean late for her period? She'd downplayed her encounter with Leo Frost after she came back from L.A. for a few reasons... Most of them having to do with guilt and embarrassment for a monumental slide into Stupidsville. "You can't possibly be thinking what I think you're thinking?"

Chelsea's lips compressed as she nodded. "When was the last time you had your period?"

Kim sat down on the chair nearest her desk before her knees buckled. She couldn't be pregnant. When *was* the last time she had her period? She covered her eyes with her palm, similar to an ostrich with its head in the sand. She definitely didn't have it last month. She'd been in between her Los Angeles and Arizona trips. Holy shit. The whole trip to L.A. had been mind-bending in so many different ways. Stephanie, her old college roommate, had been kidnapped and her house destroyed in a fire on the same night. Then Leo's embezzling accountant had turned up dead. It had been one giant bomb after another.

Then this last month in Arizona had been pretty miserable as well. She hadn't even thought about missing her period. She'd been too busy taking care of Carolyn, the house and her cousin. Although Wilson tried to do his best, he never seemed able to finish anything he started. Kim had been picking up the slack in a dozen different places.

She snagged her phone and flipped to the calendar and the last time she had her cycle. All the blood drained from her face. She was missing her second cycle now. "Oh my, God," she whispered. The loud beat of her heart pounded between her ears. How could she have not realized she was missing two periods until now?

Chelsea crouched in front of her. "You okay? You look even paler than you did two minutes ago."

Kim swallowed as she nodded and shook her head, then nodded again. Watching Chelsea's concerned face made her chest heavy. "What do I do?" she asked softly. She'd been so confident the last few years on her own. She'd lost the bad girl behavior and cleaned up her act and now after one—albeit major—slip...*this*.

Chelsea patted her thigh. "Want to tell me what really happened in Los Angeles?" Her knowing eyes saw right through Kim.

"Honestly, you know most of it." Kim stood and paced in

front of the desk as Chelsea waited. "After Stephanie left the club, Leo drove me back to her place later that night. We discovered the house was on fire and I needed someplace to stay after that. I didn't want to stay with *The Asshole...*" She'd started calling Stephanie's husband Carl, *The Asshole,* soon into her trip. "So when Leo offered a room until I left town, I took it."

"You told me he offered a room. Not a bed," Chelsea commented drolly. "How could you fail to leave out that tidbit?"

"Because," Kim wailed. "I was afraid you'd look down on me." She'd not only left her one-night stand days long behind her, but she'd cleaned up her act in a big way. Yes, she still liked to go out, but alcohol wasn't usually on the table and in turn she'd made wiser choices. She'd quit looking for Mr. Moneybags and just wanted to meet Mr. Right. She snorted at that idea. Two encounters with Leo Frost. That's all she'd had. Two encounters with a gorgeous Hollywood movie star who didn't know the meaning of the words *settle down* or *parenthood.*

"Ever since that night four years ago at the hotel." The night that Chelsea's husband, Matt, had saved her from a drunk creep. "I swore I'd never mess up like that again. And here I am. Messing up worse."

Chelsea walked back toward her desk, the hurt in her eyes as clear as the bright day outside. "You're an adult, Kim. You're allowed to drink. The fact that you think I judge you really hurts. I thought we were best friends," she scolded softly.

"We are. I didn't want to disappoint my best friend by telling her that I slept with an egotistical, mega-famous, Hollywood A-lister." She shook her head. "God, I can't even believe it myself. It seems like a dream. Like the whole thing never really happened." Her phone buzzed and indicated a voicemail. Wilson had left another message.

"Wow," Chelsea said, after taking a minute to absorb the news. She perched at the end of her desk and looked sheepish as she asked her next question. "Was he...you know...really good?"

Kim canted her head. She was probably pregnant and that's the information Chelsea wanted to know. "You did not just ask that question."

"Uh, yeah, I'm pretty sure I did." Chelsea matched her gesture.

Sighing, Kim rolled her eyes. She'd never hear the end of it if she didn't come clean. "Let's put it this way. I wouldn't have gone back for seconds if the firsts weren't really delicious." She went behind her desk to distract herself with all that had piled up. Fat chance of that happening.

Chelsea fanned herself. "I think I just swooned."

"Look who's talking? The girl with the gorgeous husband…"

"I know, but I can still appreciate a handsome man. Do you like the guy? Maybe he won't freak out. Too much," she added, since this was obviously going to be a huge freak out for any guy much less a hugely famous one.

Did she like him? What a question. Kim sat down in her comfortable leather chair. "I didn't think I liked him in the beginning, but he changed my mind. He's not what the press makes him out to be. I mean we parted friends, so I guess that's a step up from my norm back in the day."

"Is there a chance that you guys might…?" Chelsea tipped her head from side to side indicating they might make a go of it.

Kim laughed. "No. Not a chance in hell. He made it very clear that the last thing he ever wants to do is be a parent. Ever." That made her sad. The guy had no idea what he was missing out on. "If I do this, I do it on my own."

"If," Chelsea said. Her forehead winkled in concern. "You know you don't *have* to."

"I know." An abortion? Maybe she would've considered it ten years ago, but now…? She couldn't do it.

A baby… Someone to love and cherish for the rest of her life.

She looked over at Sophie, sleeping peacefully in her bassinette, and emotion knotted her throat. To think that she'd get to hold her own child, nurture a baby of her own and give all the love in her heart… It was something she had been beginning to think might not happen.

"I never thought I'd be a single mother, but what if this is my only chance to be a mom. What if I don't meet *the* guy until all my eggs are dried up and useless? How can I blow what might be my only shot at motherhood?" Kim looked away from the empathy in Chelsea's eyes. "I want a taste of it," she murmured.

Chelsea's small grin spoke volumes. "Seems like you've kind of made your decision."

"Maybe I have." She was going to have a baby. A full body sweat made her light-headed, and she didn't have time for it. "I need to tell Leo and I can't do it over the phone. I have to see his face."

The baby gurgled and Chelsea eased in her direction. "When are you going?"

Running a hand through her hair, Kim squeezed her eyes shut. It was all happening too fast. It was as if her Los Angeles trip had started a never-ending roller coaster of one life change after another. "As soon as I see my doctor and get the best guess on how far along I am. Leo will probably want to know the dates."

Chelsea adjusted the blanket over Sophie and came toward Kim with a hand on her hip. "You don't think he'll believe you?" The instant anger and indignation in her voice made Kim smile. "Maybe I should go with you and—"

"And what?" Kim asked. "Beat him up?"

"If I have to!"

Kim hugged her friend. "You're the best. But I think I can handle it." She pulled away and went behind her desk. "Look, it would be different if I thought he cared about me or if I had some delusion that we might be a couple. But that isn't the case. I just need to tell him and make sure he understands that I don't want anything from him."

Chelsea crossed her arms. "It's not like he has anything anymore anyway, is it? I thought he was in debt up to his eyeballs."

"I think he's in better shape than I originally anticipated. He sold all his property. Sold his memorabilia and anything and everything that would help his situation. Honestly, I was really proud of him. I didn't think he'd do it."

"Where's he living if he sold his house," Chelsea asked. "I didn't think there was too much left standing after the last earthquake."

Kim had never been happier than to have missed that epic event, but she had worried about Leo. It had taken her hours to get in touch with him the day of that 7.1 quake. "He's renting a smaller place in the hills. I haven't seen it, but he told me a little about it."

"How many times have you talked to him since you were there?"

"I don't know. A few times a week. Sometimes less. We email more than we talk."

Chelsea took a step toward her. "If you need me, I'll go with you."

Kim waved her off. "You're sweet, but you're lying. You've got a new baby. You can't come with me. It's okay. I can do this. Leo won't have to do anything. I'm not asking him for any money." Money! She had money now!

"What?" Chelsea said, watching her face. "What just happened? Why do you look like that?"

"I didn't tell you about the inheritance." Kim paced across the room. She could actually do this. If she was pregnant, she could totally afford to have this baby. She sat down again. A baby.

"Right! You wouldn't leave a message, so spill it." Chelsea lifted an eyebrow.

"You know how Aunt Carolyn lived in a modest three bedroom house in Arizona?"

Chelsea nodded. "I do. I never would've met you if you hadn't moved from the desert and gone to school in Chicago."

"Correct. It turns out that Aunt Carolyn had money. A lot of money."

"Like...how much money?"

"Ten million dollars' worth...and she left it all to me."

This time Chelsea's eyes widened to half dollar proportions. "You said what now?"

"Crazy, right? You mentioned the word *late* and my mind totally went somewhere else and I forgot to tell you. I think I'm a millionaire." Kim would've pushed Chelsea's mouth closed if she'd been close enough.

"And you thought you'd save that information to tell me face to face?" Chelsea said, with her arms spread wide.

"You have to admit. It's some serious news." So was her pregnancy if that was in fact the case. "I should get that pregnancy test." Kim grabbed her purse and stood up again.

"Whoa, whoa, whoa. Not so fast. Ten million dollars? This is amazing." Her smile slowly disappeared. "You realize that two trips in the span of as many months have completely changed your life."

"I guess that's an understatement." Kim watched the sparkle

dim from Chelsea's eyes. "Uh oh," she said. "I know that look. What's wrong?"

"Nothing's wrong, really. I mean, I was just thinking about this." Spreading her arms, Chelsea encompassed the office. "I know you're not happy here, Kimmy. You have the chance to go someplace that makes you happy. Back to Chicago or L.A. or even New York. I know moving here wasn't on your list of places to live. But you did it for me. So I'm thinking that your life is changing in all sorts of ways and maybe you've outgrown our little operation."

"Don't say that, Chels." But she couldn't deny her friend had a point. She had a chance to make her life what she wanted. To move and experience what a bigger city had to offer. "I need to take things one step at a time. Right now the first step is to take a pregnancy test."

"Right. And see your doctor," Chelsea added. "They'll want to test you too." She waved toward the door.

"Right. I guess I'm doing this now."

Chelsea nodded. "No time to waste. Sounds like you might be a little behind already. Need to get those results and get you on a program."

"Program?" Kim didn't like the sound of this. "What kind of program?"

"Diet, vitamins, exercise. It all makes a healthy, happy baby." Chelsea escorted her out of the office. "I'd come with you, but Royal Oil is coming in for a meeting in a couple of hours and I need to get ready. Will you be okay on your own?"

Kim scoffed. "Of course. But I feel bad I'm leaving you here to deal with all of this alone."

"I've got it handled. I hired a temp. She'll be here in another half hour."

"Oh. A temp. That's the new desk in front. You didn't tell me."

"I didn't want you to worry. It's all handled. Do what you need to do."

Kim's phone rang again and she checked the screen. "What is Wilson's problem?" she muttered as she shoved the phone back in her purse.

"Problems with your cousin?" Chelsea asked.

"He's been calling me nonstop since I left him at the airport.

Questions about Carolyn or about the house. Legal issues, house issues. You name it and he has to ask me about it. I wonder if this is what Carolyn went through the last few years."

Chelsea gave her a sympathetic smile. "Just collect all the voicemails and answer them in one shot."

"Yes, Mom. Thanks."

"Haha. You're welcome. Now go." Chelsea pushed her out the door.

Kim made a quick trip to the pharmacy before going back to her condo. Her pulse hammered and her palms slicked with sweat. She'd been pacing in her bathroom for two full minutes already. Not even the soothing earth tones in the stone tile could calm her now.

She didn't want to look at the stick. Really, what was the point? She knew the results. She'd felt it in her body. Her breasts were more sensitive, her stomach had been weird and she'd been a little green for more than a couple of weeks. Not to mention the fact that she'd missed two periods. Two.

"Do it," she ordered herself. Mustering up her courage, she looked. The air froze in her lungs and the room tilted precariously.

A plus sign.

She grabbed the counter to steady herself. "You called it, Chels," she muttered. Kim sat on the covered toilet seat and put her head in her hands. "Oh man."

She should see her doctor. Get her diagnosis confirmed by a professional. Find out how far along she was.

"Oh, God." Pregnant. This was not how she envisioned this moment. She was supposed to be married first, preferably for a couple of years. Hopefully to a man she loved and who loved her in return. If living in this state had taught her anything, it was that she missed the big city, but was that the best place to raise a baby? She missed going out and meeting people with her same interests.

Now her interests included parenthood.

What else did she have to do? The list seemed never-ending.

Oh God. She had to call Leo. Kim rubbed her temples with her index fingers then stood and looked into the mirror. "What did you do, dummy?"

Chapter Four

Sitting at the counter that separated the kitchen from the den, Leo hung up his phone and dropped his chin to his chest. "Shit." Vivienne had categorically refused to take Cat. Again. He'd been trying for days. The feline stared him down with stunning yellow eyes from her perch at the end of his leather sofa. A real looker, just like his Porsche had been. He missed Stella something fierce. Cat actually reminded him of Stella in a sleek black way.

The phone rang and he checked the caller ID. His agent. Hot damn.

"Hey, Rich. What's up? You got something?"

"Leo! How are you, man? We just got wind of a new project from Jess Bryant and we're working on getting you the script. Everything she does so far is box office gold. The crowds love her."

"Tell me something I don't know," Leo murmured. His co-star, Julie Fraser, from *Dangerous Race* had scored an Oscar with Jess Bryant's first film. One of her movies could put him in the black both financially and critically. "I don't care what the part is. I want it. I need this job, Rich."

"I'm working on it. Don't worry. I'll get back to you when I know more. I just wanted you in the loop. Listen, I have to run. I've got a meeting in two minutes. We'll talk soon." The line went dead and Leo hung up the phone carefully.

He really needed this job. Something had to pan out soon or he was in the deepest shit of his life.

Looking around at the few belongings from his old house depressed the shit out of him. Most of his furniture had been sold with the house, but the things that had followed him only reminded him of what he lost. From a ten thousand square foot spacious home to this twelve hundred square foot stacked matchbox. He'd initially liked the dark muted green of the walls, but now it just looked glum. The space seemed to close in on him on a daily basis. Nothing of any value had followed him here, which meant he was stuck with the few pieces of artwork that meant nothing to him, but filled up the dreary spaces on the walls.

Pathetic.

Maybe having the cat around for a little while might be a good thing. Which meant...

"I know I said I wasn't naming you, but Cat seems so... I don't know...lame." Leo crossed into the room and sat next to her temporary bed. He had a litter box in the hall closet with the door halfway open. He had food and water on the kitchen floor per the vet's instructions. He smoothed his hand over her head and she leaned into the stroke with a purr. "Yeah, I know what you like...Petunia." He shook his head. "Nope. Never in a million years." He exhaled a frustrated groan. "Okay, I need a real name for you," he said, relenting. "So what's it going to be?" She was black. Sleek. Beautiful. She blinked all-knowing yellow eyes. "What do you think of Stella?" he asked. "I know it was my car, but she's gone now and you actually fit the profile."

The purring got louder.

Leo nodded once. "Good enough for me. I'm calling that a yes."

Strumming guitar notes rang in the room and Leo picked up his phone from the coffee table and checked the screen. His heart did a little double thump when he saw Kim's name.

"Hey!" he said, happy to talk to the one person who knew what he'd been through, the one person who knew more about him than anyone else. The only person he'd ever truly missed since she'd jetted out of his life almost two months ago. No woman had ever left him before. It had been just another dose of crappy reality. "What's new? How are you?"

Her silence tipped him off and the happy beat of his heart stuttered.

"A lot is new actually. I was going to fly in tomorrow or the day after if you can squeeze me into your schedule. We need to talk."

The four most dreaded words in the English language. *We need to talk.* Nothing good ever came from those words. "Sure. I'm here. I'm trying to set up a few meetings with some distributors, but nothing's set yet. Come on in."

"Great. Thanks." She didn't sound her usual confident, happy self, and warning signs blared in Leo's head. What if he hadn't really hit bottom? What if she had news that might sink him even more? Christ, he hardly had anything left to sell. He'd gotten rid of all the homes he had mortgages on. He'd sold his cars, his memorabilia and practically his soul. Renting a piece of shit home in the hills and a *previously owned* Benz nearly killed him.

Growing up, he'd watched his mother struggle to pay the bills. Meeting his little sister's needs had sucked up every last penny. He'd vowed to make enough money to keep all three of them comfortable, but his mom died when he was twenty-two, before he made it big. Everything he'd owned had been a mark of success, a milestone that he savored. Selling it all had been like taking strips of his hide one slow piece at a time. He'd been reminded all too clearly that no matter how hard you tried, everything could change in an instant.

Stella mewled and rubbed her head into his hand. She tried to get up, but had a hard time negotiating, so Leo took her to the litter box in case she had business to do.

"I should probably warn you, I have a new roommate. I think you'll like her though."

Dead silence over the phone. "What?" The word came with her exhale. "Of course...I...I look forward to meeting her. Bye." She hung up before Leo got another word in and he stared at the blank screen.

That was odd, not to mention very unlike Kim. What had her in such a rush? *Roommate?* Oh... *Her.* She couldn't possibly think... "Son of a bitch." Leo called Kim back, but he got her voicemail.

"Kim, it's me. My new roommate is a cat. The *her* is a cat. Not that you would care or anything because I know you and I...um. Well, you and I aren't..." Shit, he was screwing this up with every word. "Look, you just sounded a little—" *Beep.* The phone cut him off. "You gotta be fucking kidding me," he growled. He refused to call back like a pussy who cared. She'd find out soon enough who his roommate—temporary roommate—was. Until then she'd survive. It wasn't like they were a couple. They'd absolutely parted as friends.

So why was she constantly on his mind? Why did her soft blond hair and stunning green eyes make their way into his thoughts more than a dozen times a day?

Stella wobbled over to him and Leo scooped her up carefully before setting her on the sofa next to him.

"Wait until you meet Kim," he said, rubbing her head and making her purr. "You're going to like her. She's tough. Just like you."

Stella looked up at him and blinked with slow heavy eyes. She yawned, set her head on his thigh and promptly crashed.

"That's one satisfied woman," Leo muttered.

His phone beeped with an incoming email and Leo checked. "Hot damn." It was the distributor he'd met a few months ago at The Polo Lounge. Maybe he'd get his movie out after all. He just had to finish the damn thing. One location shoot—guerilla style and he could wrap this sucker. He had too much money invested in it to shelve it permanently. The fact that his co-star was in a mental institution would either kill the film or make it a hit. Why the woman had to go off the deep end after making his movie, he'd never understand. She'd not only screwed up her own life, she'd screwed up his.

He still couldn't believe that Carrie Ann Laughlin had actually murdered a man. His skin crawled when he thought about it. That she almost killed his co-star from *Dangerous Race* was an even bigger coincidence. He'd wondered about what Carrie Ann would think of him finally releasing the film. Would she be embarrassed or happy? Would she be able to comment on it at all from where she currently resided? Hell, would she even know about it? Maybe she was locked up so tight she didn't have television.

Leo picked up the shot list for the remaining scene. The director who'd started with the film had inconveniently offed himself six months ago, leaving Leo in a massive lurch. Combine that with his lead actress landing in the psych ward for murder and his film was screwed.

Until he decided to finish it himself. There wasn't that much left. He could do it. He'd just have to break a few rules. He couldn't afford the kind of set up he'd managed for the majority of the film. He'd broken cardinal rule number one. Never use your own money for a film. It took hindsight to see what an idiot he'd been. Not that being an idiot was new territory for him, but he just never copped to it.

He didn't have the money to finish it, so he'd have to raise money the old fashioned way and find investors and a distributor. All new territory for him. His palms sweat just thinking about it. What if everyone thought the film was cursed? Between a dead director and a mentally unstable co-star, people might not touch it if he paid them.

Next to him, Stella had a kitty nightmare. Her little paws flailed away and her muzzle crinkled and twitched. Poor thing was probably reliving being in the jaws of a coyote. He stroked her head, her fur soft under his fingers, and she calmed.

"Not so bad having someone to make it all better, huh, Stella?"

He wouldn't mind having someone like that for himself.

Kim's face flashed in his head. A blonde bombshell who walked into his life at the worst time. Or maybe it was the best time. Maybe she was the best thing to come his way in…ever. Leo shook off the thought. No way was he letting a female under his skin. He looked down, discovered he was still stroking Stella's head and snapped his hand back. Not even Stella.

Wilson hung up the kitchen phone after leaving another voicemail and rested his head in his hands. Did Carolyn—Kim. Did Kim think he enjoyed being ignored? For all its *beauty* on the surface, the house Carolyn left him with was a money pit. If Kim didn't float him a loan for a plumber, he estimated two days before the damn water heater flooded the place. On top of that, the washing machine quit and his laundry was stacking up.

There had to be another way to reach Kim, another number to catch her by surprise. Her office! Of course! He should've thought of this earlier. After booting up the computer in the kitchen corner, he found her agency on the Internet and called the number.

"Hello, Rivers and Jacobs Advertising, can I help you?"

The fact that she had her own business with her name attached sent a hot thread of annoyance shooting through his stomach. He could've had his own business too if Carolyn had given him a loan. He'd mapped out a whole plan to start a silk flower shop. It was the perfect business for desert country. People would clamor for fake green shit they didn't have to water.

"Can I speak with Kim?" he asked.

"She's not in. Would you like to leave a message?"

Why would she be in? She had a cool ten million dollars to play with. She probably didn't plan to work another day in her life. He nearly laughed out loud at the irony.

"Yes." He most definitely wanted to leave a message. "This is her cousin Wilson. I've been calling her cell phone, but it's urgent I speak with her."

"Oh, Wilson. This is Chelsea, Kim's partner. I'm so sorry for your loss. Kim told me how close you were to your aunt. I know this must be a difficult time for you."

Difficult, frustrating and aggravating barely scratched the surface. He'd never met Chelsea, but he knew she went back to Kim's college days. "Oh, thank you. I don't know about Kim, but it's almost like being orphaned all over again. What did Kim say about me?" Maybe she felt sorry enough to part with some of the money. A couple big wins at the track and he might not have to work another day in his life either.

"She just told me how much time you spent with your aunt the last few years and that this whole transition has been hard for both of you."

He rolled his eyes at the understatement. "I guess we're never really prepared for death. I mean, sometimes we might think we are, but..." Did he really just utter that inane sentence? "Do you know when Kim will be back in the office? She doesn't seem to be picking up her calls."

"She's actually headed out of town for a day or two."

"Really?" Wilson held back a fresh burst of envy. She was already spending that money. Probably taking a weekend spa trip somewhere. He'd be doing something similar. "Where's she headed?"

"Los Angeles."

"Wasn't she just there a couple months ago?" Kim had told him a little about that trip, but he'd read the gory details in the newspaper when the story of her old roommate's kidnapping went national.

"Yes. She had some…business to attend to."

Business? The hesitation in Chelsea's voice made it sound like something other than actual business. "Is she okay?" he asked.

"She's fine. A little morning sickness, but other than that, she's okay."

Blood drained from Wilson's head quicker than water poured over Niagara. "Morning sickness?" he repeated numbly. He remembered a few of the mornings in Arizona with Kim and her queasy stomach. The silence on the phone told him all he needed to know. "She's pregnant?"

"Oh my gosh. I can't believe I said that. I'm so sorry. That was a complete slip on my part. I'm sure she'll tell you. She just found out herself."

"Don't worry about it," he assured her. "I suspected as much. She wasn't feeling great when we were together and she mentioned a guy, but didn't tell me his name." He had no clue what he was saying, but he didn't want Chelsea to think he was out of the loop. "So this trip to L.A.…" Kim had confided how Indiana wasn't really working out for her, so maybe with the new influx of dough she'd decided to move. Or maybe the baby's father lived there…? "Is she buying a house or… What is the trip for?"

"You can ask her yourself. I'm sure she'll be calling you back as soon as she can. She's got a lot on her mind right now."

Right. Like how to spend an extra ten million dollars. His cousin was going to have a baby, was she? And his little second cousin would end up with his money. That burned him like nobody's business.

"Chelsea, do you know when she arrives in town? What airline? I'll be in L.A. myself later in the week, but maybe I can change my schedule to meet her there. I'd love to surprise her." He still had no idea what he was saying, but the faster he talked the more a plan came to him.

"Hold on. Let me check. She gave me her itinerary, so I know I have it somewhere." He heard shuffling before she came back on the line. "Here it is," she said. She rattled off the airline and flight number.

"Tomorrow?" What the hell had her flying to Los Angeles at the drop of a hat? "I guess that rules out me picking her up at the airport." He hoped his chuckle sounded sincere.

"No worries about that. She's getting a rental."

"Ah. Of course. Well, maybe she'll stay an extra day or two and we'll meet up. Thanks for the information anyway. It was good talking to you." He needed to make the most of this phone call.

"You too, Wilson. And my condolences again on your loss. I'm so sorry."

"Thank you. I appreciate it. Listen, I was thinking since you and I are so close to Kim that maybe I should I have a direct contact to you. You know, just in case of emergency."

"Oh." She paused and it made him wonder if Kim had already bad-mouthed him—a la Carolyn—to Chelsea. "Okay. Sure," she said before giving her number.

Wilson scribbled it down. "Great. Thanks. I feel better knowing we can connect." Chelsea mumbled something similar, but he barely paid any attention before disconnecting the call and heading to his room to pack. He had a seven-hour drive ahead of him. If he waited in the baggage claim area of the airport and watched her check in with the rental agency, he could probably get to the rental lot at the same time she did, once he got his car out of the parking garage and once she caught a shuttle. It was going to be dicey, but it was worth a try. If that didn't work, he'd find her somehow.

Kim hadn't said a word about a pregnancy in Arizona, so maybe she just found out. Hell, she hadn't even mentioned a guy and they talked about both their nonexistent dating lives. She'd just taken a recent trip to California, so maybe this visit had something to do with the baby's father. Or maybe he was grasping at straws.

Either way, Kim was single and pregnant and this trip to Los Angeles was the perfect chance to get even more reacquainted with his cousin. He'd make her dependent on him, or he'd just take her out of the equation. Because if he couldn't have that money, then neither would she.

The next afternoon, Leo's doorbell rang. He hadn't heard it since he moved in and the high-pitched chime had Stella lifting her head from her spot on the sofa. He opened the door and his heart did that same gallop when he saw Kim.

Two months hadn't changed his attraction to her. In fact, she looked even more beautiful than before. Loose blonde curls hung around her shoulders and those spectacular green eyes stared at him from beneath long dark lashes. Dressed in a slinky hot-pink top, a form-fitting black skirt and her signature stilettoes, she made him think of cotton candy and sex. Not necessarily in that order.

"Hi," she said. All cool ice princess. She'd worn the same expression the day they'd first met. Of course, now, he had a good idea why she had that hard look in her eyes. She thought that along with the new house, he'd shacked up with a new woman.

He didn't bother with a greeting as he leaned against the door frame. "You never listened to my voicemail yesterday, did you?"

Her stony face answered his question. "No," she finally said. She'd obviously had time to replay their short conversation in her head. He also hadn't seen her this perturbed since the day he'd met her. If he didn't know better, he'd think she was jealous. But she was the one who walked away two months ago. The one who told him to go home. So he had. He'd walked away with every part of him hating every second.

Taking her hand, he brought her inside. He'd forgotten how soft her skin was. How many times had he stared at her delicate fingers while watching her at his desk two months ago? "Kim, I'd like you to meet my temporary roommate, Stella." He stopped in front of the sofa where Stella had gingerly sat up. "Stella, this is Kim."

Kim's face melted in a sorrowful pucker as she sat down. "Oh, baby girl. What happened to you?" She eased Stella onto her lap and smoothed her hand over the feline's head. "Why didn't you tell me you were talking about a cat?" She shot him an annoyed look before giving her full attention back to Stella.

"I would have if you hadn't hung up on me." He loved being right. Mostly because it didn't happen that often. Especially when this woman was involved.

She eyed him while shifting the cat on her lap. "What happened to her?"

Leo told the coyote tale, not minding that he came off as a real-life hero for once. The E.R. story reminded him of her friend and the last time Kim had been in town. "How's Stephanie doing? Still in New York with her sister?"

Kim nodded, her gaze softening with the subject. "Yeah. I think she might relocate there. She's doing better. It's a long road."

Stephanie had been kidnapped and nearly sold in a sex slave ring. The circumstances had been bad enough, but discovering her husband was behind the ordeal—mainly to keep her from divorcing him and getting half his net worth—had sent her running back to family.

Sometimes Leo wished he could do that.

"Can I get you something to drink?" he asked, gesturing toward the kitchen.

"No. I'm fine." She waved him off, then looked him straight in the eyes. "Leo, sit down. I need to tell you something."

Shit. He knew that tone. He may not have known Kim long, but he knew her well enough to hear bad news before she spewed it. It made sense, didn't it? Bad luck came in threes. His movie had been shelved, he'd lost all his worldly belongings and now this…whatever Kim had to tell him.

Taking her advice, which so far had always been right on the money, Leo sat on the chair across from her. Was it more financial shit? He thought they'd tackled all his financial issues. What else could it be? "Hit me," he said, with more confidence than he felt.

She stood and started pacing in front of him, her heels muffled by the taupe carpet. He'd never known her to pace before either. Seemed very out of character for her. She usually tackled problems head on with her business savvy and sharp mind. Of course, watching her ass in the fitted black skirt that hugged her curves in a man-eater way took his mind off the impending dilemma. The way her bright pink top draped over her full breasts didn't hurt either.

He's missed her. He'd missed her smart mouth and her take-charge attitude. Mostly he missed having someone to confide in. Someone to listen. Though she'd judged him when they first met, somehow they'd struck up a friendship and ultimately she'd saved his ass…financially speaking. Then she'd stolen part of his heart.

"It can't be that bad," Leo said, focusing on her face. Staring at her ass would only get him into trouble.

"I guess that depends on your definition of bad." She faced

him and Leo's heart stalled in his chest. She was about to drop a bomb. He felt it in his gut. Clenching her hands in front of her, she looked him straight in the eye. "I'm pregnant."

Whoa!

Everything shut down before clicking back into function mode. If there was one thing she could've hit him with that would knock his lights out, that was it.

"Wow. That's, that's... Why are you tell—" The words died on his tongue as the implication hit harder than the original news. He stood up. Sat down. Stood up again. "Are you saying you're pregnant and *I'm* the father?" Pretty dumb as far as obvious questions went, but she'd thrown him off.

More like over a cliff.

She swallowed hard and nodded, watching him closely.

He ran a hand through his hair and strode past her, taking over the pacing as his mind spun in a thousand directions at once. She couldn't be pregnant. He couldn't be a father. There was no way in hell he could do it. "Are you sure?" he asked, turning toward her. The mix of frustration and sympathy warred in her eyes and irritated him.

"I'm sorry to surprise you with this. Trust me, it was a surprise to me too." That was the frustration.

"I haven't seen you in months. How far along are you? Are you sure it's—" He cut himself off at the narrowed gaze she leveled at him. "We used protection," he reminded her, his own frustration making an appearance.

"Apparently, either not soon enough or it failed." She had more steel in her voice now, more like the Kim he'd first met in his accountant's office two months ago. Two fucking months ago. How could she be pregnant after a couple of encounters? Granted he felt like he knew her and they'd certainly gotten close, but...

He didn't want kids for so many reasons. None of which she knew. "This is too surreal."

She sat on the sofa. "Tell me about it." Her confidence sputtered a little and the fear she must have been feeling bled through in her words.

In their two short month relationship, she'd taught him a lot about humility. Or maybe going broke had done that. Maybe selling off all his possessions had done that. But she'd stressed the importance of looking at all angles of every situation. *Put yourself in someone else's shoes and try to see how they'd feel.* So he did. He put himself in her shoes, a single, pregnant woman. She must be fucking terrified.

His initial reaction embarrassed him. Of course he was the father. She wouldn't be telling him otherwise. But it didn't change the fact that he couldn't have kids. Yes in the physical/literal sense, since obviously he *could* have kids, but he couldn't *deal* with having kids. There was too much room for error. Too much could go wrong and they could wind up like his sister, Megan. He couldn't watch his own children end up like his sister. It would break him.

"Have you got a plan?" he asked. Because maybe she didn't want to be pregnant.

"Kind of," she said, not making eye contact. She exhaled hard and stood in front of him. "I've decided to have the baby, but want you to know that I don't expect anything from you. I know how you feel about parenting and I don't plan to force you into anything. I'm happy to sign an agreement to that effect if it makes you feel better."

Boom, boom, boom. One-two punches all the way around. "*You've* decided," he said, his anger building slowly from a hell storm in his gut. "Did you ever think that the decision isn't strictly up to you alone? Maybe I've got a say in this too?"

Her eyes widened. He'd surprised her. Good. She thought because she knew his finances inside and out that she knew him too, and nothing could be farther from the truth. He had every right to feel the way he did about having children and bringing them up in the world. She didn't own the right to make this decision completely by herself.

"Actually, since it's my body, you *don't* really have a say. I choose what happens to me." The deadly calm tone should've warned him, but he didn't care.

"You can't have this baby, Kim." He shook his head because she'd obviously put a lot of thought into it, but that didn't matter. She didn't know what she might face having his baby. "I'm sorry. You can't."

Her jaw tightened and she stood taller. "*I'm* sorry you think you can tell me what to do, Leo, but *you* can't. I told you you're off the hook so don't worry about it." She headed to the door. "I think it's best we end our business dealings as well. No sense of having any contact with each other now that I know how you feel."

Bullshit. Leo grabbed her arm and spun her around. "Nope. Not that fast. You don't get to tell me how this plays out. You don't think I have something at stake in this?"

"What? The tabloids? Your precious reputation, which by the way sucks and has for a lot of years. You know after we met and I got to know you, I really didn't understand all the stories the press ran about you. You seemed nothing like what they made you out to be, but I think I've finally gotten a taste of the real Leo." She clenched her jaw. "It's too bad," she said softly. "I liked the other guy better." She spun on her heels and marched toward the door.

Leo kept right on her tail. "You're right about one thing. You don't know me or my reasons, but I'm serious. You can't have this baby, Kim. It's a bad idea."

"Bad for you?" She threw over her shoulder as she reached the door. "I don't see why. You don't have to participate. You wouldn't even know if I hadn't said something to you, and now I'm wishing I hadn't." She grabbed her purse from the entry table and opened the door.

"Would you just wait a minute?" he said, stopping her again with a hand on her arm.

She faced him. "Why? What's the point? Look, just so you know...I didn't plan for this, but everything happens for a reason, right? I got pregnant, so maybe I'm supposed to have a baby. Do I wish I wasn't going to be a single mother? Maybe. But I'm not ready to toss away a shot at motherhood when I don't know if I'll get the chance again." She stood defiant. He didn't have a chance in hell of convincing her otherwise.

Would it matter if he told her about the fucked up genetics in his family? Would it make a difference to her either way?

"Kim, I have my reasons, okay. Obviously it matters to you that I know or you wouldn't have made the trip."

"Having the right to know doesn't give you the right to decide what I do. Those are two different things."

"What if..." God, how did he say this?

She tilted her head a fraction. "Yeah? What if what?"

"I don't know. What if something is wrong with the baby?

You know how expensive a baby is? And if something's wrong then you're expenses just double or tripled or quadrupled."

She straightened up to her full height and the fire in her eyes blasted him. "Gee. That's a nice thought. Scare the shit out of me while I'm pregnant. Nice going, Leo. Good-bye." She spun and walked out the door. Her world-class ass shaking right out of his life for good.

So she thought.

Chapter Five

The sting of hot tears burned Kim's eyes as she cranked the engine of her gray midsized rental and backed out of the steep driveway. "Son of a bitch," she seethed, spinning the wheel hard on the narrow road. "You cannot and will not tell me what to do, asshole." Shifting into drive, she hit the gas and lurched forward.

She'd played a lot of scenarios in her head, but none of them had turned out like this. Why did he have to be such an asshole about it? The first curve came up fast and she hit the brake to stay on her side of the road.

"I have my reasons," she mocked as she took another curve, tears leaking down her cheeks. "Well, I have reasons too, dickhead. You're off the hook so why should you even care." She swiped at her cheeks and immediately grabbed the wheel when she couldn't control it one handed. She took two more curves, gripping the sluggish wheel tightly in her hands. "What the hell?" A sharp turn came up and the wheel barely responded. "Oh shit," Kim breathed as she slammed on the brakes. The car skidded on gravel, maybe left over remnants from a hill slide because of the earthquake a month ago. It didn't matter because the car just kept going and she had no way to turn. No way to avoid the guardrail that loomed straight in front of her or the massive drop that lurked behind it.

Jump!

Self-preservation kicked in. Kim unbuckled her seatbelt, opened the car door and jumped before impact. The crash exploded next to her as she hit the gravel road. The car went airborne and over the cliff while a deafening roar of adrenaline filled her head. Gravity yanked her in the same direction as her car and Kim skidded, out of control, scrabbling for hold as she slid. A second later, her legs went over the edge and she was falling, still trying to grab something, anything to hang onto. She caught a ledge for a couple of seconds, but lost it and dropped onto another ledge and bounced. Still grappling for something, she caught a thick bush and held on to the body of it, her heart slamming against her ribs, her breathing harsh.

Brittle branches poked against her torso and shredded her shirt, but she was still breathing, still alive, so she counted it as a win. "Don't look down. Don't look down," she muttered softly. She looked up. At the distance she had to somehow climb to save her stupid ass.

She shifted to find purchase with her legs and the bush threatened to give way. "No, no, no." Hot tears clouded her vision. She couldn't die. The baby inside her depended on her. Maybe if she went sideways and got a foot on the flat rock protruding from the mountain, she could leverage herself up. But any type of movement might yank this bush out even faster. Indecision and fear kept her completely still despite all those branches poking mercilessly into her torso.

"Kim!" Leo! The panic in his voice matched her shit-in-the-pants fear.

"Leo! I'm here!" The roots of the bush slowly came loose from their hold. "I don't have much time. This bush is about to drop me." *Don't look down.* She didn't want to know how far she had to fall. The longer she waited, the less chance she had of this damn shrubbery holding her.

"Hang on! I'm coming!"

Rocks whizzed past her and she didn't look up. The bush dropped her another six inches as more roots popped out of the mountain. He wasn't going to make it in time.

Kim kicked her right leg sideways to get a swing going. It was the only way she'd reach that ledge. The bush didn't like the new distribution of weight and told her so with another lurch. Her high pitch scream cut the silence. With a fresh burst of adrenaline, Kim tried one more shot at the ledge. She swung her leg up and caught the edge, hanging horizontal and parallel to the canyon bottom. More roots yanked from their spot in the mountain wall as the bush slowly pulled out completely. A scream tore from Kim as she started to follow it down.

Strong hands snagged her left arm and she reached up blindly with her right and grabbed onto Leo's bicep with everything she had.

"Gotcha," he huffed, dragging her up his body until she was tightly against him.

She had no idea how he managed it and didn't care. She held on, breathing hard, every inch of skin burning with cuts and scrapes.

"Easy, easy," he soothed. "Let's try and move over to that ledge you were aiming for," he said, his voice calm, cool and in control. He sounded just like the action hero he played in the movies. With her nose buried in his neck, she caught the mouth-watering, spicy scent of him.

Shaking uncontrollably, Kim opened her eyes. Leo had a rope wrapped around his chest. He moved sideways the couple feet necessary to reach their little ledge and together they got their balance, hugging the mountain like sap on a tree.

Leo manipulated them so he was behind her, keeping her safe between him and solid rock. "I've got you. You're not going anywhere."

Under normal circumstances, Kim might have enjoyed the scenery, the beauty of the rock and the green vegetation scattered within dry brush, but the only thing on her mind was moving air into her stricken lungs. Her teeth chattered too loudly for her to talk. She should've been relieved, not freaking out, now that she was safe.

"Help is coming, babe. Another car coming up the hill saw what happened and called it in. We just have to hold on. Can you do that for me?" He said the words softly in her ear with all the confidence and sex appeal she remembered from a couple of months ago. His warm hand nestled right under her breasts and hugged her tightly against him. He sounded so calm, like this was just another average day.

Kim nodded as her scraped fingers searched for handholds. "You had r-rope in your car?" she asked numbly. If he hadn't, she'd be at the canyon floor splattered on the wreck of her rental.

"Hey, after a 7.1, you can bet any self-respecting Angelino has an up-to-date earthquake kit including all the incidentals for emergencies in their house *and* their car. So, yeah, I have rope that was already tied into a slip knot and a forty pound survival pack in the trunk."

Lucky her. Long minutes ticked by before Kim's breathing evened out and her teeth stopped clanking together.

"Are you okay?" The quiet concern in his voice chipped away at the anger she harbored. His question reminded her how much she hurt. Between road rash from the slide, the branches poking her torso and the bruises forming everywhere else, she felt like she'd been through a shredder. A hell of a ride for the little bun in her oven. God, she hoped the baby was okay. In the scheme of things, though, this was just a really painful amusement ride…without the amusement.

Thanks to him, she was alive. "Yeah. I think so. Just kind of shaken up." It was hard to stay angry at Leo after he risked his life to save hers, and it was doubly hard to resist that rough-tender tone of his voice, but she still didn't know what to say to him. As minutes ticked by, the presence of Leo's growing erection against her ass brought her focus back to the man's shamelessness and away from her cramping fingers holding protruding rocks.

"You're kidding me, right?" she said, trying to edge closer to the mountain to escape the pressure of his dick between her ass cheeks. Just because he saved her didn't mean she had to put up with this crap.

He chuckled, his breath fanning her ear. Little pinpricks of sensation prickled her skin. Probably all those scrapes again. "I can't help it. You have a very nice ass. Really, when you think about it, I'm complimenting you."

Frustration bubbled out. Leo's sex life was no big secret, but like a fool she'd added her name to the notches on his bedpost. Look where that got her? She tried to shift, but only succeeded in rubbing against Leo and settling him more firmly against her. "Can you *not* compliment me this very *moment?*"

"Out of my control, babe."

Frustration warred with gratitude and she rolled her eyes. Sirens wailed in the canyon and relief washed through her like cool water in a soothing brook. "Thank God," Kim breathed.

"Not sure he's the one to thank. I'm the one who caught you, remember?"

"Oh for God's sake." She felt the curve of his lips against her temple. "You think this is funny?" Kim braved a head turn to look him in the face, but any humor that might have been there quickly vanished as he squeezed her tighter.

He stroked some hair off her cheek. "This is the farthest thing from funny I've ever dealt with." His blue-eyed gaze drilled into hers. "When we get on solid ground, you're going to tell me just what the hell you were thinking taking these curves at fifty miles an hour. Were you trying to kill yourself?"

"No!" she snapped. "I mean, I was upset, but I didn't do it on purpose." God, what if this *had* been her fault? Had she lost control of the car because she wasn't paying attention? No, the car had definitely been tough to control. "Something was wrong with the steering wheel." The sirens got louder and stopped almost directly over them.

"What?"

"I hit the brakes and because I couldn't steer, I went into the gravel and lost control in the—" she sniffed the air, "—skid. Do you smell that?"

Leo took a whiff of her hair. "You smell great." Did he just nuzzle her? No. She was hallucinating. Near death experiences probably did that to a person.

"Not me." She sniffed again. "Smoke. I smell smoke."

Looking over his shoulder, Leo nodded. "You've got insurance on your rental, right? Because it's burning."

Kim knocked her head against the rock in front of her, totally defeated. "Of course it is." Her luggage and purse were still in it because she'd come straight from the airport. Her second trip to L.A. in as many months, and for the second time in a row she'd lost everything but the clothes on her back. And if the scratches stinging her skin were any indication, then she didn't even have the clothes on her back. The cramping in her fingers moved into her hands and arms.

"Looks like you're going on another shopping spree. I'm beginning to wonder if you like any of the clothes you pack."

She ignored his attempt at humor. The last time they'd shopped together he'd taken her to a posh store in Beverly Hills. What a disaster of a trip that had been. At least this time she could afford the clothes. That thought perked her up. She kept forgetting she had money. Not that she had it yet, but it was coming. Thank you, Aunt Carolyn.

"Hey, you two all right?" someone called.

"Just hanging around," Leo called. "Could use a hand ASAP."

"Coming down as we speak," the guy replied.

A minute later, two firemen slid down next to them. They strapped a harness around Kim before taking her out of Leo's arms. Leo got a harness of his own. Kim and her rescuer went up first and Leo followed with his guy. Two more firemen helped pull her up and away from the edge.

Her jaw nearly hit the ground when she looked down at herself. Her legs were scraped, bloody and bruised. Her tattered shirt barely covered anything. One of the men brought her a yellow synthetic blanket and covered her. When she spotted Leo coming over the edge, she breathed her first real sigh of relief.

Oddly, the scenery started spinning. For a second she wondered if it was an earthquake. She'd only experienced one small one at Leo's house during her last visit, but it had been enough to freak her out. Except now, no one seemed the least bit concerned, so maybe— Darkness closed in from the outside and suddenly her knees felt like Jell-O. Then—poof—everything went black.

Leo saw Kim's eyes roll back in her head a split second before she went limp. He scrambled out of the harness and leaped forward just as the paramedic caught her before she hit the hard-packed earth. His relief at actually having Kim safe quickly disappeared with her faint.

"Her pulse is elevated," the paramedic said. He had two fingers on her wrist and his eyes on his watch.

Kind of a no-brainer, but Leo didn't say it out loud. "That's normal, right? Under the circumstances?" He ignored the sharp pain in his knee as he crouched on her other side. He must have tweaked something going over the mountain.

The guy nodded as he checked out a cut along her hairline. The vivid trickle of blood, although tiny, cut a sharp contrast against her pale skin. All around them the firemen scrambled to get hoses over the cliff so they could douse the burning car.

"She was fine a few minutes ago," Leo added. "Maybe it was just the stress of the whole thing. Or the relief of being rescued." Or her pregnancy. "Oh shit. I forgot, she's pregnant."

The paramedic looked up. "How far along is she?"

Double shit. "I don't know. She didn't tell me." But if he was the father and they did the deed two months ago, then… "Maybe eight weeks."

"Do you know if she's a high risk pregnancy?"

"A what?" The blood drained from Leo's face. High risk pregnancy. Is that what Megan had been? Is that why she'd been born with so many issues? Down's Syndrome, cleft palate, seizure disorders. You name it and Megan dealt with it. "No," he blurted, because if he said it, maybe it would be so. Maybe Kim had a healthy baby growing inside her right now. His baby. "I have no idea. She's healthy. She's fine." At least he prayed so. What if something was seriously wrong with her? What if she hit her head and this was some kind of delayed reaction? They might not have seen each other for a couple of months, but they'd talked and emailed. She'd stormed into his life like a trooper on a mission and now he couldn't imagine her not being there at all.

The paramedic listened to her heart with a stethoscope. "How long have you known her?" Premature silver streaks in his black hair glistened in the sun.

Leo took offense at the question. "What the hell does that have to do with anything?"

"If you don't know her that well then you probably don't know if she has any health issues."

Tamping back his raging annoyance, Leo clenched his jaw. "Two months." It sounded stupid to say it out loud. They barely knew each other and she was pregnant with his baby. A sick sense of dread coated his intestines. Pregnant.

"Your baby?"

The question hit him like last month's major earthquake. Hard, fast and painful. The paramedic took his silence as an affirmative.

"Let's get her—"

"Hey, what happened," Kim murmured, her lashes flickering open.

"You about took another header." Leo took her hand and

squeezed, relieved to see her pretty green eyes open and alert.

"How do you feel?" the paramedic asked.

"I'm okay," Kim said, trying to sit up. "I guess I got a little lightheaded. Going over a cliff can really take it out of you." She crinkled her nose. "And I haven't had much to eat today, so that isn't doing me any favors."

"You're pregnant," the paramedic said. "You need to take care of you and the one you're carrying. Don't forget to eat."

"How did you know?" Her wide eyes narrowed before she shot a glance to Leo then saluted the paramedic. "Ah. Yes sir…" She checked out his name badge. "Mr. Lora."

"Call me Dan." He handed her a bottle of water along with a lethal smile. "Here. Drink this. It's important to stay hydrated."

Leo hated that face. All straight white teeth and sex appeal.

God, he'd never cared whether a guy smiled at someone he was dating or not. Here he was, not even technically dating Kim and his insides felt as if they might snap apart from frustration. Was that jealousy? "So, Dan," he said to break up the love fest and put an end to all his mental gymnastics. "Maybe it's time we take her to the hospital to get checked out."

"I'm fine," Kim said, drinking the water. "I mean aside from all the scratches, I'm really okay, just a temporary lack of oxygen to the brain. I don't need to go to the hospital."

Dan began cleaning the worst of her scratches. The fire department doused the car fire and another unit needed to be called in to handle the subsequent brush fire. Police arrived at the scene and took a statement since the whole mess had been so destructive on so many levels and any insurance companies involved would want answers.

Hours later, when all was said and done, the burnt out rental had been hoisted up the cliff—minus Kim's purse with all her ID. She sat in the passenger's seat of Leo's Mercedes. All the bandages made her look like a real life Raggedy Ann doll.

"You know there's not really a choice in the matter," he told her. "Your ID, clothes and credit cards are toast. You kind of have to stay with me. Again."

"I kind of don't have to do anything I don't want to do," she snapped.

Touchy. But he couldn't blame her. She'd had a stressful afternoon. Plus she was kind of cute when she pouted like that.

"I know you're not pissed that I saved you. So you're either mad that I got turned on before the fire department came or you're mad because you're pregnant."

She faced him, her eyes blazing with heat. And not the good kind. "I'm pregnant because we had sex." Didn't make it his fault that their birth control efforts didn't work, but now wasn't the time to remind of her that. "I'm mad that you think you can tell me what to do about this pregnancy."

"And then there's that." Leo dragged a hand through his hair.

"Besides…" She turned away from him and checked out a ripped fingernail. "We don't know if my ID is *toast* or not. It might have ejected out of the car and is just waiting for me to find it."

Was she for real? "At the bottom of the mountain?" he asked with a big dose of *are you nuts* in the subtext. "None of the guys who hoisted up the car saw it, so chances are everything is gone."

"Not acceptable," she said softly. "I need to look."

The woman never gave up. She might've been in a bind two months ago when she lost her luggage, but at least she'd had her ID. He couldn't fault her need to exhaust the possibilities. But it warranted a very important question.

"How exactly do you plan to look for it?"

"I'm going to hike down there tomorrow. I may as well. I'm going to have to wait for temporary ID, credit cards and all the other stuff I need. I have nothing to lose."

Leo shook his head and almost laughed, but managed to keep it buried. "Uh, hello? You nearly lost your life today. A few hours ago? Did you forget that already?"

"No. Don't be a…" She bit back the slam and growled instead. "That was an uncontrolled descent. With the right gear, I can hike to the spot and look for my stuff." She eyed him with speculation. "Don't feel obligated to join me." She sounded way too hopeful.

Like he'd let her do that kind of a trek by herself? It was just another indication of how little she thought of him and it stung more than he wanted to admit. "Should you be hiking a big mountain in your condition?"

"Pregnancy doesn't make me physically challenged. As long as I have plenty of water and some granola bars, I'll be fine." Her look softened as she watched him, her dark lashes framing her amazing green eyes.

No way in hell. "There is no *I*. Don't think for a minute that you'd be going alone."

She had the sense to look sufficiently reprimanded. "Okay. I'm sorry I snapped. Sorry I'm being a pain in the ass. I'm sorry the car went over the edge and I nearly got you killed trying to save me. Thank you for coming to my rescue." She paused and took a deep breath. "I owe you one." She met his gaze, truce in her eyes. "You never told me... How did you even know I was in trouble?"

He had to come clean about this. "It wasn't that I knew you were in trouble. I just wasn't finished with our conversation. You dropped a bomb on me then stalked out of my place pretty fast afterward. You didn't give me much time to process. So, I followed you to continue the conversation. You're what...? About eight weeks along at this point." At her nod, he continued, "When did you discover you were pregnant?"

"A few days ago. I saw my doctor right away to confirm it. Look, this was just as big a surprise for me, okay. I didn't plan it. I told you not to worry about it."

"It's not that simple." Leo wiped a hand down his face. As much as he liked her, he wasn't ready to confide in her about Megan. It was too soon. Hell maybe he never would. Besides, maybe with some gentle persuasion, he could convince her she really didn't want to be a single mom. "Hey, I know it was accidental, okay." He sighed, frustrated and scared. "C'mon," he said, cranking the engine. "Let's go back to my place and get you some clothes. We'll hit the mall before everything closes."

The faintest smile curved her lips. "The mall? I never would've believed it."

Because Leo Frost didn't do malls. He'd told her that before. "Trust me. That makes two of us."

"Do you think Cesar is open now?"

Leo shot her a look. "Cesar? In Beverly Hills?" At her nod, he checked his watch. "Yeah, he should be open. If not he'll keep the store open for us." One little problem did exist. "Um, you do remember the last time we were there, correct?"

"Correct." She nodded. "That's the reason we need to go back."

"That makes no sense whatsoever," Leo replied as he pulled a U and drove back up to his place.

"Trust me. It makes perfect sense." But she didn't elaborate.

Chapter Six

Back at Leo's house, Kim stripped off what remained of her clothes, which didn't happen to be much. Another outfit ruined. It seemed every time she encountered Leo, she also managed to destroy the clothes on her back. She wiped off the sweat and grit with a damp cloth since she couldn't submerge her freshly bandaged cuts and scrapes in a warm bath. After pulling on a pair of his workout shorts and a T-shirt, she glimpsed in the mirror and shook her head. She looked like a twelve year old wearing her father's clothes. She couldn't walk into Cesar's shop like this. A mall trip was definitely in her future and she couldn't do that without a credit card.

She placed a hand over her flat stomach, a wave of protectiveness washing through her. Clothes didn't matter. What mattered was the baby growing inside her. A little girl? A boy? Names...she needed to start thinking of names. Maybe Susan after her mom, or David for her dad. Kim wiped at the wetness from her eyes and took a deep breath, shoving the loneliness aside.

First order of business: call the credit card company. Second: get along with Leo for the rest of the night. Maybe if she chose to block out the callous way he'd treated her pregnancy she could do that. He had saved her life after all. She had to remember that.

Kim came out of the bathroom and looked down the hallway. This house was so different from Leo's spacious Beverly Hills home. It was a fraction of the size with not nearly as much open space and light. She took a quick peak into the master bedroom before walking back down the hallway and down the stairs.

From what she could tell, he hardly had any of his old belongings. Maybe he'd sold the house with everything intact. A wave of sadness hit her chest and she vowed to have more patience and understanding. She *had* delivered a big bomb. Plus, she'd had a few days to get used to the idea so the least she could do was give him the same amount of time.

Since she'd lost her shoes sometime during her accident, she padded quietly downstairs.

"What do you say, Stella? Any words of wisdom? Because I could use a little good advice right now." Leo's words drifted from the kitchen, sounding very lost and they stopped her cold.

She was a bit lost herself. Maybe if they talked it out, Leo would understand where she was coming from. She hadn't even had the chance to tell him all the things she wanted to tell him. She'd been too angry with his initial response to do anything but leave.

Entering the small galley kitchen, Kim saw Leo holding Stella as he gazed out to the terraced back yard. In a perfect world, she might glide into his arms, kiss him senseless and live happily ever after. Too bad they lived in the *real* world.

"You're very stealthy without your heels," he said, turning when he sensed her. The half grin kicking up his lips faded as he caught site of her. "You and Stella are in the running for most battered female in the house." He stroked Stella's head and her purring got louder. "The guest bed is made up if you want to lie down for a little while. Might be good to rest after the last few hours you've had."

"I think we should talk first."

His jaw ticked, but his serious gaze held steady as he nodded. "Okay. Talk."

She exhaled a measured breath. "I just don't think you heard me or didn't believe me when I said I plan to take care of this baby. I'm not going to come to you for anything. I'm not looking for you to support either of us. If you're worried about me going public for any reason then you shouldn't. I won't tell anyone."

Those very blue eyes of his didn't bat a lash. "What if it's more than you can handle?" he asked quietly. "I know your parents are gone, but do you have any siblings? Any people around to help?"

"Not really," she admitted, leaning on the tile counter to her right. "I have a cousin, but we don't live in the same city. I just have me. But I just received an inheritance, so I can handle it."

"Oh." He blinked at that and seemed taken aback. "I guess that's good and bad. Was this the aunt you mentioned in your email last month? The one in Arizona?"

"Yes." She was a little surprised he remembered since she'd barely grazed the topic. She'd let all her clients know that a family emergency was taking her away from work. "It happened fast. Stage-four cancer. I got there quickly, but she only lived another few weeks. My cousin and I took shifts so we were both there at the end."

"Sorry to hear that." He watched her intently, almost as if he could see through to her very soul. Sometimes, she thought he could. "C'mon, let's sit down before you fall down." He gestured for her to go first and followed her into the den.

Kim gingerly sat on the sofa and Leo took the spot on the opposite end. Stella limped off of his lap and into hers. "She's sweet," Kim murmured, cuddling the cat.

"She's a man eater," Leo countered. "A couple of meows and a round of purring and I'm her fucking slave."

Kim chuckled as Leo's phone rang. He checked the screen and quickly stood up. "Be right back. I've been waiting for this call." He punched the screen as he went into the kitchen. "Hey, Scotty. How are ya? Yeah, so I'm hoping you're in the market to do a little investing. Remember the film I was making a couple of years ago." He listened. "Yeah, the western." He huffed a laugh. "Yeah, Carrie Ann Loughlin. I know. Hindsight is everything right? Who knew? So I've decided to finish it— mostly second unit stuff is left—so it shouldn't be too expensive. You in?" He listened for a long time with an occasional *Uh-huh* and *yeah* dotted in the conversation.

Kim hated eavesdropping, but she didn't have a choice if she stayed in the den. The kitchen was too close and she regretfully heard every word. She'd seen a few of Carrie Ann Laughlin's movies, but had no idea Leo had done a film with her. A western? Kim couldn't picture it.

Although she could picture Leo in a cowboy hat and chaps over faded denim. She could definitely picture him on horseback with a sun setting behind him outlining his square jaw and broad shoulders.

Stella's claws dug into her thigh as she stretched and shook Kim out of her daydream. It was those kinds of thoughts that got her into trouble in the first place.

A few minutes later, Leo came back into the room. He tossed his phone on a stack of magazines on the worn oak coffee table and sat at the other end of the sofa.

"I didn't know you'd made a film with Carrie Ann Laughlin."

"No reason you would. We never finished it."

"Really? A big budget film and the studio never finished it? Does that happen often?" She rubbed a hand over Stella's soft head and the steady purr vibrated against her arm.

"It wasn't a big studio film. I was trying my hand at producing so it was a small Indie film."

That seemed weird.

"Why do you have that look on your face?" he asked.

"I guess I don't understand why an actor used to making big money and getting awards for them would bother making an indie film. Seems counterproductive."

He sighed. Seemed to debate his answer. "It's not common knowledge, but I'll tell you the truth. I wrote it. I used a pseudonym because I didn't think anyone would take it seriously otherwise."

"Can you get investors if no one knows who wrote it?" Stella nudged her hand when she stopped petting.

"That was my first mistake. I used most of my own money. Once I had a certain amount, a few other guys followed suit, but not nearly as much as I would've hoped. Then Carrie Ann went off the deep end. I didn't have the money to reshoot her stuff and I still had a couple of scenes to go, but by that point, I didn't want to sink more money into it because I didn't know how Carrie Ann's real life issues would affect my film."

"You're afraid her trip to a mental institution might affect your box office?"

"You have to admit, I run the risk of complete failure. The woman killed a man and nearly killed Julie Fraser. She's certifiable." He had a point, because Academy Award winning actresses usually weren't in the public eye because someone tried to kill them. Repeatedly.

"But the curiosity might be a draw."

"I thought of that." Leo nodded and shrugged. "It just feels sleazy to try and make money off her misfortune."

She learned more and more about him with every sit down. The same thing had happened two months ago. The man who started off so suave and callous had a conscience. He just rarely let people see it. "You're not making money off her misfortune. You're making money from a film you wrote. What she did after she shot your movie shouldn't matter. The work she did for you should have no bearing on what she did in her real life."

"You make it sound very reasonable."

"Isn't it?"

"I don't know anymore." He looked around the place, disappointment clear in his eyes. "This isn't how I imagined my life." And suddenly they were on a whole new topic. Clearly he meant the house and his surroundings, but he must have meant her pregnancy too.

"Tell me about it," she muttered. She never dreamed she'd be a single mother.

Together they were pretty damn pitiful. A mega-famous movie star who'd lost everything, and a business owner and financial manager with no one who loved her and a baby on the way.

Leo's phone kept ringing with calls about his movie. Since he needed to straighten out the details to get back on his feet financially, Kim let him handle business, which put their conversation on hold. At this point, they had a lot of time to talk and he liked the truce they'd come to. It beat having her walk out again. Not that she could go far without clothes. Or a wallet. Or a car.

She made the call to her credit card company. As Leo expected, it was going to take twenty-four to forty-eight hours before they could reissue and overnight a new credit card. Then she still had to worry about ID to fly back to Indiana. That was going to take even longer, but since she couldn't get through to DMV before they closed, that conversation had to wait.

Kim kept petting Stella's soft head and the cat closed her eyes in a state of bliss. Shifting, Kim winced and Leo's heart took a hit. He hated that the two sweetest things under his roof were both suffering.

"I forgot to get you some ibuprofen when we came in," he said, moving into the kitchen. He came back a minute later with three pills in his palm and a glass of water. He wished he could do more.

Kim accepted the offering.

"You know you're going to be sore as hell tomorrow."

She nodded. "You mean *more* sore."

It didn't take long for her to fall asleep on the sofa. With Stella snoozing on her lap, the two of them made quite the battered pair. He quashed the urge to keep them both. He couldn't. Wouldn't. But he'd never forget either set of eyes as they'd looked at him for help the last two days.

Leo looked around the new—old—place he now called home. Kind of a dump if he wanted to be picky. Though it had the illusion of being upgraded, it was still small, too dark and not at all what he'd pick if given half a choice. But the two females sleeping on the couch seemed to soften the humiliation. They didn't seem to care about the dim lighting or chipped floors. Not that it mattered what they thought. He wanted his life back. At least part of it. The part that afforded him the good things in life.

Fresh determination blossomed in his gut. He'd get his movie made if he had to shoot the damn thing himself. He felt bad for Carrie Ann, but she'd chosen her path, just like he needed to make his.

Right now he needed to think about Kim and her present state of wardrobe. She couldn't wear his stuff during her whole stay and she'd probably balk if he offered her money. Not that he had much to offer. Avoiding the fight, Leo snagged his keys and snuck out of the house for a very rare appearance at the mall. In ninety minutes, he got a little bit of everything and hoped like hell it all fit. Back at the house, he placed all the bags in Kim's room and waited for her to find them.

Four hours later, Kim was still sacked out on the couch curled under the navy chenille blanket Leo had used to cover her. He checked his watch and glanced again at Stella's pitiful eyes.

Meow. Code for *food.* Or *feed me.* It was past her dinnertime.

The can opener was going to wake up Kim, but he felt bad for the cat. Hell, since when did he care so much about either one of them?

"C'mon, Stella. Let's get you dinner." Leo pulled a can of cat food from the pantry shelf and checked the label. "Duck and salmon." He eyed the cat and stuck the can under the opener. "You're eating better than me." The instant hum of the appliance had Stella nearly bouncing on her toes. "Easy, girl," Leo said as he spooned the smelly meal onto a plate. He set it down for her and she went to town, ignoring everything but the food.

"What time is it?"

Damn. He knew the stupid opener would wake up Kim. "It's about eight." He looked up from Stella and his heart took a solid hit. Her cuts and scratches looked absurdly pronounced in the bad kitchen lighting. Kim's mussed blond hair framed her face in a come-hither sex-goddess do that hit straight below his belt. She'd washed off most of her makeup when she'd cleaned up, the soft smooth skin peeking out of his clothes begged to be touched. His brain might've decided that he had no future with her, but his hands wanted to touch, and his dick wanted to dive into all parts wet and warm.

"Eight? God, I can't believe I fell asleep for so long. Can I use your phone? I need to make a couple of calls."

"Sure." He handed over the receiver to his landline, since living in the hills made cell phone reception spotty. "You hungry? I can make us some sandwiches or something."

Her eyes widened. "Really? You cook now."

He shook his head at her teasing tone. "No. But I can make sandwiches. That's not cooking."

She snorted. "It is in my book." She lifted the phone. "Thanks." And started punching numbers.

First she called her best friend and business partner. A woman he'd briefly met while shooting *Dangerous Race.* That movie had been one of his biggest box office successes. It killed him every time he thought about the fortune his accountant had embezzled from him. All the gorgeous property he'd purchased with that money now belonged to other people. Leo shook it off. No sense in mulling over old news. He had to move on.

Her next call went to her cousin in Arizona. That conversation sounded a little more cautious with her declining a lot of offers. *No, it's too far. No, you don't need to. Yes, I'll be fine.* Sounded like someone cared a lot. *I'm staying with a friend. No, I lost my cell phone too. His number? Is it really necessary?* She covered the mouthpiece with her hand. "My cousin wants your number so he can reach me. It's totally cool if you don't want to share, but…"

"Will it get him off your back?" Leo asked. He'd already pulled bread and deli meat out of the fridge and plates from the cabinets.

She nodded.

"Give him the land line. I don't care. He's family, right?" He stuck bread in the toaster and heaped turkey and cheese slices on a plate.

She smirked at that question as Leo wiped his hands, wrote down his number and handed it to her.

"His name?" she said into the phone after relaying his number. "Uh… Leo. His name is Leo. He's a client." She glanced up and they locked gazes. "And a friend."

The word hit him on a basic level. He didn't have too many people he could call friends. Not the kind of friends that kept your secrets to the grave and went out of their way to help you. The kind that told it to you straight or offered an unconditional shoulder to lean on.

It took another couple of minutes for Kim to end the conversation. "God," she breathed hanging up the phone.

"Some people just can't take no for an answer." The toaster popped and he slapped their sandwiches together.

"He's just trying so hard to do the 'right thing' that he's driving me crazy." She hobbled into the kitchen and looked around. "Can I help you with anything?"

He pulled up the stool from the counter separating the kitchen and den. "Yes. You can sit your ass down. You're moving around like an eighty-year-old woman."

"Gee. Thanks." When she tried to set her butt cheek on the stool, she winced, so Leo put his hands around her waist and helped her up. Big mistake. Kim yelped and grabbed onto his forearms and their gazes locked tight. Just like today when he'd been right behind her on the mountain, his body went into search mode. His dick searching for her hot, wet center.

Damn, he'd forgotten how much he liked her. Their two-month separation had been good, because he'd been able to focus on other things besides how much he wanted to be with her. Touching her set his blood on fire. She blinked a few times, fast, as if their contact was another shock to her system. And standing there, with his legs between hers, with their mouths so close together, the only thought in his brain was *kiss her. Now.*

"Leo," she whispered. Her lips seemed to move in slow motion as he slowly bridged the gap between them.

"What?" he growled.

"I don't think this is a—"

He kissed her before she finished the sentence, because she was right. It wasn't a good idea. But damn if he could stop himself. She was his Achilles heel. His weak spot. The more distance she put between them, the more he wanted her. He started slow, worked his way into the kiss, waiting for her to push him away or move back. She did neither, so he took it farther and tasted her lower lip with a gentle brush of his tongue. A little moan vibrated from her throat as their lips stayed connected. She tasted different...she tasted like a luscious cinnamon stick, all hot and spicy. "You found my cinnamon gum in the shorts pocket, didn't you?" he breathed against her mouth. The gum was her fault. Whatever perfume she wore smelled like cinnamon and he'd started to chew the gum. Whether to remind himself of her or not was something he purposely hadn't analyzed.

She barely nodded, her wet lips brushing against his in an erotic glide. "I had nap breath," she murmured.

He smiled against her lips before going in for more. Still slow, still sexy as hell, still doing his best to inhale her without scaring her off. They had history, yes, but her unpredictability always threw him off. He missed the softness of her hair under his fingertips. The way her pulse beat rapidly right before contact.

"Leo," she murmured, her mouth still moving against his as his hands moved down her thighs.

"Mmm," he managed.

"We should stop. This isn't going to get either one of us anywhere."

Just like last time, she was relying on his will power to stay away. Hadn't he failed that test already? In a colossal way?

"But it feels good," he said. "I thought after the day you had, it might be nice to feel good."

She made that sound again and it about killed him. Her fingers twined around his neck and dove through the hair at his nape. Leo took that as a positive sign and slipped his tongue inside her mouth. The groan he heard was his own. The wet slide of her tongue against his was like the perfect homecoming.

The kiss stayed slow and molten hot. He wanted her closer…wanted her against the rock-hard erection straining the zipper of his jeans, then he wanted inside her tight heat. It didn't matter that there'd been so many women before her, because he had no recollection of anyone but her. All he'd done the past two months was fantasize about Kim, about how good she'd feel if he managed to get her in his arms again. Holding her thighs apart, Leo leaned in.

Kim's yelp coincided with Stella's claws landing on his hands and Kim's legs. He jumped back and lifted the cat off her at the same time.

Breathing hard, they stared at each other. *What the hell?* Why did he always do this to himself? Starting something with Kim was as stupid as washing his car before a rainstorm. He'd regret it when the storm passed. And that's what Kim was. Her own category-five hurricane dressed to kill.

"Saved by the kitty," she whispered. Her wet lips glistened, begged for another kiss.

"I can always put the cat in another room."

Then his phone rang.

"Saved by the bell then." Her words came with a little bite. She always did that. Worked to separate them. It was starting to piss him off.

"I don't have to answer it. What's wrong?"

"Nothing's wrong." Except her posture said otherwise. "Might be your investor." The sing-song rhythm of her voice sounded almost like a warning, a tone he needed to be leery of, but he checked his caller ID.

"Oh shit! You're right." Holding his index finger in the air to indicate one minute, he set Stella in Kim's lap and took the call. "Yeah, Scotty. That was fast, what's up?"

"I'm in. Will thirty large finish the movie?" Scotty asked.

Leo pumped his fist. Relief nearly made him light headed.

"Absolutely. Thanks, man. You won't regret it." The amount of work he had in front of him suddenly seemed mountainous.

Scotty laughed. "I better not or my wife will kill me."

Leo laughed too. "No worries. I'll outline all the costs so you'll see the plan. I might not even need it all."

"That would be brilliant. So let me know when you have the numbers and I'll cut you a check."

"Great! Talk to you soon! Later." Leo punched the screen and watched it go black. He grabbed Kim around her nape and kissed the living hell out of her. Tongue, teeth, lips. He kissed her like he might die if he didn't. He'd have wrapped both arms around her if it hadn't meant crushing Stella between them. When he finally pulled away, her lips were swollen and red.

"Good news, I take it?" Her smile seemed almost reluctant, but it reminded him of a California sunrise, full of light and promise.

"More like great news!" He went to kiss her again, but stopped. "Shit, I'm going to be up all night figuring out what's left to shoot and what it's going to cost me." He stepped back and ran a hand through his hair.

"I think it's for the best. Really Leo..." She gestured between the two of them. "This thing between us isn't real. It's a mistake to fall into some kind of sleep together pattern just because I happen to be here."

She was forgetting a very important aspect. "Are you saying you haven't noticed that we're really good together?"

"I noticed that we make each other hot, but that's not enough for me. Maybe you're ready to get back on the one-night-stand trail, but I'm not. You know what I want and we both know you're not the man to give it."

Wham! Right in the balls. Leo took Stella, backed up and leaned against the counter. He scratched the cat's head as Kim's words wrestled in his brain. It was his own fault. He'd told her as much during those first few days they were together. He'd said a lot of things and he'd kept just as much to himself. So where did that leave him now when he wanted her so much?

Now that she was pregnant with his child.

He swallowed back a wave of panic at the thought. A baby. It scared the living hell out of him, enough to put some distance between them.

He flashed a smile and nodded. "Of course. I don't know what I was thinking. You and me, we're tight, but..." He snorted. "No way, no how are we in the market for the same thing. Guess I'll get to work on my movie." Leo headed to his tiny office on the other side of the stairs, his stomach turning at the idea of losing Kim, a woman who never belonged to him in the first place.

Chapter Seven

Wilson looked at the blank screen of his mobile phone and nearly threw it across the hotel room. Aggravation boiled in his blood and threatened to erupt. *No, it's too far. No, you don't need to. Yes, I'm fine.* All responses he didn't want to hear. He had to admit to hoping for a phone call from the authorities that his loving cousin had suffered a terrible injury in a horrific crash. Maybe even a miscarriage. At least then she wouldn't have that money. Especially when it rightfully belonged to him.

Didn't matter. He had not driven all the way to L.A. from Arizona to fail. Kim hadn't told him the reason for this trip, but he saw the opportunity as a sign to take action. She was in his part of the country, so it was up to him to make sure she turned to him for help. It wasn't as if anyone would suspect him of any wrong-doing. Why would they? Kim didn't have the money yet and he wasn't the beneficiary. He had nothing to gain if something terrible happened to his poor cousin. Nothing but satisfaction. If he took Kim out of the picture completely, chances were good that Amanda might get the rest of the inheritance and as her father, he'd be in charge of it. With a few million at his disposal, he could wager enough to double the money.

He'd done such a great job with the hose to the power steering too. His tiny blade had been sharp enough to peel off layers of rubber then shaved it down so it was worn to a thin sheet. Then he'd poked tiny pinpricks in the rubber so his tampering would be undetectable. He'd seen plenty of belts go bad from age and use. Of course, most rentals these days were nearly brand new cars, but he'd gotten lucky with the fire. Hell, he never expected her to fly down the damn mountain at warp speed. Going over the edge had been her fault. He just wanted to be the person she turned to when she needed someone. It was a rush watching that rental burn even knowing Kim had survived. He liked all the trouble he caused... Couldn't remember a time ever feeling that powerful. It invigorated him. Gave him a piece of himself he'd been missing for a long time. Maybe years.

Good things come to those who wait. Carolyn had told him that hundreds of times, leading him to believe that he was in line for her money. She also said if he got his act together that Chloe would come back to him. But that sure as hell never happened.

Wilson got to his feet and paced the small room as emotion clogged his throat. Chloe's betrayal still stung. She'd said the vows...'*til death do us part,* but she hadn't meant them. Instead she'd ripped his heart out when she'd walked out with Amanda. Now she wanted child support, she wanted living expenses. She wanted a whole lot of shit that money could buy. Money he didn't have.

Kim had a successful business. She didn't need all that money. Any day now, he'd have guys on his tail, aiming to break his legs. He needed that inheritance not only for his daughter, but to survive.

"You do not get what I've been working for, cousin. I haven't been busting my ass the last three years for Carolyn for nothing." He caught his haggard reflection in the mirror. He didn't used to have dark circles under his eyes, or the tiny bald spot growing at the back of his head. Time seemed to be running out everywhere. His heart rate picked up and he recognized the anxiety attack before it hit.

Taking a few deep breaths, Wilson looked away from the mirror and got his mind back on track. There had to be a way to get Kim on his side. How did he syphon some of that inheritance his way?

First, he had to justify his surprise trip to Los Angeles without causing suspicion. He paced the room, sorting it out. He needed information. He looked down at the number he'd scribbled on the hotel pad. Who the hell was Leo and since when did Kim have a client in Los Angeles when she lived in Indiana? What if she met him during her last trip? She'd only mentioned the nightmare her old college roommate had endured, so there had to be more to the story. Time to find out.

Wilson sat at the desk and booted up his laptop. He plugged the phone number into the search engine and found a website that offered a reverse phone lookup.

Perfect.

He plugged the number into the site and waited. He had a few options and chose *owner's name.* It only took a second for an answer to appear. *Private caller.* Of course. Because nothing came easy.

Okay. Plan B. Her business partner seemed to be good for information. Thank God, he'd thought ahead to get her direct number. Nervous, he tapped his foot on the carpet as he scrolled through his contacts. He punched Chelsea's number and waited.

"Hello?"

Bingo. He recognized her voice. "Hi, Chelsea, it's Wilson again. I hope it's not too late."

"No, in fact I just hung up with Kim."

"Really? What a coincidence. I was hoping you could help me one more time. I got a return voicemail from Kim and she said she was with Leo, but the rest of the message was garbled and now I can't seem to get through to her cell phone. Do you happen to know Leo's last name? I'm hoping I can track his number down."

"Oh. Sure. It's Frost. Leo Frost."

That information blindsided him. "Leo Frost? You mean *the* Leo Frost?"

"The one and only."

What. The. Hell. Since when did Kim have multiple clients worth multi-millions of dollars? "Wow. That's...that's very cool. I didn't realize she knew him." Maybe his cousin was hiding as much as his aunt. Kim probably didn't even need Carolyn's money if her clients were all as wealthy as Leo Frost.

"Yeah. She met him the last time she was in Los Angeles. But I'll let her tell you about it."

"I'm looking forward to the story." A picture blazed through Wilson's mind from a rag magazine at the market checkout stand months ago. He'd seen the headline. Who Is Leo Kissing This Time? She'd been blond with a traffic-stopping body and Wilson would bet his next alimony payment that it was Kim. Which meant Leo was the baby daddy. Holy shit. Wilson thanked her and got off the phone ASAP. "Leo Frost. You've got to be kidding me." He sat back in his chair. There had to be a way to make this work even better.

But how?

He'd think of something. In the meantime, he needed to keep a close eye on his cousin. He eyed the shotgun and handgun he'd brought from home. Guns seemed so cliché, but with the right time and right place, one of them might be the perfect solution.

Wilson checked his watch. Kim wasn't going anywhere tonight. He'd catch up with her first thing in the morning.

Kim woke up early the next day, and took a closer look at Leo's small guest bedroom. Plain white walls and a few of the pieces she recognized from his old house like the teak dresser and matching mirror above it.

She'd been a bitch yesterday after their kiss. Not because she was mad at him, but because she was angry with herself. Angry for wanting him despite knowing he didn't love her or the baby growing inside her. It was something she needed to get over. He'd made himself perfectly clear when they'd first met. He didn't believe in forever and he'd never do parenthood. If she could just get past the crazy attraction she had for him then life would be a hundred percent easier. She *wanted* to get along with him. It didn't mean she had to sleep with him.

Stretching, Kim felt every bruise on her battered body. She eased out of the soft sheets, before padding to the bathroom. Studying her scrapes and scratches in the mirror, she noticed the subtle changes in her body, the way her breasts seemed fuller and her hair and skin seemed healthier. She laid her hands over her still flat stomach, taking a deep breath at the wonder of it all. If she stayed in Indiana, she could raise her baby with Chelsea's daughter. But this inheritance was her opportunity to leave, a chance to live in a big city.

Decisions, decisions.

After a warm shower, she stretched out her sore muscles and started work on getting a replacement for her driver's license. She managed to do it online, but it was going to take at least ten days for the reissue. Next, she called the car rental agency and gave them the bad news. The police had the car and planned to investigate the accident. After this conversation, they could take it up with her insurance company.

Now she needed to see if she could book a flight without any ID. Wait! Her passport! Chelsea would bail her out. Her best friend could open her safe and overnight it. That solved the immediate ID dilemma.

Still, she had nothing left to lose if she hiked down the mountain in search of her license. Since Leo had surprised her with clothes, she no longer looked like a twelve-year-old in her father's wardrobe. He'd even bought her some workout gear and a pair of running shoes. They weren't hiking boots, but they would do the trick. The fact that he got her sizes right only showed how much he'd been paying attention a couple of months ago when they'd gone shopping in Beverly Hills.

Leo had been up most of the night working on the numbers for his movie, so she felt confident that she wouldn't wake him when she left for her hike. She needed some serious space from the guy. He jumbled every one of her senses. He was a man who didn't want commitment and she was a woman who did. Her head knew he wasn't the guy for her, but her heart didn't care. And her duplicitous body...forget about it. Her heart pounded like a damn drum whenever he was around, her eyes always searched him out and her hands ached to touch. Stupid. Stupid. Stupid.

She'd just finished writing him a note when he showed up in the kitchen, looking bleary-eyed, rumpled and gorgeous as hell in shorts...and only shorts. His washboard abs made her mouth water for a taste. For all the hours she'd spent last night hardening her heart to this man, all it took was one look for the traitorous organ to pound out of control.

His sleepy eyes narrowed as he took in her outfit. "What the hell are you planning now?"

She ignored his tone and the way it made her girl parts tingle. "I'm going on a little hike. If you don't see me back here tonight, then call the fire department again. I may need rescuing."

He shook his head slowly as his tired eyes opened wider. "Don't even think about it."

"Uh oh. Too late." She zipped past him, but he caught her arm and twirled her about face.

Leo exhaled a measured breath. "Nothing I say is going to

stop you, is it?" She shrugged a shoulder and opened her mouth to tell him she was a grown woman, perfectly capable of taking care of herself, but he cut her off. "Fine. Give me time to get dressed and pack us some provisions." He gestured to the tiny pack she had over her shoulders. "That doesn't hold nearly enough water for the amount of energy we'll be expending." He leaned forward and touched his forehead to hers. "Give me ten minutes or else."

Kim smothered a grin. He was kind of funny when he ordered her around. "Or else what?" She kept a straight face. Sometimes she liked goading him just to see what he would do.

"Or else when I see you next, I'm going to put you over my knee and spank that sweet ass of yours."

A blast of heat exploded in her stomach and moved directly south. Though the picture he created sounded erotic as hell, Kim was totally not into *that*. "Don't count on it," she breathed. "That is not on my to-do list. Ever."

"Don't knock it 'til you've tried it." He pulled away. "Ten minutes starting now. You better be here."

Checking her watch, Kim eased onto the sofa next to a sleepy Stella. The minute she put her hand on the cat, the feline started purring. Leo didn't wait for confirmation and jammed up the stairs three at a time.

Thirteen minutes later, Leo parked on the side of the road more than a mile south of his place. Several lots hadn't been developed yet and, although a lot of dried brush and rock stood in their way, it seemed like the smartest starting point. At this level they were almost even with the crash site. They just had to hike through some rough terrain to reach it. They could also pick their way through without having a gravity-defying fall. Though the sun was out, the air was crisper than yesterday. Kim figured she'd be thankful for that once they got into the hike.

Leo adjusted a black *Dangerous Race* baseball cap on his head and slapped a pair of black Ray Bans over his eyes. He looked like a model for an adventure magazine dressed in cargo shorts, hiking boots and worn baseball jersey with his muscles bulging the material. He gestured with his arm. "Ladies first."

Kim watched him for three full seconds. He was so predictable. "Don't think I don't know you're watching my ass,

Frost. I totally know your MO." She started off, debating on giving him a show since he wouldn't be getting the goods.

"Admit it. You still love me."

She heard the smile in his voice and ignored the statement. "What I would love is to find my purse and everything inside of it." Then she could get back home and continue with life. The life of a single mother-to-be. Her heart pounded faster just thinking about it. She couldn't wait to go shopping, to set up a nursery and buy all the baby paraphernalia. Right now she had to concentrate on not falling over the treacherous path she'd chosen to take.

They walked in silence for the better part of twenty minutes. Birds chirped, bees buzzed and the bushes rustled with unseen creatures. Evidence of the recent earthquake showed all around them, from cracks in stones to fallen trees and mini rockslides. It made for tough going.

"You really don't have to do this," Kim said, picking her way through a group of dense bushes and wiping sweat off her forehead. "It's not too late for you to turn back." She saw the charred edge of the mountain in the distance, but had no clue how long it might take to reach it.

"Yeah. I'll just leave you here to face who knows what all alone." He swatted at something in the air. "Do you think that little of me?"

"I don't think little of you at all." She glanced over her shoulder and noticed he was barely sweating when she was already exhausted. Maybe she needed more time at a gym. "If you want to know the truth, I think you're amazing. You've handled this whole shitty deal pretty damn well. I'm proud of you. I know how hard it was to sell everything." He didn't say anything, but he looked at her as if she'd said something he'd never heard before. "What? You don't believe me?"

His serious face morphed into a devilish smile. "No. I believe you. I'm definitely amazing."

"Oh, jeez." She huffed, rolled her eyes and picked up her pace. Clearly he hadn't lost any ego in the time she'd been gone. Some things never changed.

It took just over an hour to get to the burned spot. They had to zig-zag over miles of uneven terrain. "What do you think the drop is from the road?" she asked, shielding her eyes from the blazing sun. Too bad she'd lost her sunglasses too.

Leo followed her gaze. "I don't know. Seventy feet. Maybe eighty. Hard to tell."

Kim looked around the charred bushes and black dirt. "This is going to be dirty work."

"You're just figuring that out now?" Leo glanced around. "What are we looking for specifically and what color is it?"

"My purse and it's kind of a brown and black mix."

Leo spread his arms to indicate the terrain: a mixture of brown and black. "You couldn't have a bright blue or yellow bag, could you?"

"Oh, stop being grumpy," she said, beginning to scour the ground. "The sooner you start looking, the sooner we find it and get out of here."

Leo's gorgeous smile added more shine to the warm day. He was hard to resist when he flashed those pearly whites. "I forgot what a slave driver you are."

And she'd forgotten how hard it was to resist him. She scanned the site, walking the burned out area slowly. "Yep. And this is me cracking the whip, so stop talking and start looking." She glanced over her shoulder. "Not looking at my ass, Leo. Looking for my purse and my cell phone."

She wasn't sure, but thought she heard him mutter, "Fun killer."

The sun had started arcing downward and Leo checked his watch. He was hot, hungry and up to his neck in soot. Time to call it a day. "How much longer did you plan to keep up this useless expedition?"

A few yards away, Kim stood straight from where she'd been hunched over as she walked another blackened grid. She looked adorable in his cap. He'd tossed it to her hours ago when he noticed the sun burn on her scalp. "You want me to give up? Is that it?" When he didn't say anything, she stretched her back and sat on a nearby rock. "Okay, fine. I'm sorry. I give up, okay. Maybe an animal dragged it off." She looked completely done— with a capital *D*—and his heart split for her. Maybe he could cheer her up.

"Yeah, the coyotes here are really into Gucci." He sat next to her on the big rock.

"Smart ass," Kim muttered. She pulled a strand of hair out of her face and left a streak of soot across her cheek. Damn, she was cute. "I had a fresh pack of cinnamon gum, and a half of a granola bar left from the airport. An animal might've sniffed the food and carried the whole thing away."

He'd started buying cinnamon gum, too, after she left town. It reminded him of her. Of the way she tasted and smelled. Leo gave himself a quick mental shake. He needed to toss the cinnamon gum and get her out of his head.

She leaned over, still scanning the ground when she gasped and launched her body forward. The rock behind her exploded. Pieces of stone flew up and the shards hit Leo's side as he dove for the ground. Kim yelped and ducked from the flying debris.

Leo's pulse revved lightning fast as he yanked Kim next to him behind the protection of a rock cluster. Two more rounds hit a few inches away and splintered more stone.

"What's happening?" Kim yelled, covering her head. "Is this an earthquake?"

Leo kept her tight within his arms, covering her as best he could. "Earthquakes don't shatter rock like that." But he knew what did. "Bullets do."

"What?" Kim's head shot up. "No!" Her wide green eyes hardly looked convinced. "That wasn't a bullet."

"I think after years of working with squibs, guns and blanks, I can honestly say that no one planted a squib in this rock and that was definitely a bullet." To punctuate his declaration another chunk of rock exploded over their heads.

Kim jumped in his arms and Leo held her close. "Why would anyone shoot at us? What did we do?"

"I have no clue." He shifted to keep Kim protected between the rock and his body. The birds and insects had grown quiet and all the rustling stopped as nature quieted to detect the danger.

Halfway beneath him and breathing hard, Kim lifted her head. "So now what?"

Good question. He didn't see too many options. Jumping out might get them shot or killed. "We wait."

"Wait?" She sounded baffled. "What do you mean *wait*? For how long? This is ridiculous." Her anger was taking over the fear and he liked that better. An angry Kim was a force to behold.

Still, he felt obligated to be honest and reassure her at the same time, even if he didn't know what the hell was happening.

"Someone's out there with a shotgun and he's got his sights set on us. I don't know about you, but in my book it means we keep our heads down and wait."

"But I finally found my cell phone," she grumbled. Her pout only pronounced the fullness of her lips. Lips he'd kissed until they were red and swollen. Lips she'd dragged across his skin in all sorts of places that made him shake, rattle and roll.

Shit. Not good thoughts to have at the moment. The last thing she'd want is to feel evidence of how much that streak across her cheek turned him on. Or how good she smelled despite the hint of perspiration...or maybe because of it. Come to think of it, she smelled like this after their all-nighter before he drove her to the airport two months ago. He'd been fantasizing about that night ever since. About the way her soft skin felt beneath his fingertips and tasted against his tongue... The way she'd smiled at him as she straddled him and rode him to her cli—

"Did you hear me?" she asked. "I said I think I found my phone."

Man, he needed to snap out of this shit. It wasn't going to get him anywhere. "Is that what you went after?" he asked.

"Yes," she huffed. "It's right over..." She started to rise up, pointing as she lifted a little higher and another shot had her scrunching down and tight against his chest...which he had to admit he didn't mind.

"Well, good thing, because it saved your ass."

She swallowed hard, fisting his T-shirt. "We need to call for help. What about your phone? Do you have a signal down here?"

Leo reached for his phone in the side pocket of his shorts and checked the screen. He didn't tell her his battery was nearly dead. In all the excitement yesterday, he'd forgotten to plug it in. "I've got two bars." He punched in 911. "Let's see if I can get a connection." He waited a very long minute as the call tried to connect, all the while straining to hear anything around them.

"911. What is your emergency?"

Leo huffed out a relieved breath as Kim's eyes widened hopefully when she heard the operator. He explained the situation and waited for the person to connect him, then he explained it again to the dispatcher who answered. When he gave his name, she paused and asked him to repeat it, so he knew she recognized him. She assured him help was on the way and to stay on the line.

"Thank God," Kim sighed. She leaned her head against his chest, but pulled away just as quickly. The panic in her eyes read like the twirling red light outside a working soundstage. "What if the guy shooting gets here before the police?"

He hadn't considered that scenario. He really did hate the fear in her eyes. It was so unlike her. Not that he could blame her. Leo moved the phone away from his mouth. "With all this dry brush around, we'll hear him coming. We'll be ready." He hadn't used his improv skills in a long time, but he wanted to convince Kim they were safe. "I'll move up the rocks and distract him and you stay hidden here."

"I hate that idea," she said.

"Hopefully it won't come to that. The police will move fast."

"This is crazy. It doesn't make any sense. I mean who would—"

"Hey." He cupped her face and waited until her gaze connected with his. "We're going to be fine. We've got cover and help is coming."

"What if he's holed up in a house somewhere along the mountain?" She blinked as the thought took form in her head. Houses on stilts covered half the canyon. "What if he just picks off anyone who comes to help us?"

"Then they'll catch him faster because they'll know where he is. The cops aren't clueless. And they'll have body armor. Something we didn't think to pack with our water and granola bars. For all we know, he took off already. We can test the theory." Leo snatched the hat from Kim's head and reached for a small charred branch on his right. Using the branch to hold the hat, he raised it so it peaked out from the rock. Another shot blew the hat off the branch, and Kim jolted in his arms.

"Oh my God. This is crazy," she breathed.

He agreed. And damn, now his favorite cap had a hole in it. Should've thought that one out beforehand. "Not sure if you heard that or not," Leo said into the phone, "but we're still being shot at. How long before we get some help here?"

"Just a few minutes," the dispatcher said. "Hang in there."

Leo only wished this nut job was in one of the houses,

because if he was staked out closer, he could be moving toward them this very second. Mustering courage he didn't really feel, he caught Kim's gaze. "So who the hell might want to shoot at us?"

She lifted a frustrated hand in the air. "You haven't had any death threats lately, have you? You're the one in the public eye."

"No death threats lately," he assured her. "What about you? You said the steering wasn't working yesterday. Maybe that wasn't a mechanical failure. Any ex-boyfriends you've left in your wake who might want permanent revenge?"

She shook her head. "Seriously, there is no reason for anyone to want me—" Her eyes rounded wide.

He knew that look. "What? You just thought of something. What is it?"

She shook her head. "It can't be. It doesn't make sense. No one knows."

"No one knows what? Spill it."

She met his gaze. "About the money I inherited last week. I mean, three people know, but I'm not even sure I have access to it yet."

"Who knows?"

"My aunt's lawyer, my best friend and my cousin Wilson."

"The guy you called earlier?"

"Yeah. But the lawyer and Wilson are in Arizona and my best friend is not trying to kill me, so..." Her tone indicated neither man could be a suspect.

"Did your cousin inherit as much money as you did?" he asked. "Because money is a hell of a motivator."

She shook her head. "No. He got my aunt's house." Her brows slanted as she considered his suspicions. "He might be in debt, but I can't believe he'd try to kill me over this. Besides, like I said, he's in Arizona. So now what?" she asked.

"Now we wait for the cops to come to the rescue and hope they get here before a killer."

Chapter Eight

Despite the blazing sun, Kim shivered. Leo hadn't meant to scare her. He tugged her closer and ran his hand along her arm. The LAPD wasn't going to let some nut with a gun take them out. It would be bad for their public image if one the city's most famous citizens died.

Didn't he hope.

They needed to figure out who might be behind this. Two incidents in two days was no coincidence.

"So your cousin, Wilson. Sounds like he's the only family you have left."

She nodded. "We were practically raised together. Our mothers were sisters. I was actually a surprise. None of them could conceive. It's one of the reasons I was so shocked to be pregnant myself. Anyway, Wilson was adopted and my mom was looking into adoption when she found out she was going to have me. The older we got, the more distance separated us. Wilson got married, had a baby. We lost touch until recently when my aunt got sick."

A visible sadness colored her eyes. She cleared her throat and tucked her head into his neck as he continued to rub her arm. "I can't believe all the sisters are gone. Some days I still can't believe my parents are dead." She swallowed hard. "I still reach for the phone when I have some news to tell my mom. Then I remember."

"I'm sorry," Leo whispered. He felt the small shrug of her shoulders.

"I sometimes wonder what would've happened if I hadn't moved. They liked to travel and just take every day as it came, but I'll never understand why my dad didn't pull over if he was tired." She paused, mulling over the accident. "I get so mad thinking about it."

"You can't do that to yourself. You have to let it go. If you don't, it'll eat you alive." Kind of like how taking care of Megan had slowly eaten away at his mother. Oh, she'd loved her daughter, but all the E.R. visits and constant care had taken the joy out of her life. Leo may have been a teenager, but he'd seen how hard his mother had worked to take care of his little sister.

Kim pushed some hair behind her ear. "Sometimes I tell myself they're just on vacation and I'll talk to them when they get home." She cleared her throat again. "Sometimes it's really fresh, like it happened yesterday and sometimes it feels a lifetime ago. I miss not having them. At least having my Aunt Carolyn was like having a little piece of my mom around, but now she's gone too."

Something rustled in the bushes nearby and they both froze. Fresh sweat broke out on Leo's nape as he turned and kept Kim at his back. "Hold this," he whispered giving her the phone. He stayed low and eased away from her, toward the threat. A second later, a rabbit popped out and bounded in the opposite direction, his little cottontail bouncing like a fluffy ball.

Kim let out a shaky breath as Leo dropped his chin to his chest.

He hated this shit. He moved back to his spot near Kim and took the phone back. "You were saying?"

"I have no clue. That scared me to death." She looked up at him. Soot streaked her face. "Oh. Parents. What about you? Where are yours?"

He never talked about his mother, just as he never spoke about his half sister, Megan. Never. How'd he dodge *this* bullet? "Well…"

"Mr. Frost," the dispatcher said. Nothing like perfect timing to save his ass. "Officers are—" The line went silent.

"Hello. Hello!" Leo checked the screen. Black. No signal. "Shit. Perfect," he muttered. A bead of sweat trickled down his cheek.

"What? What happened?"

She wouldn't like this. "The battery crapped out."

"What!" She glanced around. "Now what? I mean, this idiot could be making his way to us right now. He's got us pinned down."

"He might've also cut his losses. Like I said, we'll hear him if he's coming, just like we heard Bugs over there."

"Are you sure this isn't some old girlfriend with a grudge?" she asked. "The list is kind of long. No offense."

"Trust me. None of the girls I dated know how to shoot, though I guess they could hire someone who does." But hardly anyone knew his new address. And both yesterday and today had targeted Kim. If all the people who knew about her inheritance were out of town, then who the hell wanted her dead?

The answer came like the bullet.

"Stephanie's husband," Leo said.

"What?" Kim's brows slanted down. "Carl? He's in jail. He's not shooting at us."

"But he could be pulling strings from jail," Leo suggested. "The man still has people running his business." A nasty business at that. Although the sex slave ring had been busted, Leo didn't doubt that some part of it still existed somewhere. "You still need to testify. Maybe this is his way of getting rid of witnesses."

"But I'm not even a major witness. Stephanie and that last girl he abducted, Abbey, are the primary ones."

"Maybe, but it's worth checking out. Have you talked to Stephanie lately?"

"I checked on her a few days ago. She's okay. She's got her family supporting her." Kim looked away from him, her gaze shuttered.

He felt her loneliness as keenly as if it were his own. It seemed as if the world was closing in on both of them. Having Kim around after missing her for two months made him realize that he was changing. More and more lately, all he wanted was one person to have, one person to confide in.

In many ways, Kim was already that person. She'd seen him through the worst financial crisis of his life. She didn't belittle him or mock him. The last couple of months, she'd been his biggest support system.

And he was pretty damn sure she had no idea exactly what she meant to him.

She's pregnant. The reminder blazed in his head. A reminder that had his heart thumping faster and his palms sweating.

If he could just wrap his brain around her decision to have the baby, maybe he could deal with it better. But she was basing a decision without having all the facts, and telling her the facts meant outing Megan, which meant outing himself. He couldn't do it. Had too much at stake. Megan deserved her privacy. She deserved the best care money could buy. He could take any amount of scrutiny when it came to his own life, but he couldn't when it came to his sister. She needed the familiarity and routine of the institution, not the crazy mixed up life he lived when he worked.

The whap, whap, whap of helicopter blades sounded in the distance. "Maybe that's the police. We'll make sure they investigate Carl," Leo said. A minute later, a black and white chopper came into view, the LAPD logo on the side.

"Thank God," she murmured against his chest.

"Maybe they scared away our crackpot. I'll check." He slowly raised his hat again with the same branch. Nothing happened. He edged it along the rock and still nothing happened. "I think our guy ran."

Two officers dressed in heavy armor repelled from the copter in seconds flat. Both carried extra vests that Kim and Leo happily pulled over their clothes. With no way to go back up, the cops escorted them out of the canyon, their guns drawn as the helicopter hovered above.

With sheer will, they kept a blistering pace on the walk out. By the time they got to the road they were both sweating, out of breath, extremely hungry and cranky as hell. A contingent of cops waited for them as they neared Leo's car. They gave a statement and the officers assured them the detectives investigating the accident yesterday would be in touch.

Soot coated Kim from the top of her blond hair to the bottom of her new, formerly white sneakers. She was going to have a heart attack when she looked in the mirror. Leo quashed the urge to pull her in for a hug. Hell, he was covered too.

Leo unlocked the car and they piled in.

Kim kept looking out the window as if she'd spot the joker who'd shot at them. "If I get my hands on the asshole who kept us buried like weasels all day, I'm going to wring his neck before I make sure he spends the rest of his life in jail." She muttered the words between clenched teeth. Talk about angry.

Leo hoped she never got that pissed at him. He cranked the

engine, put the car in gear and got back to his place in just a few minutes. To think they'd been so close to home and in so much trouble most of the day.

Stella greeted them with a series of extra loud meows, rubbing herself against their legs until Leo picked her up. "You okay, Stell?"

Meow. She pushed her head into his palm and purred.

Kim went straight for the cabinets and pulled out a can of cat food for Stella. "Poor baby," she said, just before the whine of the can opener buzzed through the kitchen. Didn't matter that she was exhausted and tired, her first instinct had been to feed the cat. And Stella didn't even belong to her. Her actions said a lot about her capacity to care for others. She'd been watching out for *his* hide practically since they met.

Stella quickly abandoned Leo for the food bowl. Her tail swished as she chowed down. Kim eyed her for a second before heading to the stairs, moving much slower than she had when they'd made their way through the mountain. "I think every part of me hurts."

"Hey, leave me some hot water," Leo called after her.

"I'll think about it."

By the time Kim got to the top of the stairs, she was angrier than a cat in cold water. Every muscle ached. Even her damn fingernails hurt. With trouble—and gut turning fear—behind her, she thought back on the day. She'd been so close to snagging her phone, but instead she'd dodged a bullet. What the hell kind of luck did she have in this town? Maybe better luck than she realized because after all, she did still have her head attached to her body. Still, she was zero for two so far. Every visit had been a colossal pain in the ass.

Kim trudged into the hallway bathroom and her jaw dropped open when she got a look at herself in the mirror. She was practically a brunette and nearly every inch of skin was buried under black, smelly soot. It was a wonder Leo hadn't run screaming at any point in the afternoon. "You are Bride-of-Frankenstein scary, girl," she mumbled.

It took a few rounds in the tub to get her hair and skin back to their normal color. The road rash on her arms and legs from yesterday looked fresh, pink and gross, and she had a sunburn that made her nose bright pink. At least now she was clean. She took her wins where she could.

She could go back to her plan A and have Chelsea overnight her passport. That seemed easiest at this point. Once she got her credit card she could replace her phone. No way in hell was she scouring the crash site two days in a row. Just because she thought she spotted her phone today didn't mean she'd find it tomorrow. Plus, what if the shooter was watching? Waiting for the next time she showed her face? She had to admit that having Leo with her all day had saved her life. He'd kept her sane, kept up the conversation as he absently stroked his hands down her back or her arm, comforting her without even realizing it.

Or maybe he did. Because no matter how much he pissed her off sometimes…sometimes he was just a damn good man.

Kim shivered as she stepped into a pair of new black sweats from Leo's mall excursion. The soft material draped loosely on her legs. She combed out her wet hair, slathered moisturizer on her sunburnt skin and called it good.

She made her way downstairs and the mouthwatering smell of a home-cooked meal filled her head. She found Leo, freshly showered, wearing loose black sweats, white socks and white T-shirt that molded to his ripped chest. They were almost a matched set. "I don't know what you made, but it smells like heaven."

"Grilled cheese sandwiches and vegetable soup."

"The sandwich king strikes again." She winked when he glanced at her. She liked how he took her teasing with a sexy smile. He made it hard not to like him in general. But did she know better than to fall in love with a man who'd been as brutally honest about what he wanted in life? Absolutely.

Leo scooped their sandwiches out of the pan and onto plates. Kim grabbed glasses from the cabinet and poured them both water from the fridge door while Leo set the sandwiches and two steaming bowls of soup on the bar. They worked as if they'd been a team for years. Too bad the rest of their relationship couldn't be as easy. Kim placed the drinks next to their plates, grabbed napkins and they sat down at the same time. They practically inhaled their food.

"I need to figure out what I'm going to do," Kim said when

most of her sandwich was gone. "I'm not sure the airline will let me fly without ID."

"Let's worry about it tomorrow."

He had a point. She was too tired to think about anything right now. After she cleaned her bowl with the last bite of her sandwich, she sighed and finished off her drink.

Leo stacked the dishes and put them in the sink before grabbing her hand and leading her to the sofa. He set the ottoman close so they could stretch out. He turned on the TV, grabbed a blanket, plopped down next to her and covered them both.

He made it hard to stay mad or frustrated with him because he always did something nice. Just a little gesture like the ottoman or wrapping a blanket over her knocked down the defenses she built. "This is cozy," she admitted, yawning on the last word as Leo channel surfed. It was more than cozy. It was the exact thing she wanted in a relationship. Intimacy with the normal things in life. Someone to confide in. A partner. That reminded her of the question she'd asked him earlier. "You know, you owe me an answer from earlier."

"Answer about what?" He sounded guarded.

"Your parents. What happened to them?"

He sighed. It took him a minute, but he finally started talking. "I can't tell you anything about my dad since he was never in my life. My mom remarried when I was a teenager. My stepfather died from pancreatic cancer a couple years after they got married. My mom had high blood pressure and died from a heart attack a handful of years after that."

"I'm sorry," she whispered. She couldn't imagine growing up without her father and he'd essentially lost two. "It's hard sometimes, isn't it? Being alone." When he didn't answer she kept going. "Sometimes I think I'm lucky because I have no one to answer to. I can eat ice cream from the carton. I don't have to be considerate of anyone else in my condo. I can keep my own hours." She shook her head. "Then other times, I wish I had someone to watch football with. Or someone to make breakfast for. Or someone to just hold me when I watch a sad movie."

Leo hugged her tighter. "You like football, huh?"

Kim sputtered a laugh and looked at him. "Of all the stuff I just said, that's what caught your attention?"

He shrugged. "I'm a guy." Then he went back to channel surfing.

Shaking her head, Kim chuckled. He did know how to make her laugh. "Wait," she said, pointing to the screen. "What was that?"

Leo flipped back. "Where?"

"There!" She wiggled in her spot and got more comfortable. "*Dangerous Race* is on. You can tell me all the insider stuff while we watch. It'll be fun. I only got to visit the set for a few days, so I'd love to know some of the trivia." She pushed at his bicep. "Pretty please?"

A groan vibrated through his chest. "Fine." Leo hit the sound and the ending notes of the movie's score finished as the opening credits blasted off the screen.

Kim settled in next to him, her thigh brushing his. The opening scene was a spectacular car accident, and Kim's heavy lids drifted closed as she listened to the dialogue, waiting to hear Leo's voice.

Leo glanced at Kim and did a double take when he saw her asleep. Crisis averted. Rule number one. He never watched one of his movies with a date or potential date...or the mother of his child. He hated how that reminder kept jumping into his head. It was like a jack-in-the-box wearing a Freddy mask, scaring the shit out of him every time. He lowered the sound and leaned his head back along the sofa.

What a day. He really did want to know who was shooting at them and why. Was it a random thing...some whacked out guy getting his rocks off with moving targets? Or was Kim right. Did he have a stalker or someone who wanted him dead? Or did she? He closed his eyes as he made a mental list of possible people. He lost count at twenty-seven.

Vibrations woke him and Leo's adrenaline spiked as a small earthquake shook the house. Kim stiffened in his arms. Somehow he'd ended up spooning her on the sofa, their legs stretched out on the ottoman. She smelled like his shampoo and the turn on was instantaneous.

"Leo," she whispered.

He heard the apprehension in her voice. "Yeah?" She was

probably going to blast him for getting another hard-on while being pressed up against her ass. He eased away from her backside.

"What the hell was that? And please don't tell me it was an earthquake."

This was a much easier subject to tackle. He remembered how much the small earthquake two months ago at his house had scared her. It really was the last thing she needed after the day they'd had. "Okay. I won't tell you it was an earthquake."

She bolted to a sitting position, her eyes wide and her muscles tense. "Oh my God. This is the exact reason I can't live in this city."

"Take it easy," he soothed, bringing her down next to him. "That was just a baby. Doesn't even count." They'd been having tons of aftershocks since the big 7.1 a month ago. "I'm surprised we haven't had one sooner than this since you've been in town."

"Oh, man!" Damn, she sounded sweet when she was stressed.

Leo chuckled and pulled her closer. "C'mon. You're tough. You're not going to let a little aftershock get you down, are you?"

She turned over and faced him. "What was the earthquake like?"

Leo saw the mix of curiosity and fear in her green eyes. "I won't lie to you. It scared the shit out of me. It happened later in the morning, which if you ask me is better than the middle of the night. I hate when they wake you up out of a sound sleep." He eased some hair behind her ear, enjoying the silky softness. "I was going through my memorabilia in the garage when it hit. Everything came down off the shelves, everything was jumping up and down like popcorn. It was crazy."

"How'd the house survive?"

"Pretty good in the scheme of things. Just cosmetic damage. Nothing structural." Which was lucky since the house was still in escrow and the buyers could've pulled out. He never would've ended up in this house if it hadn't been the only one of his choices to remain standing after the quake.

She shivered and Leo pulled the blanket over her. Her skin gleamed in the moonlight shining through the skylight and he smoothed his thumb across her cheek.

"You know what earthquakes do?" he asked.

Shaking her head, she took his hand and linked her fingers in his.

"They make you glad to be alive." He brought her hand to his mouth and kissed the abraded skin on her knuckles from yesterday's accident.

"I guess after the last couple of days, I should be very glad to be alive." Her gaze roamed to his lips and Leo's dick took immediate notice.

Long moments passed as they watched each other. The attraction they worked hard to avoid pulled them together like a giant magnet. Leo couldn't say who moved in first. It might've been a mutual thing, but her warm breath wafted along his lips a second before he brushed his mouth over hers.

Her small inhale set him on fire, but he didn't rush into anything. He liked her like this. Liked the gentle brush of her lips against his, liked the soft caress of her fingers through his hair. He especially liked the way her curves molded to his chest as she wrapped a leg over his thigh. His heart pounded like a drum and his blood flowed hot as he skimmed the dip of her waist and rise of her hip. She melted his thought process until the only thing that mattered was touching her, tasting her, feeling her.

Leo pulled her beneath him until he lay nestled in the vee of her legs. She moaned, a sound of need that cut straight through him. "Want you. Now," he said between deep, drugging kisses. She gave him her tongue in response and he took the offering like treasure, sucking and licking and making a meal of it.

Her legs locked him to her and he pushed his hips against her to take the edge off his raging erection. As if. The only hope of that happening came with burying himself deep inside her.

"I thought we agreed not to do this anymore," she panted between kisses before opening her mouth for his questing tongue.

"Circumstances have dictated otherwise." He nuzzled her jaw and nibbled her sensitive earlobe.

"Circumstances?" The dreaminess in her voice spurred him on. He had to have her. He needed her like California needed rain. Like fish needed water. Like man needed air.

"Between your car yesterday, the gunfire today and the earthquake tonight, I think it's a sign from above that we should live each day to the fullest." He pushed his hard-on against her and she met him, locking her legs around him even tighter. His heart threatened to burst out of his chest.

They usually kept their relationship friendly. Kim wasn't a woman to hang on to his arm or demand attention. But it was the times they let their attraction speak, the times they touched and gazed and couldn't seem to stop from taking the next step until it was too late and they ended up locked in an embrace that neither had the desire to extricate themselves from.

Skimming his fingers under her sweatshirt, he groaned at the warm smoothness of her skin and the way she arched into his touch. "Arms up," he whispered and he pulled her top off in one quick motion so he had her at his fingertips. Though her full breasts filling out a delicate lace bra made his chest ache with her beauty, he didn't take the time to admire the sight. He pulled one cup down and took her pebbled nipple into his mouth, sucking, teasing and laving the hard bud until she was panting.

"Oh God, Leo. So good," she whispered.

He loved driving her crazy. Loved taking her to the edge where nothing mattered but the way he touched her, so he did the same thing to the other side. Every once in a while she lifted her head and tongued his ear, or grabbed his ass and squeezed him tight and every time she revved him up even more. Regardless, her hands stayed busy, either running through his hair or digging into his back. The beast inside him roared.

Leo hooked his thumb into the waistband of the soft cotton sweats and eased them down along with her underwear. Kim pulled a leg out of one side to expedite the process at the same time she grabbed the hem of his T-shirt and pulled it over his head.

Nothing felt better than the soft crush of her bare breasts against his chest. Nothing tasted sweeter than the slow, deep penetration of her tongue in his mouth. He loved her boldness, loved the way she let her body do the talking when they made love.

She yanked his sweats over his ass and cool room air kissed his bare skin as she held him tight. "Leo, come inside." The whispered invitation made his heart race faster. Sweat slicked their skin.

He took her mouth a little harder, a lot deeper. He cupped her head and held her steady as he plundered her mouth and took everything she offered. Easing his hand up the inside of her thigh, he struggled to slow down, to savor every second.

"Hurry," she said. "Need you. Want you."

All those words went to his head and made him fuzzy. How many times had he heard the same thing the past two months, only to wake up and discover it was all a dream? How many hours had he spent remembering his time with this woman? How often had he had to convince himself that he'd never have her again?

Leo pushed a finger inside her, smoothing the hot cream around her clit as she jerked and gasped into his mouth. God, he loved her like this. Out of control. He loved her begging for him. Loved to see this businesswoman let her hair down and give it up to him. It wasn't until he got the head of his penis right at ground zero that he remembered something.

"Shit. I forgot a condom." He lifted up. "I need to grab one."

She held on tight as she stared up at him. "A little late for that, my friend. The horse is long out of the barn. No need to close the door now."

Because she was already pregnant. With his baby. It was like a tidal wave of information he'd somehow forgotten while enjoying these last few minutes.

Intuitive woman that she was, she read his every thought. "I know. Scary, right?" She swallowed. "But what I said when I came in the door still stands. I don't expect you to—"

"Shut up," Leo whispered before kissing her. He pushed inside a second later, electricity flashing through him as his dick found home. He didn't want to talk about it. Didn't want a reminder that she thought so little of him. How could he just ignore the fact that she was going to have his baby?

Wrapping her arms around him, she arched up and met his every thrust. He went at her hard, driving himself deep inside her heat as her gasps fueled his fire. Hot. Wet. Tight. His head nearly exploded from the sensory overload, from the sheer physical sensations of their connection.

Until he touched a rough patch of skin on her thigh and stopped, buried to the hilt, his heart pumping hard and fast. A wave of disgust washed through him.

"What?" She searched his eyes, hers were bright, dazed and heavy lidded. "What's wrong?"

He moved out slow and pushed in slower. "I don't want to hurt you. I got carried away." He took her mouth in a gentle kiss and let the build start over, taking her to the top with long slow strokes and deep penetration.

The only time he'd gone without a condom had been with this woman. The hot clasp of her body hugged him tight as he moved inside her. The perfect friction sent his blood pumping hotter and harder. All Leo wanted to do was give her an orgasm. Her muscles tightened with every new thrust, her short, panting gasps drove him closer to the edge.

"Come, dammit," he whispered harshly in her ear. "Come." He tilted her ass up a little higher and moved inside her harder, faster.

A few strokes and she broke apart with a cry as her climax shook her harder than the last aftershock. She bucked into him and Leo's control snapped. A groan rumbled from his chest as his own orgasm blew through him like a volcano, taking out everything in its wake. The repercussions hit him hard, rocked him to his bones. Nothing had prepared him for the feeling of coming inside her, the euphoria, the freedom, the chest pounding sensation that he'd marked her as his.

Leo collapsed next her, his mind blown. No one had warned him about this kind of emotion, for the blinding almost paralyzing fear that nothing would ever be the same again.

Long minutes later, when they both had their breath and a few brain cells working, Leo pulled her closely against his chest.

He could run from his feelings or he could face them. "You know you mean something to me, right?" It was as close as he'd ever come to being honest with a woman about his emotions and he waited for Kim's response. He swallowed when she didn't say anything. "Kim?" he looked down.

Moonlight slashed across her smooth cheeks. Her long dark lashes curved over her closed lids and her steady breath wafted softly over his skin. She was sound asleep.

Didn't it figure? He finally got the courage to tell the woman something important and she was out cold.

Chapter Nine

The telephone woke Kim the next morning. She rolled over, still on the sofa with two soft, thick blankets covering her bare skin. Every inch of her hurt, but a few private spots celebrated with a full aria, complete with a rousing *hallelujah* at the end. As she stretched, she spotted Leo in the kitchen as he took the call. Wearing his low hung sweats and bare everywhere else, he looked like a poster ad for health and fitness. Really, he looked good enough to eat. She loved running her hands along his abs and down his biceps. He was chiseled beyond beautiful. She wasn't sure what made her mouth water more, his broad shoulders, deep tan or the way his back muscles played as he worked at the stove.

The smell of bacon and eggs made her stomach rumble. Maybe that's why her mouth watered. No...it was Leo.

"Yeah, we're a go for Saturday. I just heard back from Oliver. It'll take a few hours to get there and a few more to get the shot." He listened and shook his head. Something scraped against a pan on the stove. "No, I'll get Rex to do the fall. With my luck I'll break something. I'll mount and ride, but—" He nodded. "Yeah, that's the plan. Once we get this shot, the rest is easy. It's all transition shots." He listened some more. "Okay. Let me know, otherwise I'll figure you got it and I won't need my contingency plan. Okay, see you then." He hung up his phone and glanced over his shoulder. "Ah. Damn. Sorry about that. I was trying to do everything by email so I wouldn't wake you up, but..." He shrugged and gestured to the phone. "Some people would rather talk it out."

"That's okay," Kim said as she leaned up on her elbows, very conscious of the way Leo's gaze took in her bare shoulders. She reached for the closest sweatshirt and pulled it over her head, making sure to keep the blanket in place before covering herself.

Leo turned back to the stove and gave her a very clear view of his sculpted posterior.

"Sounds like your movie's coming together pretty quickly." Kim shimmied into her sweat bottoms and padded over the carpet and onto the cold kitchen tile.

Stella swished her black tail along the floor, her woe-is-me eyes watching Leo for any sign of food compassion.

Leo dished out scrambled eggs from a pan and *accidently* let a little hit the floor where Stella pounced. "My cinematographer has a six-day window before he starts his next gig. If I don't grab him now, I lose him for the next six months." He turned as she got glasses from the cabinet and poured the orange juice he'd taken out of the fridge.

"What about the rest of the crew?"

"I'm doing this bare bones. We'll all be doing double duty. Which reminds me, I'll be leaving before dawn on Saturday, so if you want me to rent a car for you so you can get someplace, we need to do it in the next day or two."

With everything he had going, he was still thinking of her. Just as he had yesterday when they'd been trekking through the canyon then been pinned down by some nut with a gun. Kim considered the generous offer. He always did that. Kept her off balance with his words and his actions. "That's very nice of you." She sipped her juice. "I'll think about it." She really didn't want to ask more of him.

"Or if you'd rather, you can hang here and bond with Stella."

Stella had given up her begging and lay curled on the blanket that had fallen off the sofa.

"Or..." It wouldn't kill her to return some of his generosity. Their difference of opinion didn't have to screw with every part of their relationship. "I could come with you and help out. Sounds like you could use an extra hand."

He hit her with his blue-eyed gaze as his lips curled up in a smile. "If you're not careful, I might take you up on that."

The seductive tone of his voice said he might do more besides taking her up on her offer, and a full-body flush spread from her center and radiated to all parts north and south when he looked at her that way. "I'm very careful," she said, managing to hold a straight face.

Leo dropped his plastic serving spoon and wrapped her in his arms so fast that Kim squealed. He brought his lips within a fraction of hers. "You're also sexy as hell wearing my sweats after a night of sofa sex." No wonder the top had seemed big on her. She'd put on his instead of hers. His lips covered hers and Kim could only go along for the ride. He tasted like citrus and bacon, like morning and sun. And when he cupped her ass and brought her flush against his erection, she forgot about breakfast and feasted on him.

It was crazy. Spontaneous. They'd always managed to keep sex on the back burner on the morning after, and now they couldn't seem to get enough of each other. Leo lifted her and set her on the opposite counter, moving between her legs as his mouth continued to possess hers. He stroked her everywhere, his hand warm and firm as he explored all the curves and dips he'd reacquainted himself with last night. He edged his thumbs in her waistband and pushed down when the phone rang.

Breathing hard, Kim pulled back and held his face in her hands when he followed her lips. "The phone," she panted. "You should answer your phone. Your film's important."

She'd never seen his blue gaze so intense. He took a breath like he meant to say something, then abruptly closed his mouth and nodded. He grabbed the phone off the counter, glanced at the caller ID and walked out of the kitchen. "Hey, Rex, we're definitely on for Saturday." His voice faded as he got farther into the next room and Kim took a deep breath.

What was happening? How come she couldn't control her lust anymore when it came to this man, especially when she knew they didn't have a future together?

"Get your head out of the clouds, Kim," she muttered aloud as she jumped off the counter.

By the time Leo returned, she had breakfast on the table and her libido in check. Even if Leo had wanted to make another move on her, his phone kept ringing and he didn't get the chance. Then, detectives investigating the car accident came by and took their statements. They took definite interest when Kim mentioned her connection to Carl Wyncott and his impending trial. The man was rich, powerful and could've orchestrated both incidents. Leo mentioned the three people who knew about her inheritance and the detectives planned to check their alibies.

Early that afternoon while Leo's ear stayed glued to his phone, the doorbell rang. Kim saw the FedEx truck and her heart took a giant leap. She opened the door and signed for the delivery. Ripping open the slim envelope, she pumped a fist when she pulled out her new credit card. "Hallelujah," she said. "First stop, Cesar's boutique."

Leo came from his office on the other side of the staircase, the phone tucked between his head and shoulder as he made notes on a thick yellow pad. Dressed in a pair of worn jeans and a white T-shirt that outlined all his gorgeous muscles, he looked like the movie hero he usually played on the big screen. "Got it," he said. "I think that covers it." He listened and laughed. "I can only hope. Yeah." He nodded. "Sounds good. See you Saturday bright and early." He disconnected and stopped when he saw her. His gaze raked over the jeans and sandals he'd purchased for her. The heat in his eyes made her flush. "Credit card?" he asked.

Her smile probably said it all. "Shopping?" His phone rang and her grin faded. "Probably not," she said, answering her own question. "You're too busy."

Leo checked the screen. "It's a toll free number. You couldn't pay me to answer it." At her lifted eyebrow, he reconsidered. "Okay, if you paid me...I might answer it." He checked his watch. "We can go. I've got most everything covered and if someone needs me they can leave a message or call my cell." He grabbed his keys from the counter. "Where do you want to go?"

"Cesar's store. I want to repay his kindness from the last time."

"Uh..." Leo stalled and looked almost panicked. "Okay. Let me just give him a quick call and make sure he's in."

While Leo did that, Kim changed into one of the outfits Leo had brought her the first night. Considering she hadn't been with him, he'd managed to pick out something that was totally her style. A black skirt that hit midthigh and a deep purple button-up top with three quarter length sleeves fit her just right. So did the size seven black heels. She couldn't walk into Cesar's place like she had two months ago in torn up clothing and she wanted something nicer than jeans. Cesar was a man who knew and appreciated style, and Kim felt a kinship with him on that respect.

Before they left, Kim took the opportunity to call Chelsea and get the ball rolling on her passport. Everything was coming together.

Leo found parking at a nearby lot and together they strolled toward Cesar's shop. After opening the door, he followed her inside. He scanned the place, probably looking for the owner and seemed to sigh in relief as he met Kim's gaze.

The shop catered to the sophisticated woman. Track lighting highlighted the bright white paint. Delicate outfits filled the racks lined up against the walls. Shoes, bags and all sorts of lacey underthings filled the tables in the middle, while black-and-white stripped sofas created a comfortable sitting area outside the dressing rooms.

Cesar came from the back room, his arms outstretched. His pink silk shirt peeked out from beneath his black suit and his matching pink tie had black hammers on it. Interesting. Definitely different. "Ah! My favorite customer!" he said, kissing each cheek. He held her shoulders and looked her up and down, his scowl evident. "What is this?" he said. His gesture encompassed all of her, from her scrapes to her clothes.

Apparently he could spot mall wear in the blink of an eye.

"I'm fine and the clothes are temporary," she said. "Until you find something for me here."

His smile beamed wide as he linked her arm in his and pulled her deeper into the store. It was probably the only place she could shop and not need any ID to prove herself. Besides, she owed him for discounting everything she purchased two months ago. She didn't deny the buzz of anticipation as she looked around at the beautiful collection in Cesar's store. For the first time in her life, she could do some damage. Provided she could let herself spend so much money. Maybe just this once she could do it. Her heart thundered thinking about dropping ten thousand dollars on clothes. It wasn't in her nature to spend large amounts of money, at least not since losing everything she had four years ago.

Kim picked out a few pieces that worked well together and Cesar showed her to the dressing room. It wasn't until she came out, dressed in a new outfit, that she spotted the open door to the back room. Leaning against the wall on the floor was a *Dangerous Race* poster.

Leo's poster. If she hadn't recognized the custom frame, she would've seen the inscriptions to him personally from his co-star in the movie and the woman who inspired the film. So what was the poster doing here when Leo had insisted it be one of the few items he planned on keeping? Had he changed his mind? Well, obviously, but why?

She didn't plan to hire a detective to figure out this mystery. She'd go to a source.

Leo waited on the comfortable sofa for Kim to come out of the dressing room. Cesar stood next to him, adjusting clothes on the nearest rack. "Thanks for taking down the poster," he said, pocketing his cell phone after checking the latest emails. "If Kim saw it, she'd want to know why it was here and there's no reason for her to find out."

"Why the big secret?" Cesar asked. "It was a fair trade."

"I think so, too, but she doesn't need to know it involved her."

Cesar shrugged and shook his head. "I don't get you. You play tough macho guys in the movies, but in real life you're a big chicken."

Chicken? No one called him that. Leo stood up, his hackles rising. "What do you mean, chicken? I'm not chicken."

"Please. You've fallen for this woman who is kind and beautiful and strong and you don't have the guts to tell her. Chicken." One emphatic nod of Cesar's head punctuated the word.

"She's not interested in me," Leo protested. "Not for the long term. Besides, who wants long term? I don't."

"You're chicken *and* you're stupid," Cesar muttered.

"Hey, I heard that," Leo groused. "I don't see you in any long-term partnership," he added.

"Not because I don't want one. Who wouldn't want a companion, a lover, someone to talk to and keep you warm in the middle of the night? Who doesn't want to be loved?"

Put like that, Leo didn't have much of a defense. "Not everyone wants the same things, Cesar. Sometimes life is too complicated and it's easier to be alone."

"Like I said, chicken and stupid."

Leo opened his mouth to argue when Kim came out of the

dressing room hallway. The turquoise dress molded to her figure cut off any thought process. The low-cut neckline gave a hint of her cleavage without being raunchy, and the slits in the arms showed off the definition in her biceps.

"Now that is how my dress is supposed to look." Cesar beamed as Kim stopped in front of the three-sided mirror. He lifted the dress's zipper the rest of the way up making Leo jealous that he hadn't thought fast enough to do the same. Any excuse to touch her smooth skin.

"What do you think?" she asked, glancing over her shoulder with a critical eye.

Leo moved closer as Cesar backed off with one lifted brow and headed to the counter. "I think you look amazing," he whispered. He caught the little shiver and inhale that came when his breath tickled her ear.

"It just occurred to me that I won't get to wear this much longer."

He opened his mouth to ask why and shut it just as quickly. Because she was pregnant. "You can wear it now and after," he said.

Holy shit. After she had his baby.

Their eyes met in the mirror and Leo didn't expect to see compassion.

She faced him, her head tilted to the side. "I need to ask—"

"Mom! It's him!" A boy ran up to Leo. "I told my brother you really drove that race car in *Dangerous Race* and he said no way. Did you? Did you?"

"You're too young to see that movie," Leo said, facing the boy. He couldn't have been much more than ten.

"I only watch the racing scenes. Mom won't let me watch anything else."

Speaking of his mother, she landed next to her son. "Sorry about that. We're still learning about privacy." She looked down at him. "Say good-bye and let's go. You can tell Jared that you saw him, but don't bother him." She took his arm, ready to haul him away. "Sorry about that."

"No problem." He crouched in front of the dejected boy. "You can tell your brother that I did drive the car." At least he had in the close-ups. A stunt man had taken it around the track for the race at the end.

"That's the coolest!" The kid glanced up at his mom and back to Leo. "Will you sign my shirt? That way I can prove I really met you."

"Uh." He glanced at the mom who looked at him with hopeful eyes. "Sure, as long as your mom doesn't mind me signing your shirt. She's the boss." He gave her one of his patented smiles and she flushed.

"Okay," she said.

"I just need something to…" Leo looked around for a pen just as Cesar ran up with a marker. "Thanks," Leo told his friend. He scribbled his name on the sleeve of the kid's T-shirt. "How's that?"

"It's great! Thank you!" The kid beamed, happy as his mother dragged him out of the shop. Leo turned back to find Kim perusing another rack as Cesar pointed out more options. She nodded her head as she glanced at him and smiled. Cesar handed her a few more hangers of clothes and she took them back to the dressing room.

Cesar's words circled in his head in a never-ending record. *Chicken. Stupid. Chicken. Stupid.* He was all of the above.

Chapter Ten

Back at Leo's place, Kim hung up her new clothes—all but the turquoise dress she'd worn out of the shop—still in sticker shock. Or tag shock. Whatever shock came from spending thousands of dollars on clothes. Was this the reason Aunt Carolyn lived modestly? Because she had a hard time spending money on name brand items or wildly expensive clothes? Money or not, Kim hadn't found it easy to fork over that kind of dough. She'd mainly done it since she owed Cesar a huge favor for discounting all of the clothes two months ago when Leo had first taken her to his shop. Technically, she probably still owed him more money. Or she owed Leo more money.

The *Dangerous Race* poster flashed in her mind. Was that why it was in Cesar's shop? Had Leo bartered for her clothes with it? She never had a chance to ask him about the poster because people had started returning calls. Leo had even arranged things on the phone in the car ride home while she scribbled notes for him.

With Leo *still* on the phone getting ready for Saturday, Kim took a few minutes to check her email and surf the Internet. After a half hour, she logged off and pushed the chair back. Something crinkled on the floor and she picked up Leo's last bank statement where it had fallen from the desk.

Though she'd gone through all his finances with him a couple of months ago and she'd been proud of the way he'd consolidated his life and holdings, her curiosity got the better of her. She flipped to the second page and glanced at the numbers. A direct withdrawal from his account for twenty-one thousand dollars made her blink. She looked at the code, not surprised to see The Marion. She'd told him he couldn't afford to keep this estate, so what had he been thinking? His balance was precariously low, telling her he was still barely treading water financially.

A wave of anger rose up from her stomach. How could he spend twenty-one thousand dollars on a place he didn't visit, much less live in?

She scanned his deposits and saw several that added up to twenty-three thousand dollars. Why would he blow that money into a vacation place when he could start rebuilding his savings or begin investing in something that gave him dividends? It made no sense. Kim trekked through the living room to find Leo, but his phone rang before she could ask him about it.

"It's the LAPD," he said, reading the caller ID. "Hello." He listened, nodded. "Really? I guess that's good." He glanced at her, his brows slanted as he listened some more. "But they could be lying," he said. After another minute, he said, "Thanks for the call. I'll let her know. And you'll let me know if you find anything else."

"What happened?" Kim asked after he hung up. "News about yesterday?"

"Cops talked to a man in one of the canyon houses last night. Turns out his kid broke into his gun cabinet and fired off a few shots with his shotgun. Kid claims he was only aiming at tin cans with his buddies, but..." Leo shrugged. "The trajectory from the house doesn't match where we were pinned down, and the kid swears they didn't leave the house, just fired from the balcony. Time frame doesn't match either."

"You think he's lying?" she asked.

"Don't know. It's possible. Either way they're in a shitload of—"

The phone rang again and Leo answered, glancing up at her. "It's for you."

For her? Who would be calling...? Shit. Only one person had this number. Taking the phone, Kim set her annoyance aside. Maybe he had a good reason this time. "Hello?"

"Kim!"

Just as she suspected. "Hi, Wilson. Everything okay?"

"Yep. Great news!" Kim had to take the phone from her ear because he was practically yelling. "I just rolled into town for an engineering conference. Where are you? I thought I'd pick you up and we could grab a bite to eat."

She glanced at Leo since he'd obviously heard the invitation and he shrugged. "Uh…" Now wasn't the best time, especially since she wanted to have a talk with Leo, who was nice enough to pull her favorite tea from his pantry and silently ask if she wanted some. She nodded.

"Hey, at least tell me where you are?" Wilson asked. "I thought we could catch up since we barely see each other. This will make it twice in two months."

He sounded so happy to see her and he'd been so upset after the meeting with the lawyer that she felt obligated to see him. She'd still have plenty of time to knock some sense into the man standing in front her. She covered the mouthpiece. "Do you mind if I give my cousin your address?"

"I don't mind. Sounds like you do though," Leo whispered.

Honestly she was more torn than anything. She didn't want to think badly of Wilson. She just wanted him to grow up. He'd let his good looks open doors and when those doors started closing, he had no idea how to deal with life. Carolyn might not have been able to help him, but maybe a peer, someone closer in age, might be able to help guide him.

Kim went back to the phone. "You got a pencil?" When he was ready, she gave him the address to the house in the hills and disconnected.

"This is your favorite cousin?" Leo teased as Kim got a mug from the cabinet and filled it with water from the fridge.

"He's the only cousin I have any contact with. Not sure that's a good thing anymore," she mumbled, setting a mug of water in the microwave. "He's here for a conference."

"So I heard. That's good timing," Leo said.

"For who?"

Leo laughed, but the phone rang and cut short his joy. It also cut her opportunity to ask him about his vacation place.

Wilson arrived forty-five minutes later, looking much his usual self in tan Dockers and a navy polo shirt. He hugged her— a little too hard—before pulling back and taking a good look at her. "What happened to you? You look like you went through a paper shredder."

Kim didn't need to look at the scratches on her arms and legs.

Scratches the dress did nothing to hide. "Gee, thanks," she uttered. She waved him into the house and introduced him to Leo, who promptly took another phone call and disappeared into his office.

"Wow," Wilson said, taking a seat on the couch. Stella eyed him from her corner, but didn't make a move to get closer. "I didn't realize my little cousin had so many famous clients."

"I don't really," Kim said, holding back her annoyance at the way he got comfortable. This was the kind of thing that put people off. Instead of waiting for invitations, Wilson just assumed they were forthcoming and helped himself to anything. Kim held back the words, *cut this shit out* because she didn't want a family argument in front of Leo. "Can I get you something to drink?" Damn. Shouldn't have offered.

"Sure. I'll have whatever you're having." He stretched out his legs and looked around the place like it was a four-star hotel just waiting for him, while Kim headed to the kitchen, cursing her hostess gene. "Hey," he continued, "is your cat ni— Ouch! Shit! Damn cat." Sounded as if Stella had made up her mind about Wilson, and Kim felt guilty for smiling. "Well, it was one long drive from Tucson. I'm ready for a nap."

Don't expect to take it here. "Maybe you should check into a hotel and do that," she suggested from the kitchen. "Where's your conference?" She poured him a glass of water from the fridge.

"It's downtown. I'm pretty sure the hotel's booked, but I thought I'd come in anyway since I knew you were here. Any chance you could put me up for a few nights?"

What the hell? Kim felt a surge of fresh compassion for Aunt Carolyn, along with a strong urge to throttle Wilson. Was this what Carolyn dealt with before she got sick? Before Kim could formulate an answer, Leo bounded down the stairs, still on the phone as she entered with the water.

"No, I have it right here. Give me a sec." He rummaged through stacks of papers on the small kitchen table until he found what he needed. "Yeah, I was right. Twenty feet should be enough. I just want that close up before the dolly stops and we get the scenery in the background." He listened and nodded. "Great. I'll see you Saturday."

"What's Saturday?" Wilson asked as Leo disconnected the call.

Kim couldn't believe Wilson asked before she'd even introduced them, but Leo didn't seem bothered. "I'm finishing my film," he said. He scribbled more notes on a yellow pad.

Damn. She didn't want Wilson to know because—

"That is so cool!" Wilson sat forward. "What's it about?"

"It's a western," Leo said.

Wilson's handsome face scrunched up into a ball of doubt. "A western? Why?"

The air in the room turned suddenly icy.

"Okay!" Kim said, breaking up the conversation and handing her cousin the glass of water. "Has your conference already started? Do you need to register?" How fast could she get him out the door? Not to mention hoping he didn't bring up sleeping accommodations again. It wasn't her house to offer Wilson a bed and besides she already occupied the only other bed in the place.

Taking a drink, Wilson waved his hand in the air. "I can hit it tomorrow. There's not much happening today." He looked at Leo. "Would you mind if I watched you on Saturday? I'd love to tell my friends that not only did I meet Leo Frost, but I got to see him shoot a scene for his movie."

Leo's silence said more than any words and just as Kim opened her mouth to tell Wilson it wasn't possible, Leo said, "Sure. Not a problem."

"Great!" Wilson set his half empty glass on the table and sat back, making himself at home, and Kim had the absolute knowledge that she'd made a huge mistake inviting him over. She'd bet a bundle he got away with murder with that face.

Wilson slid the cardkey into the slot and opened the hotel room door. Anger simmered under the surface as he tossed his bag on the green comforter of the king sized bed. The strong smell of disinfectant permeated the room and he opened the window facing the parking lot. He'd hoped to not have to come back here. It was close enough to the damn conference to actually back up his story and he'd needed that alibi in case Kim asked him or came with him. "Fucking assholes think I don't know what's going on between them." He paced the room. "Sorry, there's not enough space," he mimicked his cousin. He inspected the claw mark on his hand. That was the last time he tried to be nice to an animal. "Bullshit. Move the rabid cat off the fucking sofa and I can sleep there, shitheads."

It made him glad he'd kept them pinned all day yesterday. He chuckled again. How many hours had they stayed behind that rock cluster after he'd gone home? Two? Three? Had they waited until dark? He'd wanted to ask about the cuts and scrapes on Kim's arms, but since he knew about her car accident, he had no reason to think those injuries had been caused any other way, and there was no sense inviting questions from her.

Speaking of questions, he needed to cover his ass with an alibi so he called his old buddy Nick. The guy owed him a favor after Wilson had dropped out of a card game and given his seat to Nick. Bastard had ended up winning a nice haul of almost ten grand that night. All Nick had to do was tell the cops they were together yesterday and Wilson would be in the clear. With that done, Wilson paced the room.

Something about the way Kim looked today reminded him of Carolyn. Maybe it was the dress or her hairstyle. No. It was her attitude when she'd shown him to the door. It had been all Aunt Carolyn and he despised it. They thought they were better than him. Thought he was a failure. "Well, Carolyn, if I'm such a failure, why are you six feet under and I'm still here."

Taking a deep breath, Wilson stopped moving and looked up to the ceiling. "Fine," he said, stretching his neck and tilting his head back and forth from one shoulder to the other. "You don't want me under your roof, but I sure as hell will see you on Saturday. And maybe it'll be the last time you see anybody." He took out the headshot of Leo he'd swiped from the stack on the table. "You too, asshole. You too. You couldn't even get off the phone for more than two minutes to talk to a guest in your house. I knew you were a prick."

Chapter Eleven

Saturday came way too fast. Leo had so much going through his head as he got into wardrobe, he wondered if he could pull off this last minute shoot. Outside his makeshift tent in the desert, crewmembers readied for the shot.

Thank God Kim had decided to stay because she'd turned into his right hand. They'd both been glued to phones for two days. Kim's crash course in production 101 had been an ongoing success. A smart businesswoman, she was quick to get the hang of pulling together a last minute shoot. Coordinating schedules, equipment rental, transportation, costs, food on site and a hundred other details sometimes took a magician.

Every single crewmember he'd hired had agreed to work the day for a cut rate and a piece of the profits. Provided he had profits to give. If Kim's cousin was any indication, then he might be fighting a losing battle to finish this film. Would anyone go see a western in this day of zombie/techno warfare?

The small group who'd come here today did it because they liked him and respected him. He might have a shitty reputation when it came to women, but crewmembers loved him. At least most did. He had made one huge error in judgment over the years and it still haunted him.

Most people didn't realize the amount of work that went into making a film. The amount of very creative, talented people needed to shape and produce the visions on the big screen. They looked at a costume and enjoyed the flair, but had no real concept of the work that went into designing or building it, the same with the sets or makeup or the script itself.

So, yes, though Leo had managed to make the majority of this film and pay his crew so long ago, it was the people who'd shown up here today to finish these final shots who he planned to share some of the profits with. They were the ones who'd believed in him and this film from the beginning and he felt the need to reward that.

He sure as hell hoped this thing broke even.

Leo took one last look in the mirror at his wardrobe. The dust-covered brown pants with dust-covered black leather chaps. Spurs jingled when he walked. A holster hung low on his hip and strapped to his thigh. A brown leather vest hid most of the black shirt, and his black Stetson sat back on his head. Two days growth of dark stubble covered his jaw and cheeks. Because of his lack of sleep the last couple of nights, and since he'd risen at three a.m. to get to the location, he looked road weary and tired. It worked perfectly for the part.

He didn't have any dialogue to utter, but this scene was pivotal to the movie. He'd planned to shoot it many months ago, but after Carrie Ann had gone off the deep end and been institutionalized, he'd put it off. Finishing and releasing the film had seemed like the wrong thing to do, but when it came to defining importance, Megan's health care beat Carrie Ann's any day of the week.

Family came first and Megan was the only family he had.

Not for much longer.

His brain wouldn't shut down the commentary on the new arrival due in about seven months. His palms sweated just thinking about it. Kim didn't look pregnant, so his brain had a hard time processing what it couldn't see. Pretty soon, he'd have more than just Megan to care for. Didn't matter what Kim said, he couldn't walk away no matter if she wanted him to or not. If she seriously intended to have his baby, then he had to be involved. No matter how cold-hearted some people assumed him to be, he wouldn't turn his back on his flesh and blood.

Now that he had that decision made, he needed to tell Kim. He hadn't had a minute to talk to her once they'd set Wilson back on the road toward his conference. Which didn't seem to be that important since the guy took the day off to watch him film. But for some people, watching a film being made was a once in a lifetime thing…even a film as small as this one.

Leo came out of the wardrobe tent, a tiny enclosure a couple of the guys had constructed for him to change. He went to the cooler under a bigger tent they'd erected for craft service. Not that this could be considered crafty. It was more like a table piled high with granola bars, and fruit in a basket. Bread and peanut butter sat in the corner. Two coolers filled with water, Gatorade and soda took up space on the ground. Two more coolers with deli meat, cheese and condiments hid under the table for lunchtime.

Kim had helped him buy and organize everything and for that—for everything she'd helped him with—he might've fallen in love with her.

Leo chugged some water as he walked into the blazing sun. A cool breeze took the edge off what might've been a blistering day. Not one cloud drifted in the sky. He spotted Kim in the dark blue skinny jeans he'd bought for her with a white tank top that outlined her sweet figure. A pair of brown boots with a three-inch heel gave her the height she loved. Cesar's clothes didn't really work for this desert shoot, but Kim had the ability to make even her casual outfit look custom made. She stood next to Smokey, the dark Mustang he'd be riding, patting his sleek neck and talking to the horse wranglers.

His phone must have rung, because Kim slipped it out of her pocket and checked the screen as she moved toward him and answered it, kicking up tufts of dust with each step. She'd been fielding his calls all morning so he could get some work done setting up the scene. "He's right here. Here you go." She handed him the phone. "Your stuntman, Rex."

"Hey, Rex. What's up?"

"Oh, man, Leo. I'm sorry, bro. Some douche bag rear-ended me going forty. My car is totaled. There's no way I can be there in time."

Shit. Leo's heart sank. The biggest part of the day relied on the stunt. Just another in a long line of hurdles keeping him on his toes. "You okay? You got an ambulance on the way?"

"Nah. No ambulance. I'm a little sore, but I'm fine. I'm ready to throttle this idiot though, and my car's not going anywhere. I feel terrible. I don't want you to do this stunt."

He hadn't wanted to either, but now he didn't have a choice. Sweat prickled along his neck. "Don't worry about it. I can handle it." He pretended not to see Kim's eyes narrow.

"I have the saddle, man," Rex said. "And you need a step on the saddle for the fall you're planning." The step was an L shaped metal piece that replaced the stirrup. It hooked into the fender or looped over the saddle horn and provided the support the rider needed while on the horse, and at the same time made a jumping off point when it came time to execute the fall. It also prevented the rider from getting their foot caught or twisted in the stirrup.

"Kyle has a saddle and a step, so we're good," Leo told him. "And we already prepped the ground. I think we fluffed it to your usual standard. Your nice soft landing pit will now become my soft landing pit." Yeah, right. Leo wasn't dumb enough to think that just because they'd used a pick and shovel to dig up a square section of land to soften the fall didn't mean it wasn't going to hurt. What he wouldn't give for a crash pad. And now Kim had her hands on her hips. Battle mode.

"Dude. I know you've done a lot of your own stunts, but I'm not comfortable with you falling off a horse. That's one you haven't tried before."

"True. But you're a good teacher, Rex. I can handle it." He hoped.

Rex groaned. "I hate this. Be careful. Don't make me have to visit you in the hospital."

Leo chuckled. "Quit worrying. I'll be fine." He said it to Kim, too, as she glared at him. "I'll give you a call when it's over." After listening to all of Rex's last minute words of wisdom, Leo hung up, watching the group surrounding the horses.

"No way, Leo," Kim said, not hesitating to blast him. "You canno—"

"Yes. I can. I have to. No other choice. So if you can't say something positive, don't say anything at all." The longer he stood there, the more he realized what could happen if the stunt went wrong. Yeah, he had a trust, but now he had no holdings in that trust to provide for Megan. She'd only have his life insurance and that would run out in a handful of years. What happened to her then?

Holding his yellow notepad, Kim clenched her jaw and stewed in front of him. She may have called his financial shots the past two months, but this rodeo belonged to him. He took the notepad out of her hands along with the pen behind her ear. "I'll give this back to you in one sec," he said. Then he took a few steps and scrawled out a note to Kim about his little sister: where she lived and what it cost to keep her there. Kim would make sure his money got there. She'd earned his trust in very little time with her no-nonsense approach to business and life. Not only that, but she'd been a rock through this whole miserable ordeal and he counted on her.

So far he'd been making enough money in residuals to keep Megan at The Marion Institute, but those would eventually dry up. Every day when the mail came, he prayed for envelopes from his agent and when they arrived, he ripped them open, hoping there were enough to cover his payment. He'd barely made last month's payment and knew this month's or any after that weren't guaranteed.

After finishing his note, he folded it multiple times and handed the pad and pen to Kim. He tucked the note in the inside pocket of the leather vest.

"What's that?" Kim asked, eyeing him carefully as if she could read his mind.

"Just a note." He didn't plan for her to see it unless she picked it off his dead body if this stunt didn't go right. "I see you met Smokey," he said.

She scowled at his change of subject, but grudgingly went with it. "He's gorgeous. I haven't been on a horse in years. He makes me want to ride."

"You ride?" No matter how hard he tried, he couldn't picture her on a horse. Then he had a vision of her on Smokey in a short skirt and sky-high heels in the stirrups. He could totally imagine climbing up behind her on the saddle and feeling that spectacular ass against his crotch.

"I do a lot of things," she told him cryptically, breaking into his day dream. "But, yes, I do ride. I learned at summer camp when I was a kid and I've always enjoyed it."

"Maybe if you play your cards right, Kyle will let you take Smokey for a spin after we do the stunt."

"Really?" Her face lit up with genuine interest. "I would love that!" She turned back to the horse. "He's gorgeous, isn't he?"

"He's not the only one," Leo murmured.

Kim slowly pivoted and faced him, her head cocked. "What?" Her smile had faded, but her interest shone bright in her eyes. She'd heard him loud and clear.

"Leo," Kyle, his grizzled old horse wrangler called from the trailer. He broke the spell Leo always fell into looking at Kim's eyes. "Rex just called and told me what's going on. Let's set the stirrup and the step and get this show moving along. I've got a date tonight." Perfect timing.

He headed off, walking backwards as he tipped his hat to Kim. "Gotta run. Catch you later. Don't worry, we'll be done with this before you know it, then you and Smokey can get acquainted." He winked and continued on. Hopefully, since he'd covered his bases, everything would go off without a hitch.

Kim checked her watch again. It had been a full forty-five minutes since Leo had told her it would be done before she knew it. Apparently, he'd been mistaken. Seriously mistaken. She'd had to take cover under the craft service tent because the breeze had disappeared and sun was starting to melt everything—and everyone—in sight.

Whatever Leo had written on that note was important enough for him to keep from her, and the longer that piece of paper stayed in Leo's vest, the more she wanted to read it. What did it say? Was it for her? About her? Was it something about the baby? The questions tumbled on.

His *gorgeous* comment still had her flushing like a teenager. She knew better than to let any man sweet-talk her, but somehow Leo managed to get past all her defenses.

To take her mind off the stunt and his earlier observation, Kim had hung around Smokey for a while. She'd never ridden a Mustang before. He was a sleek, dark machine at fifteen hands.

Leo walked the track that had been built for the camera. From what Kim had overheard, the track would stay even with Leo as the horse galloped along, then as the animal picked up speed, the camera would slow down and watch Leo ride into the sunset. At the last minute, Leo would get hit with a bullet and fall off the horse.

For the better part of an hour, he'd walked and talked out the stunt. They'd "fluffed" the landing pit by turning the soil and creating a soft spot on the desert floor. Kyle, the horse wrangler took Smokey's reins and met Leo near his starting point or *first mark* as they called it.

Still holding Leo's phone, Kim looked down as it vibrated in her hand. Rex had sent a text message.

Don't do the stunt!

A cold wave of chills shot down her spine as she looked up at Leo on the horse. No, it wasn't her phone or her business, but she cared about the jerk and if the stunt man thought it was a bad idea, then she agreed with him.

She heard Leo calling out final instructions as he adjusted the Stetson on his head and got low in the saddle. Kim felt heat rise in her cheeks as she took a breath to yell, but Leo barked, "Action!" The camera started its move and Leo's horse bolted forward.

"No, no, no," Kim said, jogging closer to the action. A sick roll of panic churned in her stomach as she clutched the pad and phone in her hands. She squinted into the bright sun.

A shot rang out and Leo tumbled off the horse. He landed with a thud and dirt jumped in the air before settling around him. It seemed as if he landed in the spot he'd prepped earlier, but a terrifying silence settled over the crew and Kim started running.

"Cut!" Leo lifted his head. "Got that?"

Kim stopped, her heart beating out of control, her mouth parched and limbs shaking as she watched Leo get up and head toward the horse, taking the reins and walking him back.

"Let's roll that back and see how it looks," Leo said. "If I don't have to do it again, I won't."

Kim liked that idea, and watched as a few crewmembers gathered around a monitor set up under a blue tent. After a few minutes of discussion, some of the guys dismantled the track and started moving equipment.

"One more from a different angle," Leo said, sauntering up to her. "I want to get one from the front with the guys on the chase. Then you can have a crack at Smokey."

She'd seen this option on his shot list. The riders "chasing" Leo were the horse wranglers he'd hired for the day and all they had to do was follow Leo and pretend to be shooting at him.

Leo headed toward the water bottle he'd set down before the stunt and took a swig. Kim took the opportunity to give him Rex's message.

"He's a worrier. He was a girl in a past life," Leo said. "I'm fine. I only need it one more time and we're done with that shot."

"I don't like it," Kim grumbled. "It's too dangerous." Leo grinned and her heart took an extra bounce for a different reason. "Don't look at me like that," she threatened. "Don't think that one smile is going to distract me or make me happy."

Leo moved right in front of her. Close enough that she smelled the leather and horse and sweat that burned off his skin. Standing next to him like this tested every speck of will power she owned. Because she'd never wanted to touch a man more than she wanted to touch Leo right this second. He bent close to her ear, his hat tapping the side of her head. "What would make you happy?" His sexy whisper reeked of Leo the player.

Instead of making her angrier or turning her off, it lit her fuse. All her girl parts saddled up for the ride. She leaned back a fraction to see his eyes. They sparkled with humor…and heat.

"It would make me happy if you didn't do this stunt again." She showed him the text on his phone. "If your stunt double thinks it's too dangerous, then shouldn't you listen to him?"

Leo set his hand on her shoulder and quickly readjusted to cup her neck so his thumb stroked under her jaw. The caress sent tingles all the way down her back. With his every touch, her body responded.

"I'm not going to lie to you," he said, his gaze glued to hers. "I like that you care." His thumb did that little graze against her skin. "But I have to do this. This is my best chance to pull out of this money issue. I've got to get this film out as soon as I can. No film, no money." He leaned in, brushed his lips against hers and it was the first time they'd shown any affection to each other in public. Kim felt a flush from her neck to her cheeks as Leo pulled away. "One more time and I'm done. Don't let Rex freak you out." He sauntered away and Kim let out a sigh. Whether from the situation or his kiss…she wasn't sure. She just knew that Leo was growing on her more and more.

So far this whole day had been a complete waste of his time. Wilson swatted away a fly as he stood in the shade of the horse trailer. Watching his cousin sink her claws into Leo Frost pissed him off as much as her getting Carolyn's inheritance. Apparently ten million dollars wasn't enough for her. Now she needed to snag a guy worth millions of dollars too.

His plan of getting alone time with Kim had derailed like a train on a bent track. So maybe he should go back to his other plan of plain old extermination. Of course, if she had some kind of terrible accident that scarred her for life, no guy would want her, but that meant her bastard baby would get the inheritance. Shit. She had to go and get pregnant.

Next to him, the horse sneezed and blew nasty snot all over his sleeve. "Shit!" he muttered. He wiped at the mess then eyed the horse staring at him with one giant brown eye. "What the hell are you staring at?" The horse shook his head and snorted again, but Wilson dodged the spray. He'd seen Kim petting the animal earlier and talking to the wranglers.

He'd even heard Leo say she could ride him when the stunt was over.

Well now...the stunt was over and everyone was crowded around the monitor watching it, which meant Kim would probably get her ride.

Wilson held back a smile. Not everyone could ride a horse as well as Leo Frost. He'd bet money his cousin couldn't. Especially if the horse got out of control.

He bent down and tied his shoe, picking up a little something that fit in the palm of his hand as he stood. Too big to be a burr, but much too small to be a tumbleweed. Once he tucked the strip of cactus under the horse's saddle blanket and once Kim kicked him, it was bound to be a hell of a ride. Falling from a horse, might even be good cause for a miscarriage. No baby meant he had a better chance at that inheritance.

Loving this impromptu plan, Wilson took a few steps toward the horse and patted his neck. "Easy does it, boy," he murmured. He checked around him one last time then lifted the blanket and placed his gift right where Kim's knees would squeeze the horse to get him moving.

Wilson could see it now. A hospital waiting room, a doctor explaining Kim had sustained life-threatening injuries and despite all their capabilities they were unable to revive her. A bad fall from a horse could accomplish that.

Oh, yeah...too bad the cameras wouldn't be rolling when Kim mounted the horse. Wilson couldn't wait. A lot of terrible accidents happened from getting thrown from a horse. Look what happened to Christopher Reeve. And even if it didn't kill her, it might put her out of commission for a while. Long enough to make sure he was the only one she could count on. Long enough to get her alone.

"One more take!" Leo called out.

Wilson glanced up as the crowd around the monitors separated and a few of the cowboys headed his way. "Oops," he muttered to the horse. "Looks like you get to toss the movie star after all." He patted the horse's neck. "I don't care how I get Carolyn—Kim—alone as long as it happens."

Chapter Twelve

Leo felt stupid for writing the note about Megan. Though he'd been a little nervous about the stunt, he'd landed right on "fluffed" soil and the fall wasn't as bad as he expected. After that run he felt a hundred percent more confident about doing it again from another angle. Besides, he kind of had to get the shot.

Forty minutes later when they had the track set up and all the equipment moved, Leo grabbed the reins and mounted Smokey. Unlike last time, the mustang pranced and skittered and Leo had a hard time keeping him under control. He'd been on horseback plenty of times and not much scared him, including a testy horse, but this seemed out of character for Smokey.

"Easy, boy. Easy," Leo soothed, leaning forward and patting his mane. "Let's get this going," he called out. "All set?"

His cinematographer, Yanic, gave him the high sign and so did the riders behind him.

"Call it when you've got the shot," Leo yelled, since this time the camera started on him unlike the last shot.

"Aaaaand..." Leo readied for the word from Yanic. "Action!"

Leo dug his knees into Smokey and the horse bolted forward like a bullet. Instead of running straight as they'd done during the first take, Smokey started bucking like he was a wild stallion needing to be broken. Leo held onto the reins and horn with white knuckles, struggling to keep his seat. It was nearly impossible with only one stirrup to balance himself on. The step worked against him. As familiar as he was with riding, he'd never experienced the bucking bronco scenario. His head whipped back as his legs went forward. Every time Smokey landed it was like a shockwave of pain up his spine. The scenery blurred as Leo whipped through the air like a rag doll. His hand went numb in the reins because he'd wrapped the leather around it in hopes of keeping a grip. Smokey continued to buck and kick and one particular twist took Leo out of the saddle for good. He flew sideways, sailing through the air, an unearthly silence deafening his ears. When he tried to turn in the air to at least land so he could roll, his body snapped tight as his foot caught in the single stirrup at the same time Smokey bolted forward.

Oh shit. The bad was just beginning. The thought splintered in his head as he hit the ground moving, sliding over the desert floor as helpless as a baby.

Smokey ran like he didn't have a hundred and eighty pounds of man attached to his saddle and Leo felt every rock, tumbleweed and cactus that skimmed the entire length of his body. Pain ruptured from every place at once. He finally managed to twist his foot when Smokey turned and whipped him sideways. His freedom came exactly when his head connected with something solid. A bright flash of light exploded in Leo's head before everything went black.

"Leo!" Kim screamed as she sprinted for him along with every other crewmember. Fear and panic ran a race as her heart thundered. The EMT Leo had hired at the last minute was the first to reach him. He'd started moving the second the horse had lost it.

"Call 911!" he yelled over his shoulder and three different crewmembers stopped in their tracks and pulled out their phones.

Kim saw the blood from ten feet away. It splattered along the rock Leo had slammed into and covered the side of his face. She crouched next to him, her hands shaking as she set her palms on his arm. Dirt covered him from head to toe. His chaps and vest had protected him a little, but the fabric on his arms was torn, bloody and filthy.

The EMT worked on him quickly and quietly, searching for the hole where all that blood came from. "There it is," he muttered, finding the gash along Leo's eyebrow. It bled down his face in a sheet of bright red and Kim swallowed back her panic-induced tears. "Shit," he swore, rifling through his kit one handed while he held gauze to the wound. "I need my other box." He glanced up at her. "Hold this here tight. Keep pressure on it. I'll be right back." He scrambled up and made a dead run for his truck fifty yards away.

Leo's eyes fluttered open and Kim shifted to block the sun from his face. He didn't try to smile or joke it off. The fear she saw was as real as the blood flowing out of the gash. Despite pressure on the wound, the gauze pad quickly turned bright red, staining her fingers with his blood. "Note in my vest pocket," he muttered. "Take it."

"I don't care about the damn note, Leo," Kim said, terrified at the resolute tone of his voice. She used anger to keep from falling apart on the spot. He never should've done this stunt.

"Important," he said, his eyes fluttering closed. "Need you to do this for me."

"Stop it. You aren't going to need me to do anything. You're going to be fine." But what if he wasn't? What if he went into a coma or hemorrhaged? What if this was one of the head injuries that slowly bled in the brain until—?

He grabbed her arm, his knuckles bloody. "Not about me. Take the note." His eyes rolled back as his lids closed and Kim felt every hair on her skin stand up straight.

"Leo? Leo!" Her vision blurred as she reached into his tattered vest and pulled out the folded note he'd tucked away earlier. She stuffed it in her back pocket. Kim hadn't been much on praying since her parents died. Though she considered herself spiritual, she had trouble believing in a God that let useless or tragic things happen. Miracles happened every day, she knew that, she'd witnessed it herself when Chelsea had nearly been beaten to death. Her best friend had recovered a hundred percent. But what about her parents useless death? How was she supposed to reconcile that?

The sun glared down on her and sweat prickled her back...probably because she was a hypocrite.

Maybe it was wrong to ask for help now, to pray for a miracle when she'd quit praying after her parents' accident, but she had nothing to lose. *"Please...please,"* she murmured, "if you're up there, don't hold anything against Leo because of me. Help him through this. Get him through this. Not for me, but for him, for his child. *Please.*"

Looking deathly pale, Leo had never seemed so vulnerable and Kim vowed to see him through whatever the future had to bring. He was stubborn and proud and he wouldn't want help because he didn't want people to see him weak or at his worst. She knew that much about him. She just needed him to survive.

Kyle and a couple of other crewmembers ventured closer, offering silent support. She knew they'd do anything she asked of them. She just didn't know what to ask.

She eased some hair out of another cut on Leo's forehead. His skin was hot and clammy. She glanced over her shoulder, looking for the medic. "Leo, I'm here. I'm not going anywhere, I promise. Just hang on, dammit." Fresh tears nearly blinded her. "You, jackass," she whispered. "I told you not to do the stupid stunt."

The EMT returned, skidding to a stop and kneeling next to Leo. A few minutes after he'd readied an IV, the whap, whap, whap of a helicopter sounded in the distance. Kim didn't ask if she could go, she just jumped on board after they'd loaded Leo on a gurney.

Yanic yelled something to her, but the sound of the rotors drowned out everything, including the loud beat of her heart. She didn't hear anything anyone said, she only watched Leo, waited for him to open his eyes. To smile at her the way he did when he teased her. To wink with that cocky attitude that reeked of playboy. Kim held his bloodied hand in hers, praying the whole ride. The weight of the disaster turned her stomach in knots and the flight made her lightheaded.

The helicopter landed on a grassy area right outside a Las Vegas hospital emergency room and several personnel wearing scrubs ran out to meet them. They rolled Leo into the building at a run with Kim dashing behind.

Once inside, they whisked Leo into a treatment room and left her in the dust. Dazed, Kim looked around. She'd made it past the initial waiting area, but now stood out in the treatment room hallway. Doctors and nurses bustled by, not taking any notice of her or the blood staining her clothes. The white walls and white tile seemed to close in on her and Kim shut her eyes. A replay of Smokey going ballistic rolled in her head...the way Leo had fought to hold on and struggled to keep his seat. She'd never forget the excruciating seconds of watching him fly through the air before he hit the dirt and Smokey dragged him God only knew how many feet. Kim blinked her eyes open banishing the gruesome pictures.

The EMTs who'd flown on the chopper emerged from the room, wheeling their gurney and equipment between them. The taller one with sandy hair gave her a sympathetic smile. "He's in good hands. Someone should be out soon and give you an update."

"Yeah," his partner said. His red hair glistened in the bright lighting. "This place is top notch and we made good time."

Kim thanked them and they moved to the nurses station and took care of whatever paperwork they had to deal with. She'd never been very good at waiting, so she paced. When she caught her reflection in the treatment room window, she realized the scary picture she made. It wouldn't do any good to be a mess when she finally got to see Leo, so she found the ladies room.

A look in the bathroom mirror told her more than she wanted to know. Blood streaked her cheek and forehead where she must have pulled hair out of her face and left a trail. Red smears and spots covered her clothes as well. Her eyes looked wide and wigged out, her skin pale. But it was the absolute fear of losing Leo that really scared her. The man had snuck under her skin without her even realizing it.

Yes, she'd been ready to walk out of his life, to raise their baby on her own, but she never imagined not having him alive.

Kim washed her hands and cleaned up as best she could, then went back to the treatment room hallway. A lone chair sat outside the next room so she scooted it over and sat outside his door. Something crinkled in her back pocket.

Leo's note.

What could it be? He'd said it wasn't about him. Was it about the baby? Her?

With shaking hands, Kim unfolded the piece of paper. Leo's messy scrawl filled the space.

Kim,
If you're reading this, then something happened to me. I have a trust set up, but with everything that's happened in the last

couple of months, I need your help. I know the money is scarce, but along with taking care of our baby, I need you to make sure my estate takes care of my little sister.

Little sister?

I told you The Marion was an estate of mine on the East Coast. It's not. It's an institution that specializes in special needs patients, and my sister has lived there for the past fifteen years. Sorry I didn't tell you sooner, but I had my reasons. The important thing is to keep her where she is for her health and anonymity. I have a sizable life insurance policy that will ensure her care, along with the residuals my estate should get over the years to come. Please make sure the money is used for Megan's care. She's alone in the world now.
Thanks,
Leo.

Kim re-read the note three times. Her palms moistened the page the longer she held it in her hands. Her heart sunk to her stomach and that lightheaded feeling returned.

Leo had a sister. Not only that, but he wanted Kim to oversee her care. Sure they got along and she'd helped him a lot the last couple of months. Yes, they'd had some amazing sex and they laughed a lot and got along…but this? Was he serious?

She thought he trusted her two months ago when she helped him with his books, but he'd given her a bold-faced lie about his monthly twenty-one-thousand-dollar expense. The pain in her chest could've been the invisible knife he'd sliced through her heart. She shouldn't be feeling this betrayed, so why did she? What did it mean that he trusted her with this information now? Didn't he have anyone else? Was he as alone in this world as she was?

A sister? How ill was she if she lived in a facility that cost so much money, and how could Kim possibly take care of her?

And what about her baby? How was she supposed to take care of his sister and a newborn?

Leo's head felt like a bowling ball stuck in a soda bottle. He tried to pinpoint one part of his anatomy that felt normal and couldn't come up with anything. He opened his eyes slowly as he registered the sound of a machine humming next to him and caught the strong sterile smell in the air. The white walls of a hospital room came into focus. He wasn't prepared for the shot to his heart when he saw Kim sitting in the chair next to his bed. He vaguely remembered nurses waking him up during the night, and Kim had been there to make him comfortable before he'd slid back into oblivion. With her legs tucked up close to her chest, she rested her head in the corner of the recliner, her eyes closed. He spotted the yellow note he'd penned crumpled in her hand.

Hell.

Shifting into a new position pulled the IV in his hand and he glanced at the stand next to the bed, dripping fluid into the attached line. Were there pain meds in that concoction or was that pure saline? He didn't hurt nearly enough for what he'd gone through and that floaty sensation had him blinking slowly. Oh, yeah. Definitely pain meds.

Though a serious headache made him feel as if someone had jackhammered his brain, Leo had enough sense to know that he'd screwed up with the note. But one look at all that blood in the desert and he'd been pretty sure his number was up. How many stories made the news about people who fell, bumped their heads and ended up dead hours later from bleeding in the brain? Maybe that's why he didn't die...because he bled all over the place like a stupid faucet.

Once again, Kim had stayed with him. She'd been there for his financial crash and now his physical crash. Nothing seemed to throw her off. She wore a pair of blue hospital scrubs and looked like his private nurse. He sure as hell couldn't have gotten through the day without her. She'd put out all the small fires while he'd dealt with the big ones. Hell, without her help the past few days, this whole shoot might not have happened at all. Not that he'd finished it.

Shit. So much for saving his movie and his finances.

He stared at the damn yellow paper and would've shaken his head if didn't hurt so badly. She knew his secret. Not that he expected her to run to the press, but oddly, the fact that someone else knew about Megan almost relieved him. Even the lawyer who'd drafted his trust had died, so though everything was spelled out in black and white, it was nice knowing he had someone he could count on to make sure Megan would be taken care of.

Her eyes fluttered open and when she saw him, she was wide-awake in half a second. She sat forward, the tilt of her lips an indication of her concern. "Hi," she said, her voice barely a whisper. In her eyes, he saw a mountain of worry and a ton of questions. He searched for the anger that must have been lurking since he'd lied to her. A giant lie that was going to destroy any trust she might've given him since they met. She'd been working her hardest to save him and he'd blatantly lied about The Marion.

"Hey." He had no clue what to say and he sure as hell didn't want to feel guilty for protecting his sister, yet that was exactly the emotion shredding his intestines.

They watched each other in one of the most sobering minutes of their two months together. There was so much on the table between them. So many sorrys and thank yous with more to come. So much history in so little time. Leo had no clue where to start. "Did they get the shot?" Definitely a stupid question, but he needed something to break the tension.

She closed her eyes, then glanced up at the ceiling like she might be looking for heavenly intervention. Leveling him with wide eyes so beautiful, she said, "I have no idea and frankly I don't give a shit. Rex was right. The stunt was too dangerous. You shouldn't have done it."

At least she was talking about the stunt and not Megan. He felt obligated to remind her. "First stunt went off without a hitch."

"You got lucky." She was never one to pull a punch.

"No. I just got unlucky the second time. I rode Smokey through the whole production before this and he was fine. Something was wrong." He was biding time with the Smokey subject, but he'd take any reprieve he could get. "Did anyone figure out what had him so spooked?"

"I have no idea. I stuck to you, so I don't know what happened to Smokey."

A hint of anger laced her tone. Because he was asking about the horse, because she'd been worried about him or because he'd lied to her? Probably all of the above. A perfect storm to piss her off. Either way, he liked that she cared enough to be mad. He liked it a lot. "You never got your ride."

She snorted and he loved her sarcastic smile. "Ha. Trust me—I won't ever get on a horse again after watching what happened to you today."

He flexed his good hand, hoping to get the circulation moving. "It was a fluke."

"It still scared the living hell out of me. I don't know how you stayed in the saddle as long as you did."

He didn't either.

Another silence settled between them and he waited for her to bring up the elephant in the room...that damn note.

Her anger and sarcasm seemed to fade as she watched him. "How's your head feel?"

It didn't take him long to come up with a good analogy. "Like someone blew up my brain to double the size, but didn't bother making my head bigger. Quit stalling." May as well get this over with.

She didn't pretend to play dumb, which only made Leo like her that much more and that was dangerous territory. She smoothed the paper out on her thigh and glanced over it before meeting his gaze. "How old is your sister?" she asked quietly.

"Nineteen," he said, surprised at her calm. He'd expected more anger. Especially since his lie was out in the open. The Marion was obviously not a vacation spot nor had he unloaded the monthly cost. It was the only thing he hadn't been honest about.

Kim nodded. Since she was a numbers girl, it would only take her a second to figure out that Megan was four when she went into The Institute. "Do you mind if I ask why she's there?"

He didn't have a right to withhold the information, especially after what he'd asked of her earlier. "She was born with Down Syndrome."

She nodded again, but Leo saw the tightening of her jaw and guessed her thoughts. *Who institutionalized a little girl with Down Syndrome?*

"Megan is one of a small percentage who experience the worst side effects of the syndrome. She suffers from epileptic seizures, sleep apnea and thyroid disease. Those are just the top three. She has trouble communicating because she was also born with a cleft palate, totally unrelated to the Downs. Her IQ is probably twenty-five at best. My mother needed help taking care of her and when she died, I found The Institute. There was no way I could take care of her without the media finding out and I didn't think Megan deserved that. She deserves her privacy. I can see a rag magazine plastering her on the cover and making me out to be some kind of monster for hiding her away, but..." Leo shook his head and wished he hadn't when a sharp pain zipped behind his left eye. "I think she deserves the best I have to give, and that's professionals who know how to help her. I sure as hell don't know how."

Leo chanced a look into her eyes. The silent reprimand was gone and in its place was compassion.

"I'm so sorry," she whispered. "I couldn't imagine having to worry about something like that."

It was a bitch. How many times had he second-guessed himself early on? Especially in the very beginning before he'd found The Marion. Megan had been in two different facilities before Leo found the one that took care of her the best. He shrugged. "I've been doing it a long time."

"Do you ever visit?"

"Yeah, just not as often as I should." He'd tried to keep Megan on the West Coast, but hadn't been satisfied with her care. The Marion had been head and shoulders above the rest and ultimately the place where Megan thrived. "I'd hate to see what happens if the media found out."

"No reason they should. You know I'm not going to say anything."

Leo swallowed the knot of emotion in his throat. It wasn't that he needed to hear Kim say it because he knew she'd keep his secret. It was the knowledge that he could trust her so implicitly that touched him. Two months ago, he hadn't considered telling her all his secrets, but now it seemed like the right thing to do. "Thanks. I appreciate it."

"I wish there was something I could do," she said, leaning over and taking his scratched up hand in hers. "You know, besides beating the hell out of you when you get out of here." Her words lacked the heat to back them up, but verified Leo's assumption. "I kind of get why you didn't tell me, but I'm still pissed. Makes me wonder if you've got any other skeletons in the closet." She lifted one eyebrow.

"No. That's it." Leo gave her hand a tight squeeze. He would've tugged her next to him if he'd had any strength. "I'm sorry I didn't tell you. I've just been programmed to hide it. It wasn't something malicious."

She canted her head. "I know. That's the only thing that's saving you right now." Her smile stretched wide and the playfulness in her eyes lifted his spirits like a double dose of the pain meds in his IV. She was grinning, holding his hand and not screaming at him. He couldn't ask for much more than that. Unless he asked her never to leave him. Yeah, right. He blamed the drugs.

And there they were, back to that silence where they just watched each other and Leo caught himself falling hard.

"There's one thing you do need to know and I didn't want to tell you now, but your agent is a real bulldog. I guess he heard what happened and called immediately. He said the Jess Bryant role went to Channing Tatum."

"No fucking way." He couldn't catch a break. Except he wouldn't trade anything for the way Kim looked at him now, with as much frustration as he had boiling in his gut. He had to finish this movie. It was his only hope.

When Kim leaned in and touched her lips to his, Leo figured maybe he had died and gone to heaven. Her smooth lips whispered over his in a feather-light stroke, barely a touch, but it had him wanting more, wanting all of her, mind, body and soul.

Chapter Thirteen

Hours later, Kim got off Leo's phone and began clearing away the trash from his hospital dinner. As word of Leo's presence zipped through the hospital, more and more people passed slowly by the door, all hoping to get a sneak peek at the action star.

Kim pulled the curtain closed. She'd never put herself in his shoes before. Never considered how the constant lack of privacy or anonymity could eat away at your life. In fact, the more time she had to watch the circus unfold, the more she realized why he'd hidden his little sister from public scrutiny. It was one thing to handle all of it when it centered on you, but it was something else altogether when the frenzy involved someone you loved. Someone defenseless and unable to speak for herself.

The whole idea was still hard to comprehend. This gorgeous, larger-than-life personality had a secret and he'd been dealing with it for more than a decade all by himself.

If she had to be honest, her first response had been anger. He hid his sister because she had Down Syndrome? What kind of person did that? But once he explained her condition, she understood. It took a team of professionals to care for someone with such major challenges. It was only lucky that he had a job and career that could afford the care Megan needed.

Although at the moment, those two things were debatable.

Kim hadn't pressed Leo about his decision or asked too much about Megan. He was a private man and this was a private issue. Had he not had to do the stunt, she had no doubt she'd still be in the dark about it. But his note made her wonder who he'd named as his trustee if he didn't have anyone else. Probably a lawyer, which for some reason made her sad.

Hoping that Leo would be released tomorrow, Kim had been on the phone, working on transportation. The helicopter had got them there, but now they needed to get home. They were just outside of Vegas, but that was over four hours from Los Angeles via car or an hour in the air. She couldn't book anything until she had a definite release day and the doctor was leaning toward keeping Leo a second night.

They'd learned Leo's cinematographer had finished shooting everything on Leo's shot list—thank God—and took the footage to the editor, so that took a load off Leo's bruised head. Kim fielded the dozens of phone calls from his team so he could get rest. Besides the different crewmembers calling to check on him, the list included his agent, manager, publicist and a number of women who quote, "had his number."

Kim set the dinner tray on the windowsill and moved the rolling cart next to Leo's bed as he surfed the limited channels of the hospital television. Hearing footsteps behind her, she expected to see the nurse.

"Hey, Leo. Hey, cousin."

It was the last voice she expected to hear. It probably shouldn't have surprised her. A combination of annoyance and relief blew through her in a sudden wave as she took a deep breath and readied for the next few minutes. At least it wasn't a stranger looking to spend time with Leo. It might not be too bad depending on how obnoxious Wilson acted.

"Hey, Wilson. You didn't have to come all the way out here," Leo said as she faced her cousin.

But Kim knew why he'd done it. Yesterday's sun had deepened his tan and he looked as carefree as a puppy in a dog park. "Hi. This is a surprise. What are you doing here?" *In Las Vegas instead of getting back to your conference?*

Wilson's smile spread wide across his face and showed off a dimple he loved to flash. It was a dimple she'd teased him about for years. All the girls fell hard and fast for that little divot in his cheek. "I figured Leo might need some things, so after I helped take down the tents and reload the equipment yesterday, I brought his clothes and a few things you both might need to last you another night or two. I didn't know how long he'd be here so..." He shrugged and handed her a stuffed backpack.

"Thanks, man," Leo said, downing the last bit of juice in his cup.

"Wow." He'd helped take down the set. That shocked her. "Thank you." She took out a few items from the top. Leo's clothes, his wallet and personal items that Kim hadn't thought to bring along because she'd been so worried about him. She would've checked the contents of Leo's wallet, but didn't dare do that in front of Wilson. Besides, Leo didn't carry that much cash on him anymore simply because he didn't have that much money to flaunt.

Wilson had just done her a giant service by bringing this bag. Now a whole huge heap of guilt settled on her chest along with a side of extremely grateful. The tiny niggle of doubt had to do with owing him something. But she shoved that aside for now.

"This was really nice of you," she said, stuffing everything but the clothes back inside. She opened the small closet and set them on the shelf at the bottom.

"Just glad I was here to help." Wilson gestured to Leo's head. "What'd the doctor say? You're going to be fine, right?"

Leo gave him a thumbs-up. "Good as new in a couple of days."

"Great!"

The three of them stared at each other in an awkward pause and the genuine smile on Wilson's lips actually brightened her spirits. Leo was going to be okay and Wilson had done them both a huge favor. Life could be much, much worse.

"So, where are you staying tonight?" Wilson asked her after looking back and forth between the two of them.

Kim wouldn't be surprised if he was looking forward to a night in Vegas. What better place to feed a gambling addiction. Part of her wanted to send him off with some money because he'd gone so much out of his way for them, but even as the thought materialized, she knew she couldn't or wouldn't put him in that position. Carolyn would probably haunt her from the grave if she did. "I planned to stay here," Kim said. "I doubt the nurses will let both of us stay," she added, in case he thought he'd pull up a chair and stay the night as well. That wasn't going to happen. No way, no how. Though she completely appreciated everything he'd done, she wanted to be alone with Leo.

"Oh." His smile faded, but he nodded. "It's okay. I can get a motel close by and hang around until Leo is released. That way I can take you both back to L.A."

"Wilson, you don't need to do that. We can rent a car or take a flight."

"I won't take no for an answer. Really." Wilson waved off her excuse. "Leo was nice enough to let me come watch the filming and if I know you, you've been busting your butt making him comfortable for the last twenty-four hours. Besides, I drove all the way back here after helping the crew get everything to L.A." He lifted his eyebrows, almost daring her to say no.

Without Wilson they would have spent an exorbitant amount of money on a car service or an airline flight. Leo would've insisted on paying the bill when he couldn't afford to. So, yes, her cousin was saving their butts and Kim would be pretty heartless not to appreciate it. Though *she* didn't want to do anything that would indebt her to him, this favor was for Leo.

Wilson lifted his phone. "You've got my number so just text when you're cleared to leave. I'll be here in a flash." He patted Leo's knee and didn't seem to realize the grimace on Leo's face at the contact. Both of his knees had serious road rash from the desert floor. "Hey, feel better soon." Wilson sauntered out the door like he owned the place.

Kim let out the breath she'd been holding.

"Why do you look like you've swallowed poison?" Leo asked. He played with the edge of the bandage over a particularly nasty gash in his arm.

He had enough on his plate without hearing her bitch about Wilson. She laughed off his question. "No reason. I'm just surprised Wilson came all this way for us."

"Nice of him," Leo said.

It *was* nice of him, so maybe it was time she had an attitude change toward her cousin. What if he *had* quit gambling? What if he had been helping Carolyn because he loved her and wanted to be there for her? What if Carolyn had it all wrong when she didn't split her inheritance more evenly between them?

Kim put herself in his shoes and thought about his reaction after meeting with the lawyer. She might've been just as angry.

So, yeah, maybe he had a few bad habits, but maybe he wasn't the heartless guy Carolyn had suggested. Maybe she should consider giving him part of the inheritance. She'd have to rethink all of it.

Just like she'd had to rethink Leo. At the moment, she didn't want to talk about her cousin. She wanted to talk about the man in the bed next to her. "Can I ask you something?"

He adjusted gingerly under the sheet and shut off the television. "Sure. What?"

"I've been thinking about you. About your reputation." His eyes narrowed and she continued, "I don't know if you remember what I said two months ago about you changing, but I think I understand something now."

"What?" He still had that hard skeptical look in his amazing eyes.

"I think you've always been a good guy, you've just made sure the world hasn't seen it. You deliberately give the press rag-worthy material to keep them busy so they don't find out about Megan. Deep down, you're a good guy."

It took him a few moments before he answered and he looked away from her when he finally did. "I guess that's a matter of opinion."

She nodded. "Very true. And it's my opinion."

Leo glanced out the door then back to her. "Don't spread that around," he warned her. "It'll be our little secret." Despite the big white bandage on his head and all the scratches on his face, the man oozed as much sex appeal as an Armani model dressed in a tux. The hot gleam in his eyes all but invited her to join him in his hospital bed.

Kim resisted the urge, leaned back in the recliner and propped her feet on the footrest. What else did she need to learn about this man?

With his moonstruck cousin and Leo whispering in the backseat of his car, Wilson considered driving into oncoming traffic. He pondered driving off the side of the road and into a telephone pole. He thought about slamming on the brakes and letting the occasional semi crash into them. All the different scenarios played in his head as he cruised down the 15 freeway toward Los Angeles.

Problem was he didn't want to be dead himself. So he'd have to wait and come up with a different plan to get his money from Carolyn—Kim. Damn, why did he keep doing that? Though he hadn't intended to kill Leo Frost, he had to admit that watching them giggle and grope in the back seat made him wish he did. He hadn't *expected* to be driving them like a goddamn chauffer, but Kim had insisted on sitting next to Leo instead of turning her head to check on him the whole drive.

He hadn't realized what a tough nut Kim was before now, but he was pretty sure he was wearing her down. For a while there, she seemed to be turning into Aunt Carolyn. No matter what he did or how much he helped, he got a cold shoulder and a look of disdain. Like he wasn't worthy enough for the likes of them. But this trip had changed that.

A big orange semi with a massive grill loomed in the distance and made Wilson consider the head on accident scenario anyway. Yes, he'd die with them, but he almost didn't care. What did he have to live for anyway? Amanda? His daughter rarely even talked to him on the phone, so he doubted she'd miss him. Chloe sure as hell wouldn't care. His ex had wiped him out when she left.

Listening to the two people behind him whisper and giggle sent a red haze swirling in his brain. Their behavior only confirmed his suspicion that Leo was the father of her baby. Soft laughter had him glancing in the mirror. He didn't plan to be the butt of their jokes for the rest of his life and the more they laughed at him the more his blood pressure skyrocketed.

Bitch, bitch, bitch. He wanted her dead.

The semi drew closer and Wilson laid on the gas. It would only take a small swivel of the wheel to get in his way. He figured they were both moving at about seventy miles per hour. It would be over before he knew it.

His palms sweat furiously as he gripped the wheel tighter. He heard them laughing again and felt heat rise into his face as he shifted in his seat.

In ten seconds. He didn't have more time than that...

Nine. Eight. Seven. Six. Five. Four. Three...

Chapter Fourteen

The car seemed to be moving especially fast and Kim reluctantly sat up to see what was happening. Wilson was fixated on the road, his knuckles white on the wheel. A drop of sweat rolled down the side of his face. Of all the things she had to worry about, she hadn't expected getting home in one piece would be one of them. "Wilson, are you okay?"

He jumped as if she'd scared the hell out him and the car swerved. A semi-truck in the opposite lane whizzed past them and his draft shook the car.

"Wilson!" Kim's pulse skyrocketed as she gripped the bucket seat in front of her. "Do you need me to drive? Are you okay?" That was a little too close for comfort. A few more inches and they'd be dead right now, splattered across the highway in pieces. A quick picture of what her parent's accident might've looked like flashed in her head and Kim blinked it away. "Wilson?" she pressed when he didn't respond.

"Sorry," he said, his breathing forced. He seemed almost winded and he wiped the side of his face with his arm. "I was thinking about something and lost focus. I'm okay." He glanced at her from the rearview mirror and Kim slowly eased back, unsure if she should force the driving issue.

Leo wrapped his arm around her and she leaned against his solid chest. His warm breath wafted by her cheek and sent a wave of chills across her nape and down her arms. "You smell good," he breathed in her ear, his low voice sexy and all male.

Kim tilted her head and faced him, looked into his beautiful thick-lashed eyes. "I smell like hospital soap," she said, a smile curving her lips. "Clearly you hit your head harder than we all thought."

His grin cut a direct line to her girl parts down south and Kim forced herself to breathe normally. His hand spread wide over her stomach and Kim nearly stopped breathing. Had he done it intentionally, thinking about the baby or was it just his roaming hands at work? It made her very aware of the way he held her so possessively. Somehow they'd fallen into some kind of relationship with no boundaries. What were they? What did they mean to each other? They had great sex, they got along like best friends. He trusted her with his most important secrets—well, at least *now* he did—but when push came to shove, they weren't a couple and he didn't want the baby growing inside her.

So why was she deluding herself? Why did she let him pull her close and whisper in her ear? Why did she fall into comfortable playfulness when it ultimately meant nothing to him? What was she doing falling for a guy who didn't return her budding feelings?

Hadn't her past taught her anything?

It wasn't like he was rich, she argued with herself, so in that respect he wasn't anything like the men in her past. And he treated her well when they were together. Problem was he didn't want to be together with anyone permanently. He'd made that clear two months ago. Part of his charm was making a woman feel special...treating her like she was the only one in his world. Yes, they'd talked all the months she'd been gone, but the man wasn't a monk. Even though he'd told her he hadn't had sex in a long time before they'd gotten together didn't mean he hadn't jumped back into the swing of things once she left town. And he had every right to.

Which broke her heart.

Dammit. Why did she do this to herself? The same damn question kept revolving in her head. She was a dope. An idiot to the fifth power.

"You're thinking way too hard down there," Leo whispered into her ear and Kim felt the ripple all the way to her toes. Just more torture for the woman who couldn't seem to stop torturing herself.

Kim extricated herself from his hold and sat next to him, facing him so she wouldn't be tempted to lean on his chest again.

"I was just thinking about my passport. Hope it came in the mail while we were gone." Chelsea had sent it as requested, but somehow it got lost. The shipping company had located it and assured Kim it was en route, but by that time she'd been knee deep helping Leo with the movie. The sooner I get home the sooner I can..." *get on with my life without you.*

He waited, his brows lifted in expectation, almost as if he'd heard the words she hadn't said.

"Um...get back to work...and stuff." An actor she wasn't.

He chewed his lower lip. "Back to work...and stuff." He nodded, clearly not buying her excuse. He opened his mouth to say something, but Wilson cut him off.

"Did the Indiana DMV say how long it would take to send your license?" her cousin asked from the front seat.

"A week to ten days," Kim replied, thankful for the first time that she had a distraction from Leo. Maybe sitting in the back seat with him wasn't the smartest idea. Not when she wanted to do more than just be his friend. If she had to admit it, she wanted the whole fairy tale ending and she knew that wasn't going to happen with Leo.

It had been years since she wished for something she couldn't have. Leo wasn't good for her. He was too much. Too big. Larger than life. And she'd promised herself she wouldn't go down that road again.

But he's nice.

She hated that voice in her head. The voice that argued with her resolve the rest of the way to L.A. as she sat next to Leo wishing she could rest on his chest, or play another game of thumb war. But the closer she stayed to him now, the more it was going to hurt when she left. It had been hard enough two months ago, standing in the airport security line with Leo. Although he hadn't said the words, his actions spoke for themselves. He hadn't wanted her to go. She'd been seconds from postponing her flight, from telling him she'd stay a little while longer, but that would've only prolonged the good-bye. So she'd told him to "go home." And he had. Leaving her heart to chip into pieces with every step he took.

The dotted white lines of the freeway zipped by in a blur. Wilson actually made pretty good time back to Los Angeles. He pulled up to Leo's Hollywood Hills home and cut the engine.

Leo's Mercedes sat in the short driveway. One of the crewmembers must have delivered it. Hopefully they'd left the keys somewhere safe.

"Who brought my car back?" Leo asked, voicing her thoughts.

"I did," Wilson said. "I didn't want to drive it all the way to Vegas so I took my rental. I have your keys right here." He dug in his pocket and came out with Leo's keys. The man had thought of everything.

"Thanks, man. I appreciate it," Leo said, climbing slowly out of the backseat.

Kim's sucker of a heart made her guilty and she hustled to his side to steady him. The cool canyon air felt good after the stuffy car. Together, they took the steep stairs to the front door, Leo's arm over her shoulder as she held him around the waist. Wilson brought up the rear with their bag.

Leo unlocked and opened the door, snatching an official note posted on the frame before scanning the house as he walked in.

"What's wrong?" Kim asked, following closely behind. "Afraid Stella's going to attack because we left her?"

"No," Leo scoffed. Then he reconsidered. "Okay, maybe." He looked around the empty den. "I feel guilty for leaving her so long. What was supposed to be one long day turned into three. Stella? You here?"

Meow. The cat leapt on the banister from the stairs on the right and before Leo had a chance to say anything else, she took another flying leap straight for him. Apparently, she was not only feeling better, but her bandages weren't slowing her down either.

"Whoa! Ouch!" Leo caught her deftly against his chest and her instant purring made Kim melt. She got in on the love fest and they both gave Stella the attention she needed. Kim was glad they'd left out plenty of dry cat food and a second big bowl of water.

Wilson came in behind them. "I'll just set this here. Here's your mail too. It was still in the box." He placed the pack and mail on the nearest leather chair. "You probably want to rest, so I'll catch you later."

Leo stuck his hand out and Wilson grabbed it. "Thanks again, man. I really appreciate everything you did. I don't know how soon you planned on leaving town, but I hope you let me take you to dinner as a thank you. It's the least I can do."

Kim knew the answer to that before Leo finished the invitation.

"That'd be great," Wilson said, smiling between the two of them. "I probably won't be going back for another two or three days, so just give me a shout."

"Will do," Leo said. Stella still basked in his arms as Kim opened the door to let Wilson out.

"Thanks again, Wilson," she said as she walked him across the porch. "You really saved us. I owe you." She probably shouldn't have said those exact words, but they were true.

He smiled, flashed his dimple and looked more carefree than she'd seen him in months. "Like I said, glad I was here to help." He waved as he took the steps toward the street. "Talk to you soon. Later, Carolyn."

What? "Who?" Kim asked as Wilson walked away.

He turned. "What? What's wrong?"

"You just called me Carolyn."

He tilted his head. "Did I?" Before she answered, he went on, "Oh, I guess I did. Never done that before." He watched her for a second. "You know you really do look a lot like her."

"I know, I know. I was born to the wrong sister."

He gave her a tired grin and started walking, "Bye. Call me if you need anything."

Kim took a deep breath as she watched him go. Birds chirped and squirrels played in the trees across the street. The picturesque view of the city made her long for a change from Indiana. She could almost see living here if it weren't for the earthquakes. Closing her eyes, she steeled herself to get through these remaining days. The idea that her passport had arrived cheered her up and she hurried to check.

Back inside, Kim found Leo in the kitchen watching Stella as she feasted on a can of cat food. Her tail swished back and forth in contentment as she ate. It was a scene she never expected to see. Leo almost domesticated with a pet. Her traitorous heart liked what it saw.

"FedEx tried to deliver your passport. They left a tag." He waved the Post-it note from the door. "We can pick it up tomorrow." He looked almost sad at the idea.

"Great." Kim turned away. Finally. She didn't want to see his eyes or even guess what he might be thinking. She made them soup and sandwiches since that's what Leo seemed to have handy and after dinner she walked him to his bedroom.

He spent a few minutes in the bathroom as she tossed dirty clothes in the hamper. After getting him settled in bed, she got into her pajamas and came back to see if he needed anything else. He took her hand in his and dragged her closer until she sat next to him. Then he just watched her. It was hell trying to ignore his bare chest and ripped abs staring her in the face. Even with all the scrapes and bruises, he was gorgeous.

"What?" she said, grazing her thumb over his scratched knuckles. They were both still pretty marked up. Quite a pair actually.

"You look like you're leaving. I want you to stay."

Leo saw the indecision on Kim's face. It wasn't the sex that had her considering his request because that particular activity between them ranked off the charts. Which meant maybe—just maybe—she was fighting the same emotional attachment he was. And why wouldn't she with what he'd told her already?

When she didn't answer him, he tried something else. "I need to finish a conversation we started in the hospital," he said. "Will you stay?"

Kim nodded and Leo kept her hand in his.

"I told you about Megan, but there's something I didn't spell out for you. You may have figured it out or not. I'm not sure. But you need to hear it from me so you know where I'm coming from." Leo swallowed and dove in. "I know what I said the first time we met about how some people are meant to be parents and others are meant to make fun of those people. But I didn't mean it the way it sounded." He faltered, wasn't sure how to continue, but Kim squeezed his hand and he looked into her supportive eyes and saw something he'd never seen before. Compassion. Usually he saw intent or excitement in a woman's eyes, but none of them ever showed him compassion.

"Basically, I just always thought I was better off not having kids, not so much for me, but for the woman having my baby and maybe the baby itself." He paused for a second before continuing. "I mean, let's be honest, clearly my gene pool has issues." He exhaled a slow breath. "What if because of me, there's something wrong with the baby? What if he or she is a Down baby or has other issues because of me?" He shook his head. "I can't put someone through that. I mean, I have no idea if Megan understands her limitations or if she's inside there trying to get out..." Swallowing hard he looked into Kim's eyes. "That's what I'm afraid of." He glanced at her still flat stomach then back to her eyes. "That's why I don't want you to have this baby."

Her brows slanted in frustration.

"Look, I realize that it's not my decision because I'm not the one who's actually going to give birth. I get that you have the right to choose what path you take and I respect that."

"But?" The subtle change in her expression told him she was preparing for the worst.

"But I'm just being honest." He saw her confusion. "You might be determined to have this baby, but now that you have more information, maybe you'll think about other options. And if you do decide to keep it, I can't let you do it alone. I won't abandon a baby the way my father abandoned me. Am I terrified the baby might not be healthy. Hell yeah. But am I willing to forgo my place as the baby's father? Not on your life."

"Leo, you don't have to do that. You have enough to worry about with Megan. I don't expect you to..."

"To take care of this baby too?" He tipped his chin toward her stomach again. "What if there's a problem? You shouldn't have to deal with it by yourself."

She held her hand over her stomach for the first time and it made Leo ultimately aware of their situation. "This baby is healthy." Her tone grew almost angry. "I'm sorry about Megan, but I refuse to believe that this baby is going to have her issues. And you can't assume it either." Her back went rigid and Leo felt her drifting away from him. "I have the ability to take care of this child no matter what happens, so if you're worried about my finances, you don't need to be."

He blew out another breath. "I'm sorry. Maybe you thought you were going to get rid of me, but you're not. You can't. If you have this baby, then we do it together."

She stood slowly and pulled out of his grip. She didn't look mad, but she didn't look happy either. "It's late and you should get some rest." She backed up toward the door. "I'm going to…" She pointed behind her toward the door obviously looking for an excuse to be anywhere but where he was. "Going to take a shower," she finished. She slipped out of the room before he got another word out.

He heard her pad downstairs and he stared up at the ceiling. The only shower was up here, which meant he'd been right. She didn't want anything to do with him.

Maybe money did matter to her. The fact that he had none at the moment and she was rolling in it. Or maybe it was his reputation. Or maybe it was the fact that he still didn't want her to have this baby. Didn't she get it? He couldn't bring someone into the world who might suffer the way his sister suffered. And she barely had the mental capacity to understand what was wrong with her. All she knew was the hospital beds after a seizure and the sleep apnea machine that helped her get through the nights. How was Leo supposed to deal with that again with his own offspring?

He hated not having Kim next to him now. She'd been a fixture in his life for the past few days and now she'd barely been gone for five minutes, and he was lonelier than he'd been in years.

Leo threw the covers off and headed downstairs. They may not see eye to eye on this, but he wanted his friend back. He wanted to know she at least understood where he was coming from. And yeah, he just plain wanted her. Lately he'd been so busy and then the hospital stay had put a wrench in his life, but the whole time, in the back of his head, all he'd been thinking about was the next time he got Kim alone.

Every time he'd glanced at her, he'd mentally stripped off her clothes and thought about how it would feel to be inside her again. To feel her legs wrapped around his hips and her heels digging into his ass. He wanted to hear her whisper his name as he took her higher and feel the vibration of her orgasm when she came.

Yeah, no doubt about it, he was pretty much fucked.

Kim scooped Stella off the sofa and hugged her close as she sat down. Her brain felt like it had been scrambled and she didn't know what to focus on.

Leo had been honest with her and she had to appreciate that. Didn't mean she agreed with his assessment of their situation. A small part of her understood his worry, but the logical side wanted to smack him upside the head.

No one got guarantees. Ever. Life was one big-ass crapshoot, and you played the hand you got dealt. She'd learned that lesson on a few different levels. If she lived her life afraid to have a baby, then where did that leave her? No one to love. No one to raise.

Stella purred as Kim rubbed behind her ears. Hell, she didn't even have Stella. Once she left here, she was on her own. *With a baby on the way.* She couldn't forget that. In less than a month she'd be able to screen for Downs. She'd know as soon as possible exactly what she faced, and she'd be ready. Just because Leo wanted something didn't mean he got it.

She should use his excuse as a reason to hate him, a way to keep her distance from him, but even that didn't fly. Her rational brain said *of course he's scared, look what he's had to deal with his whole life.* But her emotional side wanted to break down like a child because he didn't want their baby. Or her. It wasn't as if she expected him to profess his love and welcome her with open arms. It was just what she wished.

Foolish. Should have been her middle name. Because despite knowing better, she'd gone and fallen for the dope who got her pregnant. And though he said they were in it together, she didn't want him around if he didn't love her. Or the baby, for that matter.

Together. What was his definition of the word anyway? Did he mean *together* together? Like live in the same city or same house? Probably not. He probably meant in the decision making process. Which still sucked because she'd have to deal with him on a regular basis.

Leo's footsteps padded down the stairs and Kim looked up as his muscular legs brought him closer. His workout shorts were loose around his legs, but his T-shirt fit snug enough to outline his sculpted chest. Even with the stitches over his eyebrow, the scrapes on his face and the road rash on his legs, he was totally drool-worthy.

"Change your mind about the shower?" he asked. She didn't catch any cynicism in the question. If anything he seemed to understand she needed space. Not that he was willing to give it to her.

"Yeah." She barely got the word out and focused on Stella since she didn't want to see the pain in his eyes. There was no way in hell she was going to feel guilty about having this baby.

He watched her for a few seconds before sitting next to her. Stella—who clearly loved him like all women did—pushed her way into his lap and rubbed against his chest until he began stroking her. "Seems like she's not too mad at us anymore."

Kim nodded, afraid if she said anything her voice would crack. She'd never been so attracted to a man and at the same time known they'd never work out.

"You're mad at me." His statement came out of the blue and held no anger.

"No." She shook her head. "Not mad. I just don't get how it's going to work. And honestly, I don't want to talk about it right now." It was all too fresh. This absolute realization that they'd never be together. Which only proved that her deluded little brain had hoped for that all along, because she did genuinely like the guy.

"Will you come upstairs with me?" He looked at her then, his blue eyes steady, but unsure.

"Why?" she whispered. Not because she didn't know what he was asking, but because she wanted to know why he thought she should.

"Because I need you," he answered softly.

The immediate explosion of nerves in her stomach sent an instant flush up her chest and to her cheeks. How many years had she wanted to be needed by someone? To be loved? Yes, she realized they were two different things, but it didn't change the way it affected her.

She didn't want to need him, too, but the longer she stayed with him, the more it happened. She didn't want the damn sting in her eyes, either, because the serious look on his face cut down every defense she tried to erect. "Leo..." She barely got his name out. He was killing her.

"Aw, babe. C'mere." He pulled her close until her head tucked neatly into his neck and she was in his arms, holding tight to the man who'd changed her life. He made her want. He made her dream. He made her hope again when she'd lost hope. His arms felt so good wrapped around her and his heat warmed her through the fabric of their clothes.

"It was a long day. Hell, it's been a long four days," he whispered in her ear.

Kim took a ragged breath and nodded. So now that it was over, what did she do? But even as the question circled her brain, her body already had the answer. So did her heart. Pulling back, she looked into his eyes.

"Don't look at me like that," he scolded softly. "You know I don't ever want to hurt you."

"I know." Not intentionally. And that was the problem, because he would eventually hurt her. She tried to give him a smile but it lacked conviction.

"I can't make you..." *be with me.* The words went unspoken but they hung in the air. He set Stella next to him and smoothed his thumb across her cheek. "But..."

Something in his eyes made her breath catch. He was struggling as much as she was with their predicament and even that fact...just another thing they had in common, made her heart lurch.

She set her hand on his nape exactly the way he touched her. A half sob escaped before she caught it and stilled her trembling jaw. "We're a pair, aren't we?"

He nodded, but his eyes brimmed with moisture just like hers. "I'm sorry," he said, searching her eyes as if he needed an answer.

"For what?"

"For needing you."

Something broke apart in her chest and instead of letting him see her cry, she moved forward and put her lips on his. The soft contact only lasted a few seconds before she dove in with all her heart. She needed him, too, and wished she didn't.

One second they were sitting on the couch, practically glued to each other and the next, Leo pulled her up the stairs to his bedroom. He laid her down on his bed and moved on top of her, his mouth insistent and delicious against hers.

"We shouldn't do this," Kim breathed when his lips blazed a moist, warm path across her neck to her collarbone. "You have a concussion. You're still banged up."

"All I've been thinking about is being with you. For the past four days, this has been eating me up inside. Having you so close and not being able to touch you the way I want." His big hands stroked beneath her silky nightshirt and lifted the material over her head until she lay topless. He proved his words when he sucked a pebbled nipple into his mouth.

Kim arched into the touch with a moan. Her breasts had never been this sensitive. If she thought his hands had been lethal, his tongue might kill her. It was stupid to deny she wanted him. Stupid to fight this time with him. Walking out on him right now wouldn't change the way she felt about him. Misery was up ahead no matter how she looked at it, so instead of living with the pain longer, she decided to stay for now. Now was all she had with this man, so she might as well take it.

"This is what I need," he murmured as he stripped her bottoms down her legs. His nostrils flared when he saw her lack of underwear. Again. "God damn, that is so fucking sexy," he whispered.

She swallowed as he took in every inch of her, his hands skimming her hips and down her thighs—almost reverently—as he knelt between her legs.

"I owe you a thank you," he said, meeting her gaze with a very serious expression on his face.

"You do?" Her heart thumped a primitive beat as his thumbs stroked the private crease between each thigh, so near to where her body pulsed in expectation.

He nodded. "I couldn't have pulled off the shoot without you." He eased a thumb directly across the wet seam of her vagina and circled her clit.

Kim gasped as the electric shock stoked up her arousal. "You didn't need me," she managed, though her brain was barely working.

The hint of a smile disappeared from his face and he shook his head. "Wrong. I did. And do. I think I should show you how much I appreciate everything you've done the past few days." He shifted lower, hooked her legs over his shoulders and nuzzled the same crease of each thigh.

The expectation killed her. She felt his hot breath stroke over sensitive flesh and her lungs faltered as she waited. "Leo," she pleaded. God, she hated that she sounded so needy. She lifted the tiniest fraction, offering herself up to him, body, heart and soul.

"Thank you." He said the words so softly, almost as reverently as his touch, right before his mouth closed over her. The heat, the soft suction lifted her to another plane, a magic carpet ride of sensation. "Thank you," he said again, right before his tongue circled her sensitive clit. He laved, he licked, he made her crazy and took her higher with each stroke. He teased her mercilessly, taking her to the edge, but holding off on the final show.

Sweat slicked Kim's skin as she fisted the sheets and pushed into Leo's mouth, silently begging for the push that would take her over. He ran a finger from her wet center all the way back to uncharted territory and Kim bucked up, her muscles tense, every inch of her strung taught. She rode that line of no return, the pinnacle before the fall. When he pushed that finger inside her, the line snapped. Kim came on a cry as wave after wave of satisfaction blew through her. Breathing hard, her mouth parched, she slowly came down to earth, barely aware of Leo licking her softly. He hadn't budged. His hands stroked over her stomach and down her sides, over her hips. He looked up at her from that spot between her legs and Kim expected him to move over her, but he just grinned. "Thank you," he said again.

She suspected he had plans to stay where he was and she beckoned him over her with an index finger. As he moved up her body, she gently pressed his shoulder back until she had him under her. He didn't complain...just lifted up into her kiss as she settled over him. "These shorts have to go," she murmured.

"Burn 'em," he panted because she had her hand on his sizable erection.

She laughed, then stifled the sound. She didn't want to have fun with him, or like him, or need him, or God forbid...love him. So she wiped her brain clean and focused on sex. She stripped off his shorts and wrapped her hand around a very magnificent part of Leo.

He thrust into her hand and because she didn't plan to be with him again after this last time, she gave him the full party. When she licked the creamy pearl at the tip of his penis, he moaned and when she wrapped her lips around the head, he swore. He tasted salty and tangy. All male and all hers. At least for tonight. She'd never felt more power in this position. Never felt as if a man needed her more. That feeling fed *her* need.

She didn't hold anything against him. He had a reason for his feelings and beliefs the same way she did. So no, she didn't blame him and she wanted him to know that. So she took him deep and loved him with her mouth, intending to take him all the way. But after a couple of minutes, Leo snuck his hands under her arms and pulled her off him.

He took her mouth in a fiery kiss...teeth, tongue and lips as he settled her on top of him. Together they adjusted until he sunk inside her. The sudden invasion had her gasping into his mouth. Fulfillment washed through her with each new thrust and Kim rode him with matching pace. His hands roamed everywhere as she moved over him and with each stroke she got closer to another peak. When his fingers wrapped around her hips in a death grip, she knew he was close and she adjusted a fraction so that she got the most from their connection. He hit her G-spot and Kim tensed with the impending climax.

Leo's jaw clenched tight and he growled. "C'mon, right now. Right now." He tightened up everywhere and Kim felt the undeniable throbbing and the warm wash of his orgasm inside her. With a last powerful stroke, he set off her climax and she threw her head back and let it have her. It went beyond sex, beyond reason. Being with a man had never felt like it did when she was with Leo. There was something in the way they touched, in the fiery looks they exchanged as they came together and broke apart. Bucking on him as the last aftershocks washed through her, Kim knew no one would ever measure up to this man.

She collapsed on his chest, careful of his scrapes and sore muscles as she gasped for air.

His arms wrapped around her in a perfect moment.

Chapter Fifteen

When Leo opened his eyes in the morning, he rolled over and got nothing but cold sheets. He'd wanted to wrap himself around Kim's warm, supple body...then pull her underneath him and continue where they'd left off. The change in plans left him empty. Morning sun streaked in from the opened curtains. A jackhammer pounding in his head indicated he might've overextended himself last night, but he figured every second with Kim was worth it. So... Where was she? He didn't hear her in the bathroom? Maybe downstairs.

Leo eased from under the sheets and winced as his feet hit the cool hardwood floor. He'd definitely overdone it last night with the monkey sex. Turned out the more he had Kim, the more he wanted her. A new phenomenon for him. He'd blame it on the head injury, but he'd been leaning in this direction anyway, so that argument didn't fly.

Instead of heading downstairs smelling like sex, he took a quick shower and threw on a pair of comfortable sweats. Now that he was home, he needed to find out if his editor, Tim, had cut any of the footage. He'd let too much time get away from him since Saturday. He checked his watch on the nightstand. Tuesday, noon. Already? How the hell did that happen?

Time to get back in the saddle. He cringed at the thought. No saddles for him in the near future. Which reminded him, he needed to call Kyle and see how Smokey was and he had to make a trip to FedEx for Kim's passport. Just another item on his growing list of things to do. He had a ton of phone calls to return since most of the crew had checked up on him during his hospital stay. Seemed as if Kim had been answering his phone for days now.

Leo took the stairs gingerly to make sure his head stayed on his shoulders since he did have a 9.0 on the Richter scale of headaches. He hoped the few ibuprofens he swallowed would take the edge off, because he didn't want to use the pain meds prescribed by the hospital. That shit made him loopy and he needed to think clearly to finish the movie. His stomach rumbled like a bear out of hibernation. Food would definitely help his case.

If the smells coming from the kitchen were any indication, there was some serious cooking going on. Leo slipped into the doorway and saw Kim at the stove, manning a couple of pans. The body hugging yoga pants and form-fitting, coordinating pink tank set his mouth to salivate. Or maybe it was breakfast. Could've been both. A ponytail kept her blond hair out of her face.

"I thought you didn't cook," he said easing behind her and tugging her against his chest. She smelled like cinnamon and morning. Her firm ass cheeks cradled his growing erection.

She didn't fight him, but she didn't turn into him for more either. She snorted. "This doesn't count. Anyone can scramble an egg and you had premade pancake mix. All I had to do was add water and shake. They'll probably be horrible." She flipped a couple pancakes as she spoke then did the same with the eggs.

Leo bent and nibbled her earlobe. She shivered and he smiled against her soft skin. He could get used to mornings like this.

"Oh, forgot the orange juice," she said, easing out of his grasp and heading to the fridge. She barely looked at him as she handed it over. "You can put that on the counter."

"Okay..." Something had definitely happened since last night. The woman in front of him now was not the woman who'd been in his arms or in his bed for the last eight hours. Last night, she'd been a hot tamale spicing up his life and this morning she was a cold potato. "Is—"

"I made a list of all the people who called while you were in the hospital," she said, tipping the pan and sliding eggs onto a plate. "I mean besides all the crew members. Word got out and you made big news." She plopped a couple of pancakes along with some strawberries next to the eggs. "I also made a list of all the things you still had left to do from your original list on Saturday." She glanced up at him. "I hope that's all right."

"All right? It's better than all right." No one had ever worked this much—or as hard—for him and not received a paycheck. But why was she acting as if last night never happened? Like it was nothing out of the ordinary? Yes, he'd definitely had a lot of good sex, but nothing compared to what happened when he was with Kim. So what the hell changed between last night and today? "If there's—"

Her wide green eyes blinked when the phone rang, and she seemed to breathe a sigh of relief as she passed it to him.

Leo answered, but didn't take his eyes off Kim.

"Leo! It's Yanic. How you feeling, man? I swear to God, I nearly had a coronary when that horse went ape shit. I seriously thought you were a dead man when you hit that rock."

"I think that makes two of us. Thanks for dropping the load with Tim. I owe you." Kim slid the plate of food in front of him on the counter and stuck a fork in his pancakes.

"I've delivered more than one," Yanic said.

"How's that possible?" Leo asked. "We only used one."

"*You* only used one," Yanic informed him. "Once you left, we consulted the story board and finished the shot list. We got almost everything you wanted."

"How was that possible if I wasn't there?" Leo asked. Kim set down syrup and orange juice next to his plate.

"Wardrobe had doubles so we put Chad in your clothes and shot the scenes with the cameras behind him."

"How the hell did he get on Smokey? You couldn't match the shot without the horse." Leo forked some eggs into his mouth. She'd sprinkled on cinnamon sugar. Perfection. She settled next to him with her own plate and started eating. Her shower-fresh scent snuck its way into his brain.

"Kyle pulled out a chunk of cactus from his saddle blanket. When you kicked him, you must have nailed that piece into his side and he lost it. We found it after you were airlifted away."

He swallowed his bite. "So once the cactus came out, Smokey was okay?"

"Pretty much," Yanic said.

"How the hell did a chunk of cactus get under his saddle blanket? He was fine the first take. No problems at all." He tried the pancakes next. Not bad, although he was so hungry, he probably would've eaten his leather boot and been happy.

"It's a mystery. Kyle has no clue. He swears it wasn't there when he saddled Smokey and since Smokey seemed fine after the first take, it means the cactus found its way there before the second take."

"You studying to be a detective?" Leo asked around his breakfast. It was easier to make light of the situation than to think someone purposely set him up.

"Amateur sleuth," Yanic replied. "Mysteries fascinate me."

Leo couldn't say the same. He liked his mysteries on paper. Who wanted him hurt or dead? Why would one of the crewmembers be out to sabotage him? What could possibly be the motive? Yanic wouldn't have those answers, so he went with the question he needed answered most. "Okay, Columbo, tell me you got a shot of the trio moving in on me, thinking I'm dead, before riding away."

"Got it. It added some good tension to the scene." Yanic chuckled. "You might have a career in this business."

Smiling, Leo sipped his OJ. "Let's hope."

"The other good news is that Tim finished the cut yesterday. He's just waiting for your notes to finish it off."

There was nothing in the world like having good friends when shit hit the fan. "I can't thank you enough, man. You totally saved my ass with this."

"I know. You owe me so big. I can't wait to collect."

Leo nearly cringed at the thought. In the old days, he had courtside Laker's tickets or orchestra seats at the Ahmanson or Pantages or any number of theaters in Los Angeles, but he'd had to get rid of everything, so now all he could offer was a piece of the movie and he'd already done that for Yanic.

"Give Tim a call," Yanic said. "I think he's busting at the seams for you to see his cut."

"Ha. Him and me both," Leo agreed.

Kim kept busy with the dishes after breakfast. She discovered that keeping Leo talking about his movie and the editing process kept his mind off their relationship.

The emotions she felt when they made love surpassed

anything she'd dealt with. Sure, she liked good sex, but with Leo, it went beyond good sex into earthshattering, mind-bending sex.

With the light of day, her sanity returned. Somewhat. Leo still didn't want her to have this baby and maybe she understood why, but it didn't change her mind. Everything happened for a reason and if she was meant to have a less than healthy child, then she'd deal with it, but she wouldn't consider another option now that she'd made up her mind.

Leo drove her to pick up her passport, and Kim battled the joy of being a free bird against the knowledge that she was about to leave Leo for good. She stood in line while Leo fielded another call on his cell phone in the car. When the clerk handed over a manila envelope, she didn't know whether to laugh or cry.

Back in the car, she ripped it open and pulled it out. "Yes! Finally." Free.

Leo disconnected his call. "Let me see." He took the passport and smiled at the old picture of her. "When was this taken?"

"I don't remember. A long time ago," she said.

His smile dimmed and he crinkled his nose. "You don't want to hear this." He met her gaze. "It's expired."

"What?" Kim snatched the passport and checked the expiration date. "Three months ago? It expired three months ago? Are you freaking kidding me?" She slammed her head against the seat rest. "Unbelievable."

Leo cranked the engine. "Home?"

Did she have a choice? "Home," she said.

Luckily for her, Leo contacted his editor and ended up making notes on Tim's cut of the footage. The digital world made everything instantaneous and Leo worked for hours, his eyes fixed to the computer screen while he made notes in a little pad. She kept her distance and spent a lot of time with Stella, giving the cat the attention she'd missed the past couple of days.

With an expired passport, she needed her driver's license desperately. Chelsea had assured her that everything at work was under control, but Kim didn't see how she was going to last another week or more without some form of ID. It was the key to her freedom. A call to the airlines was in order to see if she could fly without it.

Until she could grab a flight, maybe she should take Wilson

up on his offer to stay at his hotel. That would get her out of Leo's vicinity. God, sometimes she came up with the worst ideas. She just didn't want to leave before she knew Leo was well enough to take care of himself. What if he got dizzy on the stairs and fell? That would seriously piss her off.

Later in the afternoon, the doorbell chimed and Leo strode across the room to open it.

"Dude!" A handsome thirty-something man pulled Leo in for a bear hug before releasing him. "I told you not to do the stunt. You gotta leave that shit to the professionals." It had to be Rex. Funny, he looked like a Rex, handsome, with brown hair and eyes.

Yanic walked through the door next and pumped Leo's hand. He kept his dark hair slicked back with product and was a dead ringer for Adrian Brody. "When did you get home?" he asked.

"Late yesterday," Leo said, closing the door behind them. "Guys, this is Kim. Kim this is Rex and you met Yanic on Saturday."

Kim shook hands with both men as they drifted into the den. "Can I get either of you something to drink?" She shot a quick look to Leo because when the hell had she become the hostess in his house?

"Not for me," Rex said. "I'm fine."

"Me too," Yanic said, taking a spot on the sofa.

Whew. That solved that. "I'll just be in the kitchen. Cleaning up." Because that's what the little woman would do, right? Damn, no matter what she did, she came off as the girlfriend and she really *wasn't* Leo's girlfriend. *Didn't want* to be his girlfriend.

For the gazillionth time she wished for her driver's license so she could get her life back. Staying here with Leo wasn't doing her any favors. Unless she just made it clear that their sexual relationship expired early this morning after the fourth time they'd made crazy hot love.

Kim sighed and shook her head. "Face it, you're the problem," she murmured to herself, the one with zero restraint when it came to this man. He pushed every one of her buttons, the kind of buttons that had her panting and begging for more of his touch, more of his kiss. Staying here would only mean more sex because she had that little willpower when it came to him.

As Kim loaded the dishwasher, she listened to the conversation in the other room. Yanic described the Smokey debacle and how he got the whole thing on film. He suggested Leo use that clip for promotional purposes. Kim cringed at the idea of watching it again. Once was plenty. But Leo didn't seem averse to it. He just wanted to see it first.

Rex went into a few stories of stunts gone wrong and Kim couldn't imagine doing such dangerous things for a living. Rex specialized in driving and motorcycle stunts, but he sounded like a man of many talents...all dangerous.

Kim finished cleaning up and walked through the room to head upstairs. Leo snagged her hand as she passed and he stood next to her.

"Whoa, where you headed like a bullet? Come sit down." He tugged her next to him and she didn't want to make a scene so she sat. The glance that Rex and Yanic shared didn't get past her. She just wasn't sure what it meant.

"I couldn't have done anything without Kim this past week. She saved me," Leo said, squeezing her hand.

Heat infused her cheeks. "You'd have been fine without me," she assured him. Although it had been an eventful week. The car accident, the shooting, the horse... Even *she* wasn't *that* unlucky. Sure detectives had been investigating, but this was the first time she really believed someone meant to do her serious harm.

"What's wrong?" Yanic asked. "You look ill."

Kim turned to Leo and forged ahead with her thoughts. "I see how the car accident and the shooting were directed toward me." She paused as the idea took a stronger hold. "But the Smokey drama affected you."

Leo's gaze never wavered from hers as he nodded. "True." His eyes widened as he clearly thought of something. "Except. Just because it affected me didn't mean it was meant to. You were supposed to ride Smokey when we finished the shot, remember?"

"But no one there knew that," she argued. Unless someone had been eavesdropping. But no one on his crew had even met her until that day.

"Your cousin was there. The cousin that got the short end of the stick," Leo reminded her.

"But I keep telling you he wasn't even in town when the car accident or the shooting happened."

"Have the police checked his alibi?" Leo asked.

"Is this a new screenplay you're writing?" Rex asked, his smile bright.

"Hardly," Leo replied.

"How about you guys stay here and finish your visit and I'll go upstairs and talk to the police. Maybe they've found something." She pulled out of Leo's grip, satisfied that she had a good excuse, but miserable because she missed his heat. *Buck up, cowgirl.* This ride was about to get a lot lonelier. Because after she talked to the police, she planned to call the airline and see about traveling without her license. If that didn't work, she'd hang around town until her license arrived and she could fend for herself. Leo wouldn't be happy about this—hell, she wasn't happy about it—but staying here only meant more heartache and who wanted that? Not her. That was for damn sure.

Wilson stared at his phone as it faded to black, his heart pumping double time, a smile stretched across his face. "Got you, cousin." He pocketed his phone and took a steadying breath. Now he needed a plan. His luck was changing. Even if the airlines let Kim travel without ID, all flights into the Midwest were cancelled because of an epic blizzard set to strike. She'd been so preoccupied with shooting those ridiculous scenes and then dealing with Leo in the hospital, she hadn't been paying attention to the weather in her hometown.

His brilliant cousin wasn't so smart after all.

Maybe it was time to finesse Plan A and see if he could create a few sparks with sweet cousin Kim. He'd dealt with his fair share of boners growing up with her. He'd never been blind to her looks, but hadn't seriously considered a possible relationship for obvious reasons. If hooking up didn't work, then he had to figure out how the hell to make sure she'd need him for the rest of her life without any suspicion coming down on him.

He could pay someone to hurt her. Take a knife to her face and make sure no man would want to be with her. Then he could step in and be the knight in shining armor. The man who wouldn't care what her face looked like because her bank account more than made up for the lack of looks on her part.

Once she had her ID, she'd be leaving town, which gave him more time to play with once the people here thought she'd gone home. A few texts to the right number back in Indiana saying she planned to stay longer would buy time on that end.

She still hadn't replaced her phone, so that was two things he needed to do before moving ahead.

His brain circled around the problem. ID, phone, there had to be something he was missing. He had to find someone and had to have an alibi and a time frame. There seemed to be plenty of homeless people in Los Angeles. Anyone of them might be willing to help him out for a little cash.

Wilson shook his head, still grinning, still amazed that Kim had walked right into his arms. Did she have a fight with Leo? Maybe he could score some extra cash on the side with a call to one of those rag magazines.

"Yeah," Wilson muttered, pacing his small hotel room. He bet those magazines paid good money for information on famous actors. Kim's profile had already been splashed on one of them a couple months ago, but she'd been described as the blond of the week in a long line of Leo Frost's women and no one knew who she was. Now they could post the picture again, or Wilson could set up a time and place for another picture and the new headline would have her name and more personal information. Like the fact that she was pregnant with Frost's kid. Yeah, he liked this idea. Liked it a lot. It might even make the rift between her and Leo bigger and force Kim to confide in him more.

Wait. One glitch sparked in his head. Once Kim got her ID, she'd be out of here, and he needed to keep her dependent on him. Needed to keep her here until he could figure out how to set her up. That snowstorm was only going to last so long.

After checking his watch, Wilson glanced around the room and straightened up a few things. "Hanging with the cousin," he mused softly. "Nothing like a little family bonding time." She had told him to give her a couple of hours to break the news to Leo that she was leaving before picking her up. Two hours to figure out how best to deal with Cousin Carolyn. She owed him that inheritance.

Chapter Sixteen

"What? Why?" Leo figured he probably looked like an idiot with wide eyes and slack jaw, but at the moment he didn't care. At the moment, he felt like someone had drop kicked him like last week's trash and left him to get run over in the street.

Kim paced in front of him while he sat on the couch. Wearing one of her short black skirts, with a slinky top that outlined her curves and high wedge shoes, she looked like business as usual. With the exception of her wrinkled brow, she might've been lecturing him about money. He should've known when she said *we need to talk* that she was about to unload a bomb. Those same four fucking words again. God he hated them. "Because," she said, in answer to his question. "I need some space."

Space. Which meant she felt smothered? By him?

Leo shook his head, completely stupefied, but he didn't argue. "Okay, you need space. I'll give you plenty of space. I'll stay out of your way, I won't talk to you, won't look at you. But don't leave." God, was he begging?

More to the point, was it working?

Her brows slanted down and she definitely looked torn. "Leo, it's not about that. It's about…"

He waited, but she couldn't seem to find the words. Finally she squeezed her eyes shut before meeting his gaze. "I know you mean well and I think you'd try to give me room, but the fact is you and I are very…" She pressed her lips together and shook her head, still struggling for words.

"Combustible?" Leo offered.

"Yes!" She pointed at him and nodded. "Combustible. Good word. No matter how hard we try, we seem to end up horizontal and I don't... I can't..." She took a deep breath. "I just need some space."

So she either didn't like the sex—which wasn't the case by her own admission—or was scared of the kind of sex they had. Crazy-good, wreck-the-sheets, blow-the-top-off-the-roof sex. The kind that maybe led to something deeper, something not everyone found every day or sometimes not in a lifetime.

"And you want to get away from me so badly that you're going to hang out with a cousin who might be trying to kill you?" Leo stood and rubbed the headache that kept gnawing at the back of his neck. The day her cousin Wilson won out over him definitely marked a crappy day.

"I told you, I talked to the detectives and Wilson has an alibi. His buddy in Arizona said he was with him the day of the shooting. The man isn't a magician. He can't be in two places at once."

Leo felt his chest tighten.

"Leo," she finally said, her eyes so sad that it ripped him up.

What could he say? "I don't get it?" He faced her, their attraction as strong as any magnet. "What's wrong with this?" He gestured between them, letting the heat simmer while they stood inches apart. Leo knew with complete certainty that he could kiss her now and have her naked on the sofa in thirty seconds.

Her gaze drifted to his lips and his heart took an unsteady beat. He was two seconds away from making good on his mental threat, but she took a step back. Air cooled the space between them. "Ultimately we want different things, Leo, and if I lose sight of that, I'll regret it later."

Different things? Yes, maybe they did, but they also wanted each other and that should count for something. But pushing her might do more harm than good so Leo gestured to the door. "I don't want you to go, but I can't stop you."

She nodded and avoided eye contact before going upstairs. She came back a couple minutes later with two shopping bags. Presumably all her belongings and everything she had to show for this trip. "It's not like I won't be talking to you," she said. "My license will be delivered here, probably about the same time flights will open up to Indiana. I'll see you before I leave."

"Great." Yeah, he sounded pissed, but he couldn't help it. He *was* pissed. She was willing to forgo time together because…because… "Let me get this straight. You're leaving because even though I told you I'm going to be part of this baby's life, you're afraid of us?" He gestured between them.

She shook her head, which turned into a shrug, which became a look of pain so clear in her eyes, it crushed him even more.

Someone knocked on the door.

Wilson.

Shit. Leo needed more time. He was a master at persuasion given the right circumstances.

Kim skittered away like if she didn't move, she might change her mind. "Hi," she said after opening the door to her cousin.

"Hey!" He had his hands in his pockets and looked like the cool operator he thought himself to be. Leo didn't necessarily dislike the guy, especially after all the trouble he'd gone to in Las Vegas, but watching that GQ smile only pissed him off more. He looked too put together in his blue polo shirt, khakis and round glasses.

Leo wanted to punch the enthusiasm off his face. This time his ego took a solid shot in the solar plexus. He shouldn't be jealous simply because the guy was her family, but that nasty emotion swirled in his gut anyway.

"I'm ready," Kim said, her smile forced. Her real smile stretched wide and beautiful. This one looked as if she'd sucked a couple of lemons. She turned to him. "I'll give you a call a little later."

Leo nodded. The *whatever* on his tongue stayed firmly behind his lips. He doubted anything civil would come out of his mouth at this point anyway.

"Okay. Thanks. Bye." She scrambled out of the house in a blur of streaming blond hair, the door closing firmly behind her.

Leo caught the surprise on Wilson's face at the quick departure, but he didn't argue. He just followed Kim like a stray dog waiting for attention.

Like the sap he was, Leo watched Kim load her bags into the back seat of Wilson's rental. Before sliding into the passenger seat, she glanced up. For a second, Leo wished he hadn't been at the window, but the pain he saw in Kim's eyes mirrored his own. He thought he'd hit bottom a couple of times already, but the hollowed out feeling in his gut told him he'd just found a new bottom.

"Fine," he muttered, heading to his phone. He had a shitload of work and a film to distribute and if everything went according to plan, he'd be back on his feet, with or without Kim, in no time.

A stupid thing. A real stupid thing to look back at the house and see the hurt in Leo's eyes. Kim never intended to hurt him. Very much the opposite. She wanted to make him happy. She wanted to comfort him any way she could, including under the sheets, which was what made it impossible to stay. No matter how many times her heart told her to get comfortable and stick around, her head knew better.

Leo had too much stacked against him. His reputation, yes, but mostly his opinion on her pregnancy. She couldn't look back on her decision. Couldn't regret it. Her peace of mind—and maybe the state of her heart—depended on it.

"So, what do you want to do?" Wilson's question prodded her out of her thoughts.

"Do?"

"Yeah?" He glanced at her as he drove the winding canyon toward the city.

She wanted her driver's license so she could go home and resume her life without Leo—and God, that thought killed her— but it wasn't what he meant. "I thought you had your conference?"

"It's optional."

"Optional?" Did that mean he didn't plan to go? "I thought this was a business thing. Don't you have to learn new things and report back to work?"

"All the handouts come in a conference binder." Wilson checked his rearview mirror. "I don't have to go to any of them if I don't want to. Everything I need is in the handouts."

"Why bother coming to the conference if you're not going to attend any of the seminars or workshops? Or take part in the networking?" Maybe she was more like her Aunt Carolyn than she thought because the lack of ambition on Wilson's part had her bristling. Carolyn had mentioned on more than one occasion that she thought *Wilson thought* he could get by on his looks.

He glanced at her as if she was dense. "I can't get the handouts if I don't sign up for the conference. Duh."

Kim bit her tongue—literally—to keep from snapping a surly reply. Who spent a week in a hotel for a conference they didn't plan to attend? Sure, he'd been to a couple of meetings, but nothing that required the amount of money he'd probably shelled out.

That piece of information swirled around in her head. Had the conference been a convenient way for him to be closer to her? To buddy up or be around in case she needed help. Or—what if—there was no conference to begin with and he'd come in just to find a way to get closer to her? That seemed crazy.

Wilson had been like this in Tucson, too, before she'd flown back home. Maybe she should just ask him point blank if he needed money. But even as the thought flickered in her head, she knew the door that would open and the mistake it would be. He'd take it as an opportunity to ask whenever he needed something and her patience would wear thin real fast. And what about her idea of just giving him part of the inheritance? That idea didn't sit well with her only because it went against Carolyn's wishes. What if she knew something Kim didn't about Wilson's gambling. Maybe he hadn't stopped despite saying he had. The possibilities swirled in her brain.

"How much longer is the conference?" He'd have no reason to stay once it ended.

"It ended yesterday," he said.

"What?" She faced him. That was a very convenient answer in case there had never been a conference to begin with. "Then why are you still in town? Don't you have to get back to work?"

"They can wait a few days. I told them I had a family emergency. I do," he said, after glancing at the surprise on her face. "You need me until your ID gets here. You're the only family I have, I'm not going to leave you stranded in a big city." He adjusted his shoulders as if he'd been affronted. "I know what's important in life. Family. And you and I are all that's left. We need to stick together."

If he meant to make her feel guilty, he'd done a pretty good job of it.

The rest of the drive to the hotel stayed fairly quiet. "Is there anything you need?" Wilson asked as he pulled into the parking lot. "Oh, a phone, right?" he said, answering the question. "We can set your stuff in the room and head to a phone store."

"We could if I had my license. I doubt they're going to let me buy a phone without ID for my credit card."

"We can try. And if they don't, then I'll pay for it."

She shook her head and opened her mouth, but he cut her off.

"Don't argue with me. You'll pay me back. I'm not doing it out of the goodness of my heart. You need a phone, so you should at least get one while we wait for your ID."

It was hard to argue with his logic. She *did* need a phone and she *could* pay him back. It was the IOU factor that made her itchy. Carolyn's wording in her will popped up in Kim's head. *I know that's why you started sucking up to me.* How could she *not* think of it?

Nevertheless, after dropping her bags in the room, they headed out for a new phone. As she suspected, Kim couldn't purchase the phone without ID and Wilson shelled out his credit card to the tune of several hundred dollars, making Kim feel like she'd just crossed some kind of invisible line.

The good thing about getting a new phone was the solitude she got while setting it up and adding all the contacts she could remember. Instead of waiting with Wilson in his room until a room of her own was ready, she sat in a corner of the no frills hotel lobby.

An overwhelming urge to text Leo had her pressing her lips together in doubt. "Don't be stupid," she muttered to herself. It wasn't like she didn't plan to ever talk to him again. She just needed space. She punched a quick message. *Hi. Got a new phone. Same number as before. Will stay in touch so I can pick up my ID when it arrives.* How did she sign off? *Catch you later.*

Part of her felt guilty for leaving him when he was still dealing with his concussion, but her emotional survival depended on her ability to stay strong, to stay independent. Independence meant she needed to rent a car. Or needed Wilson to rent one for her because she refused to let him be a taxi service until she left town. It was just one more thing she'd owe him, but at this point she didn't care.

Wilson stretched out on his bed, waiting for Carolyn to return from the lobby. He'd listened to the maids cleaning through the thin walls and called the front desk to make sure Carolyn got the adjoining room instead of one farther away. He had her now, so close. Right at his fingertips. No need to chase her or worry about the next time he'd see her. God, he hadn't felt this liberated in months. Too many months.

It was just so damn hard to wait to have to deal with her. He wasn't even sure he'd get his hands on her inheritance if he had to dispose of her, but it was worth the try. Because he knew damn well the only way he'd see a dime of it if while she lived was to create a bond that went past the type of family dynamic they usually shared. It wasn't unheard of. Cousins hooked up in a lot of places in the country.

So what did they do in the days until the mail arrived with her precious driver's license? Sight see? Shop? He doubted Carolyn would let him pay for more than the necessities, which meant they had a lot of nothing in their future. But, who knew…maybe with a few days to get to know each other better, his dear cousin would have a change of heart and give him everything he wanted.

Yeah, that sounded good to him.

Chapter Seventeen

Leo met Tim the next evening at Tim's home office after the editor finished working on a sci-fi thriller due out next year. The headache from hell had stayed with Leo no matter how many pain relievers he tossed back. At least today, the pounding in his skull had receded to a doable level four.

A cool breeze wafted through the magnolia trees not too far from Leo's house. Bypassing the front door, Leo opened the gate and let himself into the backyard where Tim's guest house/edit bay sat in the corner of the yard. Tim waved Leo in, his puffy eyes and tired smile told Leo it had been one long day in this little dark room.

"I know I'm asking a lot," Leo said, sliding into the comfortable leather seat next to Tim behind the control panel. A bank of monitors dimly lit the dark room with a still photo of Leo riding Smokey. "I really appreciate this, man."

Tim shook his outstretched hand. "We'll just add this to the growing list of things you owe me." And, boy, did Leo owe him. Squeezing him in to finish this film when the guy was already working outrageous hours, Tim was nothing short of hero material.

Slapping Tim's back, Leo grinned. "C'mon, you only put in twelve hours today. Another two is nothing." That number was probably shy of the true count.

"Haha," Tim said, but he had a genuine smile on his face. He punched some buttons and Leo's footage began moving on the screen, the lone rider in the wide-open desert. "This was beautiful stuff," he said. "Your idea or Yanic's?"

"Mostly mine. I wanted that first shot close then open it up to see the scenery." The camera started on a close up of his face, then widened out as he rode hard and fast into the barren, brown desert, one of the toughest, most experienced riders the Pony Express had ever employed.

The first shot had been golden. Lightning in a bottle as it were. Tim's cut had been nearly exactly what Leo wanted and Leo's minimal notes wouldn't take long to incorporate. Next, Tim rolled the footage of Smokey throwing Leo. Although Leo remembered the initial ride, the unholy way that Smokey had tossed him around as if he'd weighed nothing, he didn't have too much memory of being dragged. Yeah, he remembered the burn and trying to get his foot out of the stirrup, but he hadn't thought about the whole picture or what he might look like as it was happening.

"Wow," he murmured, watching with narrowed eyes as Smokey bucked and ran, all while dragging Leo behind him like a rag doll. The end came when Leo got his foot free but slammed into a giant rock.

"Fucking ouch." Tim's words came through gritted teeth and puckered face as he seemed to feel the impact just from watching it. "No wonder you've got a shiner the size of Texas."

"Yanic thinks I should use this for promotional material."

Tim nodded. "A great idea. I can see how it would bring people in."

"Maybe we'll just cut before impact. That's pretty gruesome." His headache throbbed worse after watching the footage.

It only took a couple hours to finish the edit and they both agreed on the final cut.

Leo had booked a sound mix for tomorrow and he could steal the music already laid in at the beginning of the movie for the score. After that it was final visual effects and final color. Then he had to send the finished product to the potential distributors and wait for their decisions. He didn't expect it to be a cakewalk, but he had a leg up because of his name.

For the first time in a long time, Leo saw a light at the end of the tunnel. This film could pull him out of his hole and once he got on solid ground, he planned to focus on one other very important thing in his life.

Kim Jacobs.

Days later, the lunch crowd buzzed in the packed restaurant. Kim set her fork down and leaned back in the booth. "The rest is yours."

Wilson's eyes lit up like winning slot machines in Vegas as he pulled the rest of their shared dessert closer to his side of the table. "I'm not going to argue with you." He took a giant bite of the chocolate chip cookie pie and rolled his eyes in dessert euphoria.

"You don't have to rub it in." Kim loved dessert as much as the next guy, but she wanted to eat as healthy as possible because of the pregnancy. She'd have to check on the nutritional value of pickles since she'd been craving them like a lunatic.

"I know," Wilson said around a mouthful. "I'm trying to eat it really fast so that you don't have to stare at it."

He said it with such a straight face that Kim had to laugh. Wilson slapped a napkin over his mouth and laughed too. And nearly choked himself in the process. That made them laugh harder.

Spending time with Wilson hadn't been nearly as bad as she expected. She'd forgotten how funny he could be. Plus, he'd surprised her by being a good listener. He hadn't looked past her at the television screen showing football game highlights or stayed glued to his phone. He'd listened to her talk about work and Chelsea and Chelsea's new baby. He'd even rented a second car under his name so she had her own wheels. She'd never been pulled over, so there was no reason to think she'd get caught driving without her license.

Wilson had shared his heartbreak over his divorce and strained relationship with his ex and his daughter. She hadn't been aware that his wife had cheated on him and the devastation of the affair showed clear in his eyes.

"So, it's been a few days and still no license," Wilson said after a moment of silence. "The weather's cleared up in Indiana. You think you might take a flight out before it gets delivered here?" He took the final bite and washed it down with the last of his water.

The weather had cleared up early yesterday, but Kim had been procrastinating, holding out hope that her ID would show.

"I probably should, but I keep thinking about the extra delay that's going to cause when Leo has to stick it in the mail again to send it to me."

"So what. Express mail is only twenty-four hours." He shrugged as he wiped his hands with a napkin. "On the other hand, you've waited this long, so another day or two isn't going to make that much difference at this point." He wrinkled his forehead. "Did you hear that a mail plane actually crashed a few months ago over the ocean? Can you imagine if something like that happened with your license? That would suck." He wadded up the napkin and tossed it on the table.

"Gee, thanks for the positive thoughts." Kim signaled to the server for their check.

"Oh c'mon, the plane already crashed, which means it's not going to happen to you or your ID. Murphy's Law doesn't work that way. Or does it?" He lifted a sandy brown eyebrow.

"Enough already. Don't freak me out."

"I'm not freaking you out. I'm trying to relax you. That was the whole point of this lunch." The server arrived and Wilson snatched the bill from his hand. "I've got this one."

"I should get it. You wouldn't still be here if it wasn't for me."

"You got last night's dinner. I've got this. I can even afford the extra side of pickles you ordered." He lifted a quizzical eyebrow almost as if he was waiting for an explanation.

She avoided it. "Okay, okay, it's yours." She'd write a check for everything she owed him in one shot once she got home. He really had been good company the past few days. He'd convinced her to do some of the touristy things she'd never done. They'd checked out Disneyland and Universal City. They'd even walked around Hollywood for a couple of hours.

"Oh," he said, a smile lifting his lips. "I've got one." They'd been coming up with memories from the old days when they were little and spent so much time together. "Remember when we used to play Monopoly in my room."

Kim nodded. "I was always the dog. And you used to sit with your legs all cockeyed and backwards." She shivered. "I still don't know how you sat like that for so long. It couldn't be good for your knees."

"Well, you used to lie on your stomach, propped up on your

elbows and I didn't know how you could stay like *that* for so long. Guess we're even." He went back to figuring out the bill.

Probably so. They each had their quirks and history. Ultimately, they'd been raised together and he was like a brother to her.

As they walked to the car, Wilson draped an arm around her shoulders. "I have to apologize."

"For what?" She glanced at him as they strolled.

"For wigging out when the lawyer read the will. I'm really sorry. I'd just talked to Chloe and she was being a real bitch about me seeing Amanda. It was just the straw that broke the camel's back. I get why she did what she did. She hadn't trusted me in a long time. I can't say I blamed her." He clicked the car alarm and it double chirped as they approached. Wilson stood in front of the door and kept her from reaching the handle. "I have changed. I just wish she'd taken the time to notice." He stroked his hands down her arms and Kim blinked. He couldn't mean anything by the close contact.

"Maybe she was too worried about the cancer to really see how you changed," she said, taking a step back.

Wilson didn't seem to be deterred and grabbed both her hands in his. "I think you're right. I felt so terrible for her. I hated not being able to do more for her."

Kim squeezed once and tried to pull her hands back. "C'mon, you did everything you could. I'm sure she appreciated everything."

Wilson kept his grip tight as he smiled at her. "Thanks." He squeezed back. "I guess I know that deep down, but it's nice to hear it from someone else." He tugged her forward and wrapped her in a hug.

Kim patted his back, giving him the comfort he seemed to need. But one hand moved slowly down her back...so far down that Kim's eyes snapped open as all sorts of warning lights went off in her head. Abruptly, she pulled back before that hand landed on her ass.

She reached for the door handle and forced Wilson back when she opened it wide then she scrambled for a topic. "The house really is pretty," Kim said, sliding into the passenger side as Wilson held open her door. He'd been so attentive the last few days, she didn't quite know what to make of it and the last few minutes really threw her off.

"On the outside, yes, you're right. It's a shame I'm going to have to sell it." He closed the door after dropping that bomb. Her stomach dropped. It was like another death all over again.

She'd spent so many hours in her aunt's house. They both had. It seemed like the last remaining piece of significance when it came to their family. She waited until he sat behind the wheel. "You're selling it? Really?" She hated that idea more than black jelly beans. "Why?"

Wilson shrugged as he started the car. "I need the money."

"Can't you at least get a loan? Take some equity out of the house."

He slipped on his sunglasses. "I don't know. The house requires a lot of upkeep. It's way bigger than I need. Just seems like overkill. I mean, unless someone else moved in with me." He glanced at her. "Want to move back to Arizona?" He laughed, but Kim barely cracked a smile.

"But it's all we have left," she murmured quietly. And she had no way to stop him from selling if he wanted to.

"You can buy it if you want to keep it so badly."

Kim scarcely breathed. Had Wilson been playing her this whole time? Had he lured her into a false sense of security before laying out this suggestion? She hated being so cynical where he was concerned.

"Or don't buy it," he said, when she didn't immediately answer. "I can see I hit a sore spot. Look, I don't care either way. I need the money so the house is my best way to get it. The sad thing is it's falling apart from the inside out. I'm probably going to have to take a lot less than it's worth."

"How much will fix it up?" Kim couldn't believe she'd actually asked. The house was his free and clear and she got the rest. She shouldn't care what the place needed, but she found it hard to let go of that last bit of her mother and aunts.

"Probably fifteen grand should do the trick," Wilson said. Then he listed everything breaking down, starting with the water heater and ending with the cracked pool.

She could float him a loan or put the money into the house herself. Worst case scenario she *would* buy it.

Back at the hotel, Wilson took her hand and walked her across the parking lot. The freaky vibe she had before they got in the car came back with stunning force. She didn't like the way his thumb caressed her knuckles or how closely he walked next to her.

"Thanks for lunch," she said, pulling her hand away to rummage for her card key in her purse.

He stood in front of her again, blocking the door, and every nerve shot to hyper alert as her heart thudded a heavy beat. "You're welcome." He gave her a smile she supposed worked on the opposite sex, but her mind still didn't want to go where Wilson seemed to be leading. "It's such a nice afternoon. How about we go to a park or something?"

A park or something? Kim shook her head. "Actually, I was going to answer some emails from my phone and see if I could get some work accomplished that way, so..." She leaned toward the door, trying to get past him but somehow he leaned the same way and Kim took an awkward step to avoid contact. "Wilson!" What the hell was he doing?

He straightened and stepped away from the door. "Sorry. I thought..." He trailed off and edged closer to his room. "I'll see you later, then. I picked lunch so you pick the dinner spot." He let himself into his room and closed the door before she could respond.

What was that all about? Wilson had been so fun all through lunch before that weird moment just now. Kim entered her room, debating whether she should meet Wilson for the next meal.

Kim talked to Chelsea about a few accounts and returned some emails and late afternoon she checked her watch. Her heart beat a little quicker. Every day at this time she called Leo and every conversation so far had contained the same grim news. With fingers crossed, Kim punched in Leo's number hoping to hear something positive.

"It's not here yet," he said without so much as a hello. "But," he said, "you're either calling early or the carrier is running late. No mail yet."

Maybe if she hoped hard enough, today would be the day.

"How about..." he paused and her curiosity peaked. "How about you come over for dinner. Just you and me. I want to show you something."

An exhilarating thrill shot through her chest, but she forced herself to sound casual. "Is it something I've seen before?"

He laughed and the sound filled her up. She could picture the sparkle in his eyes, the flash of straight white teeth, the laugh lines that bracketed his mouth. "No," he said, still chuckling. His voice pitched lower. "But I'm more than happy to show you anything you might be missing."

He made her flush without being anywhere near her and he tempted her like candy tempted a child.

She glanced at the wall that separated her room from Wilson's and heard his TV as he surfed the channels. She'd already planned to miss the next meal with her cousin so that left her evening wide open. Besides, being with Leo made her one hundred percent happier than being with Wilson. Wait...wasn't that the reason she'd decided to leave Leo's place to begin with? Maybe, but hadn't she stayed away for days? Didn't she deserve a reward?

"What time?" she asked.

"Gimme a couple hours to finish up some work, then I'll be ready for you."

Kim checked her watch. "I'll see you a five-thirty, then."

"Don't be late."

"I won't." On the contrary, it might be hard to not be early.

Wilson kept his anger buried as he followed Carolyn up the winding canyon to Leo's house, making sure to keep a good distance between their cars. The spur of the moment invitation for *her*—and only *her*—pissed him off. He knew renting her a car might be dicey, but he'd looked at it as another opportunity for Carolyn to owe him. The meals, the shopping... He'd convinced her to do all of it and he loved how their relationship had shifted. She needed him. Relied on him. Not only had they'd fallen into the good old days, but it had turned just that afternoon when they'd held hands and almost kissed. He could tell that she was still trying to get a handle on her feelings for him, so he didn't want to push.

Although the fact that she still hadn't shared her pregnancy pissed him off. The pile of pickles she ate at every meal was a dead giveaway.

Wilson stopped a few doors away and watched Carolyn exit the car and climb the steep stairs to the front door. His blood boiled, but he clenched his jaw and took a deep breath. Why the hell had he even followed her? He couldn't sabotage another rental. "Shit," he hissed. What a waste of time. He almost pulled into the street when the postman's boxy truck passed him and made him freeze. If this guy had her ID, and Wilson got it before she did, he'd have more time with her. He immediately cut the engine and glanced up the stairs to see if Carolyn had spotted the mailman. Leo must have been waiting for her because she was nowhere in sight.

The mailman pulled up to the box and dumped a pile of letters inside before continuing up the hill. Wilson waited until he got around the curve and out of sight before exiting the car, jogging closer and reaching into Leo's mailbox. He didn't have to look far into the pile of mail. The third envelope was from the Indiana DMV, addressed to Kim Jacobs. But of course they meant Carolyn Wyatt. It was easy to get them confused since they looked so much alike. People had been doing it for years.

The smile curving his lips came from deep inside. He glanced up at the house, then back to the mail in his hands. Looked as if this trip had been worth it.

Kim lifted her hand to knock on the door, ignoring the unusually fast beat of her heart. She could blame it on the conversation she just had with one of the detectives, but she knew better. The phone call had been short, because of a bad connection, but she'd heard enough to know someone had tampered with her rental car. Coupled with the shooting and the horse accident, it seemed pretty clear that someone wanted her dead.

She heard Leo approaching and took a steadying breath. Just because she hadn't seen him in a few days didn't make this meeting special. And she'd keep saying those words in her head until they stuck.

The door opened with a flourish before she even knocked. Her dry mouth and sweaty palms hadn't paid any attention to all her calm and cool thoughts.

"Right on time." Leo gestured her inside. The area around his stitches had turned dark shades of blue and purple, but the outer edge was starting to fade. The mouth-watering smell of him made her eyes glaze over. She'd just stepped past him when he closed the door, grabbed her arm and gently swung her into his chest.

Flustered, Kim gasped. "What are you doing?"

Leo wrapped his arms around her and held her close, his bowed head next to hers, his breathing soft in her ear. "Price of admission," he whispered.

A full body flush sent a delicious shiver down her spine. "I didn't know I was getting a show." She managed the words without sounding too breathy, even though she barely sucked air into her lungs.

His masterful hands stroked down her back and came up her sides as he pulled away and watched her. His smile weakened her knees. "Not just a show," Leo said. "Dinner too. And a surprise after that."

Surprise? Or sex? Because as easy as it would be to get horizontal with this man, she'd promised herself not to. "Wow. Dinner theater in Los Angeles? Who knew?" Maybe if she glazed over it, he wouldn't push her. Because they both knew the type of restraint she showed.

The glint in his eyes as his gaze roamed to her lips nearly set her hair on fire.

"What's for dinner?" This time her voice didn't sound nearly as strong and she took a step back to get some space from the sexual fireball in front of her.

But the sexual fireball in question only followed her and brought her close again. "Why don't you ask me what's for dessert?" One hand stroked low over her back while the other eased under her hair and cupped her nape. The instant sizzle of his touch made her pulse thump faster and her lids grow heavy.

"I might not be staying for dessert." Forcing the words out took real effort.

He narrowed his gaze and the moment stretched into forever as she waited for his kiss. She'd fall into it like the Niagara hitting bottom. Coming here had been a giant mistake. Maybe Leo got the same feeling because instead of diving in for a sure thing, he let her go and stepped back. Breathing hard, Kim realized that Leo's chest might've been puffing a little extra as well. It would be too easy to jump into his arms and fuse her mouth to his. Too easy to touch all parts of him north and south and take all the comfort he was so good at providing.

"C'mon," he said, holding his hand out. "Dinner first, then the movie. I'm starving."

"Did the mail come?" she asked, taking his hand and relaxing an iota.

"Ah! I meant to check after you called and got sidetracked with phone calls and getting dinner started." He headed for the door.

"I'll check. You can finish dinner."

He nodded and she bolted out the door and to the mailbox on the street. Anticipation had her fumbling with the envelopes as she looked through the small pile.

Nothing. Damn. Kim took the stairs back up in slow motion. Leo must have heard the front door.

"Did it come?" he asked.

"No." She trudged into the kitchen and put his mail on the counter as he set a container in the microwave. A plate of barbeque chicken sizzled on a small platter.

"Steamed veggies," he said, turning on the microwave. "Almost ready."

Stella limped into the room and Kim scooped her into a quick cuddle as Leo poured drinks. The domestic quality of the whole situation made her hungry for something like this on a regular basis. Once they were both seated at the kitchen counter, Leo dove into his meal.

"What's got you so busy that you don't have time to eat?" she asked before taking a bite of chicken.

"Been meeting and talking to distributors. Hoping to get my film out ASAP. I need to get a marketing campaign going first."

"Like bus and billboard ads? Trailers? That sort of thing?"

He nodded. "Exactly." He did a double take at her. "Why're you smiling like that?"

"You've just come across my specialty. Advertising."

"I thought you were the finance end of business."

"I'm very versatile."

His gaze smoldered hot. "So I've learned." He broke eye contact and focused on his next bite before he glanced at her again. "The trailer's being put together as we speak. I just need to rent the ad space wherever I decide that should be, not to mention what I can afford...which isn't a lot," he added. He went into more detail about what he thought he should do versus what he could afford and where he thought he might get the most for his dollar.

They discussed costs and different avenues of publicity as they got through the meal.

"Tell me about your movie," Kim said as she finished the last bite of her dinner.

"I'd rather you just watch it," Leo replied, rinsing their dishes and loading the washer. He took her hand again and led her into the den where he gently pushed her onto the sofa. Using the remote, he accessed his computer on the flat screen, clicked on a link from his email and started the movie. He put his arm over the back of the sofa, which effectively settled her comfortably under his arm and snuggled right next to him.

She could've moved. Should've moved, but she fit so perfectly and he smelled so good that she decided to stick it out.

The opening of the movie began with sweeping vistas of rugged mountains. The camera zooming across the land as opening credits streamed over the view,

"I thought you didn't like to watch your movies with people," she said, cuddling closer.

"This is different. You're one of the first to see this. I want your honest opinion."

Something shifted inside Kim and she caught Leo's gaze. "Really? I'm one of the first people to see this?"

"Not including the editor and the distributors I sent it to, yeah." He nodded, as solemn as Kim had ever seen him. "You've always been a hundred percent honest with me and that's one of the things I like best about you. I want to know what you think of this film. If you think it sucks, then maybe I cut my losses now and don't spend the money on advertising. If you think it has a shot, then I'll go for it."

"No pressure." She snorted. Except that it was a ton of pressure.

He didn't bat an eye. "I'm serious. I trust you. I trust your opinion."

"But it's—"

"Shh." He put his finger against her lips and kept her from saying *so subjective.* That single touch had her thinking about sex in an instant. The devil on her shoulder urged her to lick his finger, taste him. They'd be horizontal on this sofa faster than Mach 1.

The heat in his eyes warned her that maybe he was thinking the same thing, but he blinked and leaned back a fraction. "Just watch," he said.

So Kim shifted toward to the television and did as she was told. The story obviously took place in the old west. Carrie Ann Laughlin played the lead role and Kim already had her doubts, but the longer she watched, the more she got pulled in to the story—the struggle of a widow running the ranch her husband left behind. How a stranger passing through town saved her life from a group of bandits as she drove her wagon home with supplies. The two strike up a friendship. Then a love affair. Until the job he's been waiting for comes through with the Pony Express. He vows to return and marry her, but on his way home, he's attacked by the same group of men he'd saved her from in the beginning and they leave him for dead in the middle of the desert. A wagon train passes by and saves him, but months go by before he's able to make the trip back to the Black Hills and back to the woman he loves. In the meantime, we see her struggle with running the ranch and hoping he'll return. But as the months go by, her hope fades and she's left crushed again.

Finally, when he's well enough to travel, he takes the long journey home. The reunion had Kim bawling her eyes out as the music swelled. The look on Carrie Ann's face when she sets eyes on him cut straight to Kim's heart. And when the audience thinks it's all going to end happily, that same gang of bandits returns to finish the job. It takes both characters to fight off the men before help arrives from the nearby town. The final scene, where the audience sees the threat is over and the couple survive to lead a long life together had Kim crying even harder than the first time.

As soon as the screen faded to black, the first credit flashed on the screen. Written by Leo Frost. Kim's tears welled up again and she swallowed back a sheer bolt of pride that Leo penned this amazing love story. He flipped off the player before the credits rolled.

"Well?" he asked. "What'd you think?"

She turned to him as she blew her nose into a ragged tissue. "Are you kidding me? That was amazing! How did you come up with that?"

He shrugged, but he had the sweetest smile on his face. "Really? You liked it?"

"Doesn't the fact that my mascara is smeared down my face tell you that?"

"It's not so bad. Actually, you look pretty beautiful." He took a tear with a gentle swipe of his thumb and Kim sunk into the web of his hypnotic blue eyes. "Hi," he whispered.

"Hi."

Somehow they ended up only inches apart, his breath warm on her lips.

"This house isn't the same without you. Stella misses you."

She leaned back a fraction, her interest piqued. "*Stella* misses me? Just Stella?" She wanted more than that. It was stupid, she wanted the golden egg.

He shook his head, no hint of a smile this time. "No. Not just Stella. I miss you."

Kim kept her elation under wraps. It would do no good to show him how much those words meant to her. "Oh yeah?" She stroked her thumb across the hard line of his jaw. "A lot?"

"How 'bout I show you?" His lips covered hers before she could answer. Before she could run. Like she'd ever have the common sense to run when this man touched her. Kim fell under the magic of his kiss, the sweet caress of his hands against her head, his fingers combing through her hair. He gave her everything she wanted. Everything she needed with his touch, with his kiss. He filled up all the empty spaces in her soul.

Chapter Eighteen

Leo pulled back before he couldn't stop. Kissing Kim usually led to fucking Kim and he didn't want to scare her off. He hadn't been lying when he told her he missed her. The house was too quiet without her. His bed was too cold. He was too lonely. Without studying what all of that meant, he chose to take it for what it was. He liked her. A lot. More than he'd liked any other woman in his past...enough to miss her when she was gone and think about her most every waking moment when he wasn't buried in work.

He'd made peace with the fact that he was going to be a father. He'd braced himself for the worst as far as the potential challenges. No more wild spending sprees, no more mansions in multiple cities or continents. No more expensive cars or houses or hobbies. Until he rebuilt substantially and made sure his child was set for life, he wouldn't rest, wouldn't splurge.

Now all he had to do was convince Kim that he could handle it. That he *wanted* to handle it.

So yeah, maybe he hadn't planned on being a father but he'd also never planned to meet someone like Kim. A woman with brains and beauty. A woman who knew how to take control and spoke her mind when she wanted and not just when convenient.

Leo went in for a last long kiss. Her soft lips called to him. The warmth of her mouth was addictive. And the way she kissed him back, Jesus, she knew how to light him on fire with just her mouth. Her tongue tangled with his in a perfect game of catch me if you can. And he did. Repeatedly. He couldn't stop his fingers from running through the softness of her hair or skimming over the smoothness of her cheeks. Her hands never stayed idle either and as they stroked over his neck and shoulders, he imagined them sliding lower into his lap and caressing the iron bulge in his pants. Her extra soft touch on his scratches and bruises turned him on even more.

Pulling back and breathing hard, Leo looked into her glazed, heavy-lidded eyes. He could push it. Her. He could have her if he never stopped to talk or breathe. He could carry her upstairs, strip her naked and be inside of her in the next three minutes, but he wanted her to see him differently. Wanted her to know he'd not only had a change of heart, but a change *in* heart.

"What did you really think?"

She blinked a couple of times and the faintest of smiles curved her lush lips. "Are we talking about the movie or that kiss?"

Leo held back his raging libido with a whip and a chair. "We'll get to the kiss later. I'm talking about the movie."

"I told you. It was amazing." She licked her lips and it was everything Leo could do to sit still. "I can't believe you did all that low budget."

Didn't he wish. He snorted. "Who said anything about low budget? It cost me a fortune."

"I thought you weren't supposed to use your own money if you're making a film. I thought you're supposed to get investors."

"All true." Leo nodded. "Live and learn." He swirled little circles on the soft skin of her shoulder since she was still tucked close to his side. "What'd you think of Carrie Ann? She's the wild card in this thing. Had I known she was going to lose her mind after shooting this, I never would've cast her."

"You can't see into the future. Besides, I thought she was terrific. She was the one thing that held me back but she won me over pretty quickly."

"Yeah, me too. She auditioned and it was like, boom. I was done. She nailed it. I had a few people who I was considering but as soon as I saw her, I knew. She never let me down." Too bad he couldn't say the same for himself. She'd tried like hell to reach him when they got back from location, but Leo had followed his usual MO and not returned her calls. It wasn't that he didn't like her, he just had no urge to be caught by her. He'd seen her motivation from the first time they'd hooked up. She was all about the PR and promo. She'd mentioned as much during one of their nights together...where they happened to be in Leo's trailer because they'd never gone back to the hotel. Carrie Ann had guzzled his wine and got a little loose, not only with her body, but with her tongue.

"Did I read somewhere that you two had a little on-set fling?" Kim asked.

Leo suddenly needed a shower, but he couldn't deny it. "It was very short-lived. I hadn't planned on it. I was a little busy producing and acting. But..." He shrugged. Carrie Ann was the last woman he'd been with before Kim. "She made herself very available even though I told her nothing was going to happen once we got home. I think she was hoping for a different outcome."

"Did she fall in love with you?"

Leo laughed. "I doubt it. She was in love with my standing in Hollywood. My reputation maybe. I don't know." He shook his head. "She wanted me, she didn't love me."

"She sure lost it," Kim mused, her eyes sad and full of compassion.

And he felt like shit about it too. What if he'd seen her just one or two times? What if blowing her off had pushed her over the edge? It wouldn't have killed him to take her to dinner. He just hadn't wanted to lead her on and that's what he would've been doing.

Her eyes narrowed as she watched him. "Hey, you're not feeling guilty about it are you?"

He shrugged a shoulder. "I can't help but think that things might've been different if I returned a call or went out with her a couple of times. I just didn't have the interest."

"Exactly. So why should you spend time with someone you don't want to be with, especially when you know she's using you?"

"Maybe. But she killed someone and attempted to kill two others."

"That was her deal. It had nothing to do with you."

The room got quiet as she thought about something else. "Flings are common on the set, aren't they?" She eased away from him with that question as if it just dawned on her the amount of movies he made and the potential for easy hook-ups.

Leo owed her an honest answer. "Depends on the people in the movie. If you're single, yeah, people hook up."

"And even if they're not single…"

"Maybe. Depends on the person. Depends on their marriage. Depends on a lot of things."

She eased even farther away from him and Leo watched the divide between them grow bigger. So how did he get her back?

"But some people don't even consider it," he said and she met his gaze. "There are a few people so much in love with their wife or husband that they rush back to their trailers or hotel rooms to text or Skype or FaceTime or call, or if they're shooting in the city where they live, rush home to be with that person. I've seen it. It's not fiction."

"But that's not something you've ever experienced."

"Not personally. Doesn't mean I won't." He looked her straight in the eye with that answer. Her gaze skittered away, but he couldn't blame her. Maybe he needed to back off with the insinuations. He had no business leading her on when he didn't know what he was feeling either.

"How about dessert?" he asked, pushing to his feet and heading into the kitchen. "I went all out tonight. Root beer floats."

The smile she gave him lit up the darkened room. She followed him and leaned against the counter. "I don't think I've had a root beer float in fifteen years."

"Then you're past due." He pulled out everything he needed and started scooping ice cream into tall glasses. "Have you heard from the detectives lately?"

"Oh my God, I completely forgot to tell you. Detective Browning called while I was on my way here. He said Wilson's alibi checked out. He was with a friend in Arizona the day we were shot at, so that means he couldn't have been here the day before when my accident happened."

Leo handed over her float. "Did he say anything else?"

"Something about the car, but the line started cutting out and I couldn't hear him. I told him I'd call him back, but all I heard him say was 'available' and 'tomorrow.'" She shrugged. "So. That's all I have for now." She scooped some ice cream into her mouth. "Mmmm, this is good," she said around her first bite.

It would be even better if he slathered it over her skin

and licked it off but that would have to wait for another night.

"You might not want to consider this, but is it possible that his alibi is bogus or that he hired someone else to do it? I mean, he's a cousin that just lost out on a butt load of money. Don't discount that fact." When she didn't say anything, he kept going. "You know you're welcome to come back here anytime. Actually, I'd feel a lot better if you were close by."

She stirred her spoon again before meeting his gaze. "I know. Thanks," she said quietly. "It's been pretty quiet the last couple of days. Honestly, if Wilson wanted to kill me he's had nothing but time."

Leo didn't want to push her. It wouldn't do him any good, but her answer wasn't enough. He'd have to show her his intentions and that started with tonight. It started with showing her their relationship didn't revolve around finances and sex. A little patience might go along way…if he could only find it.

There was nothing Kim wanted to do more than stay with Leo, but that would only lead to misery. He watched her closely and she'd never felt more scrutinized.

"Sounds like you've made up your mind," he replied, seeming to read her silence.

"Leo, I can't." Staying here meant a merry-go-round of great sex followed by the roller coaster of self-recrimination. She wanted a good relationship with her baby's father. She *didn't* want to end up hating him because he couldn't return her feelings and she couldn't hold it against Leo if he didn't love her. Single motherhood awaited and if she wanted to start holding her own, then now was as good a time as any to start.

"Because…" he pressed. He deserved an answer.

"It's no secret that I like you, Leo. But liking you doesn't mean I'm going to change my life for you more than I already have."

"I don't remember asking you to change anything for me."

No, he hadn't asked. He'd just accomplished it when they'd had sex and she'd become pregnant. It didn't *change* much bigger than that. "Look, I'm not blaming you. It takes two. I get it." She shook her head and turned away, at a loss for words. "I just…" She didn't want to make him feel bad, but they both knew the emotional risk he'd taken in the past. Zero. So why should this be any different? She refused to force him into a relationship on the basis of *like*. *Like* wasn't strong enough. Not even close. She wanted head over heels in love. She wanted happily ever after. The knight in shining armor. She was a sap. A sucker. A dreamer. All those endings happened in fairy tales, not real life.

Real life happened with a lot more *grit* and a lot less *happy* involved.

"You just…" Leo stood right behind her. She hadn't heard him move and the solid warmth of his presence radiated along her back. "What? What were you going to say?"

It seemed stupid to dodge the question and she'd always been honest with him. Kim faced him. Even beat up, he was drop-dead gorgeous. "I don't want to be with a man who just likes me. I want a man who loves me. A lot. Despite my faults. I want a guy who's not afraid to commit. A man who's in it for the long haul and not until the next best thing comes along."

Leo didn't budge, but his gaze flattened and his eyes lost their sparkle. She'd hurt him.

"Let's be honest, Leo. You really still don't want to be a parent. You've just psyched yourself up because it's what you think you have to do." She took a step around him to get some space. "We like each other, sure. I admit it. But that's not enough. And not only can't I force you to love me, but I don't want to make you live a life you'd regret." She faced him again with a few feet between them. "You don't deserve that. Neither one of us do."

"So you'd regret living with me. Is that what I'm hearing?" He wouldn't even look at her.

"I would regret not waiting for a man who loves me."

Leo crossed to the other side of the kitchen, his hand brushing through his hair in obvious frustration. "I guess this means you're ready to take off then." His body language didn't match his neutral tone and Kim wished she knew what he was thinking.

This wasn't how Kim wanted the night to end. Something deep and painful made her chest ache as she watched him. "If you—"

Leo's mobile phone rang and he glanced at the screen on the

counter. His face morphed into a worried frown. He snatched it up and turned, giving her a perfect view of his fine ass. "This is Leo," he said. Then he listened. "When?" He ran a hand through his hair again and started pacing his small kitchen. "Where the hell was the aide when this happened?"

This had to be about Megan. Leo didn't have any other family members who needed round-the-clock nursing care.

"Where is she now?" He checked his watch. "Yeah, I'll be there as soon as I can. You have this number, so if you can text the address and number of the hospital, I'd appreciate it." He listened for a few more seconds. "Yeah, me too. Thanks for calling. I'll see you soon." He punched the screen and gave her a cursory glance. "I need to go." He ran a hand through his hair as he passed her for the hall closet. He pulled out an oversized backpack and a jacket.

"What happened?" Kim kept her voice steady. For a guy with Oscar winning acting chops, Leo didn't seem to be hiding any of his worry. Then again, she already knew about Megan.

"What's it matter to you?" He took the stairs with his pack and Kim followed.

"Because believe it or not, you matter to me."

"After that speech you just gave me, I tend to think otherwise." He started pulling clothes from his closet and tossing them into the bag.

"Do you need me to call the airlines while you pack?" It was the least she could do.

Leo swore and snatched the phone from his back pocket. He scrolled through his contacts, then he went to the receiver on his bedside table and punched some numbers. "Hey, Jim, it's Leo." Jim must have said something funny because Leo actually cracked a smile. "Heard about that, did you? News travels fast in this town. Look, I need a huge favor. I hope you can help me." Leo nodded as he listened. "I forgot about that. But what I need goes above and beyond." He paused. "Do you still keep a pilot on call? I need the use of your airplane so I can get to New York ASAP. I wouldn't ask if it wasn't important." Leo continued to stuff his pack with essentials. He listened and checked his watch. "I totally understand. I'm packing now and I should get to the airport by..." He closed his eyes and calculated. "Ten-forty. It's going to be tight, but I'll make it." He opened his eyes and nodded. "Thanks, man. I owe you big time. Yeah. I'll talk to you soon. Thanks again." Leo pocketed his phone.

"Are you going to tell me what happened?" Kim's pulse had taken a sudden roller coaster ride, listening to Leo try to keep his shit together.

For the first time he looked at her and she saw the devastation in his eyes. "Megan had another seizure. She fell out of bed and landed face first. She might've fractured her orbit, but they still need to take X-rays. She's been unconscious since the seizure so we could be looking at something else. They're doing tests now." The more he spoke, the more it seemed to hit him.

"Leo, I'm so sorry."

He nodded and glanced around his bedroom, looking lost and alone and Kim couldn't stand for him to go through this without anyone to lean on.

"So, you have a friend with a private jet that can take you to the East Coast tonight. It's nice to have friends in high places."

He nodded again, but she didn't think he heard a word she said.

She should go, but she couldn't leave him. Getting on the airplane two months ago had been hard enough, but leaving him when he seemed so vulnerable seemed like abuse. "Can I come with you?" The words were out of her mouth before she even thought it through.

Leo met her gaze and couldn't hide the quick flash of hope in his eyes before masking it. "I don't see the point," he said, snatching his bag and heading downstairs.

Kim followed close on his heels. "I do. You need a wingman. I'll do whatever you need. Just like the other day in the desert."

He stopped and turned, and Kim nearly ran into him. They looked eye to eye on the uneven stairs. "Why?"

"Because, believe it or not, I care about you and I want to be here for you." And maybe, just maybe, she wanted him to need her beyond her body. Maybe it was a suicide mission on her part, but she couldn't leave him so absolutely wrecked.

Meow. Stella twirled around their ankles.

"Shit. I forgot about Stella," he said, lifting the feline in his big hand.

Normally that might cause a problem, but he wasn't looking at the big picture. "It's a private jet. Let's take her with us."

"Us?" He studied her. "I never said yes to you coming along."

But he hadn't said no, either. "Let me help you, Leo."

He looked at Stella and back to her before sighing. "How the hell are we going to accomplish anything with a cat in tow?"

Kim took Stella from his arms and brushed by him to her bag sitting by the front door. She took out a little black book and a few other items and set Stella inside. She smiled up at him with a flourish of her hands around the bag. "Voila!"

"Fine, so Stella has a bed. What about food, water and a litter box? What about you? You have nothing with you?" He shook his head. "It doesn't make sense. What makes sense is for you to stay here and take care of Stella until your driver's license gets here."

Kim faced him head on. "Do you want to go alone? Be honest." He opened his mouth, but she cut him off. "None of your Academy Award winning bullshit either," she said. "If you have some convoluted reason that makes you think you need to go at this alone, then fine, I won't stop you, but if you want me to go with you. Then just say it."

Leo swallowed, looked past her, then met her gaze. He shook his head, then sighed. "It."

Kim's heart took a flying leap and she blinked back emotion. "Good." This was the perfect way to begin a solid friendship based on caring and understanding. She headed to the kitchen and filled two large Ziploc bags with dry cat food and two with cat litter. Then she filled a thermos of water, grabbed a small plastic bowl and a shallow pan. Five minutes later, she returned with everything stuffed into a brown bag. She set Stella in her purse so her little head peeked out between the straps. "We're ready. Let's go."

"What about Wilson?" Leo asked as they headed toward his car.

"I'll call him from the road. He's the least of my problems."

Chapter Nineteen

Leo drove to the Santa Monica airport and tried to breathe through the guilt crushing his chest. He could only picture Megan in the hospital, lying flat on her back with tubes running from her body and into machines. They didn't say she was on a ventilator, but with Megan's health as precarious as it was, that situation might not be far off.

He didn't remember arriving at the hangar, or meeting Jim's pilot and boarding the Gulfstream V. Somewhere over Nevada, he looked down, saw Kim holding his hand and his chest tightened. "Thanks for coming with me." He hated the unfamiliar hitch in his voice.

"You're welcome." Her soft smile gave him hope. Hope that maybe the situation wasn't as bad as he worried it might be. She was the one person who could help him through this. The only one he'd confided in about Megan. Seemed that no matter what kind of shit rained down, she was there to help shield him. Sure, she cared about him, but she didn't love him, and he never thought of himself as relationship material. Never imagined he'd want to be with someone *'til death do you part.* Was that why Kim had him so off balance? Was it more than the pregnancy? His headache from hell suddenly got much worse and he rubbed his fingers over his forehead to ease the pain. Right. As if that might work.

"Looks like Stella's adapted pretty well." Curled in Kim's lap, Stella snoozed at thirty-nine thousand feet. Kim gently stroked a hand over the cat's soft head. "She seems pretty good at rolling with the punches."

He could probably take a lesson from the damn cat.

Kim had boarded this plane without a stitch of luggage. She'd packed cat food and Stella and nothing for herself. During most of the time they spent together, she had practically no personal belongings, yet she rebounded like a champ, without a whine or complaint. "You're pretty good at it too."

"Sink or swim, right?" She gave a soft smile and squeezed his hand and Leo fought back the lump in his throat. "So how long does it take to fly to the East Coast in one of these things?" She looked around the interior of the plush private jet with its tan, leather recliners and extra-long sofa across from a big screen. It was Jim's playroom in the sky.

"The usual. Five and half/six hours. I usually don't pay attention. I board a plane and sleep."

"That's probably a good idea." She pushed the recliner back, so Leo did the same. The leg rest automatically came up and they looked at each other. "This is really decadent." The sparkle in her eyes lifted his spirits and that old feeling returned. That urge to lavish her with gifts and surprises and all the girly things she loved so much. Her smile faded as she watched him. "You just let me know what you need, when you need it and I'll be here for you."

"But just for this trip," he said. He wanted to take back the words. To kick the shit out of himself for even bringing it up, but the truth was right there, staring him in the face.

"Leo, you don't *want* more of me and you're not in love with me. But you do have my support. Always. You're the father of my baby."

Leo swallowed back the hurt and regret. Her words crushed him like an avalanche. It's what he deserved. Why should she stay with him when he couldn't give her what she wanted? What she needed?

"Thanks for coming with me." He couldn't look at her when he said it and purposely avoided the expression on her face. Pity or compassion...he didn't want either.

"You're welcome." She squeezed his hand again and Leo didn't feel so alone.

He must have slept because the plane jolted him awake and the rising sun cut a blinding shard of light through the plane windows.

"Welcome to New Jersey, folks," the pilot said over the

intercom as the engine noise ratcheted down. "Mr. Carrey has arranged for a car for you."

"Mr. Carrey?" Kim repeated. Her green eyes rounded like half dollars as Jim's full name came together. "Jim. Jim Carrey?"

Leo stretched out the kinks, and his back and knees cracked in the process. "You know him?" He grinned at her surprise. He loved that look on her face. "I've known him for about fifteen years. In fact, he owes me. I turned down *Bruce Almighty* because of a conflict in my schedule, and it was the highest rated Memorial Day weekend opening of any movie."

She cocked her head to the side, her smile brilliant as she adjusted Stella in her lap and unbuckled her seat belt. "Is that why he loaned you his jet?"

"That might be part of it. I also got him a good deal on his current house when I set him up with the seller. They didn't use any brokers and saved a fortune in fees. I think that's the debt he thinks he's repaying." The plane slowed as it neared a row of hangars.

"Who knew you were such a nice guy?" Kim said as the plane came to a stop. She eased Stella back into her bag. "We're going straight to the hospital, yes?"

Leo stood and tossed his pack over his shoulder. "I'd like to if you don't mind."

"It's your show, Leo." Kim rose and faced him. "I'm here for you."

Leo watched her for a second, taking in her confidence and letting some of it bleed off on him. She rarely seemed to falter. It was something he admired about her. The urge to kiss her hit him like a club. He needed her in a way that overwhelmed his senses. She filled up every empty part of his soul when she looked at him like that. Instead of doing something *she'd* regret later, he took her hand and headed for the door. The pilot came from the cockpit and opened it. "You two have a nice stay. Our plan is to remain until Mr. Carrey calls us back or you're ready to go home."

"Thanks, Travis. I appreciate the last minute service."

"My pleasure, Mr. Frost." They shook hands and Leo started down the stairs with Kim behind him. A few clouds dotted the mostly clear sky and cool early morning air felt good after so many hours in the plane.

Leo headed toward the black stretch limo thirty yards away near the closest airplane hangar. "If you want get a taxi while I'm at the hospital, that's fine with me. You probably need to pick up a few things to get through the next couple of days. I need to make another phone call, but I've got a place for us to stay."

"I'll figure out my stuff later from the hospital."

Leo gave her a sidelong glance. She constantly surprised him. "You know when I first met you, I thought you'd be nothing but high maintenance."

"I am very high maintenance," Kim told him, a grin sliding across her beautiful lips. She kept pace with his long stride. "You've never seen me in my natural habitat."

A pink bedroom with a ruffled four-poster bed and white carpeting blossomed in his mind. Maybe a few turquoise pillows popped some color into the space. Her place would be as put together as she was. Then he imagined himself there. With her. He could see stripping her bare and taking her down on that frilly bed in her natural habitat.

"That sounds almost promising." Leo tugged her closer and put an arm around her as they walked to the waiting limo. He soaked up the happiness she brought him because he knew it was all downhill once he stepped foot in the hospital and especially after this trip ended. He worked in La La Land, so for the immediate future he planned to pretend he'd always have Kim by his side.

The drive into Bethpage took just over an hour and the six-story hospital surprised Kim with its modern glass and cement structure. Leo had told her that Megan had been there multiple times over the years. She'd just assumed that because Megan lived in a private facility, the hospital would be comparable in size. The steel gray building towered over her like an ominous giant. Kim shivered in the dark blazer Leo had placed over her shoulders in the limo, then took a deep breath and soaked up the scent of his aftershave. A quiver of something sexual made her heart flutter and she shook out of the unwanted feeling.

She made sure Stella did her business outside on a little grassy area near the E.R. before following Leo inside the hospital. She suspected he needed the few minutes to psych himself up for the visit.

Though she didn't feel very comfortable taking a cat into the hospital, Kim eased Stella into her bag and rubbed the feline's soft, furry ears. After playing in the limo for the whole trip, Stella fell asleep in seconds flat. No harm could come if Stella stayed out of sight and in the bag. It wasn't as if Kim planned on going into Megan's room in the ICU.

The long walk down a handful of sterile hallways only intensified the anxiety streaming off Leo. If Kim had harbored any doubts about making this trip with him, they disappeared as worry lines etched on Leo's handsome face.

She didn't know what to expect when she looked through the glass at ICU, but the sight put her heart in a vise and squeezed tight. She wasn't sure what struck her most, the teenage girl in the neck brace with her face swollen beyond recognition or the absolutely desolate eyes of Leo as he approached his little sister.

Leo took Megan's hand and bent low, talking to her quietly as machines beeped rhythmically.

Kim recognized her features as being Down Syndrome, but Megan had other scars on her face that indicated multiple surgeries. She couldn't imagine what that poor girl had endured or what Leo had gone through, taking care of her for so many years.

Placing a hand over her stomach, Kim closed her eyes and said a quick prayer to her baby. *No matter what happens, I'll love you with all my heart.*

A nurse entered the room and came out a few minutes later. Kim heard her call for the doctor at the nurse's station behind her. Maybe because Leo was world famous or maybe because the doctor happened to be nearby, but within five minutes, a middle aged man with glasses and wearing a white doctor's coat walked briskly down the hall and entered the room. The two men shook hands and Leo listened intently to what the man said. Leo gestured to his eye and back to Megan, obviously asking about her recent injury and the doctor explained some more.

After the doctor left, Leo stayed for another fifteen minutes before backing out of the room. He took Kim's hand and led her down the hallway, waving to the nurses and telling them he'd be back later.

"You okay?" she asked, rushing to keep up with his long strides.

"Not really." His terse response only made her feel for him more. She'd never seen him hurt like this and she'd never wanted to comfort someone as much.

She didn't ask him anything else as they hopped in the waiting limo and Leo directed the driver to an address on Waverly Place.

Leo pulled out his cell phone and punched the screen. "Hey, Gino, it's me. I'm on my way." He listened for a minute and almost smiled at whatever he heard. "Okay. I'll try to come up when I get in. Give her a hug for me until then." He nodded. "Yeah. Ciao." He disconnected the call and leaned his head against the seat rest.

She'd never seen him this distraught. Not even when he'd lost everything. Sure he'd been beaten down, but he'd bounced back. But this... This scared her. "Who's Gino?" Maybe trying to take his mind off Megan for a few minutes might help.

"Gino is an old friend of mine from the neighborhood. He and his family were one of the first people I met when I moved to New York."

She'd just assumed he was from Los Angeles. "Where are you from originally?"

"I was born in Iowa. My mom moved to Los Angeles when I was small and I grew up in the valley. After high school, I got a bit part in a small movie and from that I got an agent. I booked another film that shot in New York. Then my mom died and I was in charge of Megan. Initially I kept Megan on the West Coast, but I didn't like the facilities. I found The Marion Institute and settled her there while I worked."

"There's no way you could afford that place when you were just starting out," Kim said, amazed at the responsibility he'd had to take on at such a young age.

"First of all, it didn't cost as much then. And second, I never stopped working. I took every job my agent could get me. The jobs got bigger and better and the next thing you know, I didn't have to audition anymore because producers were offering me roles."

"What was that like?" she asked, facing him. They'd never talked about his life in show business. It was a question Kim thought she didn't care about, but now she found herself wanting to know everything about him.

He grinned and the smile changed his face. He became the world famous actor in the blink of an eye. "I'll never forget the first time I got offered a role. I'd just come off a small part in a Scorsese film and there was pretty good buzz coming from it. The phone rang and Audrey, my agent said, 'You're not going to believe this.' I was thinking that someone was stiffing me on a paycheck, but that wasn't the case. She'd just got off the phone with Ari Nepali, who wanted me for his next film." Leo shook his head. "Ari-fucking-Nepali wanted me. I couldn't believe it. He'd called from London, but he was on his way to New York so we met at Carnegie Deli. We talked about the role and just like that, I have my first job that I didn't audition for. I never looked back."

"And then you won an Oscar." Kim felt a sudden bolt of pride for the man next to her. He'd worked hard to get where he was.

"Don't forget the Emmy." If she hadn't known him she would've thought he was conceited, but having gone through so much with the man, she knew he only brought it up to laugh at himself. He'd used his resume to keep people at a distance, to create a sort of invisible barrier because of all the things he'd accomplished. It kept him separate, which kept the world at bay, which was what he wanted.

"I would never forget the Emmy." She liked that she got him smiling again. "Ari took you with him to a lot of films."

Leo nodded. "He did. *Dangerous Race* for one."

"Yes. Can't forget *Dangerous Race*. Just think, we might've met back then if you'd been there the day I visited."

"I'm glad I wasn't. I don't think I was in a good place to meet you then. I think we met when we were supposed to."

"Do you mean to tell me that you think God has a plan?"

He laughed at that and sobered just as quickly. "If God has a plan, then he's laughing his ass off right now. Especially since I have no clue what the hell is going to happen in my immediate future. I've got so many balls in the air that I'm ready for them to start coming down on my head any second."

"How about I try to help you keep some of them in the air?"

The heat in his eyes nearly scorched her and just like that she was hot for him. "You already are." The low timbre of his voice struck another chord. He took her hand and stroked his thumb over her knuckles. The foreign feeling of intimacy bowled her over. His touch meant much more than he probably intended. It was one of the things she should avoid and yet she kept falling back into the same Leo trap.

From her bag, a muffled *meow* caught their attention.

Kim eased Stella out of the bag and the cat stretched her paws on the limo floor before jumping into Leo's lap for a rub.

"How you doin', girl?" Leo brought her up to his face and nuzzled her soft fur.

Stella purred in response. It wasn't long before she sacked out in Leo's lap for another snooze. Kim never would've believed that a cat could tame the mighty Leo Frost. She held back the smile. She'd started to feel guilty for bringing Stella with them, but now she was glad she'd insisted on it. Leo needed the company.

The limo pulled up to an apartment building and Leo took Kim's hand and started the climb up three flights of stairs.

"A walk up?" she asked.

"What gave it away? The stairs?" He lifted an amused eyebrow.

"That and the lack of elevator." She smiled at his teasing. There was something different about him. Something she couldn't put a finger on.

When he got to the third floor, he walked to the last apartment down the hallway, lifted the mat and opened the door with the key he found. The apartment surprised her. It was much bigger than she anticipated with large windows that looked out over the street. The studio apartment had a small kitchen, bathroom and double bed in a room that was probably half the size of Leo's old den in his Beverly Hills house. Decorated in rich browns and tan walls, the place seemed like the ultimate bachelor pad.

"So this place was yours?" she asked.

"Yep."

"And your friend Gino lives here now?"

"Yep."

"It's nice of him to let you stay here on such short notice."

"His mom lives upstairs. She can't walk the stairs anymore so

Gino has to be close by. It worked out." Leo stood at the window and shoved his hands in his pockets. He had to be thinking about Megan.

Kim set her bag on the old leather recliner in the corner of the room and scooped Stella into her arms. Then she poured the kitty litter in the shallow pan and set it down with Stella on top. Stella didn't hesitate to do her business then check the place out. Leo hadn't said anything in the car and Kim hadn't pushed him, but bottling it up wouldn't do him any favors. "Do you want to talk about it?" she asked, "Did the doctor think Megan would recover all right?"

"He's not sure." He rubbed a hand over the back of his neck. "They have her under sedation. At least they're not dealing with a broken bone, but they're worried about more seizures. And with any type of fall, she risks more injury."

"Seems like she's in good hands. I liked the nurses." Megan probably got great care being the little sister of one of the world's most famous movie stars.

"Yeah. They were nice." Leo scrubbed a hand over his head.

"Did you sleep at all on the plane?" She'd managed to get a few minutes so maybe he had.

"A little," he said.

Still, she saw it in his eyes. He was wiped out. She took his hand and led him to the bed. "Here, lie down. When you wake up, we can grab a bite to eat and go back to Megan. I'd like to meet her if you don't mind. Now that we can leave Stella here, I can go in her room."

Leo's mesmerizing blue eyes captivated her. "Thanks for coming with me. I really appreciate it."

"You're welcome. I'm glad I could be here." But the truth was she always wanted to be there for him. Not just for this trip, but for a lifetime.

He patted the spot next to him. "C'mon. Lay down with me."

That would be suicide. "I need to run out and get a few things for me and Stella. I won't be gone long." She made her escape, wondering how she'd keep her distance from the man who tempted her like none other ever had.

Chapter Twenty

Leo walked into Megan's room for the second time that day and not much had changed. Machines still hummed and the sick sterile smell permeated his senses. His stomach still knotted in the worst way and his guilt meter soared off the charts. Realistically, there was nothing he could've done to change what happened. A nurse had been helping Megan to the bathroom when the seizure began. The nurse had lost her footing trying to get Megan back to the bed and they'd both fallen hard. Megan hadn't been the only one injured. The nurse had suffered a broken arm. Leo didn't blame anyone. He just hated what his sister had to endure. Though her face was swollen, she hadn't fractured anything. Good news in and of itself, but still...this poor kid couldn't catch a break and it killed Leo.

Pulling up a chair, he sat next to Megan's bed and took her small hand. She didn't look anything like a nineteen-year-old girl should. She looked more like twelve, her body small and her features distorted from multiple cleft palate surgeries and the fall from last night's seizure. The worst effects of Downs were bad enough, but to be born with a cleft palate on top of it seemed the like cruelest punishment to a child.

His hand dwarfed her smaller one and he noticed scratches he hadn't seen earlier.

"Leo?" Megan squeezed his hand and he glanced up to see her eyes barely open. She tried to smile. "Leo!" Her excitement gave him much needed hope. "Hi." Her low-pitched voice was like a present on Christmas morning. Then she looked around the room and blinked. "Where am I?" Her words were slow and precise as always. The fact that her speech was consistent with her norm gave him a little hope.

He rubbed her chilly hand. "You're in the hospital. You fell down and hit your head, so the nurses brought you here to see a doctor."

"You fell too," she said, pointing to his face. She looked at the room again. "I want to go home now." She said each word carefully since she had trouble speaking after her last surgery. Leo wasn't even sure if she realized what she'd had to endure or why.

"I know you do, Megs, but you fell and the doctors want to make sure you're okay on the inside before they send you home. So they're doing some tests, okay?"

"I don't like doctors." She stuck out her bottom lip. A sure sign that tears were on the way. "My face hurts."

"I know, honey. I'll make sure we get something to take away that pain." He squeezed her hand and she blinked up at him.

"I missed you," she said. "You have to see the new room at home. I can draw and paint all day and they let me. It's so fun."

Waiting for her to finish long sentences was always an exercise in patience. "That's great. I can't wait to see it." He'd seen the construction of the art center during his last visit to The Marion six months ago. Six months ago, before his life had gone to hell.

"What's your next movie?" she asked, the sparkle in her good eye giving him hope that she might make it out of the hospital sooner rather than later. She even tried to smile and one side of her mouth lifted. Megan always loved listening about his movies, but she never brought them up again. He wondered if she even remembered them.

"I just finished one that I wrote. I hope it'll be out soon."

"Can I see it?" She hadn't seen most of his films because of the content. She might be physically nineteen, but her mental capacity was more like a second grader. Nevertheless, she always asked and it always made him proud.

Leo shook his head. "I don't think you'll like this one. It's boring." He knew the sure fire way to dissuade her from the film. "It has goats and chickens in it."

"Ew!" She squinted the eye that wasn't swollen shut. For Megan's tenth birthday, Leo had paid for a mobile petting zoo to visit The Marion. He'd thought the whole place would enjoy the experience and most people had. But a goat had nipped Megan and when she'd jumped back in surprise, she'd tripped over a chicken that had immediately started clucking at her. Talk about a birthday party backfiring. "Why would you do that?" she asked, horror etched across her battered face. She may forget about his movies, but she never forgot about that incident.

He shrugged. "It sounded like a good idea when I wrote it." He shook his head and she smiled.

"It's okay. I'll just watch *Going Bananas* again. That's funny."

He'd voiced an orangutan in an animated movie years ago and Megan must have seen it hundreds of times. "I can't believe that DVD still works."

"Oh, Leo." Megan actually giggled and Leo released a worried breath before she yawned. "I'm tired."

"That's okay. Go to sleep." He checked his watch and calculated the time. "I'll come back tomorrow. I brought a friend with me this trip and she's looking forward to meeting you."

"Okay. I like making friends."

"Yeah. Me too." He stood over her, kissed her forehead, every protective instinct firing to life. "Get some sleep. I'll be back." He squeezed her hand as she closed her eyes and in the next minute she was asleep.

Leo sat back in the chair and sighed. Thank God she seemed to be okay. Bruised and battered, yes, but she was still the same sweet girl she'd always been. He missed the hug he would've received if she hadn't been flat on her back in a neck brace.

She looked so small and still in the big hospital bed. So innocent.

He pushed back the guilt at keeping Megan at The Institute. Deep down he knew it was the best place for her. They specialized in people with serious physical disabilities and Megan, with her constant seizures, needed the attention they gave her.

How could he even consider bringing someone into the world who might suffer the same fate as his sister?

Maybe once Kim met Megan, she'd understand his point of view. Although, knowing Kim, probably not. She'd made up her mind.

With a last glance at Megan, Leo left her room. He spotted

the thick dark frames and thinning hair of her doctor at the nurse's station.

"Dr. Noori, do you have a minute?"

"Mr. Frost," he said, glancing up from his paperwork. "Good to see you." Leo had read up on the doctor through the hospital website. Originally from Egypt, he'd gone to Harvard Medical School, but even after twenty-five years in the U.S., he still carried a hint of an accent. "I'd like to keep Megan one more night for observation before we let her go. We adjusted her seizure medication and I want to make sure she gets through the night without incident before we discharge her."

Leo liked that plan. If he got her back in The Institute tomorrow, he could potentially be on a plane and back to L.A. the day after tomorrow. "Sounds good. I'll be back in the morning so I can take her to The Marion myself." Megan loved limo rides. He'd have to call for one. Didn't matter that he couldn't afford it. All in all, the trip could've been much worse. He was just thankful that Megan was going to be okay.

He'd just gotten out of the elevator and walked into the lobby when some asshole started snapping pictures of him. Someone at the hospital must have tipped him off. Social media was a bitch. Like a lot of celebrities, he'd given up any chance of privacy when in public. As long as Megan's life stayed private, he didn't care.

But when he stepped outside into the afternoon sun and got bombarded with microphones and camera flashes, his surprise couldn't have been more genuine. One or two pictures from people in the hospital, he understood, but this? This was too massive to be anything but an ambush. He slapped on his sunglasses.

"Leo, why didn't you tell the world about your sister before now?"

"Leo, do you plan to sue The Marion Institute?"

"Mr. Frost, what are you hiding?"

"Is it true you're going to be a father?"

The questions hit one on top of the other as people jockeyed for position. The swell of anger that rose in his chest nearly drowned him. Rage like he hadn't experienced in a lot of years made his vision glaze over. The darkness swimming his gut sickened him.

Someone grabbed his arm and yanked him sideways. "No

comment. Mr. Frost has no comment." Kim dragged him toward a waiting taxi as photographers continued to snap pictures and reporters followed with outstretched microphones.

"Who are you?" Someone called over the crowd noise, pointing a microphone toward Kim.

His savior, but he didn't say it out loud, and Kim said absolutely nothing until they got in the car.

"Hit it!" she ordered the driver and he stepped on the gas, happy to oblige. "You okay?" It was the in-charge accountant asking, the woman who solved problems, but Leo couldn't even look her in the eye.

He punched the seat in front of him and scared the hell out of the driver. "No." He was pissed. The fake lemon smell of car freshener invaded his nostrils. He looked behind them to the disappearing crowd of reporters. "I want to know how they found out about Megan." For fifteen years, The Institute had managed to keep his secret. It wasn't as if Megan hadn't been hospitalized before. Although she'd only been to private facilities for her surgery. Shit, he'd gotten used to everyone keeping her under wraps, so he hadn't been too worried about her being admitted to a large hospital. If this was the best place to make sure she didn't have a more serious injury, then so be it. But they should've respected Megan's—and his—privacy. Now her picture would eventually be splashed in all the rag magazines and he could say good-bye to life as he knew it. Again. "And how'd they know I'm going to be a father?"

"Does it matter how they found out?" Kim asked softly. "The point is they know about Megan and you need to figure out what you want to do about it. We'll focus on the Megan issue and maybe that will throw them off the father track."

As usual, the woman was right. Leo wiped a hand over his face. "Shit," he hissed. Everything he'd worked for flushed down the crapper.

As the taxi motored through the city, Kim's heart tumbled over at the agony in Leo's eyes. He'd actually been pretty lucky that no one had found out about Megan before this. That was a hell of a secret to keep under wraps for so many years. Just because he had his reasons didn't mean the press and outside world wouldn't crucify him for hiding her. They were sure to come up with vile excuses, which was probably one of the reasons Leo had kept her under wraps.

"I'm sorry I didn't get here sooner or I could've warned you about the press and you could've dodged them by going out the back way."

"Doesn't fucking matter. They still found out about her and they won't quit. You can always tell when it's a slow news day." Leo stared out the window for a minute, then pulled his phone out and punched the screen a couple of times before putting the phone to his ear. "I need to speak with Howard Kaminsky. This is Leo Frost."

Kim couldn't put a face to the name and with all the rooting around in Leo's business two months ago, she would've remembered. Of course, he kept Megan and The Institute a very well-kept secret, so it was no wonder this name didn't ring a bell. "Who's Howard Kaminsky?" she asked.

"The director at The Marion. He's only been there a few years. He didn't strike me as a man with iron control over his operation. This just proves it."

Turning toward Leo, Kim tapped his thigh. "C'mon, be fair. That might not be true. I mean a nurse broke her arm trying to protect Megan from the fall. That has to count for something. Someone at the hospital could've leaked the news."

He gave her the stink eye and opened his mouth, but a voice sounded from the other end of the line. Kim only heard Leo's end of the conversation.

"You can tell me how Megan's identity slipped out." He listened and let out a harsh breath. "Fine. I'll see you tomorrow and I expect answers." Disconnecting without another word, Leo leaned his head back on the seat and dropped a very eloquent f-bomb.

She hated to see him this hurt. It twisted her insides into knots. "Maybe we should work on damage control." Kim searched her bag for her phone. "Do you want me to call your publicist? Your team should know what's going on."

Leo tossed her the phone and she caught it one-handed. She knew from diving into his finances who worked for him, so she called Sara Finley—his publicist—and gave her the low-down. As Kim suspected, Sara got right to work.

Kim handed Leo his phone back. "How's Megan? Did she wake up yet?"

"Yeah. She woke up. She was better than I thought she'd be. Talking...even laughing. She surprised me. She wants to go home. Back to The Marion. They built a new art building and from the sounds of it she just about lives there now."

"So what did she do when she saw you? Was she excited?"

Leo grinned for the first time. "Yeah. She was glad to see me. Her eyes got wide—well, her good eye—and she smiled. That girl deserves a medal for everything she's gone through. And she's still so happy. She could be the poster child for enjoying the little things."

"I guess we all should take a lesson on that," Kim murmured. They watched the tall buildings of the city whiz by. People bustled on the crowded streets. She wished Leo would try and see the positive side of things, but he'd been dealing with the hard decisions for so long, it seemed as if he didn't know how.

Leo glanced her way. "The doctor said he'll release her tomorrow. He just wants her one more night for observation." He picked up his phone from his lap.

"That's good. I didn't expect her to be released so soon."

"I didn't either. But the faster she can get out of that hospital, the happier she'll be. Don't let me forget, I need to call for a limo. I want her to go back in style. She gets so excited for limo rides. I figure she deserves it."

"I'll arrange it."

"You don't need to arrange it. I can do it. You're not my god damn secretary."

Wow. Nothing had upset him like this before. It was a side to him she'd never seen. "I know," she said calmly. "I was just trying to lighten your load a bit." Kim sat forward. She knew better than to let Leo's bad mood trickle down to her, but it was hard not to. So before she got mad, too, she opted to keep her mouth shut.

A long silence settled between them. The purr of the taxi's motor hummed around them. Leo ran a hand down his face and sighed. "I'm sorry," he said. He took her hand and linked their fingers. "I just..." His voice cracked and Kim looked over, shocked to see his eyes wet with emotion. "I didn't expect this today. The last thing I want to do is take it out on you. I..." He swallowed, shook his head.

"You what?" she asked softly. He'd never been this emotional in front of her before either. Pissed, angry, upset, yes, but this raw emotion scared her. And he opened her heart to him even more.

"I'm really glad you're here." A mountain of contrition laced his words. "You keep saving my ass and all I do in return is shit on you."

She didn't imagine he'd ever said that to anyone. "I wouldn't say that."

"No?" He met her gaze and the blue in his eyes melted her battered defenses even further. "Then what would you say?"

He made it so hard to fight the attraction between them. It was easier when he was an asshole. But when the flesh and blood man needed her, she couldn't ever seem to say no. "I'd say there's always some excitement when I'm around you. It's not so bad." And maybe since they were being honest, she needed to confess. "You're not so bad either."

He rubbed his thumb across her hand, the gentle caress and sweet reminder of how much his touch affected her. "You know, I'd planned to take you out for a nice dinner tonight, but after this," he gestured behind them. "I'm afraid of having it ruined with cameras and microphones."

"To be honest, I'm not really up for going out." She hadn't felt great after the plane ride, but she chalked it up to air-sickness and pregnancy. Then she'd had to do some shopping for necessities for her and Stella, and that took the whole afternoon while Leo visited with Megan. Fortunately, the nausea had passed, although the overpowering smell of the car threatened to bring back her queasy stomach. Food would probably do her good. She was glad she'd grabbed some pickles earlier. "What if we just bring in something easy? I can run down to the corner pizza joint and grab us a deep dish."

"Deep dish?" He smiled and stayed quiet for a minute as he watched her. "You remember what happened the last time we had pizza?"

She did. Very clearly. They ended up on his cabana sofa. And she got pregnant. She nodded, remembering the first time they'd made love on his back patio with the stars out and moon shining bright. They'd both been drinking, but she remembered every second of his mouth on hers. She remembered every touch, every kiss. A wave of chills prickled her skin as she nodded. "I remember very well."

Leo nodded too, his blue eyes full of heat and hope. "Let's get pizza."

Chapter Twenty-One

Kim insisted on running to the corner and picking up the pizza Leo had ordered. She slipped into form-fitting yoga pants, sharp pink sneakers and a pink hoodie. He loved when she dressed in workout clothes, because he usually only saw her dressed to kill in fuck-me pumps and high class dresses or black skirts. Not that he had a problem visualizing lifting her skirt and taking her over a desk or against a wall or on a counter. Yeah, he liked that fantasy too. But more often than not with them, it was when she dressed down that she let go with him.

So maybe the pizza innuendo in the taxi over here really meant they might have sex for dessert, but he wouldn't bank on it. He never knew with Kim, which was one of the reasons she kept him on his toes.

He heard her moving down the hallway and a reluctant smile lifted his lips. He liked that she worried about him. To the best of his knowledge, she was only one of a handful who did. Of course most everyone else who worried about him had their bank accounts in mind. He was a commodity after all, one that was about to lose a lot of stock when the news of his secret hit the airwaves.

Leo opened the door as Kim approached. She juggled their pizza and a bag from the corner market as well.

"What'd you get?" he asked, taking the box from her hand and motioning her in the apartment. He did like watching her ass in those yoga pants.

"Just a little something for dessert," she said as she kept moving to the kitchen. "It's a surprise."

Honestly, he was about done with surprises for one day, and

her attempt to cheer him up had him feeling way more vulnerable than he wanted.

The smell of pizza made his mouth water as he closed the door and followed Kim into the kitchen. He lifted the box top to a pizza masterpiece. One deep dish with everything on it. He shoved aside the shot of guilt that he'd fired his trainer Hans. Although, really, it was plain un-American to not eat pizza.

"You're thinking about Hans again, aren't you?" Kim lifted a delicate eyebrow.

Yeah, she knew him better than anybody and that hollow ache in his chest got wider, because she didn't want him. "How'd you know?" Leo took a slice of pizza and set it on the plate she offered.

"You're looking at that pizza like you'll get in trouble if you have a bite. You're allowed to eat like crap every once in a while. We'll just work it off later."

He watched her, but she didn't meet his gaze. Did she mean what he hoped she meant? Hell, why did he torture himself like this? He slapped pizza on another plate as she poured them water.

They converged on the leather sofa in front of the flat screen. Gino had updated the place in the fifteen years since Leo bought it. He wondered how he was going to break that news to Kim. She'd thought he'd sold all his property—which he had, with the exception of this place. It was bought and paid for and he saw no reason to unload it. Selling his two million dollar apartment near Central Park had helped him out of his financial pit and gotten him clear of a big mortgage. This place wouldn't get nearly as much. Besides, with Megan at The Institute, he needed a place to stay whenever he came to town. Gino lived here the majority of the time and took care of the place for almost no rent with the agreement that he had to vacate whenever Leo came to town. In those instances, Gino just went up another flight of stairs to his mother's place and his old bedroom. A win-win for everyone involved. Leo had a live-in taking care of his place and Gino had a place to escape his mother.

"Mmm, this is good," Kim said after swallowing her first bite.

Leo dug in to his piece and closed his eyes as the hot cheesy heaven melted in his mouth. He inhaled that slice and one more as Kim chowed down next to him. The last time he'd had pizza had been with Kim. They'd had scorching hot sex for dessert that night. Hot enough to make a baby.

Nothing like that reminder to kill a promising mood.

Leo put his pizza down. He turned on the TV because the silence invited discussion and he wasn't in the mood to talk about their problem. He flipped through some channels until something stopped him cold. A teaser about him and a *secret* with footage from the hospital.

Kim looked at the screen and back to him. She reached for the remote. "Why don't we—"

Leo yanked it out of her reach with a glare. They waited five of the longest minutes of his life before the celebrity trash program returned with the story. They had a few of the facts right. Megan's age and how many years she'd lived at The Institute. Then came the speculation as to why she'd been there so long. Leo was hiding her. Leo was ashamed of her. Leo was embarrassed by her.

All the shit he'd been afraid would happen was happening before his eyes. The pizza turned in his stomach and Leo thought it might come up. He'd never been so emotionally sick that it affected him physically.

"It's not true, you know," Kim said softly. She moved to sit next to him. "They don't know her condition. They don't know how hard you've worked to make sure she can stay in a facility that can take care of her."

"What if they're right?" Leo leaned forward and put his head in his hands. "What if I'm ashamed and embarrassed by her?"

"And what if you're just trying to make sure she has the best care possible round the clock? That's not a bad thing, Leo." She rubbed his thigh and her warmth cut through his jeans. "You told me she loves the place. She's not unhappy there. She doesn't beg to be with you or go anywhere else."

"Because it's almost all she's ever known. I don't even think she remembers our mom or going into the damn place."

"And that's okay." Kim set her arm around his shoulder. "She's thriving there. You told me that yourself. Her speech is better than it's ever been, she's happy."

"Yeah, except she fell and landed in the hospital. What does that say about the place?"

"It says that Megan's seizures are bad enough to even throw the professionals a curve ball." She sighed. "Leo, a registered nurse broke her arm trying to save Megan when she fell. Who's to say that someone else might not have tried so hard? Megan might have had a seizure years ago that could've killed her if she'd fallen and landed wrong. Don't let these assholes drag you down because they don't know the story." She waited, but he didn't know how to respond. "Leo?"

She didn't say anything he didn't already know, but the fact that she said it at all, the fact that she was picking up the pieces of his broken heart meant more to Leo than anything she could ever do.

He met her gaze, saw the compassion, the truth, and he didn't give a shit whether what he was about to do was wrong or right. He didn't care if she meant for it to happen or not, but Leo leaned in and kissed her. He probably should've gone slow, probably should have wooed her with soft, addicting kisses, but instead he went in for the whole combination plate with his mouth open over hers.

Her gasp gave him the room he needed to thread her lips and taste her, taste the pizza they shared and the woman he craved. She brought this on herself. She cared too damn much for his feelings and he didn't deserve it. Didn't deserve her.

She didn't slow him down, didn't stop him. She took his kiss and gave back with her heart and soul. She matched his need with pure fire, pure passion. At any other time she would've been holding him off, trying to keep her distance, but now, when he needed her most, she was there.

This kiss didn't invite second thoughts, it demanded action and participation.

And Kim complied.

Leo's need washed over Kim like a tidal wave and she nearly drowned in it. He kissed her with a desperation that made her ache. As disoriented as he'd been when he'd lost all his money, his despair hadn't been this palpable.

Keeping Megan safe had been his whole purpose and now that she was exposed, so was he.

Kim wanted nothing more than to ease his pain. Sure, it was a trip down a one-way street she'd been on before and yes, she was bound to get hurt, because as much as she tried to fight her attraction and respect for this man, she couldn't do it anymore.

Seeing him struggle after the financial mess, then watching him battle back to finish his film had made her realize he was a better man than he gave himself credit for. But after watching how quickly he got to Megan's side after her seizure, seeing how her health and privacy really mattered to him, she slid off that slippery slope.

She was hopeless.

And hopelessly in love with him.

Which probably accounted for the reason that she jumped on board so quickly when he pounced. She wanted to do something to ease the pain, but it made her sick inside to go two steps forward and four more backward. Why did she constantly put herself in these situations?

"Leo." Kim leaned back and stopped him before he went in for another kiss.

He opened his mouth to say something, but her phone rang from the counter. It was the second time she'd been saved by the bell. She welcomed the distraction, moved off the couch and picked up her mobile. Los Angeles Police Department flashed on her caller ID.

"It's the police in L.A.," she said, accepting the call. "Hello, this is Kim. Can I help you?"

"Hello, Ms. Jacobs. This is Detective Browning at the LAPD. Sorry I wasn't able to finish our conversation yesterday. I was wondering if you could come by the station."

"Did you find something?" she asked.

"I'd rather talk about it in person, if you don't mind."

He wouldn't be calling her again and asking her to talk if he hadn't found something. "I wish I could, but at the moment, I'm in New York. I'd really like to know what you've found."

"Normally, I wouldn't discuss this over the phone, but since you're out of town and I think this is information you should know, we should probably finish the conversation we started yesterday. We checked out your car and it looks as if it had been tampered with."

Kim's heart started pumping double time as she glanced at Leo. "Tampered with? How?" Leo jumped off the sofa in a second and came by her side. She leaned the phone toward him so he could listen in.

"It looks as if someone deliberately sabotaged the hose to the power steering. A small section of the hose seemed to be sliced, but not all the way through. Then someone shaved it and punched in tiny holes. Whoever it was wanted this to look like average wear and tear, but the car is too new to have this kind of issue. Between that and the incident in the canyon, I think you may be in danger."

But Leo had also been hurt. "What about the burr under the saddle? Do you think that's connected in any way?" Kim asked.

"It's certainly suspicious. Are you sure there wasn't anyone around who previously knew you?" he asked.

"Just my cousin, but he's been ruled out."

Leo's eyes widened. "Just because he has an alibi for the car accident and the shooting doesn't absolve him of the Smokey incident," he said. "Maybe he hired someone to tamper with your car and shoot at us."

"Detective Browning, hold on a second. I'll be right with you." Kim covered the mouthpiece. "What? So now you think my cousin has criminal contacts and knows how to hire a hitman? That's crazy."

"Don't you remember, I said you could ride Smokey when we finished the shot. We broke down the tracks. Anyone not under that screen at video village might've thought we were done with Smokey and planted that cactus for your benefit."

"By anyone, you mean Wilson."

"Ms. Jacobs?" Detective Browning said. "I'm going to take another look into your cousin's alibi."

"You think he's lying?" Kim couldn't believe it.

"Is he with you in New York," the detective asked.

"No, he stayed in Los Angeles. He was hanging around in case I needed help or ran into trouble since I don't have my ID."

"Well, that's either very noble or very suspicious. My partner and I will talk to him again. Also, we checked out Carl Wyncott, but there's nothing that leads us to believe he's behind this. Please call me back when you return to town or if you think of something that might help us."

"Yes, of course. Thanks for the information." Kim disconnected the call and sat on the nearby stool.

Leo took her phone from her hands and set it aside. "It's possible that someone messed with the car before you ever got in it. Meaning they didn't know who was going to be driving it."

"But what's the point of that? Unless they hoped the fluid leaked sooner. Maybe the police should be asking who rented that car before me."

Leo ran a hand over his head, ruffling thick dark hair. "I don't know." He sounded as frustrated as she felt and paced next to her. The bullets in the canyon didn't feel like anything accidental, and only a few people had heard Leo say she could ride Smokey after they got the shot, but she couldn't say for sure if Wilson was one of them. None of it made much sense.

"All this talk about your cousin has me wondering if maybe *he* made the phone call to the paparazzi and told them about your pregnancy. They pay big money for information like that."

"But they didn't mention me. They just asked if you were going to be a father. Maybe they were pulling that out of thin air, trying to shock you or something."

"Doubtful," Leo said. "Someone tipped them off and the list of people who know you're pregnant is very short."

"You really don't like my cousin, do you?" she asked.

"I just don't trust him, that's all. Not after what you've told me. I don't think you should trust him either." Behind her, Leo set his warm palms on her shoulders, gently squeezing all the tension locked in her muscles. "How about, for right now, I make you forget all of this for a few hours?" When she turned around he saw the misery in her eyes. "I guess that answers my question." He sounded so forlorn she almost reconsidered, but that sick feeling in her stomach wasn't just her emotions battling it out, she really didn't feel that great.

"I can't." She swiveled in the stool and stroked a finger down his cheek. "I'm sorry. I've got so much running in my head and I just can't do this knowing…knowing it's a dead end. I like you. A lot." More than a lot, but what was the point of telling him otherwise. "But we have fundamental differences that I can't get past. And I don't think you can either." He moved back, the desolation in his eyes nearly crippling her. "To be really honest, I'm not feeling that great either. I don't know if it was the plane trip, the shopping, the pizza or this latest news about the car, but my stomach is not happy."

Concern took over in Leo's eyes as he stood up. "Why didn't you tell me?" He pulled her off the stool and walked her across the room to the bed. "Here, lie down." He pulled the blanket back. "I'll get you some ginger ale. I know Gino keeps it stocked. It's half of his favorite drink." When she lifted questioning brows, he continued, "Seven and Ginger."

"Ah. Cousin to your favorite Seven and Seven."

"Yep. You remembered," he said over his shoulder as he went to the fridge.

"How could I forget?" How many cocktails had they shared when they first met? Too many. Kim ran her hand along the crazy soft sheets. It was too easy to imagine making love to Leo in this bed. She watched as he poured her a glass of ginger ale and brought it back. The concern in his eyes only made it harder to keep an emotional distance.

Kim sipped her drink and leaned against the pillows. "Thanks. And don't look so worried. I'm fine. It's like backward morning sickness because I get nauseous in the evening. Not the first time it's happened, but I've finally put two and two together."

Stella mewled from the floor, her yellow eyes piercing the dim room.

Leo picked her up and set her next to Kim. "Here, Stella will cure you. She specializes in cute."

Actually, Leo did too, but Kim didn't dare tell him.

"Anything else I can get you?" He sat at her side, the bed depressing with his weight. The crease in his forehead deepened with the question.

Kim ignored the warm fuzzies he sparked. She categorically ignored his sweet blue eyes and broad shoulders. She refused to think about the mouth-watering sex she was missing at this very moment. "Ginger ale and cat. I think I'm good."

Leo nodded. "It's no big deal if you're not up for meeting Megan tomorrow. She won't know the difference."

Maybe he didn't want her to meet Megan. She hadn't considered that. "I'll be fine. I'm just tired. I didn't sleep much on the plane either."

"Why didn't you say so? You should've crashed with me this afternoon."

"I had too much to do. I needed some clothes and essentials.

So did Stella. And I wasn't feeling it this afternoon. It just hit me in the last hour or so." Even as she said the words, a fresh wave of nausea rolled through her. Not fun.

"You've got to take care of yourself, you know."

"I know." Her body was speaking a new language and she was doing her best to make sense of it. "I'll be good as new tomorrow morning." She closed her eyes with Leo's hand in hers and that was the last thing she remembered.

Chapter Twenty-Two

Leo sat next to Kim for a long time before he finally crashed on the sofa. He didn't feel right taking the space next to her on the bed. Not when she'd put the brakes on what had surely been a runaway train. Granted, she hadn't felt well, but he didn't want to push her or make her uncomfortable. Sure, he wanted her almost more than he wanted to breathe, but even more than that he respected her. When the hell had that ever happened? Besides, he knew damn well if he spent horizontal time next to her, he wouldn't have the discipline to keep his paws off her. She was too much of a temptation.

He forced himself to stop fantasizing about Kim, and focused on Megan. Was The Institute still the best place for her? Had it gone downhill and he hadn't noticed because he hadn't visited in so many months? Or was Kim right and it was simply the bad timing of a seizure that made this incident so bad? Kim's words kept replaying in his head. Maybe The Institute was the best place. Maybe Megan would've been hurt worse with a seizure somewhere else where people weren't as trained as the employees there.

Kim was probably right. She'd been right with just about everything else so far.

Leo tossed and turned on the sofa. The only good thing about the night was hearing Kim's steady breathing as she slept. Luckily, she woke up feeling fine and relief chugged through Leo like spring water. She threw on a casual pale green dress that hugged her hips and made her eyes pop. No remnants of her nausea existed.

They arrived at the hospital when visiting hours started. Leo wanted Megan's doctor to sign her release papers ASAP so he could get her back to familiar and comfortable surroundings.

Kim suggested they enter through the front door, but hire a second limo to wait for them at the E.R. entrance in the back. That kept the first limo as a decoy for the paparazzi staked out front.

As a treat for Megan, they decided to bring Stella along for the ride. Kim had played hard with her in the morning so they kept her in the limo with the driver to nap when they went inside the hospital.

Leo didn't expect to find Megan sitting up in the bedside chair and already dressed. His mood lifted exponentially. "Hey, good morning." He gave her a gentle hug, afraid he'd do extra damage to her small battered frame.

Her eyes lit up. "Leo!" She wrapped her arms around his neck and kissed his cheek. "I get to go home today!" Her contagious smile let a little more sunshine into his heart.

"I know. I came to take you."

"Who's that?" Megan pointed to Kim, her smile still in intact. She loved people and especially loved meeting new people. Her innocence and total acceptance of everyone shone in her bright eyes. She took in every inch of Kim's beauty.

"I'm Kim." Kim extended her hand and Megan shook it. Leo shoved back his emotion. He shouldn't care about this meeting except that these two females were the most important things in his life.

Megan looked from Kim to him and back to Kim before an even wider smile broke out across her face. "Leo has a girlfriend."

"Oh, uh…" Kim hesitated and glanced his way.

No reason to make her more uncomfortable than she already was. In a perfect world, his sister might've been right on target. "She's a really good friend, Megan. She's been helping me figure some things out lately."

"But you guys like each other too." Her smile beamed wide.

He more than liked Kim, but he didn't know if he could give her what she wanted. Plus she seemed pretty damn sure it wasn't him. Leo was saved from answering when Dr. Noori entered the room with a chart in his hand and a nurse in green scrubs behind him. Though Megan didn't have to wear the neck brace, the doctor suggested she take it easy for a few days. She still had some serious bruising on her face.

It took some time to get Megan in a wheelchair and into the elevator. Leo kept glancing around, waiting for the boogey man to pop out and start snapping pictures. Getting her into the limo stretched every nerve taut, since she moved so slowly, and Kim took the opportunity to let Stella do her kitty business in the small grassy area along the building. Ultimately, Kim's idea worked and they got away clean.

Megan's excitement over the limo doused every one of Leo's worries as they headed back to The Marion. She *oohed* and *aahed* upon meeting Stella and the two became instant pals. She didn't seem the slightest bit aware of the nasty bruising on her face or the soreness that must accompany it.

"What happened to her? She got hurt like me?" Megan asked.

"Kind of," Leo said, dodging the real story. No need to tell Megan about the coyote attack. "She went to the hospital just like you did and she got some stitches in her side."

Stella purred in Megan's lap all the way back to The Marion.

Love at first sight.

Happy to be back home, Megan hugged the employees they passed as they walked to her room. Leo had sometimes wondered if they gave her attention because of his fame, but their genuine happiness at seeing Megan changed his mind. She waved to all the residents in the hall as she went by and the smile on her face said she was thrilled to be home.

Leo had made sure she had all the comforts of a regular bedroom. The only sign that marked her extra care was the hospital bed with guardrails in case Megan had a seizure in the middle of the night. She had round-the-clock care, and the nurses treated her like family. Leo made sure the whole staff understood his appreciation and everyone got gifts for birthdays and holidays. He still had to figure out how to manage this year, but he was determined to make it happen despite his catastrophic financial loss.

"I like your room, Megan," Kim said, surveying the space. She kept a hand in her bag, no doubt petting a hidden Stella. Baby blue paint covered the walls and stuffed animals lined the top of a four-foot-high circular bookcase filled with books and toys. His mom had sewn the old fashioned quilt on her bed.

Some of Megan's artwork was prominently displayed next to a few old pictures from home. Leo's favorite was a shot of his mom holding Megan and him smiling at something she said. It had been taken a few months before she died. He'd been a twenty-two-year-old kid without a clue how his life was about to change. He looked around the room to see if she needed anything and buried the ache in his chest.

"Come see the art house." Megan grabbed his hand after they dropped the hospital bag with her belongings on her dresser. He wasn't sure she should be out and about after just getting back. "Leo." Megan tugged on his hand. "Let's go."

"Maybe you should take a rest," he said, "You just got here. Aren't you tired?"

"No. I have to show you. It's so cool." Her enthusiasm kicked him right in the gut. Leo couldn't deny her. She took Kim's hand as well so the three of them walked down the hall together. Megan looked up at Leo. "I like her," she whispered loudly.

"Me too," he whispered back.

Megan giggled. She talked nonstop, albeit in her slow cadence, telling them both about her artwork and some of her friends. Once inside the new building, she made a beeline for the corner of the room. "This is mine," she stated, her voice full of pride. "I get this whole space 'cause I'm in here the most of everyone." She showed them drawings, ceramics and paintings. At the moment she was working on jewelry and beads.

Leo saw the patience Kim had while listening to Megan's slower speech. The woman was going to make a great mother. She asked just the right questions and Megan delighted in talking to her. Watching them together made Leo realize just how important family was. He'd been working so hard to keep Megan cared for, but he'd cheated her with the absence of real family.

A little mewl sounded in the room. Kim glanced up. "Sounds like Stella wants in the on the action."

Leo reached into Kim's bag sitting on the floor between them and pulled out the little bandaged ball of fur. Megan came between them to pet her. Kim opened bottled water from her bag, poured some into a collapsible bowl she'd purchased yesterday and set it in front of Stella. After the feline had her fill, she went straight into Megan's arms and purred her brains out. Sure, she'd purred for Leo, but never that loud. He might've been a little hurt if Megan and Stella hadn't been so cute together.

"Leo, can I keep her?" The excitement in Megan's voice filled Leo with the kind of love he'd forgotten. The unconditional kind. Megan sat in her chair and snuggled Stella close to her chest.

Kim shot him an apologetic glance. "I don't know if they'll let you. Maybe we can ask the director." She looked at him for guidance.

He'd never expected something like this to happen. What if they refused to let Megan keep the cat? "I'll ask, Megs, but I can't promise anything."

Rubbing the soft fur against her cheek, Megan didn't let up. "I promise I'll be so good to her. And I'll give her food and water and I'll clean her. Everything. Please, Leo, please!"

Kim's wide eyes spoke volumes. "I am so sorry," she murmured. "I did not see this coming."

"Neither did I. Let's not panic. Maybe I can convince them Stella's a therapy cat." He shrugged. "Worth a shot." The hope on Kim's face made him feel ten feet tall. "It's not like I intended to keep her. What am I going to do with a cat? Stella knew it was a temporary arrangement. We discussed it at length."

Kim's smile fell flat in an instant. He had no idea what he said to make her react that way, but clearly he'd landed in the doghouse. Or maybe it was the cathouse. He would've asked, except the door opened and Howard, the director, walked in with a woman following. Leo had never seen the guy as stressed. Puffy half circles beneath his eyes aged him more than a decade. The middle-aged woman behind him had her arm in a cast and looked white as the pages before he'd written his screenplay.

"Hello, Mr. Frost. So nice to see you again," Howard said. "I apologize again for the circumstances."

Leo had to admit that this guy couldn't be expected to control anyone at the hospital. He'd probably never discover who made the call that brought the paparazzi, but Leo couldn't blame this man who looked as if he hadn't slept for forty-eight hours. "Not your fault. I'm just glad Megan's okay." He looked to the woman next.

She stuck out her right hand. "Hi, Mr. Frost. I'm Janice

Leigh. I was with Megan when she had her seizure. I wasn't supposed to come in today, but when I heard you were here, I just wanted to meet you and apologize. I'm so sorry that I wasn't in time to catch Megan." Janice's eyes teared up and she struggled to keep her composure. "She's my favorite of all the patients here and I was devastated when—"

"Janice, it's okay." Leo pulled her in for a gentle hug. "I know you did the best you could. I'm just sorry you got hurt trying to help her."

She waved him off and pulled away, flushed and maybe a little embarrassed. "I'll be fine. A few weeks in a cast is annoying, but things could be worse."

A tiny *meow* sounded from Megan's direction.

Howard's eyebrows slanted inward. "What was that?" Didn't seem as if the guy was a fan of animals.

It had been a long time since Leo had practiced his improvisational skills. "That was the therapy cat we brought. I hope you'll let Megan keep her. I think she'll do wonders for my sister."

Megan shifted in her chair and lifted Stella for Howard and Janice to see. Janice immediately ran over to give Stella some love and the purring started all over again. Man, that cat was easy.

"She looks pretty scraped up for a therapy cat," Howard said.

"Which is why she's ideal for this place. No one's perfect," Leo said. Except the green-eyed beauty standing next to him was pretty damn close to perfection. Maybe he needed to tell her that.

"I don't think I can sign off on this," Howard continued. "We've never had an animal here at The Marion. It would go against our—"

"C'mon Howard. Think of how much joy Stella will bring to your patients."

Kim walked forward and held out her hand. "Hi, Mr. Kaminsky. I'm Kim Jacobs, Mr. Frost's accountant. I just wanted you to know that Mr. Frost is willing to pay for Stella's upkeep while she resides here with Megan."

He was? Leo shot her a glance, curious to see what else he was *willing* to do.

"An extra two hundred dollars a month should cover any of Stella's needs. You can keep a Stella fund and any medical expenses incurred can come out of it if necessary." When Howard seemed like he might balk at the offer, Kim continued. "And of course, Mr. Frost is willing to donate a one-time only therapy cat fee of five hundred dollars for you to use at The Marion at your discretion." She gave him a beaming smile and Leo waited for the man to fall at her feet.

Howard looked between all of them and finally nodded his head. "That's very generous. I'm sure a cat won't be too much of a bother. I just have to see if any of our residents are allergic. That could cause a problem."

"You could always make sure that Stella stays with Megan. If the other residents want to spend time with Stella, then they can come visit Megan as well."

Leo kept his mouth shut as Kim negotiated the deal. Watching her work in those heels and that dress made him itch to have her. Last night had been long and lonely on the couch and he didn't especially want a repeat tonight.

"Of course. I think we can arrange that."

Kim sealed the bargain with a handshake, and they watched Howard and Janice head back to the main building.

"That was genius. Except that I can barely afford to pay them what I'm paying them now."

"No worries. I've got it covered."

Leo faced her. "What is that supposed to mean?"

"It means, I'm going to pay Stella's fee and the retainer for her to live here. It was my idea, it'll be my money that pays for it." She put her hands on her hips. "Why do you have that stink eye on? I'm perfectly capable of paying this. And honestly, I want to."

They both watched Megan and Stella, happily enjoying each other's company.

"I'm not letting you pay for my sister's cat." It was a matter of pride at this point.

Megan looked up them, her eyes sparkling.

"Can we not talk about this now," Kim said, gesturing with a nod of her head toward his sister. "Little ears are listening."

He sighed. "Right. Fine. We'll talk later."

They spent the rest of the afternoon getting a tour from Megan. She showed them the indoor swimming pool, the cafeteria, the movie room, the playroom and even the laundry room. Stella didn't stay far behind. She weaved around Megan's legs like they belonged together. It was clear to Leo that maybe they did.

Another Stella bites the dust.

Leo checked his watch. He still had a few phone calls to make to the distributor and time was running out. "Megs, we have to leave now, but we'll be back tomorrow before we go back to Los Angeles."

"Okay. Will you be back for another visit soon?"

"As soon as I can. How about next month?" Leo asked.

"That's good. That's not too far away."

Leo tried not to let the guilt wipe him out. It happened like this every visit.

Kim left all of Stella's paraphernalia, food, treats and bowl, and promised to bring the rest at tomorrow's visit. Megan didn't really seem too crushed at his leaving because she had Stella to take out the sting. It seemed weird to say good-bye to the cat, but Stella was just as wrapped up in Megan as the girl was with the cat.

Chapter Twenty-Three

Once they returned to Leo's neighborhood, Kim took him up on the dinner offer from the night before. Leo decided on the Italian place a couple of blocks from his apartment. The small restaurant catered to an upscale crowd. Wall sconces and candlelight provided an elegant ambiance. A middle-aged host with balding gray hair greeted Leo with a welcoming hug and seated them in a back corner table for privacy.

Despite feeling positive about the day's outcome with Stella and Megan, Kim readied herself for an earful regarding the cat's fee at The Marion. She never intended to wound Leo's pride, but since she made the offer, she intended to supply the funds. Sitting across from Leo, she sipped a ginger ale. "Megan is adorable," she said, setting her drink on the table.

He nodded. "Yeah, she's pretty cool." His half-hearted smile didn't trump the turmoil in his eyes. "I just wish..."

She hated the guilt that streamed off him and she leaned forward. "You're doing the best you can, Leo. You can't beat yourself up about it. Look how happy you made her with Stella."

His gaze met hers. "You made her happy with Stella." She waited for the *but* or the *earful*. Instead he smiled. "Thank you." He took her hand and his instant warmth sent a thrill up her arm. "You are one giant surprise after another."

"Me?" she scoffed, pretending that his innocent touch didn't make her as giddy as a baby goat. "I'm as predictable as it gets."

"Hardly." His shocking blue eyes made her self-conscious and she sipped her drink again. "Thank you for today, for being so awesome with Megan, for handling Howard and Stella. I don't know what I would've done without you."

"You're welcome. It was no big deal."

"You're wrong. It was a huge deal to me." His gaze never wavered and her heart kicked hard against her ribs. "I've never seen Megan so enthralled with anyone. She fell in love with you in two seconds. So did Howard."

Too bad the man watching her hadn't done the same thing. Kim kept her disappointment buried and forced herself to match his smile. "Howard fell in love with the money. Megan just liked having the attention of a new face." A waiter came by and Leo ordered the house special for both of them, a sample plate with small versions of their best dishes. "Megan's lovely, Leo," Kim said when the server left. "She's not unhappy at The Marion. Yes, she might miss you, but she stays busy and she's being well taken care of. Janice wouldn't have come back two days after breaking her arm if she didn't feel the need to apologize, and she felt that need because Megan is special to her." She reached across the table and took Leo's hand. "You did good when you found that place. Megan needs specialized care. There's no need for guilt."

Leo blinked a few times and Kim saw the emotion he struggled to hold back. Something in her heart snapped and all she wanted to do was comfort him. Though he'd complained about not wanting a cat, she had a feeling that Stella's unconditional love filled a void in his life. In one fell swoop she'd accidentally flushed that relationship down the crapper.

They ate in relative silence, but every time Kim looked up, she met Leo's hot gaze. Just looking into his eyes, sent her heart racing faster. She saw so much inside him: need, desire. Two things she'd always wanted from a man. But she didn't have his heart and that was the one thing she wanted most.

When they finished, Leo escorted her back to the apartment, his hand warm and strong around hers.

"You've been awfully quiet," she finally said as they took the stairs to his place.

He nodded. "Just thinking."

She wanted to take away the grim expression on his face. "Okay. I'll allow it, but just this once."

His smile melted her bones. When they reached his apartment, he trapped her against the door. "You know, you keep making me smile and I might do something to return the favor."

"Impossible." The second she said it, she realized it sounded like a dare and that hadn't been her intention.

The determination in Leo's eyes warned a second before his mouth closed over hers. She had zero will power when it came to this man. Less than zero. Because she kissed him back just as she had last night. The man had a set of lips to die for, and God, did he know how to use them.

He nibbled, sucked and kissed the bejeezus right out of her.

He pulled away after a few minutes, looked into her eyes and stepped back before unlocking the door. Was he putting on the brakes because of last night? She remembered everything she said to him and it was all true. But it didn't stop her from wanting him.

His mood took a complete one-eighty and she hated it. The last thing she wanted was to be another load of shit on a rough day.

Did all his visits with Megan give him this much guilt? Did he struggle this much after every trip to the East Coast?

Leo dropped his sport coat over the back of the sofa and stood at the window, looking out to the dark, quiet street. He looked so alone and she didn't want that. Yes, they had a major gulf between them, between what she wanted and what he could give, but it didn't mean she didn't care for him.

Kim stood behind him and wrapped her arms around his waist, offering her warmth, her comfort. Offering more than she should, and she realized it. She just couldn't help herself. If her body was the thing that would help him right this minute, then she didn't mind giving it. In fact, she wanted to.

Leo faced her, the confusion in his eyes disappeared as soon as he got a look at her. The heat that took over nearly set her aflame. When his lips touched hers, she melted into his arms.

Nothing was going to change after this interlude. He'd get distant and she'd feel alone, but for this minute, when his hands traveled her curves and his tongue tangled with hers, she didn't care. She wanted him and wanted to give him the solace he needed.

When he scooped her in his arms, she gasped into his mouth. He didn't say a word as he carried her to the bed. Last night she'd had the bed all to herself. She'd woken up alone and surprised that Leo had crashed on the couch. No chance of that happening tonight.

Leo kept his mouth on hers. Maybe he worried if he gave her a chance to breathe, she'd put a stop to the amazing foreplay he'd started. Not even if hell froze over. Clearly old habits died hard with her. She kept going back to all the wrong places despite knowing she'd be crushed in the end.

This isn't about you. She had to keep reminding herself of that. This was for Leo because he needed her. That was all she ever really wanted. Well, that and someone to love her.

After laying her down on the bed, Kim helped Leo peel off her clothes. She tackled her dress and bra and he divested her of her thong in one quick motion. His clothes came off next.

He never slowed the pace. He kept his mouth and hands busy, working her into a mindless sexual haze where nothing mattered but his skin against hers, his mouth on hers, and his body filling hers.

With a couple of pushes to test the waters, Leo finally plunged deep, taking Kim's breath and most of her sanity. She'd never felt so full, so needed. So with every fresh thrust, she lunged up to meet him. She let the sensations take her where nothing mattered but release. She locked her legs around him and dug her heels into his ass to keep him connected, to let him know he wasn't on this train alone.

The guttural sounds coming from his chest tore her up as he battered into her. All she could do was grip him tighter and hold on for the ride. And, God, what a ride. He knew what she liked. Knew how to hit the exact right spot that would send her off into a euphoric abyss.

Sweat slicked their skin as Leo moved over her with deliberate hard strokes and, with every new glide, Kim got that much closer to the edge. Leo hooked an arm under her knee and levered it back, opening her wider as he thrust, the fierceness in his eyes an aphrodisiac like none other. When he growled and clenched his jaw with his muscles straining above her, he pushed her over...a slow motion fall that wiped her mind clean of everything but the pulsing between her thighs. Nothing mattered but the pleasure rippling through her in delicious waves.

Leo set his mouth over hers as he froze over her, his muscles stiffening as his climax rumbled through him. Kim breathed him in, the salty taste of his sweat, the smell of sex. She loved this part as much as the sex itself, the immediate afterward, the closeness, the bond, the little aftershocks that rocked them both. Leo collapsed on her and rolled to his side, taking her with him, keeping them close. He held her tight and she put her lips to his neck, spreading kisses and nibbles so he knew she was all right. He'd worry about her, worry that'd he'd been too rough and she didn't want that. She wanted this time to mean something to him because it meant something to her.

He was still semi-hard inside her and Kim didn't want to break the spell that happened when they were together. Much too soon they'd be apart for good, so she wanted this time to last.

She rolled him to his back, kissed his lips softly. "Don't move. I'll be right back."

He watched her with those gorgeous blue eyes of his, eyes that sometimes seemed to see right to her very heart and soul. He opened his mouth and Kim shushed him with a kiss.

"Shh. No questions. I'm not done with you yet."

The hot spark in his eyes coincided with the fresh twitch of him between her legs. Kim gave him a seductive smile as she eased off him. After a quick stop in the bathroom to clean up, she went to the kitchen and grabbed the chocolate ice cream from the freezer. Leo watched her from the bed, leaning on his elbow, a predatory look in his eyes as he followed her every move. Kim came back to bed with a bowl full of ice cream and nothing else.

"You forgot a spoon," Leo said, his voice husky.

Kim wrinkled her nose. "Spoons are overrated. And I hate doing dishes." She swiped a dollop on her finger and spread it over Leo's shoulder. The blank look on his face turned into understanding when she leaned forward and licked the ice cream off. He groaned when she shoved him down to his back.

"I want my dessert now," she murmured, then she spread more ice cream over the hard bud of his nipple.

Leo held her head as she licked and sucked the chocolate from his skin. "Jesus," he muttered. "This is the best dessert I've ever had." He dipped his finger in the bowl and spread more down the line between his abs, coaxing her, daring her with just a look.

Leaning forward, Kim took his chocolate covered finger in her mouth and sucked it, loving the cool, sweetness combined with Leo, loving the rise and fall of his chest and the animal attraction in his gaze. She released his finger and took his dare further when she added more to the line and ended right where the tip of his erection rested on his stomach. A primitive thrill of success shot through her veins as his nostrils flared when she bent low, her gaze on his, her mouth open and ready to taste.

She took a long swipe up his abs and devoured the ice cream and Leo in one lick. After she'd clean up that particular spill, she spread more chocolate to make a perfect outline of his hard-on, making sure to barely graze the edges as she worked. Then because she was feeling extra frisky, she straddled his chest backward—not only so she could do as much damage as possible with this angle—but because she hoped he took her up on the invitation.

He did.

She jerked at the cool ice cream he spread inside her thigh. She moaned as he nipped at her tender flesh. But when she felt the cold right between her butt cheeks all bets were off. Kim dipped into the bowl and spread a line of chocolate down his rigid erection and took satisfaction in making Leo twitch.

He dropped an f-bomb as she wrapped her lips around the tip and began to suck.

If it was war, Kim had to admit it was the best damn war she'd ever been involved in because Leo reciprocated by working his tongue along her sensitive seam, from her clit to her ass and back. Long strokes that set off immediate need so sharp she could barely breathe. In retaliation, she sucked him harder and deeper.

A war to come. She didn't see any losers in this battle. Not one.

But as Leo pulled her closer to orgasm, she gripped the base of his cock and squeezed at the same time she sucked. She felt his fingers pump deep inside and stroke her G-spot. With his fingers inside her and his tongue working her, Kim couldn't hold back her climax. She moaned on his cock, jerking as her orgasm jolted through her. Leo's shout warned her a second before he pulsed in her hand and into her mouth.

She loved the combination of ice cream and Leo.

When he finished, she rolled off to the side, replete and out of breath. Leo yanked her up next to him, not giving her a chance to recover before he put his mouth on hers and stole a hot kiss. He stroked his thumbs across her temple. Something different lurked in his eyes. Something she hadn't seen before.

"I..." He didn't finish, just kept looking down at her. "You..." He shook his head.

"You don't need to say anything," she whispered. "This is just us, being us. It's okay. All good."

He shook his head again, his eyes so serious. "No, it's not good. It's better than good." He kissed her again, a sweet brush of lips across her, a moment to remember, to cherish. "I don't want this to end. I don't want to be apart from you."

Longing, strong and sharp, welled up in her chest. What was she supposed to say to that? They'd hashed this out already, hadn't they? But she'd never seen him like this. Like this very second meant life or death. "What are you saying, Leo?"

He swallowed hard, never took his gaze from hers. "I love you."

The words stopped her breath, but only for a second. Words she'd always dreamed of hearing coming from a man who had never said them, the man she wanted more than anything. But he was a master at conveying emotion he didn't really feel. In fact, he made a living off it. They way Leo looked at her, she almost believed him.

Chapter Twenty-Four

Leo couldn't believe he'd actually said the words. Three words he never thought he'd utter ever in his life. Yet there they were. Out in the open for anyone to hear. Well, anyone who happened to be in the bed, which at the moment only included Kim. Although she looked as if she needed convincing. "I'm serious," he said. "I love you. I've never said it to anyone before."

"Leo..." She said his name in a tone he'd learned to be leery of. "I'm serious. We're okay. You don't need to tell me you love me because we had great sex. At least I think it was great sex. I was certainly happy with it." She gave him her playful smile, as if anything he'd said in the past minute could be construed as sex-brain and not something he really meant.

What really hurt was not hearing her say the same words back. But that shouldn't surprise him. She wasn't like any other woman who'd ever fallen at his feet. She was Kim. Strong. Independent and not one to say anything she didn't mean.

"*I'm* serious." He gripped her head a little tighter and gave a tiny shake to get her attention. "I love you. I don't want to be without you. Ever. You know me better than anyone. You can finish my damn sentences. You don't let me get away with any shit and you can stand your ground with anyone. I love all those things." He stared into her eyes and kissed her again, the softest most soulful kiss of his life on the lushest lips this side of the Mississippi. "If I love all those things, then it stands to reason I love you too." He gave her something she'd agreed with. "I'm just a dope so it took me a while to figure it out."

She shook her head the tiniest bit like she really couldn't believe him or his words. Then her eyes filled with tears. "Don't fuck with me, Leo," she whispered. She grabbed his wrists and held him tight. "Because if you're fucking with me, I...I'll..."

He loved her fierceness, even when she was naked and flat on her back. Emotion clogged his throat as he watched her. "I'm not. I swear to you, I'm not." He never wanted to hurt her, never wanted to see pain in her eyes. He wanted her again so much, to prove with his body what he knew in his heart. There was just too much more to tell her. "Today...with Megan. She loved you and you were so great with her. I'm glad the two women in my life met each other."

Kim wiped at a tear that trickled down her temple as she nodded. "Yeah. Me too. She's pretty awesome." Something serious still lurked in her eyes and Leo waited. "I'm still having this baby. You know that right?"

"Our baby. You're having our baby. Yeah, I know."

More tears slipped from the corner of her eyes. "You're serious? You love me?" She sniffed. "Because I kind of got the impression from you on several occasions that you didn't do love."

Nodding, he gave her a half grin. "That's true. It's possible that I excel at keeping women at a distance." His smile faded. "But I don't want you at a distance for another minute. I can't imagine being without you."

She studied him for a moment then leaned up and pressed her lips to his. "I love you too, you big dummy."

Leo took a second to soak up the words before they registered. It was as if someone opened up a cage and set him free. It was a free fall into heaven. It was his wildest dream come true. Laughing, he rolled over and pulled her with him, his heart soaring. No one had ever told him what this would be like. This whole falling in love shit. But Kim's serious face wiped the smile off his mouth.

"You're sure this isn't some knee jerk reaction to everything happening? I don't want you to feel trapped or think that I meant to pressure you, because—"

Leo kissed her quiet. He kissed her long and deep, holding her head steady as he plundered her mouth. "I don't feel trapped," he told her when he finally broke free. "I feel like I'm not so alone anymore. Like I have someone on my team who'll be there for me the same way I'll be here for her."

A ghost of a hopeful smile spread across her face. "I like the sound of that."

Swallowing back another damn lump in his throat, Leo nodded. "Me too."

Right before they finally fell asleep, spooned together, Leo couldn't remember why he'd been so opposed to falling in love. Then he realized it was because he hadn't yet met Kim.

The next morning entailed a lot of outstanding, celebratory sex. They packed up their few bags, collected the last of Stella's things to take to The Marion and headed out. They'd spend the first half of the day with Megan and take the plane back late in the afternoon.

In a black form-fitting skirt, a loose coral blouse that draped over her curves and her stilettos giving her an extra four inches, Kim looked as if she was ready for a board meeting. She drove him crazy because all he wanted was to strip her of the clothes and bury himself deep inside her.

Her sly smile indicated she knew exactly where his thoughts were as she shook her head. "You're insatiable."

He gave her his movie star smile. "Takes one to know one."

"You are so full of shit," she said, laughing, her eyes bright and playful. "Do you always quote lines from your movies, because you said the exact same thing to Julie Fraser in *Dangerous Race*."

"First of all, it was Mac who said it to Trace. And I only repeat them if they're if good lines and if they apply." He lifted an eyebrow. "It applied."

They made it to The Institute and Leo managed to keep his hands to himself, although it was close. What he really wanted was another ten or twenty hours in bed with Kim and a bowl of ice cream.

If Megan had liked Kim yesterday, she absolutely fell in love with her today. Walking across the manicured grounds, they held hands, giggled and talked like they'd known each other forever. Leo had never seen Megan act that way with anyone. True, he wasn't around as much as he should be and he'd never brought someone to meet her. Megan might be mentally challenged, but she was bright enough to understand this was a first. That alone held significance.

Though the bruising on Megan's face still looked as if she'd gone a few rounds with Mayweather, his sister didn't complain or seem uncomfortable.

After spending an hour in the art room, Kim excused herself to go to the ladies room and Megan waved Leo over. Stella's tail twitched happily across Megan's leg as she stroked the cat's soft fur. "Will you bring Kim every time from now on. I like her." Megan's hopeful gaze met his.

"I'll ask her." Leo crouched to Megan's level. "But I'm not sure she'll be able to visit you when I can."

Megan's smile dimmed. "Oh. But you'll ask her, okay? Because I want to see her like I see you." She cocked her head, her hands never stilling over Stella's fur. "I think you should keep her, Leo."

Leo held back a smile and matched Megan's serious face. "You do, huh? You like her that much?" He took the chair next to her that Kim had vacated.

Nodding adamantly, Megan looked around and leaned closer. "I think she's perfect," she whispered. "She's so pretty and smart. She can add all sorts of huge numbers in her head? She doesn't even need to use her fingers and toes."

Leo stroked Stella's rump, and the cat just rubbed against Megan as if she'd made her choice of preferred sibling. "Yeah, she is pretty smart," he agreed.

"It's good to be friends with smart people," Megan advised.

Leo nodded stoically. "Very smart thinking, Megs. I'll remember that."

She nodded too. "And I really get to keep Stella?" she asked, her eyes back to hopeful.

"Absolutely. I worked it out with Mr. Kaminsky. Stella gets to stay. You just have to remember to give her food, water and a lot of love."

Megan jumped up, careful to hold Stella as she wrapped the other arm around his neck. "I will, Leo. I promise. Thank you, thank you. This is the best present ever and it's not even my birthday or Christmas even."

Kim found them in the same hug a minute later. "Can I get in on this party?" She stood off to the side, glancing between the two of them.

"What do you think, Megs? Should we let her in?" Leo never imagined his heart could be so full. He not only had Megan to care for, but now he had Kim and a baby on the way. Staggering responsibility for a confessed bachelor, but he couldn't wait to prove he could handle the challenge.

"Yes! Yes!" Megan opened up and motioned Kim forward. The three of them shared their first family huddle.

Leo wasn't sure how he was going to tell Megan about the baby, but he'd have to eventually. He'd be here at least two more times before Kim gave birth, so he'd save it for another visit.

He spent one of the best days of his life with Megan and Kim, playing around in the art room, walking the grounds, and watching Stella frolic with Megan in the grass. Considering all hell was about to break loose when he got back to L.A. and faced the fallout, he managed to make the best of their time together.

He didn't expect the lump in his throat when he said good-bye to Megan and Stella. Watching his little sister holding that damn cat made him think that maybe Megan wouldn't be as alone as he always pictured. A few of the nurses stood out front with her and waved good-bye and Leo and Kim got in the limo and headed to the airport.

Kim patted his thigh. "You did good leaving Stella. One of the nurses has a good vet and she's going to make sure Stella gets regular checkups, including getting her stitches out in a few days. It's all set with Howard. Those two will be great for each other."

Leo linked their fingers. "I think so too. I also happen to think the same about us." He loved her smile, loved the way she looked at him with love and a whole lot of desire. "I can't wait to get you alone in that plane," he murmured, leaning in to give her a soft kiss. He wanted to kiss her for hours. Wanted to see her lips swollen and pink like last night when she couldn't keep her mouth off him.

"You can't possibly be talking about a mile high club. Leo, you're scandalous." Her deadpan delivery made him smile.

"I try, babe. I really try." Though they were joking, the truth of the matter hurt. He'd been scandalous most of his life to keep this one secret and now it had blown up in his face. This could kill his movie before it ever got out. It could very well end his career if the public saw him as a monster and his whole purpose in being successful was to keep Megan in the place where she thrived the most. Would the public see it that way? Probably not. Not that he gave a rat's ass what the public thought, with the exception that public opinion could make him or break him.

"Quit thinking about it," Kim said in his ear. She pulled back and met his gaze. "Everything's going to be fine. Sara's going to make sure of it. I'm going to make sure of it." The sincerity in her eyes gave him a ray of hope. Kim always made him feel better.

"I should have never let you go home two months ago." The truth of that statement hit him like a brick. "I should've dragged you out of LAX, taken you home and locked you in my basement."

"Yes, but then you'd have moved into the new place which doesn't have a basement and you'd have nowhere to keep me and—"

Leo shut her up with a kiss.

The plane ride home turned out to be much more adventurous than the East Coast leg. Kim loved every second of being introduced to the mile high club. Leo showed her the back of the plane where a gorgeous suite held a bed and bathroom. The walls were painted in desert tan and a rich brown comforter stretched across the bed. She'd barely gotten through the door when he'd closed it and pushed her against it. He had her skirt hiked up and her thong on the floor before she'd had time to process the seduction. But then he'd slowed things down. She loved the way he took his time kissing and touching every inch of her before giving them both what they needed.

Kim cleaned up in the bathroom afterward and noticed a little bit of spotting. It wasn't bad, and she knew from all the reading she'd done that it wasn't abnormal to spot. But with the additional cramping knotting her stomach, all she wanted to do was cuddle up in bed and sleep for a week. That would have to wait for a little longer.

Leo and she hadn't talked about the serious stuff yet. The couple stuff. Admitting they loved each other seemed like the biggest hurdle and now they had to face the media and the scrutiny that would come with Leo's decision to keep Megan at The Marion.

From the bit of poking around she did during their visit, it looked like a class-A establishment. The facility catered to the mentally and physically challenged alike. Many of the residents—like Megan—dealt with seizure disorders and needed constant medical supervision. People would argue that Leo had the money to hire people in house and keep Megan under his same roof, but half the time Leo was out of town or out of the country making movies, and he couldn't manage Megan's healthcare workers from long distance. He admitted that he didn't trust his privacy would stay intact with one, two or more live-in healthcare workers rattling around in his place.

Kim understood his reasoning, especially after meeting Megan. Aside from her slow, low pitch voice, she had the inquisitiveness of a second grader. She was happy and the staff at The Marion all seemed to know her and love her. Whether they kept a special eye out for her because she was Leo's sister or because Megan was just a special girl, Kim didn't know, or care. She just liked what she saw when Megan gave them the tour.

So, yeah, they had a lot to tackle before they squared away their relationship, but at least they were on the right road.

Leo leaned on his elbow, picked up her hand and linked their fingers. Kim took her gaze off the setting sun as they chased it in the sky. "What are you concentrating so hard on over there?"

"Damage control." At her words, his expression sobered. "When you address the media about this, I'll be right behind you. Everyone's going to want to know who I am, right? They already have that picture of us together in the parking lot at LAX from the last time, so seeing me again will cause speculation. I come forward, answer a few questions, including the fact that I got your sister's seal of approval at our visit. And I'll explain how much Megan loves her home and needs her home for the best possible care. And boom. In a few sentences, I take the speculation and drama out of the situation and we leave everyone with their thumbs up their asses. How's that sound?"

"Sounds like you've added another reason why I love you." His eyes shone into hers with something she hadn't seen before. A little bit of wonder mixed with some mischief.

"You have that devious look in your eyes. What?"

"Just thinking about the future. Us. As soon as we land, I want you to get your things together and bring them back to my place."

She hadn't even considered that, but it made sense.

Hopefully, Wilson wouldn't be too bent out of shape after waiting for her. "Maybe my driver's license showed up while we were gone. We can stop at the hotel, grab my stuff and head to your place if that works."

He nodded. "Have you talked to Wilson today?"

"I left him a message. He's not picking up and he's not returning my calls. I'm a little worried about him, but maybe he's busy with work. I have no idea. I'll find out soon enough."

"While you're getting your stuff together, I need to make a few calls and see if my distributor is on track."

Seemed like they were doing a bang up job of talking about everything but them. They'd covered his strategy, Megan and his movie. All important, but maybe not the most important. The most important was the bun baking in her oven.

"You know," she said, trying to ease into addressing the elephant in the plane. "I know now why you were so adamant about me not having this baby. About not having kids in general." Leo didn't say anything, he just watched her. "I'm going to love this baby no matter what. And with the inheritance from my aunt, we'll be able to afford whatever special care he or she might need for whatever reason. If we invest half of it the right way, it'll start making money for us too." She'd have to find a way to make the most of her investment, because Megan's costs alone were astronomical. She couldn't guarantee that Leo was going to work again or make the kind of money he made in the past so it was up to her to figure out the finances. "We're going to be fine. The baby is going to be fine too. So will Megan. We'll figure it out."

Leo squeezed her hand. "Megan isn't your responsibility. Let's get that straight right now. She's my sister, not your burden. I've handled her care for the last fifteen years and I'll do it until one of us dies. We clear on that?" This was as stern as she'd ever seen him aside from some of his movie roles.

It made her think that maybe she'd jumped ahead. Just because they'd professed their love for each other didn't mean he had any intention of marrying her or consolidating their lives.

"We're clear. Let's get clear on something else while we're at it. I love you. I said it last night and I meant it. But maybe we should define what *love* means. I'll go first." Because if she didn't get it out, and Leo had something else on his mind, then it was better to clear the air now. "Love means we're a partnership through thick or thin, good times and bad. It means I help you if I can and if you need, and you do the same for me when it's my turn. When things turn around for you, and I know they will, then it won't matter anyway."

Leo just watched her, a blank expression on his face. For a guy who could ooze emotion, he did a great job of making her uncertain. "I've been connected to a lot of women," he said, his gaze still shaded.

"Now tell me something I don't know." She lifted an eyebrow unimpressed with his response.

"And not one of them ever offered to help me financially."

"Leo, that doesn't count. You've never been in a financial crap-hole until now."

"I guarantee you every one of them would've bailed at the first sign of trouble. If there's no money, there's no fancy things. No fancy things means no fun. You're not like anyone else I've ever met."

But he never met the old Kim. What would he have thought of her? "I used to be," she whispered. "Does that matter?"

"I don't care who you used to be. I fell in love with the woman you are. To be honest, I'm not sure why you fell in love with me." Genuine interest clouded his blue eyes.

"A lot of reasons," she said, turning on her side and facing him. "You were there for me when Stephanie disappeared and her asshole of a husband tried to intimidate me. You listened when I needed someone's ear. You didn't judge me when you saw me at my worst and you continually offered your help without any strings attached. You showed me how much you care about your sister by the way you take care of her, how much you care about animals when you saved Stella. You're a good man, Charlie Brown. You can't hide it, even though you've tried."

He had the courtesy to flush and Kim hid her grin. "You mean you didn't fall in love with me because I'm hot in the sack?"

"Well, of course, there's that. It goes without saying." His grin made her laugh. "Seriously. You are not a hard man to love, Leo. No one ever tried to find the real you so they lost out. I'm okay with that."

Leo leaned over and kissed her softly, his lips lingering on hers as he took his time. "We're going to be okay, aren't we?"

She nodded as she cupped his cheek. "We're going to be better than okay. As long we communicate, we'll be just fine."

"I'll kiss to that," Leo said a second before grazing his lips over hers again. And again.

And again.

Chapter Twenty-Five

Wilson washed down his fifth shot with half a beer. He couldn't remember the last time he'd been this pissed off. He still couldn't believe Carolyn had left him in Los Angeles and taken off with no notice. She hadn't even packed any of her new shit. She'd just jumped on a jet with her famous asshole boyfriend and left him to bake.

He'd been getting closer to her too. They'd talked and laughed and he'd cheered her up. Told her she didn't need a putz the size of Leo Frost in her life. The man was worthless. Literally and figuratively. His accountant's scandal had been all over the news. So had the most famous people on the man's client list, one of whom had been Leo Frost. So, yeah, it was common knowledge that Leo had taken a giant hit. Not too many people knew how hard, but Wilson did. So what did that make the guy? A giant *loser* with a capital *L*. Wilson could spot them a mile away.

He happened to look in the mirror at that exact moment. The fresh circles under his eyes reminded him of his father before he died. A decent night's sleep would take care of that…along with getting Carolyn back in his sights. Wilson finger combed his thick hair. Leo Frost had nothing on him. He took the last shot on the bar and chugged the end of his beer chaser.

A nice celebration after seeing the aftermath of his phone calls to some high profile publications. Information was power and he'd happily shared news that had blown into a firestorm he never anticipated. Even better. On top of the pregnancy and financial ruin, Leo had been hiding a disaster of a family secret. Wilson chuckled at the irony. Mr. Perfect wasn't nearly as perfect as he claimed to be.

He couldn't wait to set eyes on Carolyn after the hell he hit her with. Once she walked through that hotel room door, she was going to see him and figure out just how much she needed him. He'd been there for her for years. She owed him. And he was going to get his hands on that inheritance if it killed him. Or her.

Kim opened the door as Leo killed the car's engine. Cool night air hit her warm cheeks. They'd been discussing photos for the ad campaign, but she was having a tough time concentrating. "It's probably going to take me five minutes to get my stuff together." Plus she needed to use the bathroom. Her stomach tightened with another cramp. Maybe something she ate. She remembered when Chelsea got the stomach flu early in her pregnancy. Poor thing had been miserable.

"That'll give me time to grab a coffee across the street. I'm going to be up all night going through the stills of the Montana footage. You want something?" He'd been super attentive ever since the *I love yous* and it made her heart swell every time he looked at her.

"No thanks. My stomach is doing that weird thing again. It's probably my evening morning sickness. Either that or I'm allergic to Jim's plane. I'll see you back here in a few."

"Remember, no contact with Wilson unless I'm with you," Leo said. "I still don't trust him."

"I know. But even if he did leak the pregnancy—which I didn't tell him about—doesn't mean he's out to kill me. He won't gain anything with me dead and like I said earlier, he had plenty of time before we left for New York if he really wanted to hurt me." Leo opened his mouth to argue and she cut him off. "I know. I heard you. I'll just go to my room and we'll call him later. He might not even be here." She leaned over and gave Leo a quick kiss before walking toward her door. She used her keycard, but it didn't work. She tried again with the same results.

Glancing over her shoulder, she saw Leo crossing the street to the coffee shop on the corner. She hesitated before going to Wilson's room.

"This is stupid," she mumbled. "We were raised together. He could've killed me ten times over before I left for New York."

She walked a few steps and knocked on her cousin's door.

"Wilson? You there? It's Kim. I can't get into my room." When he'd booked the hotel, he'd been next to an adjoining room so when Kim checked in, he'd requested it. Initially, she hadn't been thrilled to be next door to him, but they'd had so much fun talking about the old days that it hadn't mattered.

The door opened and Wilson stood there, his eyes red-rimmed, his hair a mess.

Kim stopped short of the hug she was about to give him. "What happened? Are you okay?"

"Of course I'm okay." He stepped back, but the stench of alcohol wafted in her face and she grimaced.

"Wilson, what have you been drinking? And why?" She followed him inside and made a beeline for the adjoining door. Her side was locked. Damn.

"Don't bother," Wilson said. He faced her, crossing his arms over his chest. "I packed up your stuff and gave them back the key. I wasn't going to spend money on two nights of a hotel room with no one in it."

She hadn't even thought about it when she left with Leo, but she never expected Wilson to cover all the expenses. "I am so sorry. You're absolutely right. You know I'm going to repay you for everything. I hope you're not worried about that."

He snorted, turned his back on her and looked out the window. "Oh no. Not worried about that at all." But clearly something had made him mad. His body language said it all, with his arms crossed and his wide stance.

"Okay. Good. Did you listen to any of my voicemails? Or see my texts? Why didn't you get back to me?" Maybe he'd lost reception, but his phone had been working fine before she left.

"Yes. I did." He turned and his eyes were glacial.

"Okay, so you're mad at me. I see that. Because I left so suddenly? Look, I'm sorry I didn't give you any notice. But I told you days ago that you didn't need to hang out here because of me. You could've left my stuff at the front desk and taken off."

"No, I couldn't." His jaw was clenched tight.

A sharp cramp hit Kim and she backed toward the bathroom with a grimace. "I need to make a quick pit stop before we finish this. Then I'll be out of your way." Kim took a second to lean against the bathroom door, fighting the shooting pain in her abdomen. She slipped into the bathroom, locked the door, and sat on the toilet, hoping to relieve the cramps. She saw more spotting on her underwear. Not good. Her rational excuses faded into escalating panic. Better to be safe than sorry. Leo wouldn't have a problem running her by the emergency room to be checked out. Once out of the bathroom, Kim saw a few of her belongings tossed in the corner of the room and gathered them up as Wilson stared out the front window.

Wilson's small carry-on bag sat on the chair at the desk. Kim did a double take at the envelope sticking from of the outside pocket, then got a closer look. The return label said Department of Motor Vehicles. Wilson sure as hell wasn't expecting anything from them. She pulled it out. Lo and behold, it was addressed to her in care of Leo Frost.

"My driver's license!" Finally! Except what was it doing here? She checked the date posted on the envelope. It came before she left for New York. How the hell...? "Wilson, what the... What are you doing with my license? How long have you had it?" She lifted the envelope high.

He turned slowly, his eyes menacing. "Oh, you found it?" The strangely calm inflection didn't match his tense body language.

Kim's anger crept up in increments. "Yeah, I found it. And I might not have if I hadn't seen the end sticking out of your bag." What the hell? "You want to explain this?"

His flat stare had her skin prickling. "Gosh, *you're welcome.* It was my pleasure to drive all the way across town every day to pick up Leo's mail and make sure you got your precious driver's license. No problem at all. It's not like I have a life."

She hadn't seen this side of him since the day at the lawyer's office in Arizona. "Oh no. You're not spinning this, Wilson. The date posted on this thing is the day Leo and I left for New York." She opened her mouth to say more, but the malice in his eyes shocked her. It made no sense for him to be so angry with her. Instead of laying into him like she wanted to do, she picked up her bags. "You could've told me a half a dozen different times while I was gone that you had it, and you didn't. You knew I was waiting for it." This was getting her nowhere. What happened to the cousin from her childhood? The nice guy she'd thought she'd reconnected with before her trip East? This Jekyll and Hyde thing was not working for her. "You know what? I don't care. It doesn't matter." Bags in hand, she headed to the door.

Wilson put his hands out to stop her. "Wait. Just wait a second." He scrubbed his hands over his head and further wrecked his hair. "Look, it's my turn to apologize. Sit down a second. Please," he said when she hesitated.

Against her better judgment, Kim sat on the corner of the bed.

Pacing in front of her, Wilson seemed more agitated than a rat in a cage with snakes. "I was just hurt when you picked up and left so quickly the other day. You didn't call until you were practically on the plane. I thought we were getting along great all week. We spent so much time getting to know each other again and talking about the good old days."

Kim released a frustrated sigh. She hadn't meant to hurt him. Still, she didn't see how any of this related to him holding onto her driver's license and not telling her. Maybe he read that in her expression.

He sat next to her, just a little bit too close for her comfort, but she didn't move. "I thought we were really good together...you know...before you left."

Good together? As in they made a good couple? "Wilson, you're my first cousin. You're making it sound like we had some type of relationship happening."

He smiled and with the sweat running down his temples it made him look...smarmy. "You're forgetting I'm adopted. We're not related by blood." He took her hand in both of his and a shiver raced down her back.

Was he serious? "Wilson, you're my first cousin." She tried pulling her hand away, but he kept a firm grip. "It doesn't matter if you're adopted."

His nostrils flared. "Yes, it does. We're not *really* related. You and I..." He gestured between them. "We could make something work between us. After everything I've done for you the last few years, you owe me the chance to make this work."

Few years? What the hell was he talking about?

"You've changed recently." His smile freaked her out. "It's like you've rejuvenated. Like our time together made you happier than before. Didn't you feel the connection all week?" he asked.

Kim shook her head, quick and violent. "No! No, I didn't feel any connection." Where was all this coming from? "And I'm sorry if you did and thought something was going to come of it." She couldn't get out of this room fast enough. "Wilson, I'm sorry, if you felt that I led you on in any way. It wasn't my intention. You know you're family to me and nothing more." She yanked her hand and he still wouldn't let go.

"We could be a family in a different way." He squeezed her hand so hard that he cut off the circulation. "I would be a great father to your baby. Our baby."

The man was out of his mind. Kim shook her head again. "No. We can't be a family because I don't feel that way about you." He *did know* about the baby. Which meant he might've meant for Smokey to give her that wild ride in the desert. And maybe Leo had been right and Wilson's alibi was a complete lie. *Get out!* The words screamed in her head. "Send me an email for everything I owe you and I'll write you a check as soon as I get home."

She stood and pulled on her hand again, relieved when he let go. But just as quickly, he was on his feet in front of her, seething and red-faced. Before she could react, he grabbed her shoulders and slammed his lips over hers. Kim struggled against the cloying stench of alcohol and sweat and kept her lips sealed together. His fingers bit into her skin, and fear and anger swirled together in her chest like a vicious whirlpool. Kim slammed her heel into his foot and shoved him back at the same time.

Wilson screamed and almost toppled over, but kept his balance. "You should not have done that," he seethed through gritted teeth.

Fresh fear blossomed in Kim's gut. Breathing hard, her pulse beating frantically, she tried to diffuse the situation. "You're drunk, Wilson. You have no idea what you're doing." *Walk out. Nice and calm. Pretend like nothing happened then run like hell.* "I'm leaving. Call me when you sober up."

A lecherous smile crossed his lips as she passed him. Wilson grabbed her arm and swung her backward so hard that she flew through the air, her bags toppling with her. She landed on the edge of the bed ass first, but her momentum kept her going and she rolled off the side. Her heart thundered as she hit the floor between the two double beds.

Disoriented and stunned, she took a second to calm her

breathing, before struggling to get her legs beneath her. He couldn't have meant to do that. This whole situation couldn't be happening.

"Wilson! What is wrong with you?"

He stood over her briefly then yanked her up by an arm. Before she got steady on her feet, he pulled back and punched her in the stomach. Hard. Air whooshed from her lungs as she doubled over. She hit the floor again, this time on her knees, fighting to get air into her lungs.

The baby.

Panic, fear and nausea rolled together in a sick wave. Situation critical. This went beyond anything she'd ever dreamed of.

"Wilson," she gasped out. "Don't."

"But you don't understand," he told her, his voice a soft whisper. "I have to. You didn't go over the cliff, you dodged my bullets and you didn't get on the horse. That means you'll take what's coming to you now."

Something slammed into her face and pain exploded in her head. Kim hit the carpet in a fetal position. Her fuzzy brain shouted one thing over and over. *Survive.* For her, yes, but mostly for her baby. But even as the thought flashed, she felt warm sticky moisture between her thighs.

No, no, no!

Wilson started a quiet rant. His words didn't register, but as his pace picked up, so did his volume. He walked the room, stopping to yell down at her or deliver a vicious kick.

She needed to fight back, needed to surprise him somehow and get to the door. But she didn't have a weapon, nothing near her to strike him with on his next pass.

Except...

She had her shoes. Shoes with sharp stiletto heels. Kim reached for one, and held on to the toe. Keeping the shoe behind her back, she waited, her heart slamming hard against her ribs as Wilson came at her again.

"Wilson," she pleaded. "Please, stop. Please hear me out." The pain in her stomach doubled.

He bent lower, his fetid breath right in her face, his eyes wide and crazed. "It's too late for that Carolyn!"

Carolyn? "Wilson, I'm—"

"You played me for years! You can't leave me out—"

The room suddenly jolted and everything inside bounced around like popcorn. It sounded as if a train was coming through the walls. Fresh heart pounding adrenaline soared through Kim.

Earthquake!

Wilson froze, his eyes rounded even wider. Possibly his first earthquake by the looks of it.

Kim took advantage of the distraction. She roared and swung with everything she had, rage and fear fueling her strength. She connected with his face, felt the contact as the heel broke skin.

Wilson screamed and reared back just as the shaking stopped. She tried to keep the shoe in her hand for another strike, but Wilson batted it away with a vicious kick. Pain shot through her hand and up her arm. Not ready to quit, Kim lunged up and tackled Wilson as he stood sideways, holding his cheek. They both went down, knocking into the other bed, but she scrambled up and made a run for the door.

"Help!" She yelled at the top of her lungs, every muscle shaking, every nerve ending screaming. She yanked the door open, but it bounced closed because of the maid's lock. A guttural groan tore from her mouth as Wilson caught her from behind and threw her back. She lost her balance on something— one of her bags—and landed flat on her ass. "Wilson, it's me. It's Kim. I'm not Carolyn. Do you hear me? I'm Kim!"

"You can't fool me, Carolyn. I know exactly who you are. You led me on for years. Kept me jumping every time you called. Well, those days are over. I did everything for you and how did you repay me? By screwing me, that's how! Well, that's not going to happen anymore." The deadly expression on Wilson's bloody face warned her that he wasn't close to being finished. Kim lobster-crawled backward, trying for space, trying to buy time.

But her time had run out.

Leo got his coffee and picked up a decaf tea for Kim. It might help her stomach so it was worth a try. He tried making a couple of calls to set up one or two meetings for tomorrow, but he only got voicemails.

Waiting at the corner for the light to change, Leo had Kim on his mind. Well, Kim and the baby. The more he got used to the idea, the more he liked it. A baby. He could totally see raising a child with her. Seeing her laugh and play with a little person they created. Yeah, that was pretty cool. The light finally changed and Leo crossed the street. An odd rolling motion made him stop at the curb and he looked around to see the trees and streetlights sway. Earthquake. Oh man, Kim was going to hate that. He hurried his pace, knowing she was going to be freaking out. He got to the edge of the building when he heard a scream. Intuition had him picking up his pace and when he heard a definite cry of help coming from Wilson's room, he dropped both drinks and ran like a wide receiver headed to the end zone.

He saw the door open a crack and slam closed a few seconds before he got there. Looking through a space in the closed curtains, Leo saw Kim cornered at the back of the room. Before he could do anything, Wilson lifted her off the floor, drew back and punched her in the stomach. She doubled over, gasping for air. Blood pooled at her feet.

And Leo lost his shit. He slammed into the door with his right shoulder over and over, but it didn't give an inch. He ran to his parked car, grabbed a crowbar from the trunk and ran at the window. Hearing Kim's screams drove him like a maniac. A few people came out of rooms, looking around. "Call 911!" Leo shouted. With everything he had, he slammed that bar into the glass. It shattered with a resounding crash and Leo dove inside.

Wilson turned just in time to take the full brunt of Leo's weight right in the chest. They flew into the back wall right next to where Kim lay curled in a fetal position.

Somehow, Wilson squirmed out of his grip. He yanked Kim up by her hair and twisted her right arm behind her back. "Stay away!" he shouted. "I'll break her arm, I swear I will!" He looked possessed, completely unhinged.

In the second it took for Leo to figure out what to do, Kim slammed one stiletto heel on Wilson's foot and slammed his ribs with her left elbow.

Wilson howled, Kim managed to duck out of his hold and Leo pounced.

Yes, he usually had a stuntman do the real work in any fight scene, but now he had the opportunity to beat the shit out of someone who really deserved it.

Leo got in a solid right hook that spun Wilson backward and into a small, upholstered chair. The burn in his hand felt good as he advanced to do more damage. Wilson recovered and lashed out with a punch of his own that caught Leo on the chin and snapped his head back.

That was the only shot Leo allowed.

Over and over, he pounded his fists into any part of Wilson he could find; face, stomach, ribs. Anyplace that caused pain. "I knew it was you the whole time, you piece of shit." His knuckles felt like fire and he welcomed the hurt.

Two strangers finally pulled him off as sirens wailed from the parking lot.

"Shit!" one guy exclaimed. "This is Leo Frost."

"No fucking way," the other guy said.

"Let me go, let go!" Leo yanked out of their grasp and knelt next to Kim. God, he'd shot a movie that had almost this exact scene, and the victim had been Kim's best friend in real life. What the fuck kind of déjà vu was that? "Kim, can you hear me?" She was lying in a pool of blood, gasping for breath, holding her stomach and her arm. A wave of helplessness drowned Leo. "Babe, I'm right here. Help's on the way." He looked behind him to the ambulance outside. Cops stormed the room, their guns drawn. The two men that pulled him off Wilson raised their hands and stood back in the opposite corner.

"Leo," she whispered, looking up at him with tear filled eyes. "The baby. I'm losing the baby."

"She needs a hospital, now!" Leo ordered with a glance over his shoulder. "No, you're not," he said, stroking some hair out of her bruised face. "You and the baby are going to be fine." Behind him, Wilson groaned and shifted. "Get this piece of shit out of here." Leo motioned to Wilson, lying on the floor.

EMTs rushed in and after checking Kim's vital signs and checking her for other more serious injuries, they loaded her onto a gurney. "She's pregnant," he told them and the look the men shared with each other made his stomach drop.

The cops wanted to talk and Leo told them he'd be happy to, but he wasn't letting Kim go to the hospital without him. He'd be damned if he was going to lose sight of the best thing that ever happened to him. He grabbed Kim's bags at the last second and jumped in the ambulance next to the driver.

Leo tried to hold his emotions in check, to keep them buried deep, but remembering the agony on Kim's face decimated him. His heart had never hurt this much.

Once at the hospital, he made it to the back of the ambulance before the doors even opened. The nurses rushed her through the E.R., and Leo was forced to wait as they whisked her into a treatment room.

Looking around, Leo saw all the faces in the room staring at him, recognition in their eyes. An older couple in one corner. A family of three in chairs off to the right and three men sitting separately on his left. He moved into the hallway and paced until a nurse showed up asking all sorts of questions he couldn't answer about Kim's history, her insurance. It made him realize just how little he knew about her.

Didn't matter. He knew the important shit. Knew he loved her. He loved her fierceness, her independence. Loved the way she looked with her hair in a bun and her glasses on as she worked at his desk. Loved how she constantly thought of others before herself. She'd become instrumental to his well-being. He couldn't imagine living another day without her.

Cops showed up a few minutes later and the nurse left them to talk. Leo told them all he knew, which wasn't much. Wilson—who seemed like an average ordinary guy—had taken a short leap into deep waters. The guy still hadn't regained consciousness. It was the only thing that gave Leo some satisfaction. He looked at his bloody knuckles for the first time and registered the hot burn. He ducked into the men's room and washed his hands, his stomach turning as he thought about all the blood Kim had lost.

There had to be something he could do. Someone he could call. Kim's parents were gone and the scumbag who'd attacked her was her only living relative. But she did have her best friend in Indiana. A woman he'd met when he'd starred in a movie based on her sister's life. Back in the hallway, Leo rummaged through Kim's purse, found her phone and searched up Chelsea Harding, now Chelsea Rivers since her marriage. He punched the screen and hoped he wouldn't have to leave a message.

"I knew it was you," a woman answered. "No one else calls this late and you're the only one I know on California time."

Leo cleared his throat. He'd never been at a loss for words before. "Is this Chelsea?"

"Yes. I'm sorry. I thought this was Kim." She must have looked at the screen again before coming back to the line. "Who is this?"

He heard a baby crying in the background. "Uh…" Leo didn't know how to tell her. "This is Leo Frost. We met a long time ago when you were in California."

"Yes. Leo. *Dangerous Race,* Leo. This is a surprise. Is there something wrong?" She knew there was. He heard it in her question and he wouldn't be calling this late at night if something wasn't very wrong.

"I, uh…" For a man rumored to be a smooth operator, he had zero tact at the moment. He glanced at the double doors Kim had disappeared through. "I'm at the hospital. With Kim. We just brought her into the emergency room."

"Oh God. What happened? Is she all right?"

"I'm not sure yet," he admitted. "They're working on her now. Her cousin lost his mind and…" Leo swallowed hard. "He hurt her. Badly. I got to her as soon as I could, but…it wasn't as soon as it should've been." There was a lot of blood. Too much blood for the damage that Wilson had inflicted, which meant that something else was happening. Something he didn't want to consider.

"Was she conscious when you found her?" Her voice cracked on the question.

"Yeah." But just barely. And, God, all the blood. Leo wiped a hand down his face. He'd never forget it as long as he lived. "I know she doesn't have any family, but—"

"I'm her family," Chelsea said.

Leo hoped he was too.

Chapter Twenty-six

Kim blinked her eyes open to bright hospital lights. An antiseptic smell invaded her nostrils and her parched mouth craved water. Men and women in various shades of blue and green hospital scrubs talked over and around her, but she only caught a few words. *Nothing broken. Vital signs stable.* The excruciating pain in her stomach was gone and she didn't know if that was because she'd been given drugs or because...

No. She couldn't go there. Wouldn't go there.

"Leo?" she asked. She felt groggy and slow. "Is Leo here?" She licked dry lips and grimaced when she encountered her cut lip. Flexing her hand only brought a sharp sting from the attached IV.

A young man with thick dark hair and wearing a white lab coat glanced at her before gesturing to a nurse, who hurried out of the room. "We'll get him now." His dark eyes studied her face. "I'm Dr. Godwin." He asked her a few questions to determine if she'd suffered a concussion. Her name, the date, the day of the week. She remembered it all. She also remembered the amount of blood she'd lost in the ambulance. She'd felt it beneath her.

With every minute that went by, an overwhelming sense of loneliness washed through her. She wanted Leo.

A minute later, he came into the room, the concern in his eyes and bruise on his jaw pushed her over the edge. Hot tears slipped down her cheeks. She didn't want to face the news she was about to hear without him. She needed him more than she'd ever needed anyone.

He took her hand and she squeezed tight as more tears

flowed. He bent low, grazed his lips across her cheek and whispered in her ear. "It's okay. You're going to be okay."

But their baby wasn't. The one thing she'd been looking forward to. Her chance to have someone to love and care for had been stripped from her in an instant.

The doctor stood at the end of the bed. "Ms. Jacobs, I know you wanted to see Mr. Frost, but I'm sure he wouldn't mind waiting outside if you'd like some privacy while we talk."

Leo glanced at her like he might bust a gasket if she sent him out and she quickly shook her head. "He's part of this too." She squeezed his hand and waited for the news that would surely crush her.

The doctor held a chart, his eyes solemn. "I'm sorry to inform you that you had a miscarriage."

Despite already knowing, the words sent a fresh round of pain to her heart and a full body flush made her hot. A tremendous sense of loss flooded her, destroyed her in its wake. She'd wanted this baby so much. Wanted to be a mother to a little baby girl or boy. She'd been planning a nursery, thinking of names, doing all the things that went with pregnancy and now it was gone.

Leo swore quietly as he squeezed her hand tighter.

"I know you went through a serious trauma tonight," the doctor continued. "But I'm curious if you had any cramping before you were attacked."

Kim wiped her eyes and nodded. "I had a little cramping two days ago, but I thought it was the airplane or something I ate. They were on and off while I was on the East Coast, but not so bad that I thought about it. Then I had more on the plane home earlier and I noticed spotting. I just thought maybe it was the altitude or something and I'd read that a little spotting isn't out of the ordinary. The cramps got progressively worse. I planned to go to the hospital tonight and call my doctor in the morning."

Dr. Godwin nodded, his eyes sympathetic. "I know it's not much consolation, but I think you would have miscarried this fetus even without tonight's incident. You weren't that far along, not even through the first trimester. Miscarriages aren't that uncommon so early. The good news is I did a D&C and everything looks fine. When you're ready, you can try again.

Just because you miscarried this time doesn't mean you will ever again. I just don't want you to have that worry."

"So this might not have been Wilson's fault?" Leo asked, his voice hard.

"Possibly." The doctor set her chart at the end of the bed. "At this stage, the fetus is so small that even a hard punch probably won't affect it. There's too much insulation. The fact that Ms. Jacobs experienced classic signs of an impending miscarriage makes me think it was inevitable. Devastating, I know. But inevitable. I'm sorry." He looked back and forth between them, compassion in his eyes. "Honestly, her bigger injuries are the cut along her cheek and lip and her bruised ribs. Those will probably take longer to heal than anything else. Ice is your friend. Apply it often in twenty-minute increments. Arnica will help the bruising." He glanced over his shoulder. "Just don't tell my staff I suggested anything holistic. They'll give me crap about it for weeks."

Kim wanted to smile at his playfulness, but wasn't in the mood. She should be asking questions, but her brain wasn't functioning on all cylinders. Thank God Leo was thinking. He asked all sorts of questions about the time frame of her recovery.

Leo.

Leo was now free to do what he wanted and not what he thought he had to do. Yes, he'd convinced her he loved her, but that was when they had something connecting them. Yes, they got along great and she loved him, but what if this gave him the excuse he needed to bail?

Then she'd not only lost her baby, but the man she loved.

Fresh tears slid down her cheeks. This morning, she had everything, and now, she might possibly have nothing.

The doctor left and Leo gave her all his attention as a pretty Asian nurse scribbled in her chart.

"It's okay," he soothed. "You're going to be okay." He pulled a chair over and sat next to her. "What can I get you? What do you need?"

Just you. But she didn't say it out loud because she didn't want to pressure him. "Nothing. I just want to get out of here." She wanted to be alone where she could grieve for the child she lost. The child *they* lost.

The nurse looked up from her chart. "The doctor wants you to stay a little while longer to make sure all your vital signs remain normal, but I doubt you'll have to be admitted."

"Good news." Leo gave her a half-hearted smile and she loved him even more for trying. But his face sobered and he took her hand again. "I know you probably don't want to talk about it, but the police are waiting outside for a chance to talk to you. They're booking Wilson on attempted murder and assault charges. You do plan to press charges, right?"

It was the last thing she wanted to think about, but when Leo looked like he might blow another gasket she nodded. "Yes." But she had other things on her mind.

"Feel like telling me what happened?" His brows quirked together in a way she'd seen dozens of time in the movies and suddenly her whole relationship with him seemed completely surreal.

"He was drunk off his ass is what happened. I found the envelope from the DMV sticking out of his suitcase and I called him on it. I realized too late that I should've gotten out of there faster. He had some whacked out fantasy that we were a couple and he kept calling me Carolyn. He wasn't making any sense. When I finally made a move for the door he swung me back and just laid into me."

"You got at least one good shot in," Leo said. "What'd you hit him with?"

"The heel of my shoe." She shook her head. "I never thought I'd be thanking God for an earthquake."

He smoothed his thumb over her knuckles. "Ever since the 7.1, we've had a little more shaking than normal."

"Well, it gave me the chance to hit him. I'm not sure he realized what was happening. Looks like my stiletto's are good for more than just height." She thought back to her best friend's fight for her life, a fight Leo knew about. "Chelsea at least had a pipe when she tried to defend herself. I didn't have anything as substantial." That was the other completely surreal part to the day...getting beat up just like Chelsea had so many years ago.

"I saw the door open a crack, then he slammed it shut," Leo said.

Kim shook her head. "He must have set the maid's lock when I was in the bathroom. I was so busy running that I didn't see it until it was too late. He was on me before I could do anything but scream." Kim shuddered at the memory and her stomach tightened in a painful cramp. A sharp reminder of what she lost tonight.

"Did he say anything?" Leo asked.

"He said plenty," Kim scoffed. "He was mad that I went with you to the East Coast on such short notice. Mad that I didn't appreciate him driving across the city to pick up your mail, which we never asked him do," she added before Leo said the same thing. "He basically confessed to rigging the car, shooting at us in the canyon and screwing with Smokey's saddle blanket. And of course, the topper…he thought I was Carolyn and that we were good together."

Leo's brows snapped together. "Seriously?"

She snorted. "Yeah. It was crazy. He kept calling me Carolyn. I mean, I know we looked alike, but he completely lost his grip on reality. It makes me wonder if he had a thing for her and that's why he spent so much time helping her out the last few years. His wife left with their daughter and he didn't have anyone, so he attached himself to Carolyn. Then he took all that time we spent together and concocted a relationship."

"Isn't he your first cousin? Your aunt's nephew?"

"Yeah. But as he reminded me, he's adopted, so we're not blood relatives. Maybe he thought he could really have a relationship with Carolyn. Or me, who he construed as Carolyn." Kim shuddered again.

Leo shook his head. "It's over, that's the important thing."

Another wave of despair crashed in her chest. So much was over. Kim met Leo's gaze. She had no idea how to bring up the subject of *them* now that there was no baby keeping them together. How could he even look at her when someone in her family had tried to kill him? The ball of guilt in her chest threatened to suffocate her.

"Why are you looking at me that way?" He sounded leery. The man had learned to read her so well in such a short period of time. Too bad she wasn't as good an actor as he was.

"You didn't happen to remember to bring any of my stuff, did you?"

"I brought your purse." He gestured to the corner of the room. "I set it on the chair."

At least now she had ID and a credit card. That would get her where she needed to go.

Away. Her heart lurched again as loneliness pressed in on her.

Leo squeezed her hand and she met his gaze. "I called Chelsea. I thought she should know what happened. I told her I'd call back after I talked to the doctor and to you. I think she's ready to jump on a plane."

He'd thought of everything. She owed him so big.

"Send her a text. Tell her it's not necessary." She'd be leaving herself as soon as she could.

The two officers who'd been first on the scene knocked on the treatment door. One came in and took her statement and the other took Leo outside and talked to him. Fifteen minutes passed before Leo joined her in the room and the policemen left.

"Thanks for being here," she said after an extended silence.

Leo's eyes narrowed. "Where else would I be?"

Her throat knotted and she shook her head. She didn't want to talk about it now. Everything was too fresh, too painful and for tonight, tomorrow and maybe the day after, she'd take whatever Leo had to give. But as soon as she felt strong enough, she'd let him go.

Leo woke up alone. Again. It didn't take a genius to figure out something was wrong with Kim, something beyond having a miscarriage. Though he never professed to being all that smart, he did know women. Kim had grown distant in the last few days. Leo practically had to beg to keep her in his bed. It wasn't like he was planning on sex. Hell, he wasn't that big of a moron. But he wanted her close. Wanted to hold her and take away the bad dreams that woke her in the middle of the night.

She'd given in, but not without a disagreement. Okay, she needed her space. He got that. She'd lost a baby, their baby. She was hurting. Hell, he was too. But shouldn't she have been turning *to* him instead of *away* from him?

While she recuperated at his place, he kept busy with meetings regarding the movie. He talked to his distributor and kept his team involved so everyone stayed on the same page with the movie's release in four months.

Leo hopped in a fast shower, pulled on jeans and a T-shirt and came downstairs to find Kim dressed in a dark green wraparound dress and high wedge heels, ready to face the world. Physically, she'd bounced back to almost a hundred percent. She still had to take medication to fight any infection from the miscarriage, and the bruises had faded enough to be covered by makeup, but sadness still lingered in her pretty eyes.

"I thought I'd go home today. Chelsea's mad that I wouldn't let her come out so I feel like I should get back so she knows I'm really okay. I just made flight arrangements for this afternoon."

She may as well have knocked him over the head with a two-by-four.

"What?" A stupid question, but the only thing he could utter at the moment.

"I'm going back home." She kept her gaze on her little black book. "I've got a lot of paperwork to figure out from my aunt's estate. She had a trust and her attorney wants to make sure I have access to everything."

"Okay." That made a little bit of sense. She did have to figure out her aunt's estate and she did have a job in another state, but surely she'd planned to move before having the baby. A cold chill swept down his spine because the baby wasn't a factor anymore. What if… "When are you coming back?"

Her bottom lip quivered. "I'm not."

Wham. She couldn't have delivered a harder blow to his heart if she tried. A combination of anger and hurt swirled inside him like a twister and Leo crossed his arms over his chest to keep the pain inside. "And why's that?" Years of training made it possible to talk through the crippling rejection.

"Because, I don't see that there's anything keeping us together anymore."

Leo moved toward her, his steps measured. "You think the baby was the only thing keeping us together." He laughed, but it lacked humor. "Funny, because for the longest time, it was the baby that was keeping us apart."

Her eyes brimmed with tears and broke Leo in two. "I just think you felt pressured into being with me and now the pressure's off." She couldn't even meet his gaze.

"You know what's off?" He got right in front of her. "You. You're way off if you think I told you I love you because you were pregnant. You're off if you think I'm going to let you walk out of my life. I let that happen two months ago and I'm not letting it happen again." He pulled her close and wrapped his arms around her. "I love you. I meant it in New York. I mean it now. It's not something I've ever said to anyone else and it's not something I *plan* to say to anyone else."

Her eyes filled with more tears. Seemed like all she'd been doing the past few days was cry. The doctor had said it was natural after a miscarriage, but Leo missed the sharp-witted teasing that Kim did best.

Unless she was crying because she really didn't love him. He hadn't thought of that.

"Is it me?" he asked. "Maybe you didn't mean it when you said you loved me." The possibility slayed him.

"No, no." She covered her face with her hands. "I meant it." She looked at him then, as serious as a heart attack. "I thought that maybe if the baby was gone, you'd be free to... I don't know. Free to do whatever you want. I didn't want you to think that you were stuck. Like you were before..."

Leo didn't know whether to throttle her or kiss the living hell out of her. "How about I show you what I think. What I want. And I hope I make myself very clear with this." He cupped her face, looked into her eyes as he brought his lips down on hers. The kiss started sweet, just his lips grazing over hers, but he coaxed her mouth open with his tongue and tasted her in increments. Small swipes that led to long, deep kisses. Kisses that reminded his sex starved body that he hadn't made love to her in too many days.

Kim finally jumped on the wagon and kissed him back. Her fingers threaded through his hair and the little rumble in her chest may as well have been a string to his dick by the way it stood at attention in just a few short seconds.

When they eventually pulled apart, they were both breathing hard. "Did you understand that?" he asked.

She blinked a few times. "I'm sorry, the connection dropped midway through. Do you think you could repeat yourself?" A trace of a smile lifted her lips.

Leo grinned and dove in for another kiss. He still had another week or so before sex was back on the table, but that was fine by him as long as Kim planned to be here.

"I love you," he told her. The force of his words brushed her hair back. "Pregnant or not pregnant, you're the one I want."

Her smile set his soul free. "And if I get pregnant again?"

"Then we'll make sure we'll do everything in our power to have a healthy, happy baby." He grazed his thumb gently over the bruise along her jaw. "I know if nothing else, we'll have fun trying."

Chapter Twenty-seven

The movie theater buzzed with a packed crowd as Kim waited for Leo in the last row. The smell of popcorn hung thick in the air and people talked and alternately used their phones before previews started.

A month ago, the premiere of *To the West* had been a red carpet event to rival any blockbuster movie. Leo and his team went all out to create as much buzz as possible. Skeptics already doubted the success of a western, but Leo didn't let the public see his tension. He'd worked so hard that everything else had taken a backseat.

She'd been busy herself, traveling back and forth, closing out her end of the business with Chelsea in Indiana and shipping things to Los Angeles in manageable sizes. Leo treated her like gold and though she felt secure in their relationship, a part of her longed for the official commitment. She knew not to expect anything. Just because Leo said he loved her didn't mean he planned to marry her. Plenty of people lived their whole lives together without the benefit of a ceremony pronouncing them husband and wife. Even before the miscarriage, when he told her he loved her, he hadn't said a word about marrying her. Not even for the baby's sake. His only intention had been to stay involved.

Marriage. Kim had let go of that dream. It should be enough that she had a man who loved her and wanted to be with her, someone who appreciated all her parts instead of just the ones visible to the eyes. She was better off focusing on the fact that she and Leo were a team. She'd even helped him get to this point.

The work leading up to this opening night had been exhausting. The morning shows, talk shows and personal appearances had kept Leo busy for weeks. Kim wanted to do something special for him, but it had taken her several weeks to figure out what he'd love most.

Though she was officially a millionaire these days, she didn't feel any different than she used to. She didn't spend crazy amounts of money mainly because she'd learned a hard lesson the first time around. She was not a repeat offender. With the exception of Leo's surprise tonight.

Leo and she had contingency plans depending on the movie's outcome, be it a massive flop, mild success or sleeper hit. Kim's money certainly kept them way above water, but it didn't put them quite in the category Leo was used to. And Leo wanted his toys back.

Kim waved at Leo as he walked in the theater. Wearing a cap and glasses, no one would've recognized him. Kim almost hadn't recognized him when he'd come out of their bedroom in his disguise. He'd been growing extra scruffy since the premiere last month and now she knew why. He liked to go to opening night of his movies in a regular theatre with a regular crowd to see the audience's reaction first hand.

So far, the critics had loved *To the West*. So much so that Leo worried about the audience reaction. "Good reviews don't mean shit if the theaters don't fill up," he'd told her last week.

Understood.

On the off chance the seats didn't fill up or the crowd didn't like the movie, Kim planned an end to this night that Leo would never forget.

Already she'd seen the movie more than a half dozen times. Her fascination came from watching Leo watch it. He didn't enjoy it like the pressure was off. He'd watch with a critical eye and always found at least one thing he would've done differently if he'd directed the whole thing and not just a few scenes. He still loved it and had pride in it as a writer and producer, but he liked that, more than anything, he'd learned from it as a director.

Kim had bought them drinks and snacks at the concession stand while Leo had been in the men's room and she dipped into her popcorn. The usher introduced the night's movie and the crowd cheered. Kim squeezed Leo's hard thigh, more excited than she'd been at the premiere. She understood now what Leo had meant. Premieres were fun, but most of the people attending were friends, acquaintances and people in the business who wanted to suck up. Few were likely to give Leo honest feedback if they didn't like it. Critics not included.

Yes, tonight was the real test. Kim didn't know how Leo looked so calm. She was ready to jump out of her skin.

The lights dimmed, and trailers for new movies started rolling. It felt like twenty minutes before the opening began and Kim nearly forgot to breathe.

For the next ninety-five minutes, she watched the crowd's reaction. She felt their tension during fight scenes and rapt attention during a smoking hot love scene.

Kim still wondered why watching Leo make love to Carrie Ann Loughlin didn't bother her. Maybe because she knew Leo's feelings toward his co-star. Maybe because she didn't know him then. Or maybe because she had the real deal and knew what it meant to be in the man's arms. Of course the last possibility was that the woman now lived in a mental institution for committing murder.

Would her indifference last with any of his future films? It did her no good to think about it. One film at a time. Besides he told her every second of what happened during that love scene. How he had to shift his head at the exact right time to accommodate a camera angle or the fact that Carrie Ann had eaten some onions during lunch and her breath stunk. It all sounded extremely unsexy.

But on screen…they burned up the theater.

Kim watched the women as Leo kissed Carrie Ann. The dreamy faces and parted lips.

Yeah, her man was a hottie of major proportions. She grinned. How the hell had she ended up with Leo Frost?

He linked their fingers together and Kim glanced over just as he shot her a flash of his signature smile. God, she loved him. She couldn't wait to show him just how much.

The last fight scene of the film had the crowd cheering for the hero. Leo inserted just enough humor to keep the audience in the reality, yet subtle enough to lighten the mood. When he kissed Carrie Ann at the end, the audience cheered wildly.

Kim's heart soared and she squeezed Leo's hand. Success. She never thought she'd feel so much pride for another person. Sudden tears pricked her eyes and she blinked them away.

If this audience was any indicator, then Leo had a hit on his hands. Kim hoped for his sake that it was.

They waited for the crowd to clear out. Leo liked to listen to comments as people walked by. Discussing the movie, the turning points, the action or love scenes. He considered every comment to be a potential learning tool. How could he make his next performance better?

Walking out hand in hand, they strolled to the exit. The parking lot had mostly cleared since this was a midnight showing and it was the middle of the night.

Kim waited for Leo to figure out the problem. It didn't take long.

"Hey. My car's gone."

She looked up from her phone, where she'd been intentionally distracted. "What? What do you mean?" She bit the inside of her cheek to keep from smiling.

"I mean, my fucking car's gone. It must have been stolen." He spread his arms wide. "I don't fucking believe this. Tonight? Of all nights? Really?" He pulled out his phone from his back pocket. "I'm calling the cops."

"Wait, Leo!" Kim stopped him. "What's that over there?" She pointed to the very corner of the large lot where a lone black car sat under a tall parking lamp.

"I don't know," Leo said, hardly paying any attention. "It's obviously not my Benz."

"Are you sure?" Kim grabbed his arm and started pulling him toward the car, her stilettos clicking on the pavement. "It could be. It's pretty far away."

"Kim, I can see just fine. That's not a Mercedes. If anything it's a Porsche." Leo slowed as he squinted at the car. "Man, it is a Porsche. A Boxter S, just like Stella. God, I miss that car." The longing in his voice proved it.

"Oh, well, if you know for sure it's not the Mercedes, then I guess we can go back and call the police." She started walking back, but Leo stopped her.

"Wait, wait. I just want to take a quick look. For old time sake," he said, pulling her behind him.

"Oh. Okay." Seriously, maybe she wasn't so bad at this acting thing. This was kind of fun.

Leo got to the car and whistled as he walked around it. "This is one beautiful car." He crouched in front of it. "If I didn't know better, I'd think this was Stella."

Kim finally couldn't hide her smile. "Really? What makes you say that?"

"Stella had two little things that made her different from the crowd. One, she had a tiny divot right along..." Leo ran his fingers over the bumper and his eyes opened wider. "No fucking way. Couldn't be." Then he jumped up and ran to the back. "She also had a tiny crack in the back window." Leo flipped the flashlight app on his phone and shone it at the window's corner. "But this couldn't—" His eyes widened more. "Holy shit! This is Stella! This is fucking Stella!"

Loving his excitement, Kim pulled the keys from her jeans pocket and tossed them at Leo. "Think fast."

Leo caught them deftly, the surprise on his face better than anything Kim could've hoped for. "What? What is this? What did you do?" He walked toward her, dragging a loving finger over Stella's frame as he moved.

"Surprise." She wrapped her arms around his neck. "Stella's home."

"What?! How? When? I..." He finally shut up and kissed her. Kissed her stupid would be a better description. He raided her mouth while holding her head steady. Yeah...like she might possibly want to pull away. *Ha.* His beard tickled her lips.

When he finally pulled back, breathing hard, he glanced over at Stella then back to her. "Explain."

Kim laughed then sighed. "Oh, where do I start? Okay, first, I thought you needed a Stella in your life. Second, I know how much you missed her. Third, I wanted to do something special for you. Fourth, I figure if we ever fight, I can use this to my advantage."

Leo lifted her in his arms and kissed her again. "Seriously. How did you do this? How'd you find her?"

"I came across the guy's number when I was in your account last month. You were working so hard and I had some extra money..." Like ten million dollars' worth. "So—"

The love in his eyes filled her up...made her obscenely thankful to have found him.

"You've hardly spent any of your aunt's money on yourself, but you bought back Stella?" He sounded truly perplexed. "What were you thinking?"

Her smile faded because she really only wanted one thing these days and it was important to her that he understood it. "That I wanted to make you happy."

Gazing into her eyes, Leo brushed his thumb across her cheek. The tender gesture made her misty. "Babe, you make me happy just being in my life. You know that, right? You didn't need to buy back Stella."

"No, I didn't need to. But I wanted to."

His reckless smile flashed in between the new scruff. "Did you at least get a good deal?"

"Hardly." She laughed at Leo's frown. "Let's just say that both parties are happy. I got Stella and Mr. Young made a good investment when he bought her from you in the first place."

Leo glanced at Stella then back to her. "Where's the Benz?"

"In your garage at home. I got Viv to make the switch while we were in the theater." She waggled her eyebrows. "I'm pretty sly when I want to be." She pulled back, summoning all her lost innocence. "Oh, I almost forgot… There might be something in the back seat."

Shaking his head, Leo narrowed his eyes. "What the hell? Now what?" He hit the alarm and Stella double chirped a hello. "God, I missed that sound." Leo opened the door and dug into the back seat. "No fucking way!" His voice was muffled, but the sincere mixture of appreciation and excitement mingled together and brought a smile to Kim's lips. Leo backed out of the car, holding the *Dangerous Race* poster she'd bought back from Cesar. He opened his mouth, but no words came out. Instead, he just shook his head as he looked from the poster to her and back to the poster.

A giant wave of love washed through Kim. She'd never seen Leo speechless before. The man who always had a snappy reply or droll comeback couldn't put two words together. Finally he eased the poster back inside the car and got close enough to pull her into his arms. "I know where you found this, but I don't know how." He lifted a dark eyebrow.

"I saw it at Cesar's. Oh, put away the scowl," she admonished when his forehead wrinkled. "He didn't realize that

I spotted it in the back room until I went back and offered to buy it. By then it was back on the wall where I'm sure he usually kept it. If I have my sleuthing skills working, I'm guessing that's what you traded for the bag of clothes two months ago. Am I right?"

He studied her before nodding slightly. "Guilty." His soft kiss plundered her mouth and she felt his emotion in his gentleness. "Thank you." After long blissful minutes, he removed his lips from hers, but stayed close. "I'm going to have to keep my eyes on you all the time, I can see that now."

She chuckled and nodded. "Very good plan. I think you should start tonight."

Lying in bed a few days later, Leo was still thinking about Kim's gift of Stella. Not much could've made Leo happier than driving Stella home. God, he'd missed her. She purred all around him as he cruised down the boulevard, taking the long way home in the middle of the night.

He distracted himself the rest of the weekend by making love to Kim at every opportunity. Not only to thank her, but to show how important she was to him, to show her how much he loved her.

Monday morning, the box office results came in. Leo just hadn't had the balls to check yet. His phone had been pinging for twenty minutes, but he avoided the rush. It could've gone either way. A major flop would have everyone sending him condolences on the death of his film. He'd find out soon enough and right now all he wanted was a few more minutes of stroking the soft skin along Kim's bare back. She hummed her satisfaction, but after another few pings, she cracked open a green eye.

"You ever going to check your phone?" She looked sexy as hell with her sleepy eyes and bed hair.

"Guess I should."

"Don't be nervous." Facing him, she adjusted the sheet to cover her breasts and took his hand. "It's going to be fine. I've been lying here dying to know and trying to be cool, but I'm done with that." She sat up and brushed her messy, sexy hair out of her face. "C'mon, let's see what the movie goers have said."

So much rode on this minute, that Leo felt sick to his

stomach. It had been years since a movie's opening weekend meant this much. The outcome was out of his hands, but this was so close to home that he had no way not to let it get to him.

He grabbed his phone as it pinged again and a tweet showed up on the screen.

Congrats @TheLeoFrost! #anotherhit

The instant high that hit him was immediately tempered with the fact that this could be one of his millions of followers fucking with him. Leo pulled his laptop over, opened it up and went to the tab with the weekend's box office results. He hit refresh and waited for the page to load.

Kim snuggled closer and looked on next to him.

Leo blinked a few times when he saw the numbers. His little film was sitting at the top of the list with thirty-four million dollars, one of the best opens for an indie film to date and the highest grossing movie of the weekend. "Holy shit," he muttered. He closed his eyes to fight the pressure behind his lids. He was in the black. No more debt, no more panic attacks in the middle of the night. No more worrying if he'd work another day in his life. He swiped a hand over his face and let out the breath he'd been holding.

"I'm so proud of you," Kim whispered. She nuzzled his ear and her warm breath caressed his cheek. Since her mouth was right there, he couldn't *not* kiss her.

"Thanks," he said, right before setting his lips on hers.

"What'd I do?" She smiled as she pulled back.

"You've been here for me almost since the day I met you. So I'm going to do my damnedest to never let you down." God, he wanted to do something for her. Something big. She'd not only bought Stella back, but his favorite movie poster, too, so she deserved an equally big gesture. What could he do for her? What did she want? Well, besides a baby and he'd already been working on that issue. Every chance he got.

The room shook with a tiny aftershock and Kim jolted and squeezed the hell out of his arm.

"I will never get used to those. Not ever." She jumped out of bed. "I'm showering now before a bigger one hits. I can't go through an earthquake with dirty hair."

Leo watched her sweet ass disappear into the bathroom.

Bingo.

He knew exactly what to get her. Exactly.

The holidays had been low-key and now he knew why since Kim had known she was going to buy back Stella. His own budget hadn't allowed for a big-ticket purchase, but Kim had promised that all she needed was him. Sweet sentiment, but now that he could do more, he planned to reciprocate for his Porsche.

The next weekend the movie made it into more theaters and *To the West* was still number one at the box office. Critics and audiences loved it. Carrie Ann's reviews were the best she'd ever received and Leo's weren't too bad either. The best part was being seen in a new light as a writer and producer. He'd just rewritten his stock in Hollywood and he loved the feeling.

Move over Clooney.

He did a tour of the late night shows and the morning shows. Sleep became something he did on airplanes and in limos between appearances. Kim accompanied him, which had the paparazzi out in force. Leo downplayed the Oscar buzz. He was just happy his film was well received. Well, that and not losing his shirt—again—in the process.

Most of all, he was thrilled to be able to pay the crew members who'd worked so hard on that last day in the desert for practically no money. Especially since they'd finished the thing without him. Giving a percentage of the movie had made every one of those guys the best payday they'd ever received.

Another thing happened after the second weekend's box office. He got a call from his manager that Global Star Entertainment wanted to secure him for a three-picture deal. Leo's team negotiated for one of those pictures to be something of his choosing and the company went for it. With the signing came a giant holding fee. Enough to warrant that surprise for Kim.

After three weekends the film was closing in on the one hundred million mark and Leo decided it was time for a change. Thanks to a few referrals, he found a realtor who sent him pictures of some terrific prospects.

Following another red-eye to New York, Leo had the limo take them to Manhattan. But instead of dropping them off at Waverly Place, the car went to Tribeca.

"Where are we?" Kim asked, stepping out of the limo as the driver pulled their luggage from the trunk. Didn't matter that they'd gone all night on a plane, she didn't have a hair out of place and barely a wrinkle in her curve defining, navy, cashmere dress. She clutched her matching coat tightly against the frigid New York winter.

Leo tipped the guy a twenty then ushered Kim into the skyscraper. A doorman greeted them with a luggage cart and took their bags. "Just a little something I wanted to show you," Leo said. They entered the opulent lobby with its massive crystal chandelier in the center. Off to the right a comfortable sitting area surrounded a square glass coffee table. To the left was the reception desk.

Working hard at playing it cool when he really wanted to sprint toward the penthouse, Leo gestured to one of the plush leather chairs in the lobby. "Have a seat. I'll be right back." He checked in at the front and got the key to the condo, then waved to Kim.

She met him halfway to the elevators. "You're being very cryptic." Her green eyes narrowed.

He saw the accountant in her scanning the place and price tagging everything. "You've got your detective face on."

"Because I think you're hiding something."

"Me? Hide something? From you? Not possible." He wrapped an arm around her shoulders.

She still looked skeptical as they took an elevator all the way to the top. The doors opened and they stepped out into a large carpeted hallway. Modern sconces created subtle lighting. Two doors marked the only two condos with about fifteen yards separating them. Leo grabbed Kim's hand and went left.

"Leo? Where are we going?"

"You'll see." He unlocked the door, his palms sweating. Even though he'd seen pictures, he wasn't sure what the place looked like in person. He took a deep breath and walked inside. The polished bamboo floors of the large entryway opened into a massive living room decked out in warm earth tones. The place came fully furnished and it was just what he'd hoped.

"Oh, my God," Kim breathed. "It's beautiful." She took a few steps in, craning her neck to get a better view of the custom kitchen off to the right.

"Not bad," Leo murmured. "I hope you like it. Because it's ours."

She turned to him in slow motion, her eyes wide, her mouth open. "What?" She barely croaked out the word. "When? How?" She sounded just like him on the night she gave him Stella.

"You know that signing bonus I told you I wasn't going to get for a few months?" He grinned as she nodded. "I lied. They gave it to me immediately. I took the check and bought this place. We still have a mortgage, but it's not anything we can't handle. We can afford it."

"Does it take up the whole floor?" she asked.

"Half. The other side belongs to Seger Hughes. But I'm pretty sure his main residence is in Los Angeles these days."

Kim nodded as she strolled over, wrapped her arms around his neck and set her mouth against his. Her soft lips enticed and teased. The things this woman did with her mouth should be outlawed. "This is very sweet," she murmured as she pulled away. "But why would you do it without talking to me?"

Leo had to get his head back in the conversation. "You mean because you're our financial advisor?"

"I mean, because I know you love Los Angeles."

"Maybe." But not nearly as much as he loved her. "I love New York too. Plus, we're closer to Megan. I can see her way more often if we're here. The best part is you don't have to worry about earthquakes."

Her jaw fell open. "You did this for me?"

He shrugged. "I did it for us. It's not like I was going to make you live in the walk-up on Waverly. Not in the shoes you wear. That's grounds for…"

She waited, but when he hesitated, searching for the right words, a ghost of a smile appeared on her lips and she stroked her thumb across his cheek. "How many bedrooms does this place have?" She always knew how to change the subject to save him from making an ass out of himself.

"Four, and four and a half baths."

Her grin spread wider. "I think the first thing we should do is pick out the nursery."

It took a second to register, then Leo canted his head. "What?" He held her face in his hands and studied her as a roaring built in his ears. "What did you just say?" As happy as they were together, he knew she wanted more. She wanted a shot at what she'd lost four months ago.

Her eyes sparkled. "I have a surprise too. Mine requires a nursery in about seven months."

Leo's heart expanded with the news. They had a baby on the way, a new place, a hit movie in the theaters. All that was missing was the ring on her finger. And that was burning a hole in his pocket. Picking her up, he spun her then promptly set her down. "Shit! Sorry. Probably shouldn't have done that."

She laughed. "I think it's probably fine."

He tugged her in his arms again. "Are you okay? How do you feel? Why didn't you tell me?"

"I was just waiting until I got past the last point. It's still early, but I'm not going to do anything to jeopardize this." She laid a hand over her stomach. "It's been a crazy few months, right?"

Leo kissed her, brushing his lips over hers in a gentle tease. "The craziest. I say we make the next six or seven decades a little less drama intensive."

She laughed and Leo's chest expanded. Felt like his heart might bust past his ribs he was so damn happy. But then she sobered. "I still have to deal with Wilson's trial. That's a crazy I could do without."

Turned out Wilson had an undiagnosed mental issue known as stress response syndrome and because he was now on medication, his lawyer seemed confident that he could get him released from jail before the trial. So far, the man was still behind bars and Leo was happy to put even more distance between Kim and her cousin.

"I'll be with you the whole time." He stroked his hands down her back. "Then we'll be drama free."

She lifted a bored eyebrow. "I'm not convinced we'll accomplish that when you're the drama king." God, he loved her sense of humor. It made him horny.

"Because..." he insisted, blowing past her one-liner, "...the only drama we're going to go through is the kind that happens on camera." He looked into her eyes and saw his present and his future. "I already told Global Star that we're spacing out those movies. I want plenty of time with you..." He placed his hand over stomach. "And our baby. And however many babies you want to give me."

"You are so good at making me hot."

He laughed. The feeling was very mutual. "I try. I really do try." No time like the present. He stuck his hand in his pocket and came out with the black velvet pouch. He dropped the four-carat diamond into his palm, got on one knee and took her hand.

Kim's eyes rounded even more. "Leo...?" He loved her speechless too. That rarely happened.

"This is in keeping with making you hot." He gazed up at her, the ring ready to slide on her finger. They hadn't talked about marriage. They'd talked partnership. They'd talked about her helping him produce his next three films. Did she really think he wasn't going to make this deal a permanent situation? "Will you marry me?"

Tears filled her pretty eyes, but her smile gave him the answer right before she whispered, "Yes."

Leo had hoped for that reply, but hearing it still put a lump in his throat as he placed the ring where it belonged. He stood up, taking her lips in a sweet kiss before holding her hand out and admiring the sparkle.

"You want to marry me?" She stared at the ring like it was the pot of gold at the end of the rainbow.

"You did hear me ask a second ago, right?" He grinned at the utter fascination she had with the ring. "Do I need to get down again and—"

"No!" She stopped him from kneeling again, her eyes watery and full of happiness. "We just never talked about it. I didn't think you ever wanted to get married."

"I didn't. Until you came along. You fit me. You make me better." He pulled her close. "You love me for me. Not for my movies or my money or my reputation or lack of reputation. You don't let me get away with shit and you keep me on my toes. It doesn't get better than that."

"You fit me too," she whispered. "I'm so glad we found each other. There was a time not too long ago that I thought I'd never be this happy. That I'd never have the chance to have it all. A family, a career, a man I love... Thanks for making my dreams come true."

"All in a day's work," he teased, bending down to brush his lips against hers.

She sighed into his mouth before pulling away. She studied the ring and the opulent condominium. "Although, I see I'm going to have to watch your spending like a hawk." She wiped at a tear. "This is beautiful. All of it." She wrapped her arms around his neck and rubbed up against him, causing all sorts of impulses to fire to life. "But from now on no more surprises. We're a team which means we talk about big ticket items."

"Said the woman who just spent a fortune to buy back my car."

"Guilty as charged. It was worth every penny to see your face." She shook her head with another glance around the room. Her smile softened and her eyes narrowed. "I've discovered that sometimes you are a dangerous man, Leo Frost."

"Baby, I'm *always* dangerous." He took her lips in a hot kiss, sure to end this conversation, then eased her coat off her shoulders and tossed it to the side. He was pretty sure he missed the chair he was aiming for, but didn't really care because she pulled at the button on his jeans, took the zipper down and made his head fuzzy with lust—and love—when she stroked her palm down his hard-on.

"So where's the bed in this palace?" She took his hand and walked backward, leading him God only knew where since they didn't know the layout of the place.

"I think it's down that hall and to—"

Kim laughed, turned and started running, her heels clicking on the floor. She really could do anything in stilettos. Leo chased her. Once he caught her, he wasn't ever letting her go.

The End

About The Author

After graduating high school in Texas, Dee moved to Los Angeles to pursue acting. For twenty years, she acted in television and worked behind the scenes as an acting/dialogue coach for sitcoms. Writing happened accidentally after a vivid dream and the urging of her husband to "Just write it down." Three weeks, fourteen hours a day, and four hundred and fifty (long hand) pages later, she had her first novel. Dee loves writing books filled with action, mystery and love. (Not necessarily in that order.) Her experience in show business led to her narrating many of the books in the Adrenaline Highs series for Audible.com. She is the wife of a wonderful man and mother to a fabulous daughter. She's a dog lover all the way, with a fondness towards Boxers and Pit Bulls. She is a member of several organizations, including Romance Writers of America and SAG-AFTRA.

For more information on Dee's books please visit:

www.deejadams.com

www.ingramcontent.com/pod-product-compliance
Lightning Source LLC
Chambersburg PA
CBHW050016180626
46810CB00002B/447